A THOUSAND STEPS INTO NIGHT

A THOUSAND STEPS INTO NIGHT

TRACI CHEE

Clarion Books
An Imprint of HarperCollins*Publishers*
Boston   New York

Clarion Books is an imprint of HarperCollins Publishers.

A Thousand Steps into Night
Copyright © 2022 by Traci Chee

Library of Congress Cataloging-in-Publication Data has been applied for
ISBN: 978-0-35-846998-8 hardcover
ISBN: 978-0-35-869407-6 signed edition

The text was set in Carre Noir Std.
Cover design by Celeste Knudsen
Interior design by Natalie C. Sousa

Manufactured in the United States of America
1 2021
4500845332

First Edition

For the awkward, the different, the brave

PART I

1

THE ABANDONED VILLAGE OF NIHAOI

LONG AGO, in the noble realm of Awara, where all creation, from the tallest peaks to the lowliest beetles, had forms both humble and divine, there lived an unremarkable girl named Otori Miuko. The daughter of the innkeeper at the only remaining guesthouse in the village of Nihaoi,[1] Miuko was average by every conceivable standard—beauty, intelligence, the circumference of her hips—except for one.

She was uncommonly loud.

Once, when she was two years old, her mother was wrestling her into one of the inn's cedar tubs when Miuko, who had no plans for a bath that day, screamed so violently that the foundations shook, the bells rang in the nearby temple, and a respectable chunk of the dilapidated bridge spanning the river a full quarter-mile away let out a horrified groan and slid, fainting, into the water.

This was mere coincidence. Miuko had not, in fact, been the cause of an earthquake (at least not in this instance), but several of the priests, upon hearing of her peculiar vocal faculties, rushed to exorcise her all the same. No matter what spells they chanted or incense they burned, however,

---

1   Niha-oi (*nee-hah-oy*): literally, "almost there." According to village lore, many centuries ago, when the Old Road was but a simple walking path, a father and son were traveling toward the nearby city. The son, growing impatient with the length of the journey, kept asking, "Where are we, Father? Where are we?" and the father, growing impatient with the child's incessant inquiries, kept responding, "*Nihaoi. Nihaoi.*" Almost there. Almost there. It is said that the son later went on to found the village as a rest stop for travelers, naming it "Nihaoi" in honor of his father.

they were ultimately disappointed to discover that she was not, in fact, possessed. Instead of a demon, what her parents had on their hands was merely a loud child. Worse, a loud girl.

Among other things, girls of the serving class—and indeed, girls of all stations in Awara—were expected to be soft-spoken, well-mannered, comely, charming, obedient, graceful, pliable, modest, helpful, helpless, and in every respect weaker and more feebleminded than men. Unfortunately for Miuko, she had very few of these qualities, and as a result, by the time she was seventeen she had discovered that she was not only able to frighten off a man with the power of her voice alone, but she also had regrettable inclinations toward spilling tea upon her guests, kicking accidental holes in the rice paper screens, and speaking her mind, whether or not she was invited to do so.

Her father, Rohiro, had the good grace never to say it—and by the time it mattered, her mother had long ago deserted them both—but Miuko knew it was her duty as an only daughter to attract a husband, bear a son, and secure her father's legacy by passing on the family inn to future generations. Over the years, she'd learned to hide her opinions behind her smile and her expressions behind her sleeves, but despite her best efforts, she was ill-suited to being a girl of the serving class. She was simply too visible, and frankly, that made her unappealing, both as a servant and as a woman.

With few prospects, then, Miuko devoted her days to the upkeep of her father's inn. Like the rest of Nihaoi, the guesthouse was failing. The roof was in need of thatching. The straw mats were in need of mending. She and Rohiro repaired what they could, and if they couldn't repair it, they went without it. All in all, it was a quiet life, and Miuko was not (or so she told herself) unsatisfied.

Everything changed, however, the day she dropped the last teacup.

It was a late August afternoon, and nothing out of the ordinary was afoot. In the village temple, the priests sat cross-legged and meditated, to varying degrees of success, upon the order of the cosmos. In the teahouse, the proprietor weighed dried jasmine against brass units shaped like emperor butterflies. At the inn, a teacup slipped from Miuko's fingers as she was putting it away and was dashed to pieces upon the floor.

Miuko sighed. Over the years, she'd damaged every single cup in the set. There were the ones she'd dropped, the ones she'd cracked as she cleaned them, the ones she'd cantered across the courtyard stones, pretending they were ponies (but that was ten years ago). Being ceramic, the teacups were nervous by nature, but Miuko's clumsiness had so increased their anxiety that it seemed all she had to do was look at them, and they'd shatter.

Given that the only remaining cups were either chipped or seamed with glue, Rohiro determined that it was finally time to replace them. Ordinarily, he would have walked the mile to the potter's himself; but, as he was currently nursing a broken foot, it was decided that he would remain at the inn to serve the only guest they'd had all week—a misanthropic silkworm farmer with one arm—while Miuko was dispatched to retrieve the teacups.

Taking an umbrella, she stepped eagerly out of the guesthouse. As a girl, she was supposed to be accompanied in public by a male relative at all times, but due to her mother's absence and the deteriorating state of the inn, her father was admittedly lax on this custom, so Miuko had in the past been allowed to collect tea from the teahouse or eggs from one of the remaining farmers. Such errands, however, had always been confined to the village, and the prospect of venturing as far away as the kiln, well beyond Nihaoi's borders, filled her with a giddiness she could not quite suppress.

Rohiro, a handsome, broad-shouldered man, watched Miuko from the doorway. Her mother used to say that Otori Rohiro was more beautiful than a man from a failing village had any right to be, and she'd often say it while threading her fingers through his thick black hair, or counting the laugh wrinkles at the corners of his eyes.

Not that Miuko remembered it very clearly.

"The potter won't like it," Rohiro muttered worriedly.

In Miuko's opinion, her father's habitual muttering somewhat mitigated the effect of his good looks, for she thought it made him seem older than his forty-three years. He'd lost half his hearing as a child while swimming in the Ozotso River, when an eager *geriigi*[2] sucked it from his skull like a yolk from an egg, giving him a poor sense of how loudly or softly he was speaking.

"Won't like what?" Miuko asked. "The fact that we won't be able to pay him until the silkworm farmer checks out, or the fact that I'm a girl without a man to escort her?"

"Both!"

She shrugged. "He'll just have to cope."

"You sound like your mother." Her father's smile turned languid, the way it always did when he was thinking of his wife (beautiful, by all accounts, but completely unable to be brought to heel). "You're getting to be more like her every day."

In spite of herself, Miuko grimaced. "Gods forbid!"

He frowned, though his eyes were too soft for it. Instead of looking angry, as other fathers might, his frown only made him appear sad—or at best, quietly disappointed, which everyone knew was infinitely worse.

"You could turn into worse things than your mother, you know," he said.

"Certainly." The words flew from her mouth before she could stop them. "I could turn into a demon."

Her father stilled, his face etched with sadness.

Inwardly, Miuko cursed her recalcitrant tongue. Sometimes, contrary to the conclusions of the priests, she was certain she was possessed, for no other girls she knew spouted off with every comment that popped into

---

2   geri-igi (*geh-ree-ee-gee*): literally, "grabby finger," a spindly-limbed demon that dwells underwater. According to the tales, *geriigisu* are said to lurk along the muddy bottoms of rivers and shallow lakes, where they will lunge for the ankles of unwary swimmers, dragging them into the watery depths to drown them—or, as in the case of Otori Rohiro, rob them of their hearing.

4

their heads. "I'm sorry, Father." She bowed deeply; for, loud and willful as she was, she had no desire to cause her father pain. "Please forgive me."

With a sigh, he leaned over, kissing the crown of her head, the same way he'd done since she was a baby. "You're my only daughter. All is already forgiven."

She glanced up at him wryly. "And if you had another daughter, would you be quicker to hold a grudge?"

Chuckling, he nudged her toward the Old Road. "Off with you now! And be quick. No one is safe at the verge hour."

She traipsed into the front garden, nearly clipping the camellia bushes with the tip of her umbrella. "Dusk is more than an hour away!" she said.

"Best not to chance it," he replied. "My great uncle's cousin once knew a warrior who got caught out at sunset and came home with his head on backwards."

"*What?*" Miuko laughed.

Rohiro shook his head. "It was terrible. First his wife left him, then he broke both his legs trying to chase after her. Finally, he tried to cut his own throat, only he couldn't get the angle right . . ."

It occurred to Miuko that the wife's departure should have told the husband quite clearly that she did not want to be pursued, but Miuko knew her father well enough to know that he'd just tell her she was missing the point.

The point, of course, was this: it was safest to be within human borders at dawn and dusk, when the veil between Ada and Ana—the worlds of the mortal and the spirit—was thinnest. Miuko's mother had always been particularly wary of the verge hours, for it was during these times that demons attacked travelers for their unctuous, buttery livers, ghouls appeared in mirrors to steal human faces, and ghosts slipped from doorways to wring the necks of unsuspecting passersby underneath.

So superstitious had Miuko's mother been that she would refuse to

5

cross a threshold during sunrise or sunset. She'd kept spirit dolls upon the rafters, written blessings for the spiders weaving in the bathtubs, left crushed eggshells for the *tachanagri*[3] living in the guesthouse walls.

Then again, she'd also stolen a horse and ridden off into the gloaming one evening while she was supposed to be fetching water for the dinner kettle, leaving Miuko, age nine, and her father at the table, watching their rice grow cold.

Since her mother had chosen braving the twilight hour over spending another second with her family, Miuko suspected, with some bitterness, that perhaps her mother hadn't been so superstitious after all.

"I'll be back before sunset," Miuko assured her father.

"With all the teacups intact?"

"No promises!" Bowing again, she left the front garden and set off through the village with a bounce in her step. She passed vacant shops and crumbling homes, noting the doors coming out of their tracks and the mice scurrying through clefts in the foundations like violet luck sprites. To anyone else, the appearance of the village might have been cause for alarm, but to Miuko, who had only ever known such deterioration, it was beautiful in its ordinariness.

The sigh of floorboards sinking into the ground.

The slow creep of vines pulling down a wall.

Through the center of the village, Miuko trotted down the beaten gravel path known as the Old Road, which had in years past served as the primary route into Udaiwa, the capital of Awara. In ancient times, Nihaoi, only a half-day's journey from the city, had catered to travelers of every stripe: noblemen and their vassals, lecherous monks, beggars, circus

---

3   tacha-nagri (*tah-chah-nah-gree*): literally, "tree goblin." In Awara, *tachanagrisu* are said to be small, green-skinned creatures, rarely glimpsed unless their trees are chopped down and used for lumber, at which point their sharp features become visible, to the discerning eye, among the fine whorls of the timber.

troupes that boasted choleric fortune tellers and dancing raccoon spirits, and, on at least four occasions, unmarried women.

Nearly three hundred years ago, in the aftermath of the Five Swords Era, the then-*yotokai*,[4] Awara's highest-ranking military officer—second only to the emperor himself in authority, and, for all intents and purposes, the actual ruling sovereign—had ordered the construction of the Great Highways to unify the realm. In the centuries since, traffic on the Old Road had dwindled, and Nihaoi had entered a sustained period of decline: taverns closed; stables, cobblers, and merchants forced out of business; farmers leaving their fields to fallow and rot; government emissaries, who had once been wealthy and complacent in their fine pavilions, all removed to other, more promising posts.

Since then, nothing in Nihaoi had gone untouched by decay: not the smattering of shops, or the temple, home to four lugubrious priests, not even the spirit gate, which marked the edge of the village. Generations of insects had left tunnels along the pillars, forming twisting labyrinths beneath the flaking vermillion paint. Lichens clung to the joists. The engravings, meant to be repainted each year with sacred indigo ink to renew their protective magic, had faded to a faint and ineffective hue.

Though she tried not to, Miuko could not help but think of her mother as she approached the gate. It had made quite the scandal for the tiny village, even sparking rumors that Otori Rohiro's wife was in fact a *tskegaira*[5] —a spirit wife—who took human form to lure mortals into marriage.

---

4   yoto-kai (*yoh-toh-kye*): "commander," or, poetically, "one who points the way."

5   tske-gai-ra (*tskeh-gye-rah*): literally, "not-long-love," or, to put it more poetically, "she'll love you, but not for long." In Awara, *tskegairasu* could be any number of spirits, including those of foxes, sparrows, cranes, and snakes, and they were not always wives, for there are several rare accounts of spirit husbands as well. While there is tremendous variation in the tales, there are two defining features of spirit wives: first, a human weds them after they take human form; second, one way or another, they always leave.

Although she did not believe in such things, per se, Miuko could not help but think that there had indeed been something odd and wild about her mother, something that now rushed through Miuko's veins like a brisk stream or a southern wind.

Despite herself, then, she could not help but wonder how her mother had looked astride that stolen horse, its mane and tail the same flowing dark as a river at night. Had her mother glanced back even once, her oval face pale as the moon, before charging off into the wild blue countryside like a warrior from some ancient tale or a queen of shadow and starlight?

How melodramatic! Annoyed at herself, Miuko kicked at a stone, sending it clattering into a nearby boulder with a *clack!* that echoed through the ruined village.

It didn't matter how her mother had looked, if she'd hesitated or not, for the end result was the same—she'd left. Miuko and her father had been abandoned, just like the rest of Nihaoi.

The borders had already been tightened once since Miuko's mother had left, as businesses failed and families departed in search of more prosperous circumstances, but the potter had steadfastly refused to relocate, for both he and his wife claimed that the spirit of their dead son still haunted the kiln. Perhaps the boy broke the occasional vase or ceremonial urn, but on the whole, he remained a chatty, good-natured child, and none of them were prepared to sacrifice their happy family for something as frivolous as safety.

In general, this situation was of little inconvenience, for in daylight a mile on the Old Road, which hadn't the traffic to attract unsavory types such as highwaymen and ravening monsters, was hardly dangerous. In fact, Miuko rather enjoyed the opportunity to stretch her legs, and with about an hour left before dusk, she had no reason for concern.

Leaving the gate behind her, Miuko walked cheerily along the Old Road as it wound through the abandoned fields. During the Five Swords

Era, these plains had been the site of a great battle, when the powerful Ogawa Clan had ridden upon Udaiwa—stronghold of their enemies, the Omaizi—and were massacred on the fields. When she was a child, Miuko had longed to dig among the furrows with the boys her age, unearthing rusted arrowpoints and scraps of lamellar armor, but propriety had forbidden it; and, after hearing a number of harrowing tales about warrior ghosts rising from the earth, she'd decided that perhaps it was better if she played inside instead.

Swinging her umbrella, Miuko picked her way across the dilapidated bridge that spanned the Ozotso River, an emerald serpent that hissed and glittered along its steep banks as it meandered toward the capital. Once, the bridge had been broad enough for two carriages to comfortably pass, but the earthquake that had accompanied Miuko's infamous tantrum had put an end to that. Now, with its half-rotten beams and a gaping hole on the downriver side, the bridge was scarcely wide enough for a single horse.

As she crossed, a lone magpie winged across the sky, clutching a golden medallion in its beak.

It was an ill omen, which Miuko did not see.

Then, among the weeds in the overgrown ditches, an insect chirped eleven times and stopped.

A portent of misfortune, which Miuko did not hear.

Finally, a chill wind gusted over the empty fields, shuffling the dead leaves in Miuko's path to spell out a message of doom.

Perhaps if she had paid more attention to her mother's stories, Miuko would have known that, in advance of some terrible calamity, the world would often be filled with warnings and opportunities to change one's fate. But she did not like stories and, since her mother's abrupt departure, had gone out of her way to avoid them, so she did not see the signs; or, if she did, she told herself they meant nothing. She was a straightforward girl with her head squarely on her shoulders, too sensible to be concerned with anything more than the look of the clouds, which appeared as if they were breaking up anyway.

If she *had* been paying more attention, perhaps she could have saved herself a great deal of trouble by promptly turning back the way she had come, although (unbeknownst to her) doing so would have had an equal chance of bringing about a cataclysm so swift and absolute that not even the abandoned village of Nihaoi would be spared.

Either way, she continued walking.

2

THE VERGE HOUR

HAVING RETRIEVED THE TEACUPS from the potter, who thrice commented on how improper it was for a girl to be running errands, Miuko was on her way back to the village center, trying to avoid jostling the cloth-lined box of teacups tucked under her arm.

Out here near the old border, the village had entirely surrendered to ruin: collapsed roofs, saplings sprouting through floorboards, birds flitting through great gaps in the walls. As Miuko passed, mist began to rise from the nearby fields, floating eerily over the ditches. Somewhere in one of the abandoned farmhouses, a cat screamed.

At least, Miuko hoped it was a cat. According to legend, the thick fog of the river plains was said to be filled with the ghosts of slain Ogawa soldiers, who climbed from the earth with the mists, heavy with bloodlust. *Naiana,*[1] the villagers called the mist "spirit vapor."

Under her arm, the teacups clinked nervously.

Giving the box a comforting pat, Miuko picked up her pace. She may not have paid much heed to her mother's ghost stories, but she was not fool enough to linger where there might be vengeful spirits about.

She was passing the old mayoral mansion, with its collapsed gate and its ruined gardens, when she spied three children, wiggling and hopping on the road ahead.

---

1   naia-na (*nye-ah-nah*)

There was a squawk, followed by a round of cheers. The children had surrounded a bird—an azure-winged magpie with an ebony head, gray body, and blue-tipped wings and tail. He limped along, dragging his right wing while one of the children circled him, prodding him with a stick. Flopping out of the way, he landed on his side and scrabbled up again as a second child struck him with a rock. The third was just rearing back to pounce when Miuko's voice rent the air.

"*Stop!* Leave him alone!"

The children halted mid-step, gazes fixed on her, feral as little foxes.

One grinned at her with crooked teeth. "Make us, lady!"

"Yeah, lady!" said another with narrow eyes.

Forgetting for the moment that she was not a warrior, but a servant girl who had never brawled with other children—and that she did not, strictly speaking, know how to fight—Miuko charged forward, swinging her umbrella in what she hoped was a menacing fashion.

The children scattered, shouting, "Lady! Lady! Lady!" The one with crooked teeth hit her across the thighs with a stick. She tried to kick him, but tripped. She cursed her ineptitude, and then cursed her ankle, which twisted underneath her.

While Miuko regained her footing, one of the children turned around and lowered his pants, exposing his pale bottom, which she promptly smacked with her umbrella.

The paper tore. The bamboo ribs snapped.

The bottom turned red with hurt.

Shrieking, the boy leapt away, rubbing his backside.

The other two laughed and shoved him, and after a moment tussling among themselves, apparently forgetting Miuko altogether, they scampered off into the mist, leaving her alone with an injured ankle, a broken umbrella, and some very shaken ceramicware.

Collecting herself, Miuko looked around for the magpie, but all she could see now was the crumbling gate of the mayoral mansion and the black branches of a cloven pine peeking over the rooftops like a fork of lightning. The fog drew nearer, closing in about her like a noose.

Standing, Miuko tested her ankle. It wasn't broken, but she'd have to hobble back to the village with twilight nipping at her heels. Quickly, she checked the teacups, touching them one by one with her forefinger: *fine . . . fine . . . fine . . . shattered.*

The jagged ceramic shards clinked against one another as she sifted through the box. Half the set was damaged, and the others were clearly rattled. Inwardly cursing her own clumsiness, Miuko tucked the pieces back into their places, smoothing out the cloth lining like a tiny shroud before closing the box again.

Could she do nothing right?

The cups were silent.

With a sigh, Miuko began limping back to Nihaoi with her broken umbrella and the cold fragments of the broken teacups sliding this way and that among their brethren.

The fog thickened. Darkness crept over the Old Road. Above, a slim crescent moon, no thicker than the needle of a silver fir, appeared in the mists. Nervously, she wondered if she were still headed toward the village, or if she had been turned around somehow, on some tortuous path spun by trickster spirits. Through the fog, she could have sworn she saw a shape, both massive and ethereal, fluttering overhead.

Had the sun fallen? Had she been caught out in the verge hour?

She stumbled through the fog, breaths coming faster with every step. It seemed like hours since her encounter with the rabid children, an age since she'd left the inn.

So when she saw the balusters of the dilapidated bridge emerge out of the mist, she nearly gasped with relief. Limping, she started forward, but before she could reach the bridge, a flood of cold struck her, frigid as winter.

The world spun. The box of teacups tumbled from her hands with a *crash*. The broken umbrella tipped into the road like a felled tree.

Reeling, Miuko peered into the fog, which swirled across her vision in dizzy spirals, shifting and parting, revealing trees, ruins, and a lone figure some twenty feet down the Old Road.

A woman.

No, not a woman.

She was dressed in the robes of a priest, but her skin was a vivid and enigmatic blue, like the most sacred of indigo inks, and her eyes were as white as snow, flicking over the road as if searching—no, *hungering*—for something.

Or someone.

Miuko staggered backward, startled. Spirits could be good or evil, tricksters or guides, but this one did not seem to be there to help her. Not with that ravenous look in her eyes. *"Yagra,"*[2] Miuko whispered.

Demon. An evil spirit.

Seeing Miuko on the road, the creature stumbled forward, arms swaying at her sides. With a hair-raising shriek, she darted forward.

Miuko tried to run, but she was too slow, or the spirit was too fast. She was twenty feet away. She was close enough to touch. She was standing before Miuko, hair cascading over her shoulders like long strands of black kelp. Her hands were tangling in Miuko's robes, drawing Miuko so close, she could feel the demon's icy breath on her cheek.

Miuko knew she should struggle. If she'd been braver, or more adventurous, like her mother, she would have.

But she was not her mother, and she was not brave.

The creature was speaking now, whispering, the words like smoke upon

---

2   yagra (*yah-grah*)

the chill air. Frozen, Miuko watched the demon's lips parting, heard the voice that was both a woman's voice and not a woman's voice at all, both human and not-of-this-earth: *"It must be so."*

Then the spirit leaned forward, and before Miuko could stop her, pressed their mouths together in a perfect, round kiss.

3

DORO YAGRA

MIUKO'S FIRST THOUGHT was that she was having the first kiss of her life, and she was having it with a demon.

The people in Awara had a word for that. *Yazai.*[1] More intense than mere bad luck, *yazai* was the result of all one's evil thoughts and deeds compounded and turned back on oneself a hundredfold. *Yazai* was the reason the warrior in Rohiro's story had had his head twisted backwards, and the reason his wife left him, and the reason he could not die honorably by his own hand. *Yazai,* or so it was said, was the reason Nihaoi was crumbling and returning slowly to the earth—the result of some long-ago transgression by one of the villagers against a powerful spirit.

Yazai had to be the reason this was happening to Miuko, though she had no idea what she'd done to deserve it. Being a mere girl of the serving class, she had scarcely considered things like divine retribution before, but given the circumstances, she was certainly starting to consider them now.

Which brought her to her second thought, or perhaps it was her third (at this point she couldn't be bothered to keep count), which was that the kiss didn't feel at all like she'd thought it would. True, she hadn't given much thought to being kissed by a demon, but what she felt from the *yagra* was not passion, nor even desire, romantic or otherwise. Instead, what Miuko felt was the curious sensation of being split open: a tree hewn by the axe, a

---

1   ya-zai (*yah-zye*): literally, "evil again," roughly equivalent to the concept of bad karma.

geode halved by the hammer. It was as if the kiss was cleaving her in twain, and inside the cavity of her chest, something was changing. A seed, taking root. Rot, spreading slowly, altering the flesh of a corpse.

Except she was not dead. Or at least, she hoped not.

Abruptly, the spirit thrust her back. Stumbling, Miuko caught a brief glimpse of the sickle moon, glowing faintly in the fog.

She lurched toward the bridge, her only thought of reaching the spirit gate at the border of the village. If the gate's failing magic still held, the demon could no longer pursue her. Inside human borders, she would be safe.

But she felt no chill breath on the nape of her neck, no hooked fingers clawing at her wrists. Perhaps the demon had let her go. Perhaps she had escaped.

Miuko squinted in the gray air, though she knew that if she couldn't even see the massive hole in the bridge, somewhere off to the side, she could hardly expect to see a demon moving quicker than her eyes could follow.

She wobbled on, clinging to the railing.

Then: the drumming of hooves.

It came from behind her—the steady rhythm of iron shoes on hard-packed earth. Miuko turned, readying a cry of warning.

But when she looked back, she saw neither the blue-skinned demon nor a horse but a light in the fog, bouncing swiftly toward her like a child's abandoned ball.

Briefly, Miuko wondered if it was a *baigava*[2]—a light carried by monkey spirits to guide lost travelers to safety.

She almost laughed. How many spirits was she going to encounter tonight? Two? Nineteen? The twelve thousand Ogawa that had been slaughtered on the river plain?

It was *yazai*—it had to be. Seventeen years of her life, and she'd never

---

2   baiga-va (*bye-gah-vah*)

met a spirit. Now she'd angered the *nasu*,[3] however unwittingly, and this was her punishment.

But as the light neared, she saw upon the Old Road not a monkey spirit or other inhuman creature but a man, a young one, and although she'd never seen him with her own two eyes, she recognized his features from the official announcements and public posters: the curves of his cheeks, the high arch of his brow. He was handsomely symmetrical in the way of all wealthy and powerful individuals, for whom money and prestige have bought generations of good breeding; although, in Miuko's opinion, the end result was a little lacking in character.

Here upon the Old Road was Omaizi Ruhai, the *doro*,[4] sole heir to the *yotokai* and future ruler of all Awara.

Miuko blinked, openmouthed.

She could have dealt with a spirit. She would have managed, somehow.

But the sole heir to the most powerful man in the realm? *This* she could not comprehend.

The *doro* was supposed to be summering in the southern prefectures with the other young nobles, as he did every year. What was he doing galloping for the abandoned village of Nihaoi with no retinue to speak of?

Although she'd known the *doro* was a few years older than she, he seemed more youthful than he appeared in his portraits, his dignified features glowing as if alight from within.

It took Miuko another second to realize he *was* alight from within, his skin as luminous as a paper lantern. More than that, he was on fire.

---

3   **na-su** (*nah-soo*): the plural of *na*, meaning "spirit."

4   **doro** (*doh-roh*): a title of nobility, similar in importance to "prince." It should be noted that, technically, the Awaran *yotokai* is not a king; therefore, his heir is not, technically, a prince. However, given that the *yotokai* is the most powerful political and military position in all of Awara, and the true authority behind the spiritual and ceremonial figurehead of the emperor, the *doro* occupies a prince-like station, which is why it is often translated here as "prince."

She watched, aghast, as fragments of his flesh charred and flaked away, revealing not muscle and bone but another face beneath, one with blazing pits where his eyes should have been and ridged horns twisting from his forehead like those of a serow. As he thundered closer, heat seemed to radiate from him, washing over her in wave after wave, making her skin slick and her grip slide upon the balustrade.

Omaizi Ruhai, the heir to Awara, had been possessed by a demon.

And he was going to run her over.

There was not space enough on the dilapidated bridge for both of them, and so Miuko grabbed for the railing, hauling herself forward on her injured leg as the spirit hurtled down the Old Road on his enormous black steed.

Perhaps the demon did not see her in the *naiana*. Perhaps he was in too great a hurry to slow down. Perhaps he saw her and did not care enough to stop.

In any case, he was upon her in seconds. Miuko was thrown against the balustrade, toppling backward as the horse and rider darted around the giant hole in the bridge. As she fell, she looked up to see the *doro* turning, the demon's eyeless gaze fastened upon her, his lips parted in an expression of greatest surprise.

Then she struck the water, and the Ozotso River sucked her, screaming, into its roiling depths.

4

THE LUGUBRIOUS PRIEST

WHEN MIUKO AWOKE upon the riverbank, it was morning, and she was missing a shoe. While the water lapped at her toes like an eager dog, she drew back from the shore, groaning. She had never been what one would call a "morning person," and the fact that this was a day following an encounter with not one but two spirits did not help.

What did rouse her, however, was the memory of the *doro yagra*[1] riding for Nihaoi. Scrambling up the bank, Miuko hoped that the neglected spirit gate had been enough to prevent the demon from entering the village, though she doubted it. She did not know exactly what sort of demon he was, but given that he could possess someone with as many spiritual protections as the *doro* surely had, she had no doubt that he was more powerful than some fading warding magic. There was no telling what sort of carnage he could have wrought upon her hometown in the night.

Climbing the slope, Miuko found herself a mere quarter mile from the village border. With a swift bow and a prayer of thanks to the river spirit for depositing her so close to home, she began limping through the soft grass toward Nihaoi.

She had not gone far when she spotted one of the lugubrious priests loping toward her, his robes flapping comically about his slim figure, a string of wooden prayer beads bouncing on his neck.

Miuko could not stop herself from grimacing.

---

1   doro yagra (*doh-roh yah-grah*): roughly translated, "demon prince."

Only one of the priests was that tall and had a gait that comical, and he happened to be her second-least favorite. A willowy man, Laido had terrible halitosis—his breath always stinking of rot and whatever pungent herbs he'd tried to cover it up with—but his breath was not why she disliked him.

"Miuko!" he cried.

She quickly bowed to hide her expression. Guiltily, she knew she ought to have been relieved that someone had survived the *doro yagra,* for it meant her father might have escaped as well.

But did it have to be Laido?

"Laido-jai,"[2] she said, "what happened? Is my father—"

"So you're alive!" he declared in a deep voice. His fetid breath billowed over her, and she bowed again to hide the way she wrinkled her nose. "Your father was beside himself with concern. Where have you been?"

So her father was safe, then. The dreadful knot of worry that had been tightening inside her began to uncoil.

"I—" she began.

"He begged us to find you, you know. We've been searching the Old Road all night."

The priest had a maddening way of speaking, for he was both overly explanatory and overly insistent, as if Miuko were simultaneously an infant and a temptress: too simpleminded to understand even the most basic of concepts, and too cunning to be allowed to speak.

"But what about—"

"He would have come himself, of course, but for his foot . . ." Laido took her by the arm, though she did not need his help and had not asked for it. "You wouldn't believe who arrived at the inn last night. It was—"

---

2   -jai (*jye*): an honorific appended to names and nouns to denote politeness. Where English speakers might use "Mr.", "Ms.", or "Mx.", for example, the people of Awara would instead use "-jai."

"—the *doro*! I know. He—"

"—so you know how important this visit was, and yet you could not be bothered to come assist your poor father? When the *doro* left this morning, he—"

"Laido-jai!" She flung herself into the conversation again, this time with the full force of her voice. "The *doro* has been possessed by a *demon!*"

Halting (and jerking her to a halt too, it should be noted), Laido peered down at her, chin tucked toward his neck as it was wont to do when he was concerned, giving him the appearance of a disgruntled turtle. "What nonsense! You must have hit your head."

She tugged out of his grasp as he reached out to test her forehead.

At her recalcitrance, Laido sighed. "Miu-miu," he said, pulling her onward again, "if you're not careful, you're going to end up like your mother."

"Miu-miu"[3] had been her mother's nickname too. Her mother, who had ridden out of Nihaoi with the same dramatic flourish as she'd once ridden into it, had always been dreaming of far-off places, fantastical stories, and adventures among the *nasu*. For a time, it had endeared her to the villagers, who would stop by the inn to listen, rapt, while she regaled them with tales beyond their limited imaginings; but the longer she remained among them, the more the rumors spread—she was too free, she did not act as a woman should, she did not belong with them, she was a *tskegaira*, poor Rohiro—and soon what had been most engaging about her became the thing for which she was most ridiculed.

"But—"

"The *naiana* was about last night, wasn't it?" Laido asked. Then, without waiting for an answer: "One can never be certain what tricks the mists will

---

3 Miu-miu (*mew-mew*): literally, "wander-wander," a nickname similar to "daydreamer" or "head-in-the-clouds."

play upon the simpleminded. Don't you fret, Miu-miu. A bath, some fresh clothes, and a good nap will straighten you out . . ."

By this time, they'd reached the temple at the edge of the village, the gardens strewn with fallen leaves, the indigo roof tiles chipped and fragmenting with age. As Miuko and Laido slipped through the bamboo gate at the back of the grounds, she could not deny that the luxuries he described sounded heavenly — warm water to soothe her chilled bones, clean hemp robes to replace her muddied ones — but neither could she deny the way she wanted to smack him across the face with the flat of her hand.

As if afraid she were going to say more about the *doro yagra*, Laido rattled on about how the villagers hoped Omaizi Ruhai's visit would compel him to repair the Old Road and rejuvenate the village's failing economy. Miuko hobbled along beside him, padding quietly over the moss that carpeted the stones of the path, growing more and more weary the closer she got to home.

Her injured ankle hurt. Her thoughts were bleary with exhaustion. In truth, all she wanted was to reassure herself that her father really had escaped the *doro yagra*, apparently without even knowing it. She was so occupied with her thoughts that she must not have been looking where she was going, because the next thing she knew, she was sliding on a patch of wet leaves, both feet going out from under her.

Crying out, she snatched for the nearest support, which unfortunately happened to be Laido. He grabbed her arm, keeping her upright. "There now, Miu-miu!" he cried. "I've got you. Soon, you'll be returned to your father, and . . ."

His gaze drifted to the path they'd cut across the temple gardens and froze there, transfixed. Surprised that anything short of divine intervention could silence him, Miuko turned.

Behind them at regular intervals were withered, blackened patches in the moss. They wound through the temple's back gate and across the dewy grass beyond the village border, like a narrow path of small black stones, each placed precisely where Miuko's bare foot had made contact with the earth.

Seizing her leg, Laido stooped to examine the sole of her foot. Miuko almost cried out again, for her injured ankle was still tender, but she stopped when she saw on her pale, exposed flesh a single blemish, brilliantly blue in color. For a moment, Miuko thought it looked as if she'd stepped in the priests' holy ink, and out of habit was beginning to apologize for her clumsiness when Laido stopped her.

"*Shaoha*,"[4] he whispered.

Death woman.

And she remembered.

The demon in the road. Her ocean-blue skin. The kiss.

Miuko's mind flew back to that moment in the verge hour—the sensation of being cracked open, of something being planted inside her. Had it been this?

A mark?

A curse?

Laido backed away, clutching his prayer beads. "Demon!"

Her?

How did he know? Because of a spot? A blue spot? But it was a sacred color, wasn't it? Divine?

Her thoughts ran together, tumbled as river stones. Her second-least favorite of the lugubrious priests was right. She *did* need a nap. Just a quick doze, and then she would feel like herself again—

Laido backed away from her, making a warding sign with his fingers. "Get out! You cannot be here!"

---

4 shao-ha (*shaoh-hah*)

Miuko's mind finally caught up to her body. Laido was screaming at her. Not only was he screaming at her, he was seizing a disused broom. He was running at her, gracelessly, the same way she'd run at the children the day before.

"Evil!" he bellowed.

She fled, his cries following her to the front of the temple, where she flew under the gate, tripping over the beggar huddled in a horse blanket near one of the pillars.

Miuko cried out. The beggar grunted.

But she didn't stop. She ran for the guesthouse, racing over spiked seed hulls and bits of gravel that in her panic she scarcely felt, and though she dared not look back, she knew that if she did, she'd see dead seedlings and tufts of grass shriveling in her footsteps.

"Yagra!"

5

A GOOD NAP

WHEN MIUKO ARRIVED at the guesthouse, near tears and spattered with mud, her father did not ask questions. Cooing in the way of pigeons and concerned parents, he dropped his cane and embraced her in the front garden, among the camellias. "My poor daughter," he muttered into her tangled hair. "Please forgive me. I would have gone to look for you myself, but the *doro* . . . and then there was also . . ." He hesitated, as if he were not sure how to continue.

Being rather beside herself at this point, Miuko did not notice. If the *doro yagra*—who, it seemed, had appeared simply as the *doro* to her father and the other villagers—had stopped at the guesthouse, it would not have been possible for her father to turn him away. He was, after all, a man of the serving class—his *purpose* was to serve. He could have no more refused a guest like Omaizi Ruhai than flown upon the winds like a cloud spirit.

That he'd asked the others to search, that he was safe, that he was happy to see her: these things were more than enough for Miuko.

"You're my only father," she said. "All is already forgiven."

He released her with a fond smile. "What a night you must have had! What happened, my dear?"

Miuko opened her mouth to reply, but to her surprise, she discovered that for the first time in her life, she did not have anything to say. Having survived, in the past twelve hours, encounters with demons, children, and one lugubrious priest, she had neither the energy to explain nor the wits to determine where to begin.

"I'm sorry to have worried you, Father," she whispered.

"We both had some excitement last night, it seems. We can exchange stories when you've rested." Picking up his cane, he gestured her toward the back of the inn, where the cedar tubs were. "Let me heat you a bath. Have you eaten? While you wash, I can fix you something. How about . . ."

Weary though she was, Miuko tiptoed carefully around the patches of moss in the path, making her limping gait even more awkward.

Her father paused. "You're hurt?"

"Not very," she admitted truthfully, for the swelling seemed to be abating and the pain was not much.

He chuckled and offered her his arm. "What a pair we make! *Si paisha, si chirei.*"[1]

Like father, like daughter.

Gently, he helped her to the porch of the bath, where he lit a fire beneath the tub, talking of the *doro* and the silkworm farmer, who had departed for the capital together shortly after dawn.

Only half-listening, Miuko stared at her dirty toes. *Yagra,* Laido had called her, and *shaoha.*

She was no demon, of that she was certain. Being a demon would surely feel different somehow, like a stomachache or a gallop upon a horse. Since waking on the riverbank that morning, however, all she'd felt like was herself: too loud, too impatient, out of place everywhere except at her father's inn.

---

1   Si paisha, si chirei (*see pye-shah, see chee-ray*): as *paisha* and *chirei* in the Awaran language are gender-neutral terms, the phrase could also mean "like mother, like daughter," but that's a meaning Miuko tried not to think about.

But that blue spot . . .

Perhaps it wasn't the mark of a demon, but the mark of a god. Indigo, after all, was the color of Amyunasa,[2] the December God and first of all the Lunar Gods to arise from the primordial waters, from which all things were created and to which all things ultimately returned. It was a color of both life and death, a color of divinity and mystery. Perhaps the creature from the road was not a demon at all but an emissary, sent by Amyunasa for some purpose unfathomable to Miuko's feeble human mind.

There was the sound of water pouring into the tub, followed by the soft *cloc-cloc* of an extra pair of wooden sandals being laid upon the flagstones.

But Laido had known what she was — *shaoha* — and he was sure she was a demon. More than that, she could not deny the malevolence she'd felt emanating from the creature on the Old Road — that ominous chill.

If this was indeed a curse, she'd have to get rid of it immediately. A few murmured incantations, some burning herbs, perhaps a soak — like a soiled rag — in some blessed waters, and then she'd be demon-free. She could return to being Miuko, daughter of the Otori and girl of few adventures.

Strangely, this thought did not fill her with relief.

"Get in when the water is warm enough. We'll talk after. I have much to tell you," her father said, kissing her on the crown of the head. He made a face, wiping at his mouth. "Pah. You're filthy."

"Ha!" With some of her usual pluck, Miuko called after him as he limped toward the kitchen, "Now I'll be able to scare off suitors without even opening my mouth!"

Waving her off, her father muttered something she could not hear.

Alone in the bath, she sat cross-legged on the floor to examine the

---

2 **A-myu-na-sa** (*ah-mew-nah-sah*): literally, "all-unknown-spirit-forming." The mightiest and most mysterious of all the Lunar Gods, Amyunasa's body is composed of the primordial waters from which they first emerged, with a face as blank and white as the moon.

bottom of her foot. The curse was still there, among the dirt and scratches. Now that she had time to study it, she thought it looked something like a kiss.

With a yawn, she lay down upon the worn floorboards to wait for the water to heat. She would tell her father about the curse as soon as she'd cleaned and dressed. It wouldn't take long, and there would be no harm in keeping the secret a half hour longer.

Miuko did not remember closing her eyes, but before she knew it, sleep had overtaken her, swift as the *doro* on his steed. Her dreams, however, were no respite, for they churned with images of priests, torches, chanting, the oil slick of panic, and something else she could not name but only felt, behind the eyes and under the skin, cold and murderous.

She sat up, tasting smoke upon the air, too thick and foul to have come from the little blaze beneath the bathtub.

Something else, something big, something near, was burning.

6

ABANDONING THE
VILLAGE OF NIHAOI

THE INN WAS on fire. Black smoke billowed from the front of the building, choking the air, as flames ate holes in the rice paper screens.

Miuko stepped from the bath, sliding her feet into the extra pair of sandals, and was surprised to find that her ankle no longer pained her. A side effect of the curse? She did not linger on this thought for long, however, for as she raced across the inner courtyard, shouts rang through the blaze.

It was her father. He was begging someone to put out the fire. Please, this was his home. This was his father's home and his father's before him.

"Give us the *yagra*, Otori-jai!"

Miuko recognized that deep voice.

Laido. He and the priests must have come for her.

"You're mad!" her father told them. "There may be demons about, but my daughter is not one of them!"

She could just see him through the charred screens. He was at the front door, where the flames were starting to lick hungrily at the beams. One of her mother's spirit dolls toppled from the rafters, mouth agape in silent horror as its body was consumed by fire.

"Father!" Miuko tried the steps, but she was repelled by a sudden burst of heat.

He turned. "Miuko, get away from here!"

She had always tried, with middling success, to be a good, obedient daughter, but in this case she didn't think her father would object to a little insubordination.

He was her *father*.

He was the only family she had left.

Now, he limped from one room to another, stopping and starting as new blazes sprang up in his path. In the front garden, the priests were chanting.

Miuko looked around. In the corner of the yard was a trough that belonged in the stables and a couple of horse blankets that should have been in storage until autumn. Briefly, she wondered why they were out of place, but she did not have time to wonder long. She was already grabbing the blanket. She was already dunking it. She was already racing back to the main building to beat at the flames.

But before she could enter the building, the rafters crumbled. The fire roared. She was thrown back into the courtyard, landing hard on the flagstones.

Undeterred, she scrambled up again, racing along the veranda, trying to locate her father in the blaze.

There he was—on the ground in what was once their kitchen, half hidden behind a heap of what had once been a wall. His full head of hair was pathetically scorched, and his neck and shoulder had been badly burned, but he was *alive*.

"Father!" she shouted.

He looked toward her. Through the smoke, she saw his eyes widen. She saw his face twist from hope to horror. Disgust flared in his eyes.

"No." He was muttering again, but Miuko could see the word on his lips. "No, no. You're not my daughter! Get away from me!"

Miuko halted. Her eyes stung. Without meaning to, she touched her cheeks, afraid for a moment that they had turned blue as waters of the sea.

But her hands were the same color of chestnut cream, her fingernails in need of a trim.

What had changed since he saw her last?

A nap? A quartet of melodramatic priests? A threat of ruination upon his family legacy? How could these things turn Otori Rohiro against his own daughter?

His only daughter?

"Shaoha!" he shouted. "What have you done with her?"

There was that word again — death woman.

"Father, it's me —"

Miuko started forward, but before she could reach the collapsed wall of the kitchen, the priests stormed around the side of the building. Two carried banners inked with magic. The others carried bamboo staves.

Seeing her, they cried out and ran at her, chanting.

Miuko couldn't move. This could not be real. The priests, their incantations, the smoke curling across the sky like the many-fingered hands of some depraved god — it was but a dream. She was still on the floor of the bath. She would wake at any second. The water would be warm, and in the kitchen her father would be forming rice balls with his sturdy hands . . .

"Begone from this place!"

He *was* in the kitchen, not puttering about but railing at her from the ruins. Though he was injured, his voice was like an avalanche, so loud it must surely have frightened off every dog and cat and sensitive *ozomachu*[1] — sleep spirit — for miles.

Stunned, Miuko understood then that he did not mutter because he didn't understand how to regulate his volume. He muttered because otherwise he, too, would be uncommonly loud.

Si paisha si chirei.

"Go!" he thundered. *"You are not welcome here!"*

Miuko couldn't help herself. She was transforming back into the good

---

1   ozo-machu (*oh-zoh-mah-choo*): literally, "lazy bear." While *ozomachusu* are not technically bears of any sort, the folktales most often describe them as round, furry spirits that can be found slumbering in the folds of bedspreads or curled up on pillows, giving them a remarkable similarity in appearance to hibernating bears.

daughter, the obedient daughter, the one who would have done anything her father asked of her.

She ran.

No longer lugubrious but inflamed with spiritual fervor, the priests chased her to the village border, but she did not stop running there. Past the abandoned markets, the overrun fields, the caved-in chicken shed, now succumbing to the earth, she ran.

She only looked back once.

At the edge of the village, three of the priests were erecting banners on bamboo poles, the fresh indigo ink gleaming in the morning sun. Beyond them, the fire at the inn was dying down, ebbing from the building like a tide leaving a wreck upon the beach. Beside the ruins, her father was standing with a priest so tall, he could only have been Laido, who seemed to be consoling him.

Her father was alive, but the notion brought Miuko little comfort. He was alive, but he thought she was a demon.

And he no longer wanted her.

7

UNSAVORY TYPES

MIUKO MUST HAVE been halfway to Udaiwa by the time she collapsed in the middle of the Kotskisiu-maru[1]—the Stone Spine Wood—and fell into a heavy, heartbroken sleep from which she did not emerge until many hours later, after nightfall. In the darkness, the trees creaked. Pale mushrooms sprouted from pulpy logs, half disintegrated in the gloom. Overhead, a shadow fell across the stars—a bat, perhaps, or a night bird on silent wings.

The Kotskisiu-maru was so named for the length of rocky outcroppings that twisted through the center of the wood, like the spines of some ancient monster, long ago defeated and turned to stone, and it was here that Miuko got up to sit upon one of the fallen rocks and bemoan her situation.

First, she was hungry. Second, far too many of the past twenty-four hours had been spent fleeing. She was certain she'd never run so much in her life, and now every muscle in her legs and torso, not to mention a couple in her arms she hadn't even known she was using, burned. It was unconscionable that girls were not encouraged to exercise more. How else would they have the strength to run away when priests they'd known all their lives and the father upon whom they depended suddenly exiled them from the only home they'd ever known?

She ought to have been thinking about her prospects for survival

---

1   Ko-tskisiu-maru (*koh-tskee-see-oo-mah-roo*)

(finding potable water would have been a good start), but instead, she sat there, fretfully picking thorns from her robes and raking her fingers through the knots in her hair.

She had almost untangled half of her head when a voice spoke from the shadows: "Hello, little dove."

With a cry Miuko started up, clutching, for lack of a weapon, a particularly dense snarl of hair.

Four figures emerged from the trees — human (or more precisely, man) in shape but with cruel demon faces. One had the tusks of a boar. One had a third eye in the center of his forehead, yellow as a snake's. One had a crown of horns and lank black hair that swayed as he bent forward, studying Miuko as if she were a fresh blossom seconds away from being de-petaled.

The last had a blood red face and the long, pointed nose of a goblin. "What's a pretty bird like you doing in a nest like ours?" When he spoke, his mouth did not move, the words coming from behind his closed teeth.

But those, she realized with a start, were not his real teeth. As he slunk from the shadows, Miuko spied the straps tied around the back of his head. These were not demons at all, but men in masks.

Which, perhaps, made them more dangerous.

"I'm not a bird," Miuko said, a little obviously, backing toward the trees.

Three of them watched her, still as statues, but the man with the crown of horns slid behind her, blocking her escape. He loomed over her, so close she could smell him — hot and reeking of mildew. She could not help but cringe as he leaned closer. Though she knew he must have had a face under his horned disguise, the darkness in his eyeholes gave no indication there was any humanity beneath.

"Excuse me," she said. "I was just on my way."

From behind her, the man in the red mask chuckled mirthlessly. "Were you, little dove?" He slithered toward her now as the others froze, as if only one of them could move at a time. "Looks to me like you're just ready to be plucked."

Miuko tried to run, but the man with the horned mask caught her by the arms, laughing as she struggled in his grasp. She tried kicking. Her sandals flew from her feet. She tried screaming.

The woods echoed with the sound of her voice. In the trees, the leaves shivered.

The men halted.

"That's a nice mouth you've got," said the red-masked man. "Wonder what else it's good for."

With a shudder, Miuko felt something brush against her back, someone's fingers, knotting in her hair, and then—

There was an explosion overhead. Light flared in the sky, edging every branch in the canopy in white. Grunting, the men covered their eyes. The one with the horns dropped Miuko, who, momentarily blinded, dug her hands into the mulch in search of a stick, a rock, anything with which to defend herself.

It was for this reason that she did not, at first, see the reptilian giant burst through the trees, four-armed and black-feathered, golden eyes aglow. Lightning crackled from its taloned hands. Along its back, an enormous set of spines raked across the clouds.

"MORTALS," it declared in a voice like the breaking of mountaintops. "YOU DARE INFECT MY WOODS WITH YOUR VIOLENCE? FOR YOUR INSOLENCE, YOU SHALL BE PUNISHED! STAND WHERE YOU ARE AND RECEIVE YOUR COSMIC JUDGMENT!"

Like many humans, however, and particularly the unscrupulous kind, these men had no interest in facing the consequences of their wrongdoings, and did not linger to see what penalties were in store for them.

They ran, squealing like piglets.

Gathering her sandals, Miuko did too, in the opposite direction.

As she crashed through the underbrush, she heard the giant calling to her, its voice transforming from earth-shattering to merely gravelly: "NO, WAIT! I'M SORRY! I DIDN'T MEAN to scare you! Please, come back!"

She did not.

On the contrary, she ran so hard and so fast that she did not see she was running straight into someone else entirely. She slammed face-first into his chest and fell to the ground like a discarded lump of clay.

There was a low laugh, and the person reached down to help her up. "I'd say it was fate, running into you here, but to be honest, I was hoping to find you again."

Startled, Miuko took his hand. It was well-formed, with manicured nails and unblemished skin—not the kind of hand one would expect to find in the middle of the Kotskisiu-maru. The arm it was attached to was clothed in fine silk, embroidered so delicately with gold that it must have cost months of a tailor's life to produce.

She recoiled, falling to the ground again with an ungainly *whump!* From her new perspective among the leaf litter, she noticed that the man's shoes, too, were of the highest quality.

A wave of heat struck her, and it was with considerable dread that she redirected her gaze upward to the noble visage of Omaizi Ruhai.

It was the *doro yagra.*

8

TWO SIDES OF A COIN

MIUKO SCRAMBLED THROUGH the dead leaves as the demon prince watched her the way a cat might watch an injured rabbit kicking feebly on the floor of a barn. He watched her until she backed right into a fallen log and was halted, at which point he took one step closer and stopped again. His face was still aglow from within; as he studied her, one of his eyes shriveled and collapsed into ash.

"How did you find me?" she gasped.

He cocked his head, as if he did not understand the question. "I could sense you, faintly, like a fragrance from a farther room. Can you not sense me?"

She shook her head.

"Are you afraid?" he asked. Flames flickered between his teeth. "Speak."

Miuko swallowed. Her fingers gripped the earth. "Yes."

"Because you see me?" He glanced down at his grand robes, his well-formed hands. "As I am?"

"Yes."

"What am I?"

She considered. He had the body of Omaizi Ruhai, the *yotokai*'s heir, to whom she owed her life and loyalty. If he'd ordered her to cut her own throat, she would have been obligated to obey.

But beneath that, he was a *na*—a creature of Ana—who wore the *doro*'s body like finery.

38

"Doro yagra," she said at last.

"Demon prince?" he repeated, chuckling. He had a surprisingly pleasant laugh, for a demon, generous and warm. Underneath it, however, Miuko heard a low crackling: the sound of flames, of hardening earth, of the ground breaking under the formidable glare of the sun. "I like it."

"I'm glad—" Miuko hesitated, unsure whether she should call him "my liege."

The *doro* tilted his head, as if listening to something she could not hear. "Are you? Glad?"

She did not respond, for she was busy praying to every god and high spirit she could think of.

"You see me," the *doro yagra* repeated.

Startled out of her prayers, Miuko nodded.

"You're the only one who sees me."

From the reactions of the villagers, who had not known they'd had a demon among them, she'd gathered that people of the commoner classes could not see the *yagra* inside the *doro*'s body, but she was surprised that the nobility and high-ranking priests with whom the *doro* must have come into contact had not seen it either.

"I find that fascinating . . . I find *you* fascinating. What's your name?"

Remembering her mother saying once that giving one's name to a spirit could bind one in eternal servitude, Miuko considered lying; although she also seemed to recall that some spirits despised falsehoods and would smite deceivers from the earth.

"Miuko," she said.

"Miuko." The *doro yagra* licked his lips, as if tasting the name. Apparently satisfied, he asked for more. "What is your family name, Miuko?"

"Otori," she said. "Otori Miuko."

"Ah, the innkeeper's daughter." His gaze traveled over her, from her tangled hair and down her tattered robes to her bare, aching feet, then to the path she'd created in the mulch, where a few shriveled ferns lay limp and black among the leaves. "I think you are considerably more than that."

Swiftly, so swiftly her gaze could barely follow, he closed the distance between them. He moved like the blue-skinned demon from the road, but he did not touch her when he knelt to examine the soles of her feet.

"*Shaoha.*" His breath was hot against her ankle.

The word made her flinch. Death woman. Demon. That was what Laido had called her. And her father.

Tilting her knee, Miuko realized with a gasp that the vivid blue stain had spread. Now it covered both her soles, from the balls of her feet to her arches, where it had begun to seep into each of her heels.

Where would it stop? At her ankles? Her calves? Her thighs? Would it *ever* stop, or would it eventually envelop her entire body, from the tips of her toes to the crown of her head?

"I thought you were a legend," the *doro* said.

Despite her horror, Miuko almost laughed. "Me?"

Still crouched over her legs, he turned his head at a most unnatural angle. "You. The Death Woman—a variety of malevolence demon the likes of which the world has not seen for many centuries." Then he sat back, wrinkling his nose, as if Miuko were emitting a foul odor. "Only you're not entirely *her* yet, are you? You're still . . . human."

She leapt upon his words, for they filled her with hope. "I am?"

If she wasn't a demon, she could go home. Her father would accept her back with a kiss, declaring how like her mother she had become, and Miuko, being so relieved to be back, would not protest.

"Yes." The *doro yagra* stood. "For now."

"Wait." Wobbly and weak-kneed, she climbed to her feet. "What do you mean? How long will it take before—"

He smiled. Sparks escaped from a charred hole in one of his cheeks. "Not long, if you're lucky."

"But I don't want to be a malevolence demon!"

"Why not?"

"Because—"

"I think you believe you ought to be small," he said softly, almost meditatively. "I think you have been taught that greatness does not belong to you, and that to want it is perverse. I think you have folded yourself into the shape that others expect of you; but that shape does not suit you, has never suited you, and all your young life, you have been dying to be free of it."

Miuko blinked. It was as if the *doro* had dug his fingers inside of her and pulled from her heart some deep-rooted weed, so long established that she'd forgotten it was there, choking her every breath.

"Do I see you?" the *doro* asked.

"Who are you?" she whispered.

"Do you not recognize me? It is I, Ruhai, the most cherished son of the Omaizi Clan," he joked, giving her a bow. "At your service."

"No," she said foolishly. The demon could surely snap her in half like a chopstick, but that didn't stop her from asking, "What's your real name?"

The fire within him guttered and dimmed. "That's a simple question with a complicated answer." He tried to smile, but it fell from his lips. "I am . . . I was . . . You can call me Tujiyazai."[1]

Vengeance.

It was not the most comforting name.

"Why are you here, Tujiyazai-jai?" she asked.

Now he answered easily, with a careless shrug, as if there were nothing simpler in the entire world. "I want you."

---

1 **Tuji-yazai** (*too-jee-yah-zye*): literally, "your bad karma," or, more elaborately, "one's own evil returned."

She glanced down. Through her torn clothes, parts of her undergarments were visible, sections of exposed flesh at her calf, shoulder, elbow.

As if sensing the direction of her thoughts, he curled his lip in disgust. "Not that way." Then, as if the idea had only just occurred to him, he cocked his head, considering it the way one might consider a choice between green and white tea. "Well, perhaps."

This did not make Miuko feel any better.

"It's more likely I'd want to eat you." Tujiyazai bared the *doro*'s straight white teeth. "Or perhaps, in all my long years, I have been as one side of a coin, alone and unmatched, searching for his other half in order to be whole."

"And you think I'm your other half?"

"Perhaps. We are both malevolence demons, after all." He grinned again. "Perhaps we could rule this world together. Doesn't that sound appealing? You're a servant, yes? Imagine, if you joined me, you wouldn't have to serve anyone ever again. You could be Shao-kanai,[2] more powerful than any mere mortal."

Lady Death. The title made her shiver, although (if she were being honest with herself) not entirely with dread.

"And," Tujiyazai added, "if we tired of things, we could simply destroy them. You were built for that, I think."

"No!" Miuko cried. She was not a demon. She was not Lady Death. She was not the stuff of legends. She was a girl from Nihaoi. Her life was small, perhaps, and at times ill-fitting, but it belonged to *her*—the failing village, the guesthouse, her father—and she refused to abandon it for promises of power and importance.

Tujiyazai looked disappointed, almost hurt. "Are you certain?"

"Yes!"

---

2   **-kanai** (*kah-nye*): a title appended to names and nouns to denote high status, used as English speakers might use the titles "Lord" or "Lady."

42

It only occurred to her then that, if she did not join him, he might very well kill her; but it was too late to rescind her response.

A smile flitted across the *doro*'s face, fleeting as smoke. "We'll see." With a final bow, he turned and disappeared into the shadows, his voice floating from between the trees: "Farewell, Ishao,[3] until next we meet."

Trembling, Miuko sank to her knees. *Ishao,* he'd called her. Little Death. A demon, or not quite a demon, possessing the power to reign over Awara or raze it to the ground.

It was not possible. It *could not be* possible. She was Otori Miuko. She was a member of the serving class. If she was fortunate enough, she was supposed to become a wife, a mother, a caretaker to her aging father, and, if her husband departed for the spirit world before she did, a widow in the care of her son. Unlike her mother, who had stolen away in order to chase a bigger life beyond Nihaoi, Miuko had long ago resigned herself to spending the entirety of her days in a failing village.

She had not sat there long, however, when she heard another voice calling from the woods: "There you are!"

She scowled, wondering if this was to be her life from now on: one thing after another, with not a moment of rest between them. Whatever it was, she planned on walloping the next thing that came at her, good or evil.

She did not, however, bother to stand up to do it, as a young man about her age came through the trees, awkwardly ducking branches and climbing over logs, his right arm tied in a blue sling. "I've been searching all over for you!"

He was disarmingly odd-looking, with delicate features, round eyes, and thin lips, and for all he was speaking to her as if he knew her, she was certain she'd never seen the boy in her life.

He bowed abruptly, as if he'd only just remembered his manners, or

---

3   I-shao (*ee-shaoh*)

if he'd never learned them in the first place. "I'm sorry I frightened you. I only wanted to scare off those ugly *vakaizusu*[4]—" The foul word made her blush, despite her shock. "Hey, what's the matter?"

Miuko blinked. "Have we met?"

The boy laughed, his eyes crinkling up, deep creases dimpling his cheeks. He had a laugh like a song, quick and sharp.

She waited patiently, more or less, for him to stop.

He hopped onto one of the fallen logs and crouched there, beaming. "I'm the magpie you saved from the fox children. My name is Geiki."

---

4   **vakai-zu** (*vah-kye-zoo*): frankly, a curse too foul to be translated.

9

BIRD BOY

MIUKO DID NOT KNOW much about the creatures of Ana, but she'd heard enough of her mother's bedtime stories to know that *atskayakinasu*[1] —magpie spirits—were tricksters, no more trustworthy than a second summer or a southern wind; so, as she listened to Geiki's story over a crackling campfire and a meal of roasted nuts, which she gobbled up with an embarrassing amount of gusto, she took in everything he said with *kei-ni-iko-sha*—that is, with all the weight of a pebble in a wave.

Which was to say, very lightly.

He had been flying home with a gold medallion he'd found lodged among the disintegrating straw mats of Nihaoi's mayoral pavilion when he'd spied something glinting through the rafters of a barn. In need of a rest anyway, for the medallion was rather heavy, he'd just stopped to tug the new thing free, when—

"But you already had the medallion," Miuko interrupted.

"So?"

"So why did you need something else when you couldn't even carry what you had?"

"Because it was *shiny*," he said with the careful enunciation of an adult explaining a difficult concept to a child.

Naturally, his spirit-logic was utterly lost on her.

---

1 atskayaki-na (*ah-tskah-yah-kee-nah*): in the language of Awara, the word for "magpie" is *atskayaki*, meaning "thieving bird," and the word for "spirit" is *na*. Hence, *atskayakina*.

Anyway, Geiki continued, he'd just stopped to tug the thing free when he was set upon by three young fox spirits, who'd caught him by the wing, throwing him about with their teeth until he'd wrestled free. As he fled, they'd chased him into the road, tumbling nose over tail as they took on their human forms.

"That's where you come in, O Fearsome Wielder of Umbrellas," Geiki said with a wink.

After Miuko had chased the fox spirits away, he'd begun limping back toward his flock, but before he'd reached their nests in the Kotskisiu-maru, he'd heard her screaming. Though he'd never been much of a fighter, he was, in his own words, a "master of illusion," so he'd conjured up a quick mirage to frighten them off, and now, well . . . here he was.

Miuko squinted at him through the smoke, trying to decide if he was being truthful or not. On the one hand, Geiki had a kind, guileless face. On the other, that seemed precisely the type of a face a trickster would use to disarm her.

There was, however, an easy way to tell.

"If you're the bird from the road," she said, "show me."

Geiki spoke through a mouthful of food: "I can't."

"Why not?" Miuko frowned, partly at his reluctance and partly at the sight of the half-chewed nutmeats visible on his tongue.

"I can't do it while you're watching."

"You mean you get nervous?"

"I mean I *can't!* Spirits can only shapeshift when no one's watching! Don't you know that? Transformations, illusions, these things only work when there are no other eyes on you. Besides," he added primly, "I don't want to."

For a moment, Miuko gaped at him. Fox children, cursed kisses, her father banishing her from the inn, the inn burning to the ground, men wearing the faces of demons, a demon wearing the skin of a prince, and now a boy that claimed to be a bird—it was too much. It was much too much.

She began to laugh.

Alarmed, Geiki hopped back from the fire. "Ack! What's happening?" He flapped his good arm at her, as if she'd fainted, which she hadn't. "Are you happy or mad? Happy-mad? Stop that!"

Miuko wiped her eyes with her torn sleeve. "What am I going to do, Geiki?"

"About what?"

Her story came out in a tumble, like a stream hurtling down a mountainside, crashing into rocks left and right: the priests, the *shaoha*, her father, the demon prince—"You met Tujiyazai?" Geiki interrupted. "I thought he was a legend!"—and the spot, which she showed him, indigo as ink in the firelight.

For a moment, he peered curiously at the soles of her feet. "A *shaoha*'s curse, huh? Never heard of one of those. What happens if I touch it?"

"Don't touch it!"

"I won't! I just want to know what happens if I do."

She had no desire to demonstrate, so she explained to him the way the grass had withered at her touch, the way the moss had blackened, as if all the green life that had once surged through it had been drained away.

"What happens if *you* touch it?" he asked.

This had not occurred to her. It would have occurred to her mother, she supposed, but this brought her no comfort.

Reaching out, Miuko touched the edge of the mark with the tip of her index finger.

Nothing happened.

Geiki sat back with a shrug. "Best put a sock on that, either way."

A hiccup of laughter fell from her lips. "I would if I had one."

47

"We'll have to get you one, then. Two, even!"

Miuko swallowed. "We?"

"Why not? My life for a pair of socks? Sounds like a fair trade to me."
He grinned at her, black eyes twinkling.

It occurred to her that she should bargain. By all accounts, the *nasu*
were shrewd dealmakers, and there were countless tales where one nebu-
lous turn of phrase bound unwitting mortals to decades of misfortune or
lives of servitude in far-off palaces, where they remained young as their
families in Ada aged and died without them.

At her silence, Geiki cackled.

Miuko blushed. Then scowled. "Look, I don't know what you want
from me—"

"Nothing! Now, I know we haven't known each other very long, but—"

"Actually," she interjected, "we don't know each other at all."

He grinned. "Fair. But it seems to me that if fate has brought us
together—you, needing a little help, and me, being a very helpful bird
—who am I to stand in the way of destiny?"

"*Destiny?*"

"Don't you feel it?"

"Not in the slightest."

"Well, I do. I've got a good feeling about you, Miuko, curse or no curse.
It's not every day you meet a human who'll fight a bunch of spirits for you,
especially when she obviously has no idea how to fight—"

"Thanks."

"You're welcome. And anyway, what kind of friend would I be if I let
you go and try to muddle through this whole curse business on your own?"

Miuko frowned. "We're not friends."

"Ack!" Geiki clutched his chest. "You wound me!"

"We *just* met."

"So? I've made friends faster than this."

"Maybe *you* have, but . . ." She trailed off. The fact of the matter was that she'd never had friends. There weren't many children in the abandoned village of Nihaoi, and of the ones that were, none of them could stand her for long. She'd been too adventurous for the girls, too opinionated for the boys, always ill-fitting and out of place.

Taking advantage of her silence, Geiki continued. "Tell you what. How about I take you to Udaiwa? They have a library there, Keivoweicha-kaedo,[2] and humans like libraries, right? Maybe they can tell you how to remove your curse."

Miuko had never visited a library. She was literate, of course, as all members of the serving class were required to be, but in Awara, women were not permitted inside such places of learning, for according to the wisdom of the Omaizi policy makers, women did not have the minds for history, politics, religious doctrine, literature, or science, and so it would be cruel to allow them access.

Now, however, Keivoweicha shone in her thoughts. She'd have to sneak in, of course, but if she could locate some scroll or instructional pamphlet that would tell her how to remove her curse, then the transgression would be worth it. She could always ask forgiveness when she was home again.

"Geiki . . ." She allowed herself a smile. "That's brilliant."

He preened. "I'm a very smart bird."

"Humble, too."

"Oh yes, I'm more humble than anyone else."

Miuko laughed—a true laugh this time, bouncing so wildly off the trees that an owl, resting upon a gnarled bough, abruptly hacked up a pellet of bones and dropped into the darkness on silent wings. And although she knew it was not proper for a girl to be laughing when she was not only

---

2 **Kei-vo-weicha-kaedo** (*kay-voh-way-chah-kah-eh-doh*): poetically, "Sanctuary of the Lantern in the Dark."

cursed but exiled, for perhaps the first time in her life Miuko was in the company of someone who didn't seem to care one whit about what was proper. He accepted her—liked her, even—human or demon, clean or cursed, rude or polite, just as she was.

"Geiki," she said, "I've got a good feeling about you too."

10

ON THE IMPORTANCE OF TRADITION

THE NEXT MORNING, Miuko and Geiki entered the outskirts of the city, passing the temple quarter where the priests were chanting their morning prayers, and made for the bustling streets of the merchant ward. They wove through shops and market stalls, avoiding farmers' carts and passels of goods displayed upon blankets: porcelain vases, brass urns, sacks of dried beans, oversize calligraphy brushes made from horse hair.

Entering a clothing stall, Geiki exchanged the gold medallion for a plain set of hemp robes and a pair of white socks, plus a little extra coin for food and sundries. While Miuko changed in a back alley, under the eye of a scarred tabby lounging lazily upon a nearby rooftop, the *atskayakina* stood guard at the entrance.

As she emerged, knotting her old clothes into a bundle, Geiki surveyed her critically. "You look respectable."

"Oh." Blushing, she lowered her eyes, unaccustomed to compliments. "Um . . . thank you."

"Not in a good way," he added. "Are you hungry?"

Apparently oblivious to the way Miuko glared at him, he beckoned her to a food stall, where he bought them each a skewer of fish, presenting one to Miuko with a flourish.

"You can eat this?" she asked, taking a bone-filled bite.

"What do you mean?"

"I thought magpies ate insects."

"When I look like a bird, I eat bird food. When I look like a human, I eat human food." He shrugged. "It's not that hard."

Sufficiently chastened, Miuko accepted his next offering, a thick slice of watermelon, without further comment.

They wound upward through the city sectors until they reached the ward of the Great Houses, comprised of the noble families closest to the *yotokai*—the estates walled and somber in the shadow of the castle. Miuko, who had never dreamed of climbing so high in the city, was breathless at the sight. All of Udaiwa was laid before her like a feast: the painted gates, the gleaming rooftops, the boats bobbing in the bay to the north.

Geiki, however, appeared unphased; and, after a moment of leaning into the wind, letting it caress his cheeks and run invisible fingers through his already-tousled hair, he quickly yanked Miuko onward.

Keivoweicha-kaedo was a vast annex of archives and gardens, twined with well-kept gravel paths. In the center of the grounds stood a massive five-floored pagoda with glazed tiles, imported from the West, adorning the roofs.

As Miuko stood there, awestruck at the sight, Geiki nudged her with his good elbow. "Well?"

"Well what?"

"Are we going in or what?"

She blinked at him. "Don't you have a plan?"

"Yeah. The doors." He gestured to the entrance of the pagoda, where two guards in ebony and ochre livery stood, stiff as dolls and equally wooden, beside a wide set of double doors.

Miuko groaned. Of course, an *atskayakina* wouldn't know that women were forbidden from entering the library.

"What?" he demanded.

"Girls aren't allowed in Keivoweicha."

"What?" He recoiled as if she'd struck him. "Why not?"

"I don't know," she said crossly. "Tradition."

Geiki made a gagging sound. "You humans and your *tradition.*"

Privately, Miuko agreed with him, but she was not about to let him have the satisfaction of knowing that. Making an irritated noise, she turned away to study the library entrance, wondering if she could sneak inside when the guards changed shifts, but she was jerked off balance when Geiki grabbed her hand, dragging her out of sight.

"Geiki, what—"

In the shadow of the pagoda, he grinned at her. "So we can't use the doors! There are other ways in and out of a place, aren't there?"

"Like wh—"

But he was already strolling away, examining the library's exterior with the practiced eye of a thief. Suspecting that she was not going to like whatever "ways" he had in mind, Miuko shuffled after him.

Her apprehension, as it turned out, was not unwarranted, for he soon stopped, pointing to an open window on the first floor. Squatting beneath it, he patted the top of his thigh. "Up you go!"

"Geiki!" she whispered, both alarmed and scandalized. Someone was going to catch them! He was going to be *touching* her!

"What? Hurry up!"

Then again, she was already breaking several customs by wandering about with a boy who was neither a blood relative nor her husband. If a little boost was all that stood between her and figuring out how to remove the *shaoha*'s curse, she saw little reason not to buck this tradition too.

She stepped onto Geiki's leg and unsteadily clambered onto his shoulders, certain she'd bring them both toppling to the ground. Before her nerves could get the better of her, however, Geiki stood, launching her at the window ledge, which she grabbed, sandals knocking against the side of the building.

"Shh!" He grabbed one of her feet and pushed her through the window and into the library, where she fell, grunting, among some dusty shelves.

Geiki tumbled after her, alighting on the floor with surprising grace.

She blinked. "How did you—"

Adjusting his sling, he glared at her, as if she should not have to ask by now. "I'm a *bird*."

As her eyes adjusted to the gloom, she slipped off her sandals and surveyed the library. Cloudy sunlight filtered through the rice paper screens, illuminating long cedar shelves of diamond-shaped alcoves, wherein thousands of scrolls were kept, tucked safely inside bamboo sheaths or knotted with silk cords. Since its founding by the Omaizi Clan, Keivoweicha had stood for hundreds of years, sacred to knowledge seekers of all kinds —at least, as long as they were men—and Miuko could almost sense the difference in the air. It felt heavy, with a silence so thick it could be sliced like a block of bean curd.

Her gaze darted to the scholars hunched over the reading tables. "Which way?" she whispered to Geiki.

"How should I know?" he chirped from behind her.

Miuko looked back at him, dismayed. "Haven't you been here before?"

"Why? I don't know how to read!"

Further argument was cut short by a priest tottering past the end of their row like a juggler in a circus act, bobbling so many scrolls they seemed to come alive in his arms, jumping and unfurling, trailing over his shoulders to kiss the hems of his robes. Miuko tensed. Though she hardly dared to move, she'd never felt louder, every intake of breath like the howling of the wind, every shifting of her weight like the shuddering of the earth.

When the priest had gone, Miuko tiptoed forward in stocking feet. "Follow me, then, I guess."

Shushing each other, she and Geiki skulked among the shelves, evading the scholars who floated through the library like ghosts, until Miuko discovered that at the end of every row were paper hangings describing the contents of the shelves. On the first floor, she and Geiki slipped past ASTROLOGY, COSMOGONY, and FLUVIAL GEOMORPHOLOGY before edging up a creaking set of stairs to CRYSTALLOGRAPHY, PHILOSOPHIES OF THE ONE HUNDRED FORTY-FOUR SAGES, and MATHEMATICS, where they were briefly discombobulated somewhere between TESSELLATIONS and TIME TRAVEL, but they finally made it to the third floor, which was entirely dedicated to the study of the spirits.

Geiki looked offended. "This is all we get?"

From the alcove nearest her, Miuko slid a scroll from its protective bamboo sheath. Upon its speckled surface, the old-fashioned calligraphy was barely legible, studded with unfamiliar words and holes left by some enterprising paper louse. "Are you kidding?" she asked. "It could take me years to read all this . . ."

"*Years?*" He clutched dramatically at the shelves. "But whatever will we eat?"

Miuko squinted at the scroll, hoping against hope that it would be, by some intervention of fate, the one that would tell her how to remove a *shaoha*'s curse.

It wasn't. At least from what she could decipher.

With a sigh, she looked up again, intending to ask Geiki to begin pulling down scrolls, but to her surprise, she found him beaming widely at her. "I have an idea," he said.

"Oh?" She lifted her eyebrows. "I do hope it's as well thought-out as the last one."

Either he did not pick up on her sarcasm, or he simply did not care, for he leaned toward her until they were nearly nose to nose between the shelves and said in a conspiratorial whisper, "Ever wonder what it's like to be a man?"

11

A DAUNTING PROSPECT

THE TRUTH WAS, Miuko had many times imagined what it would be like to have the freedoms of a man. If she were a man, she could travel without the company of a male relative. She could go bare-chested in the river! She could belch without excusing herself, and take up thrice the amount of space on public benches!

But after she agreed to have Geiki disguise her with one of his illusions, she found herself fretting over her newly deepened voice and freshly stubbled cheeks; even the men's clothes she wore did not feel right on her—too tight in the arms and shoulders for comfort—for she was not, in fact, a man.

It was too late to change her mind, however, because without any further hesitation, Geiki straightened his shoulders and sauntered out toward the center of the floor, where an elderly librarian in ebony and ochre robes was pushing a cart stacked high with rolls of parchment.

"Greetings, man!" the *atskayakina* declared with a jaunty wave. "I am also a man!"

Behind the shelves, Miuko groaned, startling yet again at the unfamiliar reverberations in her chest.

"I have many possessions, such as a roof and a mustache, although as you can see, I do not have them with me right at this second." Geiki winked at the bewildered librarian, who stared at him with widening eyes. "I also have several cats, for I do not believe them to be the spiteful, needle-clawed demon-spawn that *some birds* might think they are. Aw! Kitties! Am I right?"

Without waiting for a response, he turned to Miuko, pointing. "Oh, look! A genial colleague and not a stranger I met last night in the woods. Come here, man!"

Grimacing, Miuko almost reached for her robes as she started toward the cart, but she forced her hands down. Men didn't pick up their trousers as they ran. How did men walk? She attempted a swagger, which only made the librarian frown.

Not like that, then.

"Right. Er . . ." She fumbled for the words. "Say there, do you have any information on curses?"

"Curses?" The librarian stepped back, as if she and Geiki would break out in a pox before his very eyes. "Are you—"

"Oh, no!" Miuko tried to laugh heartily, but it came out more like a cough, which caused the librarian to retreat further, covering his mouth with his sleeve. "Nothing like that! What I mean to say is, do you . . . uh . . . do you know where . . . uh . . ."

Geiki nudged her.

"We need help," she said abruptly. "Can you help us find something?"

Despite their outlandishness, the librarian seemed relieved that she wasn't going to ask him to examine a rash or a boil or something, because he let out a breath he might have been holding since she'd mentioned curses and bowed to her. "Of course."

Briefly, she explained that they were seeking information on the *shaoha*'s curse—an esoteric affliction, she added, likely not seen in centuries.

"Fine, fine," the librarian said airily, padding off down one of the room's shadowed aisles. "Oh yes, I think I might have something on that. Hmm . . . let me see . . ."

Once the man was out of sight, Geiki grinned at Miuko. "You make a good man!"

She smacked him lightly on his good shoulder. "You don't! What was all that about cats?"

"Cats are horrible, nasty things, and yet men always seem to have so many around! I was *trying* to be relatable."

Soon, the librarian returned bearing several documents in bamboo sheaths. He ushered Miuko and Geiki to a quiet corner, where he began to describe each of the scrolls' origins, authors, and contents.

At first, Miuko was elated. All this information, at her fingertips!

Then she was irate.

If she'd looked like herself, she would have been thrown out of the library as soon as she tried to set foot in it. But because she looked like a man, all she had to do was say she wanted something? And she got it? Things were just given to her, no questions asked?

It was simply not fair. She had no desire to be a man or even to continue wearing Geiki's disguise much longer. No, what she wanted were a man's *privileges,* and at that moment it was abundantly clear to her that neither she nor anyone else should *have* to be a man to have them.

She scowled at the librarian as he opened the scroll he said was most likely to contain the information she needed.

He quailed under the force of her glare.

"Thanks, man!" Geiki cried, clapping him on the back. "Now, go away!"

Sidestepping out from under Geiki's hand, the librarian blinked, perhaps perplexed by their odd behavior, and withdrew.

"Change me back!" Miuko whispered as soon as he was gone.

Dimples appeared in Geiki's cheeks. "Already done."

She touched her face—smooth. She touched her breasts—existent. Thus reassured that she was in fact herself again, she slumped into a chair with a sigh.

"Now what?" he asked.

"Now I read."

"But that's no fun!"

"You know what would be fun?" Miuko tugged the open scroll to her. "Using that magic of yours to stop anyone from bothering us."

"You humans have a strange idea of fun," he grumbled, though he grudgingly complied.

For hours, Miuko pored over studies of the spirit world, from the academic to the apocryphal. Bored, Geiki even joined her for a time, unrolling a set of illustrations that depicted the priests of the November God, Nakatalao,[1] using spells to exorcise demonic spirits and bind them in harmless objects such as stones, empty shells, and talismans carved from the tusks of hogs.

"Look!" he declared. "Pretty!"

"Uh-huh. Does it say anything about curses?"

"I don't know?"

"Just set it aside for me and keep looking."

"But it's the only one with pictures!"

It wasn't until late afternoon—long after Geiki had begun to complain that if he wasn't fed soon, he'd waste away until he was nothing but beak and bones—that Miuko discovered a lengthy poem written by the wandering monk who had first walked the path that would later become known as the Ochiirokai[2], or "Thousand-Step Way." Beginning in the south, the road ran the length of Awara, twisting and turning like a river,

---

1   Na-kata-lao (*nah-kah-tah-laoh*): literally, "spirit-closing-attendant." One of the Twelve Lunar Gods, Nakatalao presides over the change of seasons from autumn to winter. As such, he is closely associated with closings and endings: sunset, imprisonment, the signing of contracts, the split second between the states of wakefulness and sleep, etc. His animals are the boar, the pheasant, and the moon bear.

2   Ochi-iro-kai (*oh-chee-ee-roh-kye*)

connecting the Twelve Heavenly Houses, each one devoted to the worship of a different Lunar God.

Geiki peered over her shoulder as she read the passages aloud. In somewhat stilted verse, the poem described how everyday curses, such as those inflicted by fox spirits or petty demons, could be eliminated by common priests, but only the followers of Amyunasa, the December God, could remove a curse as formidable as the kiss of a *shaoha*.

And they could only be found at the House of December, a remote temple erected upon the God's Teeth, the rugged stone islands beyond the northern tip of Awara.

Dumbfounded, Miuko stared at the crumbling scroll. She'd never been farther than a half-day's walk from Nihaoi. Even now, for all she'd been banished, it brought her no small comfort to know that if she so chose, it would take only a few hours to return to the haunted fields and abandoned buildings she called home.

How could she possibly make a two-week journey across Awara with few skills besides laundering a sheet, preparing a bath, or removing a particularly stubborn stain from a straw mat?

More to the point, how could she do it when the only resources she possessed were empty pockets and a sad bundle of muddy clothes?

Geiki nudged her. "Guess we'd better get moving then, huh?"

Miuko looked up, startled. "You're not coming with me!"

She did not know if it was a question or an order. Apparently, neither did he, for he tilted his head at her, a puzzled grin playing across his lips. "What? Didn't I tell you our destinies were intertwined?"

"Won't you miss your family?"

For the briefest of moments, she thought of her father: the way he chuckled at her impudence, the way he kissed the crown of her head . . . and then, the way his face had contorted when he banished her from the only place she'd ever called home.

The *atskayakina,* too, had grown subdued. "My family was slaughtered ten years ago," he said quietly.

"Oh no. Geiki, I'm sor—"

"Kidding!" He laughed. "They're alive and well . . . and noisy. To tell you the truth, I'm looking forward to a little peace and quiet."

Miuko stood up, frowning. She didn't know whether to feel cross at his ill-conceived joke, relieved that he was volunteering to accompany her, or pleased that he considered *her,* of all people, quiet. Giving up, she decided to feel all three at once while Geiki tugged her toward the exit, declaring, "Come on! I'm hungry!" (What she no longer felt, of course, was homesick or daunted by the prospect of the journey, which was perhaps Geiki's plan all along.)

12

THE DEMON DOCTOR

AFTER A QUICK STOP for rice balls to appease Geiki's hunger (and Miuko's too, although after all his grousing she wasn't about to admit it), Miuko set off for the edge of the city, where she planned to follow the Great Highway until it met the Ochiirokai, some distance to the west. She was walking so quickly, in fact, that she almost didn't notice when Geiki took a sharp turn at the next intersection, striding in the exact opposite of the direction they needed to go.

With a sharp cry of dismay, Miuko trotted back to the *atskayakina*. "What are you doing?" she asked, pointing. "The Ochiirokai is *that* way."

"Yes, but we're not taking the Ochiirokai. At least, not yet. It makes a big detour west to the House of November before it ever starts going north, and we're short on time already."

"So what? Are we going to fly?"

"How dare you mention flying to me, you heartless human?" Then, grinning: "We're going to take a boat."

Miuko sighed, gesturing up the road from whence they'd come. "Okay, but the harbor is *that* way."

"Yes." With a shrug, the *atskayakina* continued walking again. "But the owner of the boat is *this* way."

She jogged after him as best she could in her restrictive robes. "You know someone who owns a boat?"

"Yes." He hesitated. "But she's testy."

"*She?*"

In Awara, it was forbidden for a woman to own property. She could marry well, of course, and was encouraged to do so, for then she could manage a household of extravagant size. But not even the wealthiest of women were beyond the reach of this law. Why, even the mother of the emperor could not claim her underclothes as her own.

"Who is this woman?"

The *atskayakina* fidgeted with his sling. If Miuko hadn't seen him frighten off rapacious brigands and break into libraries without so much as ruffling a feather, she might have thought he looked nervous.

"They call her the Doctor," he said at last. "And she's not a woman."

In fact, as Geiki explained to her, the Doctor was not a doctor either, but a demon named Sidrisine who was deeply enmeshed in the criminal enterprises of both humans and spirits. Apparently, she lived here in Udaiwa in the ward of the warrior class, where Miuko and Geiki soon found themselves wandering through quiet neighborhoods inhabited by old retainer families, inactive since the Five Swords Era.

Seeing the manicured gardens and stately manors, Miuko wondered aloud how a demon could live peaceably among the gentry.

"You'll see when you meet her," Geiki said as they slipped into a narrow alley between mansions. "I stole from her once, you know. A jeweled egg. It was so *shiny*."

"And you got away with it?"

Stooping beneath a curtain of vines, he opened a gate at the back of one of the gardens. "I gave it back! Plus a bolt of cloth I thought she'd like! I just wanted to see if I could do it!"

"Do you really think she'll help us now?"

They crossed a path of perfectly placed stepping stones and knocked upon a door in a shadowed corner of the house. Geiki plucked at a stray thread of his sling. "If she's not in a mood," he said.

"And if she is?"

The *atskayakina* grinned sheepishly at her. "You were fine with walking, right?"

Miuko glowered at him, but schooled her expression quickly when a man in servants robes opened the door. He stared at them blankly, as if waiting for instruction. Then, "May I help you?" He had an odd, inflectionless voice, as if it had been stripped of all emotion.

"We're here to see the Doctor," Geiki said.

Bowing low, the man beckoned them inside.

There was something strange about his movements too, Miuko thought as she slid off her sandals: a slackness in his jaw, a disinterest in his posture. Though his eyes were open, they seemed not to focus on anything in particular as he led them effortlessly through a series of cool, dark corridors.

After a few minutes, they arrived — not at some dank cellar, which Miuko thought would have suited a demon, but at a handsomely appointed room somewhere in the heart of the manor. The sliding screens were painted with images of distant mountains fading into mist. The straw mats were so smooth they shone, and smelled as fresh as newly cut grass. More servants, like the man who had shown them the way, stood in the corners like statues.

And in the back of the room, upon a cushion of tasseled brocade, sat the Doctor.

At first glance, she looked almost human, for she had two arms, two legs, and neither horns nor tail to speak of. If anything was unusual about her appearance, it was merely that the top of her head was perfectly smooth, like a tumbled stone, and that she did not sit like any woman Miuko had ever met.

Human women sat with their legs tucked demurely under them. It often set Miuko's feet to tingling, which made her suspect that such a posture was a ploy to keep women from being able to run from tiresome conversations.

The Doctor, in contrast, sat with her legs akimbo: one knee up, one knee to the side. It would have been vulgar if she'd not been wearing an oversize robe and a pair of men's trousers. As it was, it seemed to Miuko to give the Doctor an almost contorted shape.

Miuko gawked. She could not help it. Sidrisine *exhaled* power. She commanded the entire room with nothing but her presence.

And she was a *woman*. Or a female spirit, at any rate.

Never in her seventeen years had Miuko seen anything like it, and, standing there, she could not help wanting to see more.

She bowed. Beside her, Geiki did too, but that only made her nervous, for until this moment the *atskayakina* had shown little interest in manners and had, it seemed, gone out of his way to avoid them.

"Geiki," said the Doctor, her voice soft and slick as the fine silks Miuko had seen in the merchant ward earlier that day. "You've got a lot of nerve showing up here, little bird. Why, I ought to strangle you where you stand, just to make an example out of you."

He bobbed up again, tugging at his sling. "I . . . er . . . was hoping that was behind us, Sidrisine-jai."

"Oh?" Reaching for the golden platter beside her, the Doctor lifted a cream-colored egg from a pile, angled it into her mouth, and swallowed it whole. "And what do you hope is before us?"

In a few halting sentences, he explained their predicament.

"A *shaoha*?" In one swift movement, Sidrisine arose from her cushion, shedding her oversize robe so she stood before them in only her slip and trousers, long arms and angular shoulders bare to the world.

Blushing, Miuko lowered her gaze.

There was a slithering sound, and then a cool finger was laid against her cheek. "You're a timid thing, aren't you?"

Looking up again, Miuko found herself staring into the Doctor's eyes.

Up close, the demon was huge as well as beautiful, with broad lips, narrow nose, and wide-set eyes as black as jet.

A second set of lids closed sideways over those strange eyes and retracted again.

Miuko stifled a gasp.

Sidrisine was a snake demon—an evil spirit whose gaze could turn a man into a mindless thrall. In the stories, snake demons preyed upon rapacious warriors and lascivious drunkards, men who made promises out of desire and broke them as soon as they'd been satisfied.

Were the servants men like that? They had not moved once since Geiki and Miuko entered the room. She knew she ought to feel sorry for them, but somehow she could not quite bring herself to do it.

"Don't worry, little *shaoha*." The Doctor smiled. "At times even a viper must hide her nature, if she is to survive."

"But I don't want to be a viper," Miuko blurted out. "I mean, a *shaoha*."

Sidrisine raised an eyebrow. "How dull of you."

Despite knowing the snake demon was a cruel, violent monster and therefore an inappropriate role model, Miuko could not help feeling a familiar twinge of shame—an emotion she easily recognized from all the times she'd disappointed her father.

The Doctor returned her attention to Geiki. "You're in luck, little bird. I'm in need of your talents. I host a card game every month, and *someone* has been cheating. I need to find out which of my illustrious guests would dare."

"And you want *me* to do it?" Geiki squawked.

"What better way to catch a trickster than with a trickster?" Pivoting on one heel, Sidrisine swept across the room to her cushion, where she coiled herself into another unladylike—albeit, Miuko had to admit, formidable—shape.

Geiki bowed. "I'm at your service, Sidrisine-jai."

Miuko bit her lip nervously. He had to know what he was doing, right? He must have thought of the consequences of making a deal with a snake demon.

Then again, as far as she'd seen, the *atskayakina* didn't do much thinking at all.

Another smile twisted the Doctor's lips. "Very well. I shall stake you. The game begins at —"

"Stake him what?" Miuko interrupted.

Both Sidrisine and Geiki turned their eyes on her impatiently.

"Favors." The *atskayakina* sighed. "What else do you think *nasu* gamble with?"

"Little favors from little spirits like your friend here," the Doctor added. "Big ones from more powerful spirits."

"I'd have to put in a dozen favors for just one from Sidrisine," Geiki explained. "She'd have to put in a dozen to equal just one from an even more powerful spirit. Get it?"

Miuko frowned. Like everyone else in Awara, she knew spirits had a hierarchy, just as mortals did. Common spirits, like *atskayakinasu,* were less powerful than longer-lived *nasu,* whose domains might be a very large boulder or a hoary tree. Then came high spirits, like those of seas and mountains, and finally, greatest of all in power and importance, the Lunar Gods. (Of course, this was to say nothing of demons — who could, oddly enough, be both powerful and abject at the same time.) It was all very confusing, and Miuko, like most humans, had little grasp over the intricacies of such divisions.

"So you gamble for favors," she said. "And then . . . ?"

"Cash in our winnings when we want them," said the Doctor. "Although I don't know what I'd do with a favor from an *atskayakina.*"

Geiki puffed out his chest. "You never know! Need an illusion? Need something stolen? I'm your bird!"

Sidrisine's lip curled in disgust. "Just find me my swindler, and you'll have your boat ride across the bay. Now, you'd better clean yourselves up before tonight. You, little viper, smell of servant, and that's certain to make you suspect."

13

BEYOND HUMAN IMAGINING

THE DOCTOR'S GAMBLING PARLOR was located in the basement of one of the city's largest temples, where no one would suspect to find a demon's den — or so she claimed. It was certainly the nicest basement Miuko had ever seen, with gilded walls, exotic hardwood furniture, and dozens of dangling lanterns that cast patterned shadows over Sidrisine's strange assortment of guests, both mortal and spirit.

First, there were six card players: Sidrisine; Geiki; a hornbeam spirit so tall her branches grazed the ceiling; a cloud spirit even smaller than Miuko; a man with pale blue skin and a habit of dissolving into a small blizzard; and last, a human man dressed entirely in plum.

There were plenty of other spirits too, for many of the players had arrived with entourages: *baiganasu*[1] — monkey spirits — with red faces and golden fur, goblins, bare-chested ogres, a spider woman with six arms draped in glittering lace, and still more spirits which Miuko in her limited experience could not name.

Grimacing uncomfortably, she fidgeted with her new embroidered robes. Thanks to Sidrisine's generosity, she and Geiki had been supplied with baths, fine clothes, and a choice of perfumes ranging from sulfur to sweet cherry, but these accoutrements had only made her feel even more

---

1   baiga-na (*bye-gah-nah*): in the language of Awara, the word for "monkey" is *baiga*, meaning "red face," and the word for "spirit" is *na*. Therefore, *baigana*, or, plural, *baiganasu*. According to the stories, *baiganasu* are primarily associated with journeys and have, on occasion, been known to use *baigavasu* — or "monkey lights" — to guide lost travelers safely home.

out of place, for they did not suit her. To add insult to injury, her new hair pin—carved from the carapace of some gigantic green beetle—seemed to hold nothing but contempt for her efforts to blend in, for it kept trying to slip stealthily from the girl's knot at the top of her head.

Miuko shoved the traitorous piece of jewelry back into place as she studied the crowd. "Which one do you think is the card sharp?" she whispered to Geiki, who, much to her envy, looked rather handsome in his black robes, the cloth shimmering blue where it caught the lamplight.

"It could be anyone," he replied, taking a pastry from one of the Doctor's thralls, who were circulating among the crowd with lacquered trays of refreshments.

"What about her?" Miuko nodded toward the cloud spirit, attired in gauzy white robes, who downed a cup of rice wine in a single gulp before beckoning for another.

"Beikai's a *them*, not a *her*," Geiki said through a mouthful of food. "And no. Not a chance."

Tilting her head, Miuko considered the cloud spirit thoughtfully. According to the lore, spirits had always had several genders. In ages past, humans had been equally diverse, but recent centuries had seen the reduction of their genders to male, female, and *hei*,[2] meaning "neither male nor female." Once, *heisu* had had social positions and families like anyone else, but under the rigid cultural strata of the Omaizi, they had been persecuted to the point where they were accepted only in rare corners of Awaran society, such as the priesthood at the House of December. As a result, Miuko had never met anyone who wasn't a man or a woman—at least, not to her knowledge—but she supposed there was much more to the world than she'd experienced in the limited

---

2   hei *(hay)*: a nonbinary person, whether mortal or spirit. In this text, the pronouns for *hei* (singular) and *heisu* (plural) have been translated into English as "they" and "them."

71

confines of Nihaoi, and indeed even more than that beyond the borders of human imagining.

"Shouldn't we suspect everyone?" she asked.

"Not *Beikai*." Geiki scoffed. "They're one of the Children of the North Wind! I heard they've even got a big shrine north of Izajila inlet somewhere. Do you know how powerful they are?"

Miuko surveyed the diminutive spirit, whose cheeks had begun to glow with drink, red as suns in fog. "How powerful?" she asked dubiously.

"You know how I'd need to stake a dozen favors for just one of Sidrisine's?" Geiki asked. "Well, I'd need a *hundred* to match one of Beikai's."

Miuko's jaw dropped. "A *hundred*?" she squeaked.

"Shh!" He stepped in front of her, blocking her view of the cloud spirit. "Don't gawk!"

Miuko made a face at him. "I just didn't know a demigod would even deign to be seen with a bird like you!"

"Hey, you're not so great either, human!"

As if in agreement, Miuko's green pin slid down her hair in another attempted escape, but she clapped her hand to the side of her head, thrusting it back into place.

Geiki shot her an annoyed glance. "Why are you squirming like that? You're going to attract attention."

"No one's paying attention to me," Miuko answered grumpily.

Indeed, between Sidrisine, who was beginning to call the players to their seats, and the *baiganasu,* who were clambering over the thralls, spilling cups of rice wine and something that looked suspiciously like blood, there was not much reason to notice a human girl like Miuko.

But perhaps she could use that to her advantage.

"What's your plan for finding the card sharp?" she whispered as she and Geiki drifted toward the card table.

He shrugged.

"You don't have one?"

"Why bother? They always go wrong."

"That doesn't mean you shouldn't make one!" Miuko caught her voice rising and quickly yanked it down again. "I can help. If I can slip through the crowd unnoticed, maybe I can spot our swindler."

"Great idea." Flashing her a grin, Geiki plopped down on one of the six embroidered cushions arranged for the players, where he was joined on one side by the man who wore only plum and on the other by the spirit who kept turning into a snowstorm.

"An *odoshoya*,"[3] Geiki whispered before Miuko could ask. "A demon who preys on travelers, killing them in the cold."

Miuko glanced over at the demon as he transformed back into a pale blue man with a slight paunch and a speckling of gray in his otherwise black hair. "How come he can shapeshift when we're watching him?"

"The middle-aged-man-who's-also-a-blizzard is one of his forms. The other's a lot uglier—I hear he has talons so sharp, he can rip you to shreds with the slightest touch."

Miuko gulped. "Don't get caught," she murmured.

Geiki winked at her. "I won't."

Once the players were settled, Sidrisine positioned herself at one end of the card table, stately as any of the nobility. In fact, so arresting was she in her robes of black and gold that all she had to do was lift one of her hands, and she commanded the attention of the entire room.

As the game commenced, Miuko circled the table. From what she could gather, the rules were fairly straightforward—there was some sort of betting with lacquered tokens, and bluffing seemed particularly important—although she found the nuances of the game difficult to follow. For his part, Geiki appeared to be a passable player, if somewhat gregarious,

---

3 **odo-sho-ya** (*oh-doh-shoh-yah*): literally, "lost-cold-evil."

which the other players regarded with varying degrees of tolerance, from the hornbeam spirit's creaking chuckle to the frigid glare of the *odoshoya*.

Moving among the other guests, Miuko eavesdropped on their conversations, hoping to glean some useful information, but to her disappointment she found nothing of import. One of the human women who'd accompanied the man in plum was bored. The monkey spirits, nearly as drunk as Beikai, had begun harassing the cloud spirit for refusing to help another troupe of *baiganasu* near Beikai's shrine at Izajila. The ogres, predictably, had little of interest to say.

Half an hour into the game, Miuko had discovered nothing useful, and she could feel her hair pin attempting to slip from its place again. Stepping out of the crowd to adjust it, she accidentally elbowed one of the thralls, who was passing with a tray of beverages. The man grunted. The tray went flying. A dozen ceramic cups went cascading to the floor.

Miuko groaned. These were not even the first cups she'd broken this week.

The other guests turned to glare at her.

So much for escaping notice.

Miuko felt her cheeks go hot. "I'm sorry," she said with a quick bow. "Please, continue."

Shrieking with laughter, one of the monkey spirits bowed in imitation. The goblins cackled, thumbing their long red noses.

Loudly, the man in plum demanded to know who'd brought her. Plain *and* clumsy? She ought to be sent away where no one had to stand the sight of her.

Some of the others laughed.

In her seventeen years, Miuko had wished many times for the gift of melting into the ground, and for a moment, she hoped that the *shaoha*'s curse had gifted her the power to dribble through the floorboards with the spilled wine; but, alas, she remained solidly where she was.

Then she heard Geiki's voice over the laughter: "Try that again!"

She looked up.

The *atskayakina* locked eyes with her, though he did not seem to be addressing her at all. "Try that trick again, Beikai-jai, and I'll take you for all you've got! I'm onto you now!"

He held Miuko's gaze a moment longer before grinning at the cloud spirit and cracking some joke she scarcely heard.

Try that again.

Did he mean her? Try *what,* exactly? Embarrassing herself?

Or interrupting the game?

No one was watching her now; they'd all returned their attention to their cards. As one of the goblins passed her, she extended her foot, causing him to stumble into the *baiganasu,* who leapt at him, pulling at his nose and ears.

Quickly, she slid between a pair of ogres to avoid suspicion, but no one seemed to have noticed.

She glanced at Geiki to see if she'd understood him correctly, but he was focused on the card table, where there was a flash of light.

A mirror?

No, an illusion of a mirror, winking in and out of existence beside the hornbeam spirit's cards as she turned to stare at the squabbling monkey spirits.

Geiki had seized the opportunity to spy on the other players' hands.

And she, Miuko thought with a ripple of excitement, was helping him.

As luck would have it, Miuko was not the only distraction either. One of the human women fainted when an ogre let out a particularly malodorous fart. The goblins began insulting the *odoshoya,* who withstood their jibes with a cold reserve, dropping the temperature in the basement so precipitously that for a minute Miuko could see her breath fogging in the air.

Every time their attention was turned, Geiki conjured one of his little mirrors. Every time, Miuko felt that same thrill of pleasure.

Then the hornbeam spirit ran out of tokens. After grabbing one of Sidrisine's thralls and shaking him about like a baby's rattle, she was escorted from the room. Gleefully, the *baiganasu* capered after her, some wagging their bottoms at the remaining guests in a sort of vulgar farewell.

Worried, Miuko glanced at Geiki's pile of tokens, which had shrunk to half its original size. If they didn't find the card sharp before he, too, was removed from the game, they'd lose their chance at crossing the bay.

Something in his demeanor had changed as well—he was less chatty, more subdued. When he spoke now, his voice had lost its raucous edge.

His reserves dropped to twenty tokens.

Then seventeen.

Then five.

By this time Geiki was not speaking at all, swallowing hard when he glanced at his cards. He caught Miuko's eye across the table, opening and closing his mouth as if he were a fish. Was he having trouble speaking? His eyes bulged. The tendons at his neck strained.

Was he having trouble breathing?

No one else seemed to have noticed, not even the Doctor, who was chatting idly with the spider woman.

Geiki's hands went to his throat.

"Help!" Crying out, Miuko shoved one of the goblins out of her way—or at least she tried, for instead of pushing him aside, she tripped over her own feet and tumbled directly into the *odoshoya*, who crashed to the floor beneath her.

"Oh no!" she gasped, blushing. "My deepest apol . . ."

But her voice trailed off, for from the sleeve of his robes fluttered an extra set of cards, which alighted on the floor like the last red leaves fluttering onto the snow.

Miuko blinked.

She'd done it. She'd found Sidrisine's swindler.

For a moment, no one spoke. Then the man in plum leapt to his feet, slamming his hands upon the table. *"Vakaiga!"*[4] he bellowed. "I knew no one could be that lucky!"

---

4   **vakai-ga** (*vah-kye-guh*). an Awaran swear word. Like some English curses, *vakai* is a versatile word which can be used in a splendiferous variety of insults, including *vakaizu*, meaning "one who does *vakai*" and *vakaiga*, meaning "*vakai* face."

14

CARNAGE AND RESPECT

BEFORE MIUKO COULD REACT, the spider woman flung a net of lace at the *odoshoya;* but, with more agility than his middle-aged form would suggest, he rolled aside, leaving Miuko and the goblin trapped in the web behind him.

As they struggled, there was a great howling sound, like that of a winter gale. Out of nowhere, a cloak of snow descended upon the gambling parlor, obscuring the lanterns, then the ogres' heads, and Sidrisine, who screamed in frustration as she fought through the throng.

Miuko squinted, but she could see nothing in the white-out. From somewhere overhead, there was a screech. Startled, someone—it must have been one of the ogres—slammed their fists into the table with a thunderous *crack!* Lacquered tokens came clattering down around Miuko like hail.

The goblin writhed about, pricking her back and shoulders with his long fingernails as he attempted to escape.

"Stop!" She tried to disentangle herself from the web, but one hand was lodged beneath her, and the other had been pinned above her head.

Sensing an opening, the green pin came loose from her hair at last. Its victory was short-lived, however, for it fell a hand-length and smacked neatly into Miuko's palm.

"Ha!" Blowing loose hair from her face, she yanked the sharp, stubborn pin across the spider woman's net.

As the shimmering strands parted, the goblin thrashed wildly, kicking her twice in the ribs in his haste and scrambling into the snow without so much as a word of thanks.

Standing, Miuko shoved the hair pin into her robes and flung the web aside, searching the melee for Geiki's tousled hair. As she stumbled through the blizzard, she came across spitting demons and shrieking spirits. Once, as the white-out cleared momentarily, she saw the Doctor's thralls clawing at the *odoshoya,* who had transformed into a four-armed monster made of ice.

But the *atskayakina* was nowhere to be seen.

Faltering, Miuko bumped into the broken table. Someone whimpered.

Geiki?

Not Geiki.

She knelt. Pinned beneath the table was the cloud spirit, still in their fragile human form, who blinked at her crossly.

"Beikai-jai! Are you hurt?" Miuko asked.

"Just stuck," the spirit mumbled, trying to free their arms. "I can't shapeshift—the *odoshoya*'s frozen us all in our current forms. Smart of him, but damned annoying."

Miuko gripped the edge of the table, heaving at it with all her strength.

It hardly moved.

Gritting her teeth, she tried again, resolving that when she returned to Nihaoi, she'd endeavor to exercise her arms as well as her legs, lest she be caught in such mayhem again.

"What are you doing?" Geiki appeared at her side, robes torn, scratches on his cheek. "Let's get out of here!"

"You're okay!" she cried.

"Of course I am!"

"I thought you were choking!"

"Nah, I just couldn't speak! The *odoshoya* must have caught on to me.

He can smother sounds, you know. He just had to silence me until we'd left the parlor, and then he would've caught us both! Good thing you're so clumsy, or we never would've—"

"Excuse me," Beikai interrupted with some impatience, "but since you're here, are you going to do anything about this *vakai* table?"

Grinning widely at the high spirit's foul language, the *atskayakina* actually took a moment to bow to them. "Of course, Beikai-jai."

A platter of sweets went whizzing past his head as he took hold of the table with his good arm. Together, he and Miuko began to lift.

With a grunt, the cloud spirit wriggled out from underneath the table, and Geiki and Miuko let it drop with a crash.

"Can we go now?" the *atskayakina* asked.

Beikai's gray eyes had gone blazing white. "Not yet." With a wave of their arms, they flooded the room with a frigid wind. The thick snowfall dispersed as if it were no more than a cloud of gnats, revealing guests caught in various states of violence: snapping arms, pulling hair, clawing at eyes and cheeks.

On the far side of the parlor, the *odoshoya* tore at one of the ogres with his taloned fingers, rending the thick skin as if it were no more than rice paper.

Seeing Beikai in the newly cleared air, he snarled, baring several rows of gleaming, dagger-point teeth.

But Beikai appeared unphased by the sight. Smirking, they lifted their hands and clapped once.

The *odoshoya* flew upward with such force that he struck the ceiling, cracking one of the beams, and collapsed in a dazed heap upon the floor, human again in shape.

Stunned, the other guests ceased their squabbles.

Seizing the opportunity, Sidrisine slithered across the parlor. Quick as a striking viper, she pinned something to the *odoshoya*'s chest.

A paper talisman.

The demon roared, wild as the winter wind, but the talisman seemed to have fixed him in middle-aged man form; as Sidrisine placed her foot onto his throat, he could do little but squirm.

The remaining guests drew back silently.

Sidrisine smiled.

Across the room, Miuko shuddered. Although she'd been awed by the Doctor's authority over men and spirits, she realized now that the snake demon wielded her power the same way human men did—as an instrument of fear and subjugation—and though Miuko could admit now that she was not satisfied with her station as a servant girl, neither did she wish to trade carnage for respect.

"Come on," Beikai said, tugging Miuko and Geiki toward the exit. "You don't want to see what happens next."

Quietly, they filed out of the basement with the other disheveled mortals and injured spirits, who dispersed down the streets of the temple district with murmured farewells and bewildered, listing steps.

"That ought to teach me not to debase myself at card games with *yagrasu* and men," Beikai grumbled, dusting off their robes. "At least not for another hundred years."

Still somewhat stunned by the violence she'd just witnessed, Miuko said nothing, twisting her loose hair absentmindedly.

"Hey." The cloud spirit snapped their fingers at her. "What's the matter with you, girl?"

Geiki peered at her, then shrugged. "Must be the flush of success!"

Beikai sniffed. "You were one bad hand from owing the *odoshoya* enough favors to keep you busy the rest of your natural life, *atskayakina*. I wouldn't call that success."

"Only if we were trying to win at cards, Beikai-jai, which we were not!"

The cloud spirit narrowed their eyes. "You sneaky bird! Did Sidrisine hire you to sniff out a cheater in our midst? I should've suspected when I saw an *atskayakina* at that table."

"Hey!" he squawked. "I saved you!"

The cloud spirit waved him off. "Yes, yes. And now I owe you one."

Miuko had never seen anyone flip so quickly from indignation to absolute astonishment as Geiki did now. His shoulders slumped. His jaw dropped. For a second, she thought he might have forgotten to breathe.

And then she realized what "I owe you" meant to the *nasu*.

A favor.

A favor from a *high spirit*.

In ordinary circumstances, Miuko might not have dared to ask, but at this moment, she could not help imagining herself walking back through the spirit gate at Nihaoi, past the temple of the lugubrious priests to the ruins of the inn, where she'd show her father and anyone else who cared to look her pale, unmarked feet. . . .

"Can you remove my curse?"

Beikai looked her up and down, squinting. "Curse?"

Duly, Miuko rolled down her sock, exposing the skin of her ankle, which had turned a brilliant indigo since her bath earlier that evening.

"Is that a *shaoha*'s curse?" The cloud spirit blinked. "No."

"What about a ride?" Geiki asked helpfully. "To the House of December?"

"You? Certainly. A mortal? Too heavy. You'd fall right through my clouds."

Miuko bowed, trying to hide her disappointment. "Thank you anyway."

"Well, when you want something doable—and only one thing, mind you—come find me at my shrine by Izajila," Beikai said. "I've had quite enough of the big city to last me a couple decades." As they spoke, the air thickened. Fog spilled over the temple grounds, denser even than the *naiana*. With a smile and a salute, Beikai took one step backward and was swallowed by mist.

Then the cloud bank lifted from the earth, sprinkling Miuko and Geiki with rain, and soared off to the south, leaving nothing but the stars and the crescent moon behind.

"A favor?" Geiki collapsed upon the temple steps, running his fingers through his hair. "A favor! I wonder what I should ask for. Some followers, maybe? Just call me *atskayakina*-kanai!"

Lord Magpie. Miuko could not help but chuckle as she sat beside him. "Asking for followers isn't a favor. It's greedy."

"So?"

"Greed is not a virtue."

"It is for an *atskayakina*!"

Miuko laughed, loudly this time. She would not have thought she could laugh like that, in public and past midnight in the aftermath of a violent brawl. But she supposed her standards had changed in the three nights since she'd met the *shaoha*. Perhaps being cursed put things into perspective like that.

Smiling, she swept her loose hair into a knot and fastened it in place with the green pin, which, for the first time that night, remained happily where it was.

15

A SEED, TAKING ROOT

WHEN SIDRISINE AT LAST appeared from the temple basement, she made no mention of the *odoshoya* or his fate, but Miuko could not help but notice the crescents of blood beneath the fingernails of the Doctor's otherwise immaculate hands. For their good work, she provided them with traveling clothes and provisions, and bade them follow her thralls to the harbor, where they were to depart immediately for the north shore of the bay.

Yawning, Miuko and Geiki stumbled after the thralls, and at the docks they climbed clumsily into the Doctor's boat, where the *atskayakina* curled up in a nest of rope and promptly fell asleep.

Miuko, however, remained awake, looking back in the direction of Nihaoi as the Doctor's thralls unmoored the boat and leapt aboard.

She was really leaving.

For a moment, she pictured the haunted fields, the temple, the teahouse, the inn . . . Otori Rohiro. She did not think of him now as the man in the fire, face contorted with fear, but as the father she'd known all her life: mild-mannered, hard of hearing, tolerant of all her failings as a daughter and a girl of the serving class.

If all went well, she would return soon.

But if it didn't, she would never again be this close to home.

With that thought in mind, she closed her eyes and drifted off as they left the harbor, soothed by the rocking of the boat and the sound of the wind in the sails.

These sensations were still there when she awoke, though the skies had shifted from the blue of night to the gray of morning. Ahead of them—not far at all, judging by how quickly they skimmed over the water—lay a sheltered harbor, the stone jetties stretching into the bay like welcoming arms.

"You're up!" Geiki shouted from the prow, where he was leaning into the breeze. "Did you know you snore?"

Too tired to be either irritated or embarrassed, Miuko joined him, rubbing her eyes. The sun had not yet risen in the east, but upon the western horizon, an ugly haze had emerged, swelling over the distant mountains like a water-bloated carcass washed upon a shore.

"What's that?" she asked, clutching the railing for balance.

"It showed up just after dawn." Geiki shook sea spray from his hair. "A forest fire, maybe?"

"The House of November is in those mountains," she said, frowning. "You don't think—"

"Nah. Who would burn a temple? Whatever it is, it's a good thing we didn't take the Ochiirokai, or we would've been held up there for days!"

Miuko nodded, though she could not help feeling troubled. More than that, she could not shake the strange sensation that she had missed something important—it was the same way she felt when she forgot to bank the bathtub fires at night or left the kettle boiling when she went out to muck the stables for her father. She was so preoccupied, in fact, that she didn't even notice when they sailed into the harbor, gliding smoothly for an empty berth.

"ARE YOU CRAZY?" A sudden shout jolted her out of her reverie. "GET DOWN FROM THERE, GIRL!"

With a cry, Miuko let go of the railing. Then, having nothing at all to hold onto, she lost her footing, landing hard on the deck of the boat with a *whump!*

"Miuko!" Geiki cried.

"WHAT'D I TELL YOU?" On the dock, a stevedore with weatherworn skin and callused hands was waving at them as if they were a house on fire. "YOU'RE GOING TO BREAK YOUR DAMNED NECK!"

Geiki crouched beside her. "Are you okay?"

Miuko hardly heard him. Her entire body had gone very cold all of a sudden—cold enough that she could no longer feel her feet or lower legs. In her mind's eye, she imagined herself leaping over the rail and throwing the stevedore to the dock, pressing her bare foot to his grizzled throat until he gasped horribly for air.

"What are you doing?" Geiki's voice interrupted her thoughts.

Surprised, she glanced down to find that she was holding her sandal in one hand and had begun peeling off her sock with the other. Visible beneath the hem of her robes was the blue stain, brushing her calves now, as if she'd stepped into the shallows of an indigo sea.

She gasped.

She'd wanted to *attack* that man, the same way Sidrisine had attacked the *odoshoya* in the gambling parlor.

Would she have done it, if Geiki had not brought her back to herself?

Would that have been so bad? a little voice inside her wondered.

Miuko hesitated. In her seventeen years, she'd had plenty of experience with her own private thoughts (many of them snide), but this voice was not her own. Not entirely, at least, for it was deeper and raspier, colder and whisperier.

It sounded like the *shaoha* from the Old Road.

Aghast, she willed the voice to remain silent . . . and was relieved when it did not reply.

Shaking her head, she tugged her sock back into place. "Nothing," she muttered to Geiki. "Sorry."

The *atskayakina* gave her a strange look, but before he could say anything, he was accosted by the stevedore, who began scolding him for not watching Miuko better.

Ordinarily, she would have been annoyed, but she had more pressing concerns at the moment than a self-righteous dockworker. She'd known something was different as soon as the *shaoha* kissed her. She'd felt it deep inside of her: the sensation of a seed opening, a cold tendril worming its way out. For four days, she'd allowed herself to believe that only her outward appearance had been affected, but with the arrival of the demon-voice, she could ignore it no longer. The curse had not only changed her skin.

She was afraid it was changing her heart.

16

THE OCHIIROKAI

IT TOOK THEM all morning to find their way to the Ochiirokai, which wound through the fertile farm country on the north side of the bay. Although the pilgrim road was not as busy as the Great Highways, for a few pleasant hours Miuko and Geiki found themselves caught up in a steady trickle of wandering priests, carts, and men on horses. Once, she even thought she heard the distant *whoosh* of air, coursing across the fields, that her mother had always said was the sign of a *baiganasu* sleigh careening across the countryside. Briefly, Miuko wondered if this one belonged to the monkey spirits from the gambling parlor or to another, equally boisterous troupe.

By midafternoon, however, the Thousand-Step Way had emptied. Insects chirred sleepily in the thickets. A bird sipped at a pool of ditchwater and flew away. Perhaps it had simply grown too warm for travel, Miuko thought, for the air felt wet and heavy with heat.

But as she glanced around, the back of her neck prickled. They ought to have seen *someone* — if not monks seeking to make offerings at each of the Twelve Heavenly Houses, then errand boys, market-goers, or woodcutters with bundles of kindling upon their backs.

"Something strange is going on," she said.

"What do you mean?" Geiki asked, taking her question as an opportunity to rest in the shadow of a beech tree.

"We're the only ones out here. Doesn't that strike you as odd?"

"No?" Then, seeing her expression: "Yes? How am I supposed to know what's odd for humans? You're born with extra sets of teeth, like sharks!"

"There should be more people out here." Miuko shivered, though it was far from cold, and cast another glance about her. "We'd better hurry."

Hurrying, however, was nearly impossible, for now that they'd been walking for the better part of a day, the *atskayakina* insisted on stopping every hundred steps to rest. "My feet hurt," he complained. "I wish we could fly. We'd be there in a few days if my wing were healed."

Leaning wearily against a nearby stone, Miuko imagined the *atskayakina* soaring off into the sweltering blue sky, leaving her alone upon the deserted road. "When will it heal?"

"Another couple days, probably. And then . . . freedom!"

"For you," she grumbled. "*I'll* still have to walk."

"What, you don't think I could carry you?" He puffed out his narrow chest. "I'll have you know, I'm a bird of fine size!"

Although Miuko felt guilty, for she'd apparently injured his pride, she was pleased when he quickened his pace.

They did not see another soul until they crossed the spirit gate at the edge of the next town. Vevaona, it was called—a small hamlet catering mostly to pilgrims. Along the road were a variety of shops selling everything from vials of blessed water to sun hats woven from straw, while under paper umbrellas traveling merchants displayed charms for warding off predatory spirits and talismans of good fortune scrawled in sacred indigo ink.

As they walked, Miuko noticed Geiki lagging behind again, so she stopped beside a line of vermillion prayer flags to wait. It was only then that she noticed something was wrong with him. His robes were bulging in odd places, so alarmingly that for a moment she was certain she'd caught him mid-transformation, his body fixed in some mangled shape—

She frowned.

He was not transforming. By his own admission, he could not do so while someone was watching.

"Geiki?"

"Yes?" He smiled innocently. Something inside his robes jingled.

"What have you done?"

"What?" He tried to look cross. "You don't know what it's like to be a shapeshifter! Maybe this is one of my forms!"

She raised an eyebrow, as she'd seen the Doctor do. "Is it?"

"No." Then: "I also have more than two forms. Sometimes I'm a *giant bir*—"

"What did you take?"

He bit his lip. Moments later, he pulled her into the shadow of a building, sliding from his injured arm a brass bangle she was certain hadn't been in his possession that morning.

Miuko extended her hand to take it. "Who did you—"

A silver coin landed in her palm next, followed by five others, a glinting snarl of thread, a copper incense holder, and something that looked like a decorative fingernail, scrawled with golden filigree.

"*Geiki!*"

"What? I'm a magpie!"

"You have to give this back right now!"

"Give it back?" He laughed as if this were the funniest thing he'd ever heard.

Miuko's expression, however, remained grim.

The *atskayakina*'s teeth clicked shut. "You're kidding?"

"No."

"But why? The Doctor barely gave us enough to cover a couple nights at a guesthouse! With this, we can rent a horse! Don't you *want* to get to the House of December?"

Miuko stared down at the gleaming pile of treasure. "Of course I do, but . . ."

"But what?"

She could not stop thinking about the attack on the stevedore. She had not done it, but she'd *wanted* to do it. A small part of her still craved it: the *thud* of his body striking the dock, the fear in his eyes . . .

"But I want to do it as myself," she said at last. "And I wouldn't do this."

"I would!"

She pressed the jumble of pilfered goods back into his hands. "I can't, Geiki. I'm sorry."

He shrugged. "Okay."

"Just like that?"

"Sure, if it's important to you. The fun's in the taking anyway."

Contrary to his claims, however, the *atskayakina* seemed to derive a great deal of pleasure from ridding himself of his ill-gotten gains: slipping coins into pockets, hanging the bell in a shop window while no one was looking, placing the gold fingernail upon the nose of a stone idol at the entrance to the town.

The thread he kept, for he'd found it on the ground, and Miuko insisted that they not litter.

Thus divested of their stolen treasures, they entered Vevaona's guest-house with clear consciences, or at least Miuko did. (When it came to thievery, she did not think Geiki *had* a conscience.)

The inn was larger than her father's, she observed with envy, boasting twelve rooms and an inner garden of moss and stone. Upon the veranda, a man in white robes sat cross-legged as if in contemplation, a sheathed sword in front of him and a water gourd at his side.

"Welcome to Vevaona!" An elderly man in the simple garb of the serving class bowed to them. "I am the proprietor of this guesthouse. How many rooms would you like tonight?"

Geiki said nothing.

Blushing, Miuko drew him aside. "Talk to him."

"Why? You're the human."

"You're a boy!"

He scoffed. "Not a *human* boy."

"Girls aren't allowed to rent rooms."

Or do much of anything, the small voice inside her added with mild resentment.

Miuko wanted to laugh, but encouraging her demon-voice was a dangerous business, so she bit her lip to keep from smiling.

"Fine." The *atskayakina* shook himself, as if smoothing his ruffled feathers, and approached the proprietor. "Two rooms, please."

"Ah. Brother and sister, then?"

"Us? Not a—" He coughed as Miuko elbowed him. "I mean, *yes.*"

"Good thing you arrived before dusk," the proprietor said, gesturing for them to follow. "The roads will be dangerous at the verge hour."

"More dangerous than usual?" Miuko could not help but think of the *shaoha:* white eyes, limp black hair, skin like ocean.

The proprietor frowned at her impertinence. "Yes. There have been a number of hauntings around here of late. They say that ghosts have been luring travelers from the road. They fall into ditches and drown in shallow pools."

Here, he paused, leaning toward them conspiratorially and, in a whisper perfected by all members of the serving class—except Miuko, of course —said, "You see that man over there? He's a *kyakyozuya.*"[1]

A demon hunter. Miuko glanced at the man on the veranda again. That explained his robes, she supposed. White, like the moon or the featureless face of Amyunasa, was the color of purity, unsullied by mortal affairs. Miuko

---

1 **kyakyozu-ya** (*keeah-keeoh-zoo-yah*): literally, "hunter of evil."

had only heard of *kyakyozuyasu* in tales: holy warriors armed with talismans and hallowed blades, they killed spirits who trespassed too far into human domains. This demon hunter was younger than she would have expected —around twenty or so—but, judging by the battle scars along his arms and neck, she suspected that perhaps *kyakyozuyasu* did not live very long.

Geiki let out a nervous squawk as they continued down the hall. "A demon hunter, huh? Do you think he'll catch other wicked spirits too? Tricksters, maybe? Ha! How lucky we are! I feel safer already!"

Miuko glared at him, but he did not shut up.

"Yes," he added uselessly. "Very safe indeed."

"He's come to discover the source of the hauntings," the proprietor said, sliding open a door and motioning Miuko inside. "After what happened at the House of November, we must protect the Ochiirokai."

Miuko did not enter. "What happened at the House of November?"

This time, the man looked to Geiki before answering, but the *atska-yakina* only stared at him blankly. "It's gone," he explained. "A terrible calamity occurred there this morning—all the priests have been massacred, and the temple was burned to the ground. Some say the mountain has become an *oyu*."[2]

A blight. A place of death. It happened, sometimes, when a spirit abandoned their home; for Ada, the material world, could not exist without Ana, the spirit.

At an *oyu*, the plants died. The animals fled or perished. Nothing would grow or flourish until the spirit returned.

By some accounts, it was happening to Nihaoi, although Otori Rohiro had always refused to believe it.

"The smoke we saw this morning." Miuko shook her head, dazed. "I knew something was wrong."

---

2   o-yu (*oh-yoo*)

Geiki helped her into the room, where she sank to her knees. "You knew it was an *oyu*?"

"No, but I . . ." She faltered, glancing at the innkeeper, who, sensing the sudden awkwardness of the situation, bowed and left them.

How could she explain the nagging sense that she and the House of November were somehow connected?

Had she done this, somehow?

It made no sense, of course; and, as Geiki assured her, she wasn't a *shaoha* yet. "Besides," he added for good measure, "even *shaohasu* aren't *that* powerful."

Then again, not much about her life made sense these days, and try as she might, she simply could not shake the feeling that this was not coincidence.

17

CRANE DAUGHTER

THAT NIGHT, ALONE in her room, Miuko disrobed for bed and gasped. The curse had spread past her knees, which were now a vivid, impenetrable blue.

What had happened? For three days, the curse had moved slowly and steadily up from the soles of her feet, but in the past sixteen hours, it had surged up her legs like a sudden flood.

Did it have anything to do with the carnage at the House of November? If so, *how?*

More importantly, would it continue at this speed, giving her less than a week to reach Amyunasa's temple?

She could not possibly make it so far on foot.

And if she couldn't do that, she'd never make it home to her father.

Miuko dug her fingers into her robes, fervently wishing for a horse, or for Geiki's wing to be healed. But wishes, she knew, seldom came true for plain, ungainly girls of the serving class.

Suddenly, there was a knock at her courtyard door. Upon the rice paper screen was the slender silhouette of a young man.

"Geiki, what do you—" Struggling into her robes again, she slid open the door.

But it was not the *atskayakina* who stood there smiling at her.

It was Tujiyazai, the vengeance demon. He was still in the body of the *doro*, dressed in dusty travel robes and a black scarf so fine, it fanned about him with the slightest movement, like smoke.

"Who is Geiki?" he said. "You were alone the last time I saw you."

"No one," Miuko replied instinctively, for something told her that the *doro yagra* was not to be trusted. "A friend."

Flames billowed about Tujiyazai's face as he searched the courtyard, but the air was still, and the lights were dark. Not even the shadows dared move.

"He must be a good friend, to have brought you so far," the demon prince observed. "Tell me, Ishao, where are you going?"

As before, Miuko was torn. To give him the unadulterated truth, she thought, would be like feeding her hand to a wild beast. To withhold it, however, would incur the beast's wrath.

So she told him as little as she could. "North," she said.

"Ah." He exhaled flames. "To the House of December? To the priests of Amyunasa, to beg them to make you ordinary again?"

"You knew?" Despite her fear of him, Miuko lunged forward, voice rising. "If you knew they could help me, why didn't you tell me?"

Calmly, the demon prince looked down at her, his eye sockets flickering with sparks. "Why would I endeavor to make you anything less than you are?"

Heat — his or hers, she did not know — warmed her cheeks and throat. She recoiled, unballing her fists. "What are you doing here anyway? How did you get past the spirit gate?"

"I had an errand to run nearby." Another smile flitted across his lips. "And I have been around a long time, Ishao. I have my ways of subverting human spells."

Well, that wasn't the least bit reassuring. "What do you want?" she asked.

"I want you to come with me."

She retreated back over the threshold of her room. "No."

"Come with me," he repeated, "or I shall burn this guesthouse and all its inhabitants to ash, including your friend Geiki, if he's here, and you will have no one but yourself to blame." He grinned, then. It looked awful on him—sharp and perilous.

"That isn't funny," Miuko said.

The demon's expression did not falter. "I am not joking."

Nervously, she glanced toward Geiki's room, but his screens remained dark.

Perhaps it was better that way, if Tujiyazai did not learn more about the *atskayakina* than she'd already let on.

"Fine," she said at last, retrieving her sandals. "But if you so much as attempt to touch me, I warn you, I will scream."

Bowing, Tujiyazai gestured toward the courtyard's exit. "I should like to hear that. But perhaps not tonight."

Outside the inn, the rest of Vevaona was surprisingly quiet. Along the main road, the shops had shuttered their windows and barred their gates, looking grim and forbidding in the shadows. No cats hunted along the empty streets. No night birds disturbed the heavy air. Even the tavern, which at this hour should have been radiating light and conversation, was dark and still.

"Where is everybody?" she wondered aloud.

Beside her, Tujiyazai sniffed the air. "They are here, but they are afraid."

The innkeeper had told them tales of ghosts tempting travelers from the road, but she had not known the townspeople would take such tales so seriously . . . unless they were more than tales, and there was some real danger haunting the Ochiirokai. Now that she looked closer, she could see protective talismans tacked above doorways, the wet ink still gleaming faintly in the starlight.

"How can you tell?" she asked.

"Fear is kindling to anger, and anger is my dominion."

She could not think of how to reply to this, so she didn't. In fact, they passed many minutes in silence, and, despite the company, Miuko discovered that she was rather enjoying herself. She could walk beside the demon prince, or ahead of him, for he did not seem to care, and there was no one else about to stop her. She could skip over the little stream that trickled through the center of the village and twirl under the open sky, arms wide. Of course, she stumbled doing this, but Tujiyazai, true to his word not to touch her, did not move to catch her.

They wandered to the edge of the town, where Miuko turned back at the spirit gate. "Well," she said, "that was . . ."

Fun, said the little voice inside her.

Frowning, she willed it to be quiet.

To her horror, it snickered, raspy as winter branches.

The demon prince looked confused. "Why have we stopped?"

"I can't leave."

"Why not?"

She hesitated. The truth of the matter was that all her years as a human had taught her that women were not allowed out of the village after dark, much less in the company of a *demon,* but she knew that to say so would sound as outlandish to the *doro yagra* as the idea of the rain falling upward instead of down.

Beyond the gate, the open fields beckoned, looking in the darkness much like the fallow farms of Nihaoi. How she'd longed to ramble through them when she was younger, rooting among the weeds for ancient relics dropped by the defeated Ogawa soldiers.

Propriety had forbidden it. If she'd been caught, her father would have suffered the disgrace; and, with the disappearance of his wife and the rumors about her being a *tskegaira,* Miuko had thought he'd already suffered enough.

But there was no one around to disgrace now.

"Okay," she said. "Just a little way."

As if he'd known she'd agree, Tujiyazai nodded. "We will go as far as you wish."

Under the spirit gate they went, out of Vevaona and into the farmlands that surrounded it. Orchards of apple trees stretched out on either side of them, their full canopies forming arcades over the sparse grass below. A breeze swept across the landscape, carrying the fragrance of ripening fruit—warm and sweet.

Miuko sighed.

"You're happy," the demon prince observed.

She could not help but smile. "I suppose I am."

"Why?"

At first she did not reply, for she did not have the words to explain the relief, the absence of fear (for all she was accompanied by a malevolence demon), or the glorious feeling of picking up her robes so she could stretch her legs.

The *doro yagra*'s voice was soft. "I think you could be happy all the time, if you allowed it."

Her expression soured. "You mean if I let myself turn into a demon? If being a demon is so great, why are you in the *doro*'s body?"

In the center of the road, Tujiyazai considered his hands, flexing his finely boned fingers as if seeing them for the first time. "A human body has its uses."

Though when she looked at him, she saw through his human face to the fiery eye pits and curving horns, for the first time Miuko understood that the body of the *doro* was but a costume to Tujiyazai. A masquerade of sorts.

For what purpose, however, she did not know.

Nor did she have the chance to ask, for a bone-chilling shriek rent the night, painful and tremulous with fear.

Miuko froze. "A ghost?"

Tujiyazai lifted his face to the air, inhaling deeply. "Someone is very afraid." Then: "And someone is very angry."

"Is either someone a ghost?"

Before he could reply, there was another shriek. "Stop, Father! Please, let me go! Just let me go!"

Down the road, a girl burst out of the orchards—screeching, begging, scrambling, fleeing. Her robes were torn, and her black hair streamed out behind her like a flag.

She was followed by the largest man Miuko had ever seen. He was so tall, his head brushed the lowest branches of the apple trees, snapping twigs.

Before Miuko could move, he reached out, snatching the girl by the hair. She cried out as she was yanked backward, landing hard at his feet, where she scratched and fought, flinging a handful of dust into his face.

He released her with a grunt, pawing at his eyes.

Then, quick as Miuko could blink, the girl had become a bird—a crane—with long fragile legs and wings that beat wildly at the air. She leapt from the earth, the movement so graceful it stole Miuko's breath away. For a moment, Miuko felt her heart soar, as if she, too, were on the verge of flight.

But the man caught the crane by one slender ankle, tossing her to the ground. She flapped and struggled, but he was much stronger than her bird form, and while Miuko watched in horror, he began to drag her into the trees, as if she were no more than a sled of firewood or a prize carcass he'd claimed after a protracted hunt.

"A crane spirit," Tujiyazai murmured, his voice so close, Miuko drew back in surprise. "She should shapeshift again. She's no match for him like this."

"She can't transform while his attention is on her." Miuko picked up her robes again and ran forward, chasing after the man's retreating figure.

"Indeed?" Tujiyazai's voice crackled with curiosity. "Wherever did you learn a thing like that, Ishao?"

Cursing inwardly, Miuko clapped her mouth shut to keep anything else from slipping out. They ran after the man and his daughter in silence, which gave Miuko the opportunity to marvel at how strong her legs felt, how easily they carried her compared to a few nights ago.

Perhaps she didn't want to be a demon, but she had to admit that demon-strength had its uses.

As they came to a stop at a small cabin on the edge of the orchard, light flared in the windows, though the only sound that broke the night was the *thud* of a body, followed by the heavy rattle of a chain.

Miuko crept forward, close enough to hear the man mutter in a low, measured voice: "You are *my* daughter. *Mine*."

There was nothing but the flapping of feathers in response.

"We have to help her," Miuko whispered to Tujiyazai.

"Why?"

Because there was no telling what the man would do to her.

Because it was not right that a bird so beautiful should be caged.

Because she was a girl, like Miuko, and if Otori Rohiro had not been kind and patient with his uncommonly loud daughter, Miuko could have been trapped and beaten, too, and no one would have done anything about it; because according to the laws of Omaizi society, a daughter belonged to her father, like a square of land or a sack of grain, to be used or sown to his benefit.

Miuko reached the cabin windows, where she peered through the shutters. Inside, the man had shackled the crane spirit by the ankle, locking it tightly around her thin black leg.

It fit so perfectly, there was no question that he had done this before.

"You're just like your mother. She could never figure out what she wanted either. She wanted a husband. She wanted a child. She wanted so many things, but once she had them, what did she do?" Shaking his head, he tossed a small key onto the top of a shelf. "She threw them all away. Or she would have, if I hadn't stopped her."

The crane girl dragged her manacled leg along the floor, trying to tuck it beneath her.

Her father sighed. "You'll thank me for keeping you here, one day, when you finally understand what's best for you."

Suddenly, Miuko felt cold—the same cold she'd felt that morning, when she'd imagined throwing the stevedore onto his back and using his throat as a stepping stone—but deeper, this time, in her bones.

Tujiyazai, in contrast, felt as if he had become a bonfire. What was it he'd said about fear and anger? She wondered if they fed him, the way a dry forest fed a fire. She inched away from him, certain her skin would blister if she stayed too close.

"Do something," Miuko hissed.

He blinked mildly at her. "What would you have me do?"

"You're the prince!"

"You're the one who wants to stop him."

"I'm a *girl*."

"You're much more than that, Ishao."

Miuko's thoughts spun. She could scream. It would draw the man's attention, but the girl would still be trapped, for if she transformed into a human now, the tightened shackles would surely snap her ankle.

Not that, then.

She could charge into the cabin. Perhaps Tujiyazai, who seemed to have some interest in her, would swoop in to save her.

Then again, perhaps not.

"Do you want to end up like your mother?" The man snapped a piece of kindling, feeding it into the embers of a cooking fire.

Miuko's eyes narrowed. She'd heard that question herself too many times before, used to prod her back into her proper place like a sow into a pen.

But she was not a sow. She was not even a girl anymore—or at least, she was not *only* a girl—although she knew she was not a demon either, much as Tujiyazai seemed to want her to be.

She was something else. She had to be something else. Something devious and different.

How would Geiki stop him?

By means of a trick.

Miuko turned to the *doro yagra*. "Give me your scarf."

"Why?"

"Because I need an illusion, and I don't have magic to help me." Removing her sandals, she peeled off her socks and hiked her robes to her knees. In the dim light, her legs and feet seemed to glow an uncanny blue.

She snatched Tujiyazai's scarf from his outstretched hand, flinging it over her head like a veil. As she'd suspected, the fabric was fine enough that she could still see, though her face was surely hidden.

"How do I look?" she asked him.

"Strange."

That would have to do.

Arching her back the way she'd seen the Doctor do when she attacked the *odoshoya*, Miuko threw open the sliding door.

"RELEASE THE CRANE SPIRIT." She stepped inside, revealing her exposed legs.

With a gasp, the man stumbled backward. The color drained from his cheeks. "Yeiwa?" he whispered.

A woman's name. His wife's?

She *was* dead then, as Miuko had feared, and now he believed her to be the crane spirit's ghost, returned from the primordial waters.

Miuko could work with that. And if she couldn't, well . . . she'd end up in irons like his daughter.

She took the risk.

"YOU MAY HAVE KILLED ME, BUT YOU CANNOT KILL MY DAUGHTER." Miuko took another step into the cabin, angling her stride in what she hoped was a passable imitation of a crane's stilted walk.

The man was gibbering in fear now, she observed with satisfaction. On his knees, he pressed his forehead to the floor, pleading with her. He was sorry. The girl had driven him to it. He was a good soul. Please, spare him.

She did not want to spare him, pathetic as he was. It would be so easy not to. To place the sole of her foot upon his balding head. To watch his skin shrivel. To watch the life leach out of him as water is leached from the drought-dry soil.

Oh yes, murmured the voice inside her. *It would be easy.*

"Stop that," Miuko ordered, though she did not know if she was addressing the man or herself.

Either way, he went silent.

As did the demon-voice.

Her eyes narrowed. "SPARE YOU, I SHALL," she declared. "I SHALL SPARE YOU ONE MORE MINUTE IN THIS HOME YOU HAVE DEFILED. RUN, NOW. RUN UNTIL YOUR LEGS COLLAPSE BENEATH YOU, HUMAN. RUN, AND NEVER RETURN."

Miuko never imagined she'd command the obedience of a fully grown man, but there he went, sprinting out the door and disappearing between the trees, leaving her alone in the cabin with the crane spirit.

She sucked in a shaky breath. Hands trembling, she removed Tujiyazai's scarf and lowered her robes to her ankles again. Then, taking the key from the shelf, she knelt beside the crane girl and unlocked the manacles, which she tossed aside. The insides gleamed dully in the firelight, worn smooth with use.

"You're human?" came a voice.

Miuko looked back at the spirit, who had changed into her girl form, and nodded. "Sort of. I don't have *atskayakina* magic or anything, but I guess a good costume can do the trick, too."

The crane girl staggered up, testing her ankle.

"I don't think your father will be back for a while," Miuko said. "You're free."

The spirit tilted her head. "He'll end up somewhere, though," she said softly. "And his next daughter won't have wings—or you—to rescue her."

"Then I hope he doesn't have daughters."

"Or anyone."

"Or anyone," Miuko agreed, though somewhere inside her, she knew that would not be enough. There were plenty of other men like him in Awara, and even if there weren't, even if every man in the realm was as kind-hearted as her own father, that did not change the fact that in Omaizi society, a girl was only as free as the generosity of her male relatives allowed her to be.

Crossing to the open door, the crane girl bowed. "Thank you." Then, taking a few steps, she disappeared into the shadows. Moments later, Miuko saw the graceful silhouette of a crane against the sky, flying high over the orchards.

While Miuko watched her go, Tujiyazai appeared in the doorway. "*Atskayakina* magic, hmm?" he asked. "What would you know of *atskayakina* magic, Ishao?"

Miuko bit her tongue.

Geiki. She hadn't meant to reveal him—and perhaps she still hadn't. But she could not help feeling as if she'd given the demon prince her friend's scent.

She brushed past Tujiyazai, shoving his scarf back into his hands, and began to gather her socks and sandals from among the weeds.

"You should have killed him," he said.

"I'm not a killer."

"But you could be. You could be feared and worshipped. There could be temples erected in your honor and sacrifices made at your feet."

Miuko let out a bark of laughter as she pulled on her socks. "Who would do that?"

"The entire world."

"Well, I don't want that." She slid on her sandals and turned from the cabin, not noticing, in her pensiveness, the blackened footprints she had left in the grass.

"Do you know what you want?"

She frowned. It was true that for a long time, she'd had to repress what she wanted, for all the spaces where she might have stored her desires had been occupied by duty, responsibility, obligation. To want was dangerous. To want was seditious—a betrayal of the values of Omaizi society and everyone who lived in it.

Only recently had she begun to open up those spaces again, discovering wants both old and new.

To walk alone.

To speak for herself.

To see what was beyond that distant horizon.

What she did *not* want, despite the urgings of the voice inside her, was to become a murdering demon.

"No," she said. "But I'm learning."

18

A CONFLUENCE OF GHOSTS

THE NEXT MORNING, Miuko was awoken by someone calling, "Miuko! Miuko! Get up, Miuko!" and a rattling at her door, neither of which ceased until she came stumbling groggily to open it.

Geiki was standing there, bright-eyed and fully clothed. "They're giving us a horse!"

She rubbed her eyes. "What?"

"The inn! They're giving us a horse! When I got up this morning, the proprietor said, 'There's a horse waiting for you in the stables,' and now it's *ours!* What a great town, huh?" He threw his head back and cawed. "Many blessings upon Vevaona!"

Miuko scowled. "People don't just give away horses."

"These people do!" Plopping a rice cake into her palm, he beckoned her to hurry. "Come on! We get to ride a horse today!"

With a comment like that, it should have occurred to her that neither she nor Geiki had ever been astride a horse in their lives. Certainly, thanks to her years at her father's guesthouse, she knew how to care for them, but to *ride* one? There was no law against a woman riding a horse — as her mother had demonstrated the night she left — but, like women walking alone, it was simply not done. The gift — if the *atskayakina* was not mistaken, which he may well have been — might not be the windfall it had first appeared to be.

But, given her lack of sleep and her distaste for early mornings, these thoughts did not even cross her mind until she was standing in the stables, nose-to-nose with a dapple gray mare.

She was a beautiful horse, Miuko had to admit, the kind of animal who should have her mane braided and her tack adorned with silver, the kind of animal one might expect to find in a parade of noblemen . . . or in the possession of a prince.

Was she a gift from Tujiyazai? It was the most logical explanation, for although Geiki seemed convinced that the guesthouse proprietor had handed them the reins to a magnificent, healthy animal, Miuko knew that humans were not so generous. But why would the *doro yagra* have given her the means to reach the House of December when he'd so clearly scorned the idea?

Miuko pursed her lips. "Where did you come from, girl?" she asked.

The horse sniffed her robes, but she was not a talking horse, and so she did not reply.

While Geiki paid for their rooms, Miuko poked through the saddlebags, searching for a note, but found only provisions for the road and a small pouch of coins to supplement what the Doctor had given them.

If the horse *was* from Tujiyazai, wouldn't he have mentioned it? He'd been clear when they parted—he was going to call on her again tonight. Surely he would have told her about the horse, if for no other reason than to demand her gratitude for it?

She was still puzzling over this question when the *kyakyozuya* strode into the stables, calling for his horse.

The demon hunter's curved sword hung at one side, a gourd at the other. Around his neck, covering his scars, was a scarf of vermillion, inked with spells.

"*Kyakyozuya*-jai, what's happened?" asked the stable boy, leading a skittery bay gelding from one of the stalls.

"There's been a disappearance," the demon hunter replied. "A farmer. His daughter, too. Someone found signs of demon activity near their cabin."

Still clutching the gray mare's saddle horn, Miuko stilled. She'd been *barefoot* at the cabin. Closing her eyes, she pictured withered patches of weeds drooping in the morning sun.

How could she have been so careless?

Mounting his horse, the *kyakyozuya* galloped from the stables, nearly running over Geiki, who had to hop out of the way to avoid being trampled.

"Ah!" he cried.

"We have to go." Miuko yanked him to the gray mare, who surveyed them both with limpid brown eyes.

"Watch the arm!" Geiki protested, jerking his sling out of her grasp. "What's the hurry?"

Miuko could have told him, then. She could have admitted that she and Tujiyazai had gone walking about Vevaona in the middle of the night; they'd left the town limits; they'd been together, the two of them in the darkness, alone. . . . Some part of her knew it wasn't her fault. Tujiyazai had threatened the inn. He'd threatened *Geiki*. She'd had no choice but to go with him.

But even a strong-willed girl like Miuko could not withstand seventeen years of indoctrination into a society that would brand her wanton and unwanted for such behavior, and the greater part of her was ashamed. Ashamed for going. Ashamed for her recklessness. Ashamed for liking it.

So all she said was, "I just don't want to lose any time."

Lose time they did, however; because, as she soon discovered, riding a horse was not easy, and both she and the *atskayakina* had much to learn.

The mare had the patience of a monk, thank the gods, but Geiki kept falling off, and Miuko refused to even try mounting the horse until they'd bartered some men's trousers off a fellow traveler. Propriety aside, she refused to risk her bare legs touching the mare's spotted coat, for the curse had begun climbing her thighs in the night, and in women's robes, the chance that she'd accidentally hurt the horse was too great.

After numerous failed (not to mention painful) attempts, the three of them finally settled on a configuration that seemed to suit them: Miuko, in men's clothes, clinging desperately to the saddle, while Geiki, in magpie form, perched upon her shoulder, with a little blue sling to hold his injured wing in place.

Miuko, unaccustomed to his bird form, was startled by how striking he was with his blue wings, the soft gray down of his belly, but she would have never said so, lest his head grow too big for his little bird body to carry it.

The mare, whom Geiki had decided to call "Roroisho"—meaning "dirty snow"—bore the arrangement all very agreeably, for she had been well-trained and had a good temperament for people who didn't know what they were doing—which, in her experience, was most of them.

Thus situated, the threesome made good progress throughout the morning, although their spirits were somewhat hampered by their encounters with other travelers—who reacted to a girl in men's clothing, astride a horse, with predictable scorn.

Children stared. Men shouted, "Disgraceful!" and "For shame!" and other variations thereof. An old woman, bent double under the weight of her satchel, even spat at Roroisho's feet.

Though Miuko could have drowned them all out with a few well-chosen swear words, she bit her tongue and kept her gaze on the road ahead. She was, after all, a girl alone, and could not risk them running after her. Moreover, if a girl riding a horse were worthy of such outrage, Miuko hated to think how everyone would react to the knowledge that she was, in fact, half demon.

Perhaps they'd be less offended, she thought sourly. After all, in the realm of Awara, demons were more commonplace than a girl on horseback.

"We should have bargained for a hat as well as clothes," she muttered. "Then I could have hidden my face and made this farce more convincing."

Though he couldn't speak in his magpie form, Geiki squawked and plucked at her hair, which she took to mean either that he liked her just as she was, or that he was hungry and in need of a treat from Roroisho's saddlebags.

They stopped for lunch in a stand of birches, which offered some protection from the blistering sun. In human form, Geiki watched the gray mare grazing delicately in the shade. *Atskayakinasu* did not ordinarily keep pets, he mused aloud, but when he returned to his flock, he was certain they would make an exception for Roroisho.

"Never mind the fact that horses don't live in trees," Miuko added, rolling her eyes.

"No matter!" he declared, taking a shining block of gold from his pocket. "The gods will find a way!"

As if in response, Roroisho nodded, though perhaps she was only shooing a few insects from her face.

Miuko, however, was no longer paying her any attention. "Where did you get that?" She pointed at the gilded cube, which fit neatly in his palm, geometric patterns imprinted across each of its sides.

"I found it."

She narrowed her eyes. "In someone's *pocket?*"

"No, I *found* it. It was on the side of the road this morning."

"You were a bird! When did you have time to pick this up?"

"When you were changing!"

Miuko held out her hand.

Begrudgingly, the *atskayakina* passed her the cube. "You're not going to make me give it back, are you? It was on the ground, so it's littering! Besides, I think there's something inside!"

The cube had neither hinges nor lid. In fact, except for its decorations, its sides were perfectly smooth. "What makes you think it opens?" she asked.

"It's not heavy enough to be solid."

"Maybe it's not real gold."

Sniffing, he plucked the cube from her hands. "You'd know the difference, if you were an *atskayakina*."

Miuko sighed. "Fine. You can keep it. I suppose we can always sell it if we need the funds."

He beamed.

Once they were underway again—bird and girl and horse—Miuko knew to steel herself for nasty comments, but to her surprise, the Ochiirokai emptied even sooner than it had the previous day. An hour passed in blissful calm; another, in uncanny silence.

Waves of heat rose from the dirt road, making the air ripple as if it were water.

Sweat dripped down Miuko's neck. She found herself missing Geiki's chatter, but he was dozing upon her shoulder, and, besides, in this form, he could not speak.

All seemed peaceful—the glimmering rice paddies, the endless sky— but Miuko felt as tense as she'd been when there were other people about. She didn't even understand why until she became aware of a buzzing, like the sound of a nearby hornet's nest.

More disturbingly, she could not remember when the buzzing had started. It felt as if it had been there, droning on, for hours.

The hairs on the back of Miuko's arms stood up.

"Geiki," she whispered, "wake up. Something's wrong."

The *atskayakina* stirred, yawning.

Ahead of them, in the middle of the road, was a disturbance in the air. To Miuko it looked like the lattice of cuts left by a woodsman's axe, as if something was trying to claw its way through the very fabric of the material world.

"Do you see that?" she whispered.

Then it was gone. Where it had been, the air remained smooth and untouched.

Geiki let out a soft twitter. Roroisho tossed her head anxiously.

The buzzing intensified. In the field to their right another disturbance appeared — this time human in shape — so close that Miuko could see hash marks where its face and limbs should have been.

"Ghosts," she whispered.

Geiki cawed.

"Hurry, Roroisho!" Miuko kicked her heels, like she'd seen riders do before, and, not wanting to linger any more than Miuko did, the dapple mare shot forward.

Over the road they ran, the ghosts buzzing about them, flickering in and out of Miuko's vision: the face of a girl, a hand dipped in blood, someone shrieking, an arm, a naked torso, another girl.

So many girls, each one only a little older than Miuko.

Roroisho whinnied in what must have been fear and broke into a gallop, Miuko clinging desperately to her back and trying not to topple from the saddle while Geiki clutched at her robes, flapping his good wing for balance.

It was fortunate for all of them that they were only minutes from Koewa, the next town, for they did not slow down until they'd raced beneath the spirit gate and the buzzing subsided. The horse dropped to a trot, then a walk, sides heaving with exertion and relief.

Miuko slid from her back, discovering with a cry that her entire body had seized up during the ride, muscles in her thighs and arms and abdomen stiffening and spasming in protest. Geiki hopped from her shoulder down her arm, alighting in the dirt. Shaking himself, he glared up at her pointedly.

"Oh," she said, averting her eyes. "Sorry."

He chirped.

But he did not transform. Townspeople were stopping to gawk at them now, not with the offended glare of the travelers on the road (or at least not *only* that); there was fear in their faces too, and it did not take Miuko long to understand why.

All around her, whispering behind their hands, were boys and men, and old women with wrinkled faces, and middle-aged women with marriage knots in their hair — enough people to demonstrate that Koewa had quite the population.

But besides Miuko, there was not a girl among them.

19

A SERIES OF VERY POOR
FIRST IMPRESSIONS

THE CROWD WAS growing larger by the second as passersby stopped to stare and whisper at the girl in men's robes. Miuko felt like a creature on display in the emperor's garden, with colorful feathers and a silver collar — something to be pointed at and mocked for her strangeness. She wanted to run, to bury her face in her pillow and hope that everyone would forget they'd ever seen her.

But she was surrounded. Behind her, Roroisho stamped anxiously.

"What are you doing?" A dainty woman stormed out of the assembled crowd. She wore the fine clothing that befitted a matriarch from a local, well-to-do family — nothing so grand as the nobility, but certainly of higher quality than anything in Nihaoi. With a strength that belied her delicate frame, she grabbed Miuko's elbow, shaking her so hard that a few strands of thin white hair came loose from the widow's knot at the top of her head. "You can't just ride in here in men's clothes!"

Up close, the woman's brown eyes were watery with . . . was that fear?

"You can't be here like this!" she hissed. Then, casting a glance over her shoulder: "It's not safe!"

"I'm sorry!" Miuko protested, squirming in the woman's grasp. Wildly, she searched for Geiki, who was bouncing and hopping among the townspeople's legs, trying to reach the edge of the crowd without being trampled. "I didn't mean any offense!"

She looked to the assembly for assistance, but none came. They shifted uncomfortably—afraid, Miuko thought, and disapproving, as if she deserved the woman's onslaught.

For what? The demon-voice inside Miuko dripped scorn. *Riding a horse? Dressing like a man?*

From deep inside her arose that new, piercing cold, like a glacial mountaintop sending killing frosts into the valleys below.

"Where's your husband?" the woman demanded.

Miuko's thoughts rattled in her skull like loose stones. "Um—"

"Father? Brother?" The woman shook her again. "Come on! What were you thinking? You have to get out of here! At once!"

The bartered robes slipped down Miuko's shoulder, causing the crowd to gasp at the impropriety of it.

Skin! The demon-voice laughed. *They have it too, but what a scandal to actually see it!*

With a cry, Miuko tried to tug her clothes up again, but before she had the chance, someone snapped, "Mother!"

Behind the old woman there appeared a man—perhaps fifteen or twenty years older than Miuko. Like his mother, he was small in stature and handsomely clothed. Unlike his mother, he had hard, penetrating eyes that neither blinked nor wavered from Miuko's, though he was not addressing her.

There was a murmur from the crowd.

"Laowu-jai."

"Poor man."

"To have a mother like Aleila."

"Terrible woman. Overbearing."

"Suffocating."

"A monster."

As if oblivious to their whispers, the man continued staring at Miuko. It unnerved her to be studied so.

But she could not help but feel grateful when he gently pulled his mother away. "Let her go, Mother." Then, after breaking Aleila's hold, he laid a proprietary arm about Miuko's shoulders—which reduced her gratitude significantly—and addressed the assembly in the officious tones of a practiced politician or a street performer: "Else the poor girl will think us inhospitable!"

That was an understatement, Miuko thought, but the townspeople laughed, as if this were some excellent joke they all shared.

Aleila retreated with a bow. "Of course, my son." In an instant, her expression turned from hard and panicked to soft and simpering, her round face so transformed that for a moment Miuko suspected her of being a shapeshifter. "I was only trying to help."

Help whom? demanded Miuko's inner voice, and for the first time, she did not attempt to stifle it.

Snapping his fingers, Laowu pointed to one of the elderly women in the crowd. "Your shawl, if you please."

Quickly, she handed it to him—it was patterned with pale purple blossoms, appropriately feminine—and he arranged it around Miuko's shoulders with a flourish, tugging it this way and that until he seemed satisfied with her appearance.

The crowd began to disperse.

Narrowing his eyes, as if she were a scroll hanging crookedly upon his wall, he tucked a loose strand of hair behind her ear, his fingertips lingering a fraction of a second too long upon her cheek.

Though he kept adjusting her appearance, Miuko had the uncomfortable sensation that he was still unsatisfied. "Thank you—" she began, attempting to step away from him.

His hand tightened upon her shoulder. "A girl your age has no business traveling alone."

This was the first time he'd addressed her, she realized, and only now did she recognize the anger in his voice—cold and barely restrained.

She shook her head. "I'm not—"

"There you are!" Geiki, in boy form, came racing haphazardly out of a nearby alley. "I've been looking all over for you!"

For a moment, Laowu stared at her, his expression clouded with disgust, before relinquishing his hold on her. "Is she yours?" he asked Geiki.

The *atskayakina* glanced at Miuko, who stared back at him, willing him to answer the way a man of Awara would answer.

He forced a smile. "I'm her brother."

She let out a relieved breath.

Laowu seemed about to respond when his mother took his arm, patting him on the hand. "Weren't we on our way to the teahouse, my son?" She smiled sweetly up at him. "I'm afraid that after all this excitement, I could do with a soothing cup of flower tea."

He blinked, as if he were coming out of a trance. "Of course, Mother." Then, to Geiki: "Watch her. You never know what trouble girls will get into if they're allowed to wander freely."

With that, he and his mother departed with the rest of the crowd, leaving Miuko and Geiki alone with Roroisho.

"I'm sorry!" the *atskayakina* blurted, tugging agitatedly at his hair. "There were so many people, I couldn't transform! I've never been somewhere with less privacy, and I grew up in a flock of magpies!"

Miuko watched Laowu and his mother retreat down the block. As they turned the corner, he paused, looking back at her with those unforgiving eyes, before Aleila steered him away.

"I don't like it here," Miuko said. "Something's wrong with this place."

"Should we leave? We don't have to stay tonight. Maybe we'd do better with the ghosts, huh?"

But they did not leave. She told herself—and Geiki, too—that she'd rather risk the dangers of the human world than tempt the *nasu* on the road. But the truth was that there *was* something wrong—with Laowu; with his small, vicious mother; with their town. She could sense it wafting from them like *naiana* rising from the earth, spilling over the ground until it ran down the wooded hillsides and the cobblestone streets, saturating everything—every floorboard, every footstep, every rock and weed and patch of earth—and she knew exactly who could help her find out why.

20

THE GRAVES

PACING BY HER second-story window, Miuko waited most of the night for Tujiyazai to arrive, but it wasn't until an hour before dawn that she felt the blazing heat which told her he was near. Opening her window, she found him standing on the stones below, smokeless flames drifting about his furrowed brow.

Without waiting for an invitation, she shimmied onto the rooftop and dropped to the ground, wobbling only slightly at her landing. "You came."

"I told you I would."

"You said you can sense anger, right?"

"As can you."

"So I'm learning," she grumbled irritably. "I'm just not very good at it."

Yet, added the little voice inside her.

"What do you hope to find?" asked the demon prince.

"Whatever's wrong with this place."

He bowed, the tips of his horns almost brushing her shoulders. "Very well."

He led her — though perhaps she did not need to be led, for she could feel a cold malice sweeping down the hillside that overlooked the town —through the deserted streets, their footsteps echoing on the uneven cobbles.

"Why have you not invited *Geiki* on this little adventure of yours?" Tujiyazai asked as they climbed the forested hills, where several sturdy houses, finer and larger than those below, were interspersed among the groves of pine and bamboo.

Miuko tensed. "What do you know about Geiki?"

"I know you rely on him."

"He's my friend."

The *doro yagra* chuckled. "Is that what you think? Is *friendship* enough of a reason for someone to take you halfway across Awara?"

She frowned. It had not occurred to her at the time, but now that Tujiyazai said it aloud, the idea that Geiki would come so far out of nothing but the goodness of his heart seemed rather farfetched.

"I don't know about humans," the demon prince continued idly, "but in the spirit world, some deals are made without either party ever having to bargain . . . perhaps a wish is granted for freeing a spirit from a curse, or a life is owed for a life saved . . ."

"What?" Miuko halted. She thought Geiki had agreed to come with her on this improbable journey because he liked her. Because he accepted her. What was it he'd said? *Because he had a good feeling about her.* Why would he have lied about something like that? "You mean he's indebted to me for saving him from the fox—"

But she was stopped short by the sight of a walled manor. Built into the curve of the hill, it was three stories tall, with tiled roofs and beams engraved with the faces of ogres to frighten away malicious *nasu*. The cold was stronger here, thick as a sheet of ice.

Whatever disturbed Koewa, this was its source.

Kneeling, Tujiyazai beckoned to Miuko, gesturing for her to scale the wall, much like Geiki had done at Keivoweicha.

This time, she did not hesitate. She vaulted over the wall, landing, a little fumble-footed, among the carefully pruned maples on the other side.

Surprised at her own strength, she laid a hand on her hip, as if she could feel the curse lapping at her waist. Being a demon certainly had its perks.

Alighting at her side, the *doro yagra* pointed toward the large manor house. Light spilled from the open windows, through which raised voices could be heard.

"Where did she come from?" Laowu roared. Now that he was no longer in public, it seemed he'd given free rein to his otherwise tightly controlled wrath, and it burst into the night, ravenous as a fire. "How long is she staying?"

"Why do you let it bother you?" Aleila asked. "She's just a girl."

"A girl on a horse! What else do you think she spreads her legs for?"

Stifling a gasp, Miuko hid her face in her sleeves. They were talking about *her*. "Why did you bring me here?" she muttered to Tujiyazai. "I could have told you these two were terrible, but I think there's something *else* wrong with this town . . ."

"*They* are not what we are here for." Lifting a finger, the *doro yagra* pointed to a door beneath the house.

The door was perfectly square, too low to enter except on hands and knees, and hardly wide enough for a human to pass. It must have led to a crawl space beneath the first floor, built for maintenance of the manor's foundations.

According to Miuko's mother, crawl spaces—like all liminalities—were borders between Ada and Ana, not wholly belonging to either the human world or the spirit. There, men bred with fox spirits, and *imimisu*[1]—tiny beings no taller than the length of a paring knife—rode rats through cities built of junkyard scavengings.

---

1   imi-mi (*ee-mee-mee*): literally, "star eye." According to legend, when Amyunasa created the spirit world, they made the *imimisu* with the light of the universe in their eyes.

The good, rational part of Miuko that sensed danger wanted nothing more than to run screaming from the garden. Five days ago, she would have done precisely that.

And yet she remained, like a shrew mesmerized by a snake. Whatever was under the floorboards, it called to her—thrumming in her very bones, so hard and insistent, it made her teeth ache.

She and Tujiyazai crept across the shadowed yard. Taking hold of the door, he popped the lock with hardly a sound.

The opening yawned wide, dark as a monster's jaws.

On all fours, Miuko entered the crawl space. It was cool within, smelling of floor polish, earth, and something both sweet and putrid: the carcass of a mouse rotting in the dirt, and mushrooms sprouting in the slatted light between the floorboards.

"Whore!" Laowu shouted from above.

There was a crash—the sound of pottery breaking.

Out of instinct, Miuko ducked, feeling mildly foolish when only dust came filtering through the ceiling of the crawl space.

"She's dangerous! You saw her today, looking like that! Girls her age are always flouting their—"

"Calm your temper, my son," Aleila replied in a soothing voice. "Remember what happened last time."

"Don't tell me how to feel! You're always telling me how to feel!"

As Miuko listened to them argue, the humming in her marrow intensified.

And she realized what it was.

Buzzing.

One by one, ghosts appeared along the edges of the crawl space —crouched, perched on all fours, bent double, missing feet and hands, bleeding from truncated limbs.

Girls.

All of them.

Girls in nightgowns.

Girls in bridal robes, ragged with decay.

Girls in traveling clothes, with sun hats dangling listlessly from their severed necks.

Behind Miuko, the demon prince whispered, "Vengeance."

Overhead, Laowu thundered across the floorboards. "Who does she think she is? She needs someone to show her a woman's place. It's *wrong*, Mother. *You'd* never do something like that. Why should she?"

Something else was thrown across the room.

A footstool. A wooden bowl.

"Please, my son, it's too soon! People will be suspicious! After last time . . . I can't . . . they're so heavy. You can't imagine how heavy. And they bleed so much. Even after you've killed them, they bleed so much."

In the darkness beneath the floor, Miuko went cold. Aleila had *helped* him. Instead of reporting him, instead of *stopping* him, she'd disposed of the corpses and, in doing so, allowed him to continue killing.

As if sensing Miuko's mood, the ghosts' droning intensified. A floating pair of hands clapped eagerly. A girl's head turned upside down, transforming her grimace into a grotesque smile. Miuko reached for the earth. She scrabbled at the dirt while Laowu railed on: "Don't hide from it now, Mother! Don't turn away! Look at me! *You* did this. *You* made me!"

"I *protected* you!" Aleila was weeping now. "Everything I have ever done is to protect you!"

"Protect me? You're protecting yourself. Where will you go if they catch me, Mother? You have no other family—"

Miuko dug, and the ghosts watched her—or at least, they waited for her, for they did not all have eyes to watch. She dug until she unearthed a set of bones, held together by loose threads of sinew.

Human bones.

Girl's bones.

The ghosts buzzed.

She had known she'd find them, and she'd so hoped she wouldn't.

How many girls had this man murdered? Miuko wondered. How many had his mother dismembered and buried to cover up his crimes? How many pieces would Miuko find, if she continued to look?

Abruptly, she thrust the bones away from her. They fell, clattering onto an exposed ribcage.

"What was that?" Aleila asked.

"It's nothing. You're imagining things, Mother."

Across the crawl space, the floating hands turned into fists. The decapitated head glared at Miuko. As if urging her to act, one of the torsos tried to bump into her (though, since it was a ghost and she still a human — or mostly, at any rate — it only passed through her like a chill).

But she was just a girl, too. What could *she* do?

Easy, whispered the demon-voice. She could race upstairs on her swift *shaoha*'s legs. She could vault through the manor window, Laowu and his mother freezing in their places, mouths widening in fear —

She felt Tujiyazai's hand upon her shoulder, light and warm. "Someone is here."

"Someone *else?*" Crawling to the door, Miuko peered outside.

The garden was still. Not even a leaf dared stir.

But there, upon the hillside above the manor, was a figure in white. Among the trees, his robes appeared to glow like moonlight, illuminating the red scarf he'd pulled over his mouth and nose.

"*Kyakyozuya,*" Miuko whispered. The demon hunter. She'd been a fool to think they'd escaped him.

Behind her, she felt Tujiyazai flare with heat. If she'd turned around, she might have seen sparks flying about his horns.

125

But she was still watching the demon hunter, who held a flexible bamboo pole, at the end of which dangled a circular stone with a hole drilled through the center—a spirit rod. When used properly, such tools were said to point to centers of *nasu* activity.

As he stood there, the stone began to tug him toward the manor. Was it pointing to the ghosts, who now crowded about Miuko like sisters spying on a suitor?

Or to her and Tujiyazai?

As the demon hunter hopped from his perch, skidding toward the walled garden, the *doro yagra* whispered at her shoulder: "What will you do now, Ishao?"

Kill him. The answer came swiftly, simply. *Kill all three of them.*

As if they, too, could hear her inner voice, the ghosts hummed with pleasure. She almost thought she heard one of them giggle as the amputated head turned a cartwheel, her long black hair falling across her bloody neck.

The *kyakyozuya* was out of sight now, on the other side of the wall.

"I can't," Miuko whispered.

"You are a *shaoha*," said Tujiyazai. "Nothing is beyond you."

In the far corner of the garden, where a cypress tree tilted over the walls like a drunk, there was the sound of shoes scraping upon bark. The branches shook.

Miuko flexed her fingers, tested her legs. "You want me to kill him?"

"What do *you* want?"

"I'm not a killer," she said.

"Not with that attitude."

The ghosts buzzed about her. A pair of disembodied hands made a shooing motion.

"But I—"

There was a sharp *crack!* A limb fell from the drunken tree, taking a fluttering white figure with it.

Overhead, Laowu thrust his head out a window. "Someone's outside." Then, to his mother: "Stay put."

There was a sudden commotion inside the manor. The sound of footfalls.

The buzzing intensified.

Along the wall, the *kyakyozuya* appeared, sword glinting at his side.

And Miuko panicked. "He'll find us! What do we do?"

For a moment—too long of a moment, in Miuko's opinion—the demon prince merely looked at her, as if he were waiting for something, though it should have been clear from context that *she* was the one waiting for him.

Finally, he sighed. "Go. I will draw them away."

Above, Laowu was at the door. The demon hunter landed in the garden.

Tujiyazai melted into the shadows.

The ghosts drew back into the crawlspace, only the white teeth of the decapitated head glinting faintly in the light.

Miuko ran.

There was a cry—whose, she didn't know, nor did she care to find out—as she raced across the yard's gravel paths. She flung herself at the gate, struggling with the latch, as someone crunched through the pebbles behind her.

Fearing at every second the touch of a man's hands in her hair, a blade in her back, she shoved the gate open and dashed into the lane, over the cobblestones. She ran pell-mell down the hill, toward the town, swerving along the twisted roads, through the trees.

Suddenly, her foot caught. The world tipped beneath her, and she went tumbling from the street, down a wooded hillside, dead leaves flying about her, elbows and knees striking the hard ground, until she collided with the base of a tree.

For a split second, there was a sharp pain in her forehead, followed by fear. *I'm going to be caught.*

Then darkness.

21

THE WORD OF A GIRL

MIUKO MISSED WAKING UP with a roof over her head.

And a pillow under it, the demon-voice added.

For once, Miuko could not help but agree.

Wincing, she blinked up at the canopy, through which the pre-dawn light was soft and gray as a dove. As she sat up, she tested her forehead —the blood had hardened, although the flesh beneath was still swollen and tender to the touch.

Groaning, she staggered from the trees, thanking the gods it was still the verge hour, which meant that no one was about to see her rumpled clothing or the twigs in her hair.

Rubbing her hands against her thighs, she passed the silent homes and shuttered stores of the town square. Small bits of soil tumbled down her robes, leaving smudges of dirt in the lines of her palms and upon her fingertips.

She paused, staring down at her left hand. The pads of her fingers weren't *smudged*.

They were *indigo*.

The curse had reached the ends of her fingertips, as if she'd just barely brushed the surface of a deep, inky pool. At this rate, the palm and all the fingers of her left hand would be eclipsed by the end of the day, and it would not be long before the same thing happened to her right.

Miuko curled her fingers. They'd never touch a living thing again, never feel the spiraled head of a fern or the soft nose of the gray mare, never sow seedlings in a garden, never hold someone's hand . . .

She might have lost hope, then, for she was still days from the House of December. She might have plopped down right there in the town square, as she had done in the Kotskisiu-maru, to lament her situation.

But she was not the same girl she'd been when she'd left Nihaoi. Gripping her robes in her fists, she started for the inn with renewed speed.

At least, she would have, if at that very moment she hadn't been grabbed from behind.

"There you are," Laowu growled.

She fought. She punched and flailed and tried to scream, but Laowu, small though he was for a man, was stronger than she—never mind the fact that her head injury made her dizzy and sick—and he clamped a hand over her mouth as he began to drag her from the square.

Touch him, whispered the little voice inside her.

The fingers of Miuko's left hand twitched.

Reach for his cheek.

They were almost out of sight now. If she didn't stop him from taking her, she didn't know if she'd survive.

Stop him, said the voice. *Kill him. If he's the last thing you touch, it will have been worth it.*

And for a moment, Miuko was tempted. To kill a man who'd killed so many others? If there was ever a time to use her powers, this was surely it.

But she could not do it. She could not take a life.

Not even his.

As he pulled her into an alley, Miuko set her feet against the side of a building and kicked out with all the strength in her demon-legs, thrusting them both into the opposite wall.

Laowu grunted.

His grip on her face slackened, giving her just enough room to bite down on the tender flesh between his thumb and forefinger.

With a cry, he jerked backward, striking her in the head.

Her vision swam.

But she could speak now. She could use her voice.

And she did.

She filled the town with it, rattling the windows, making the trees quiver. She called for help. She named the murderer. There were bodies beneath his floorboards. *Five bodies. Seven.* So many dead girls. Help her now. Stop him *now,* or Koewa would never be free of its ghosts.

The doors were thrown wide.

Men stormed onto the streets. Women and children peered from their houses. In the windows there appeared the faces of girls, disheveled and pale, as if they hadn't seen the sun in weeks, hidden from the monster that stalked their town.

A crowd began to converge on Laowu where he stood, still clutching Miuko's arm.

"She's lying!" he protested.

But the townspeople continued to advance.

"All those young wives you've lost," said one man. "All those poor girls . . ."

"We felt sorry for you!"

Laowu tightened his grip on Miuko, as if he could retain control of the situation if only he could control her. "She's a stranger!" he said. "You *know* me!"

"We thought we knew you!"

His lip curled. "You would take the word of a girl over mine?"

At this, the crowd halted, the men glancing uneasily at one another.

Miuko wanted to scream. Being a *girl* made her suspect? Being a *girl* made her untrustworthy? *That* was going to stop them? *That* was going to stop them from stopping *him?*

But she could not scream now, for she could already predict what would happen if she did.

They'd call her hysterical. They'd say she was overreacting. They'd say she was high-spirited, given to flights of fancy. She was a strange girl, after all, too wild. She dressed like a man. She rode *horses.* She didn't know her place. Perhaps she'd pursued *him,* and he'd rejected her, and now she was making up stories to get back at him.

So like a girl.

Miuko didn't even realize her cursed fingertips were reaching for him when another voice stopped her: "She's telling the truth."

On the edge of the crowd stood the demon hunter, his white robes befouled with dirt, and Aleila, equally filthy, cowed beside him.

"I've seen the corpses beneath the manor," he said soberly. "This woman has revealed her son's crimes, and they are many."

Aleila bowed. Tears ran in rivulets down her grimy cheeks. "It's over, my son," she said in a trembling voice. "The truth has come for us."

The townspeople turned back to Laowu, who shoved Miuko away from him as if she were evidence of his crimes. As the crowd tightened around him, he took a step toward his mother. "Stupid woman! If I die, you have nowhere to go! You are nothing without me!"

Aleila flinched.

It was true—widows without sons or sons-in-law went to live with the men of their extended families, but if those men would not take them, they would be cast out—to become beggars or nuns or women of ill repute.

Even if Aleila had an extended family to go to, there was no way they would take her now.

"Miuko!" Geiki ran up to her, pulling Roroisho behind him.

The horse did not look pleased to be hauled about so; although, after the *atskayakina*'s previous attempts in the saddle, Miuko supposed it was better than having him for a rider.

"You're hurt!" he cried. "What happened? Why are you so dirty?"

She hugged him.

He swayed at the sudden weight of her. "Ack! What's gotten into you? Are you in love with me now? Is this a love spell?"

Grinning, Miuko pushed him back. "I'm just happy to see you—"

"As you should be," he interrupted.

"But we've got to go."

Behind her, Laowu was speaking to the assembled crowd. His voice had changed—it was no longer strident but smooth—the same slippery politician's voice he'd used on the townspeople the day before. "You've seen my mother!" he declared. "She drove my father to madness! She drove *me* to madness! *She* made me this way. If I'm a monster, it's *her fault!*"

The crowd began muttering, shifting angrily as they turned their attention on Aleila, who took a step backward, glancing at the *kyakyozuya* for help.

While she was distracted, Laowu lunged.

His own mother.

The townspeople should have stopped him. Perhaps some of them tried to.

But the result was chaos—scratching, grabbing, striking. Laowu was tackled to the ground as his mother let out a frail cry. Her clothes were being torn from her narrow shoulders, exposing her wrinkled arms.

The demon hunter was shouting, but he could not be heard now over the roar of the crowd.

It was horrible to watch.

Aleila had helped a murderer. She'd protected him, as a mother was supposed to. She'd hacked up the bodies and buried them beneath her family home.

But she hadn't killed those girls.

Was birthing a monster worse than being one?

Miuko could not stand to watch any longer. Ignoring a cry from Geiki, she dove into the crowd, shouldering grown men aside, trying to reach Aleila in the cruel assembly.

The townspeople clawed at Miuko, hauling her back. Their hands dug into her hair and robes, yanking at her.

The cloth ripped.

There was the sound of threads snapping, popping one by one up the side of her leg.

Miuko froze as her robes split almost halfway up her thigh, exposing the vivid blue of her legs to the air . . . to the town . . . and to the demon hunter, who drew his blessed sword, the blade flashing in the rising sun.

22

IN THE FORESTS
ABOVE KOEWA

AT FIRST, THE TOWNSPEOPLE did not quite know what to make of her. Never having encountered a *shaoha* before, some did not know if she was a monster or merely one of the *nasu*. But others drew back, gasping. *"Yagra,"* the whisper went through the crowd. Demon.

Worse, a female demon.

Miuko felt them turn on her even quicker than they'd turned on Laowu and his mother, who now lay—unconscious and bleeding—among their former friends and neighbors, and she could not help but hate them for it. Her contempt surged through her like cold, burning in her fingertips and prickling through her veins.

She resolved to fight. She would hurt them if they tried to hurt her, for she was neither a fragile old woman nor a little girl.

She was a *shaoha*. Or half of one, at least.

She bared her teeth. She readied her blue-tipped hand.

"Stay back!" the demon hunter ordered the crowd. "This is no ordinary demon."

Miuko glared at him.

But before either of them could move, there was a crack of thunder and a flash in the sky, like the one she'd seen in the Kotskisiu-maru the night she'd met Geiki.

The *kyakyozuya* ducked.

"Miuko, let's go!"

Whirling around, she plunged through the assembly as the *atskayakina*

135

stole a shawl and flung it over Roroisho's saddle. He helped her onto the horse's back, kicking out as someone tried to grab him from behind.

Grateful for his quick thinking, Miuko reached down to haul him up after her. Even with her legs exposed, she would not accidentally harm Roroisho with the shawl between them.

Geiki climbed up behind her, clinging to her waist as the demon hunter recovered his wits and leapt at them, red scarf trailing behind him like a flag.

But he was too late. Roroisho let out a cry and cantered out of the town square with Miuko and Geiki astride her. They fled Koewa, racing off down the Ochiirokai before the *kyakyozuya* and the townspeople could muster their pursuit.

It would not be long, however, before the demon hunter came after them, so once they were clear of the town, Miuko directed Roroisho off the Thousand-Step Way and onto the narrow trails in the forested hills above Koewa in hopes that they would not be found there.

On the mountain path, Miuko and Geiki slid from the mare's back, listening for sounds of pursuit.

There were none, the silence broken only by the birds in the trees and the trickling of a nearby creek, a peace so absolute that Miuko could not help but scowl as she wrapped a bit of cloth around her cursed left hand. How could such tranquility exist when so many terrible things had happened only miles away? It felt like a violation, a flaw in the nature of both Ada and Ana.

But it had happened all the same.

Quietly, Geiki took Roroisho's reins, leading her on. "What happened back there?"

Miuko stared at the ground as they continued into the hills, her torn robes swishing about her legs.

"Miuko?"

In truth, she could no longer remember why she'd kept this secret from him in the first place. Shame? Propriety? After what she'd seen in Koewa, such reasons felt empty.

So she told him everything about her nighttime encounters with the *doro yagra*. The rescue of the crane spirit. The discovery of the graves.

"You were meeting with Tujiyazai?" Geiki flapped his good arm at her. *"He's a* demon, *Miuko!"*

A part of her knew she had no right to be angry at his reaction, but, given the events of the long and difficult morning, a much greater part of her wanted to be angry at *something,* and, well, he was there. "So?" she snapped. *"You're* a trickster and a thief!"

"Yeah, but I'm not a *demon!* He could've eaten you!"

Miuko crossed her arms. "He doesn't want to eat me."

Probably, said the little voice inside her.

She willed it to shut up, for now was not the time for snide remarks.

"He could have made you do something terrible!" Geiki cried. "Or done something terrible to you!"

"Yeah, *terrible,* like giving us this horse," she said, though in her haste to find the source of Koewa's evils, she'd neglected to ask Tujiyazai if that was, strictly speaking, true.

But who else could it have been?

"What?" The *atskayakina* drew back from Roroisho as if she'd grown fangs. "How could you?" he demanded of her.

Utterly nonplussed, the mare continued walking.

"Where did you think she came from?" Miuko scoffed. "I told you, people don't just give other people horses!"

"You should have told me what was going on." Geiki's voice softened with disappointment. "I thought we were friends."

But she did not want his disappointment any more than she wanted his outrage, for in her opinion he was not entitled to either.

"Oh?" She lifted an eyebrow. "We're *friends,* are we?"

"Of course!"

"You're not just here because I saved your life, and now you're beholden to me until you save mine?"

He was halted mid-retort, mouth hanging open as if to catch gnats.

"Tujiyazai told me," she said smugly, although smugness was a grubby sort of emotion, and it only made her feel worse.

"Of course he did," Geiki grumbled.

"Is it true?"

He looked away. "Yes."

"Why didn't you tell me?"

"It was embarrassing!"

"*Embarrassing?*" Her voice cracked. "You lied to me because you were *embarrassed?*"

"Yes! And I didn't lie! I told you it was destiny, didn't I?"

"I assumed you meant in the metaphorical sense!"

"I'm never metaphorical when it comes to destiny!"

"Don't yell at me!"

"Ack!" He ran a hand through his hair. "How would you feel if you were almost killed by a bunch of babies? And had to be saved by a human, of all things?"

"I thought you liked that I was human!" she cried.

"I do! But you have to admit, it's also a little embarrassing, right?" He tried to smile. "Come on, Miuko."

She spun on him, eyes dry and wild. She'd hardly slept. She'd escaped priests and demons and ghosts and *men,* and in the past six days she'd been chased, attacked, threatened, and yelled at for dressing incorrectly, for riding a horse, for being bad at being a woman, for being a woman in the first place, and to be frank, she was tired.

She wasn't going to make it to the House of December.

If it wasn't for Geiki and his harebrained plans, she could have spent these last days of her humanity in comfort, or at least not in the wilderness with a thieving, lying *atskayakina*.

Was this fair of her?

No.

Did she care?

Also no.

"*You* come on!" she shouted. "You lied! You're not my friend. You never had a 'good feeling' about me! You just *have* to be here because of some ludicrous *nasu* rule!"

"That's not true!"

"Do you even have to be here anymore?" The words tasted foul on her tongue, but she could not stop them, hating herself more and more the longer she went on. Inside her mind, the demon-voice was laughing. "Haven't you repaid your debt by now? Why don't you just fly home?"

For a moment, Geiki glared at her over Roroisho's withers, looking as if he'd shout back.

Part of her wanted him to. After everything, she wanted to fight something, and if she could not fight the demon hunter or the townspeople of Koewa or the very foundations of Omaizi society, she would settle for fighting Geiki.

But he did not shout. He sucked in a breath, his eyes shining with tears that made her feel guiltier and angrier. Then he turned away. "Stop staring at me," he said.

For a moment, Miuko wanted to continue glaring at him out of sheer obstinacy, but, despite the things she'd said, she still considered him a friend.

At least, she hoped he'd still be her friend, after this.

She looked away.

When she glanced up again, Geiki was in bird form, perched sullenly between Roroisho's ears.

Miuko glowered at him. She would have much preferred an argument to this corvine brooding; she may have felt ashamed for being mad at him when he was a boy, but now she felt ashamed *and ridiculous* for being mad at a bird, which only made her feel madder and more ridiculous than before.

She should have apologized.

But she did not want to.

For the better part of the day, Roroisho bore their foul tempers with great patience, but by sunset, she'd had enough, and somewhere deep in the forests above Koewa, she stopped and refused to go another step further.

Geiki hopped from her head, reappearing on her other side in boy form. Taking the reins, he tugged the mare toward the trees, beyond which they could hear the chiming of a mountain stream. "Stay here," he said to Miuko. "I'm going to find water."

"But—" Miuko caught his hand, stopping him. Now that she'd had a day to simmer in her own anger, her feelings had all burned off, leaving her feeling sorry as a scorched pot. In her palm, his fingers felt light and strong, and she was not surprised that he'd managed so many successful thefts with them. "Geiki, I—"

He slid out of her grasp, adjusting his sling. "Make a fire or something," he said over his shoulder. "I don't know."

Gloomily, she watched him lead the gray mare down toward the water, leaving her alone in a nest of ferns with only a fallen log for company.

The log wasn't much comfort either, for it was too rotten to make for good firewood. Sighing, she trudged up the hill in the opposite direction, searching for tinder and composing an apology she hoped would be good enough.

As she collected fallen branches, she noticed a streak of blue at her wrist, peeping over the cloth she'd wrapped around her hand earlier that day. Grimly, she tugged her sleeve down. She'd have to find a glove in the morning . . . maybe two, if her right hand also turned indigo in the night.

Would Geiki still be with her then?

She hoped so.

The sun fell behind the mountain. The verge hour closed in around her, heavy and black among the trees.

The pile of kindling in her arms grew until she could carry no more, and she was just turning back toward the glade of ferns when she heard shouts in the woods.

"They came this way, *kyakyozuya!*"

"See this passage through the bushes?"

Miuko froze.

The demon hunter had found her. And from the sound of it, he had brought company.

How *much* company?

And had they found Geiki?

Flinging the firewood aside, Miuko dashed down the mountain in the direction the *atskayakina* had taken Roroisho. Stones rolled beneath her steps. Low-hanging branches clawed at her face.

In the distance, the sounds of the hunters grew louder.

Water splashed against her ankles — she'd reached the stream.

She turned to follow it downhill, but she was halted by the sight of torches in the trees: dozens of tiny lights igniting, one after another, cutting her off from Geiki and Roroisho.

"What's that?" someone called.

There was a high, shrill sound — a horse, crying out in fear.

Miuko panicked. She could not let them capture her friends. Geiki was a trickster and a liar and a fool, sure, but he wasn't a *demon*. Would the *kyakyozuya* and his hunters know the difference?

She could not bear to find out.

So she did the only thing she could do at this distance. She took a breath . . . and screamed, "HERE!"

The lights in the woods halted. One by one, they turned, advancing on her position, the silhouettes of men visible between the trees.

"There she is!" someone shouted.

That's right, said the demon-voice, or perhaps it was Miuko herself. For the first time, she could not be sure. *Come and get me.*

And, turning uphill, she ran.

She was good at running now. With her demon-legs propelling her quickly up the slope, she was swift as the shadows and strong as the earth.

But she was outnumbered. The hunters seemed to be everywhere: behind her, closing in from her right, their torches flickering among the leaves, smoke thick upon the air.

She leapt over a gully, scrabbling among the rocks on the other side, hauling herself to her feet again. She had to keep running. She had to lead them away from Geiki and Roroisho.

At the top of the ridge, she glanced back.

The hunters were in the ravine already, clambering over the stones below. They were so close, Miuko thought she even recognized a few faces from Koewa.

As if sensing her watching them, one of the men halted, staring up at her where she stood above them. In the torchlight, his white robes were sickly yellow.

The demon hunter.

She ran again.

But even demons tired, and she felt her strength flagging. The hunters had not reached the top of the rise yet, but she could hear them calling in the gully below, the light of their torches illuminating the canopy behind her.

She was going to be caught.

What then? Would they drown her in a barrel of blessed water? Would they cut her cursed limbs from her torso to try to save her? Would she be run through with the *kyakyozuya*'s shining blade?

The sound of hooves jolted her out of her morbid thoughts.

For the briefest of moments, she thought it might be Roroisho, with Geiki clinging haphazardly to the saddle.

But it was not the dapple gray mare, and it was not the *atskayakina*.

It was a great black horse, taller and broader than Roroisho, with eyes that seemed to blaze in the moonlight.

Miuko had seen this horse before, she realized, six nights ago on the dilapidated bridge outside Nihaoi.

It was the *doro*'s horse, and upon his back, handsome face severe and wrathful, was Tujiyazai.

23

MALEVOLENCE DEMON

"TUJIYAZAI!" MIUKO GASPED. "The *kyakyozuya* is here! He—"

From the shadows beneath the trees, the *doro yagra* stared down at her, features wreathed in flame. "I know."

His apparent composure made her ashamed of her own fear, but it didn't stop her from babbling: "Please, you have to help me. I haven't seen Geiki. I don't know if—"

"They are coming for *you,* Ishao."

Behind her, the woods were alive with the sounds of men: hard breathing, heavy footfalls, twigs snapping like little fingers, things being scraped and broken and trampled with thoughtless ease.

Tujiyazai extended a hand to her. "I can take you away from here. But you must come willingly."

Miuko hesitated as Geiki's words echoed in her mind: *He's a* demon, *Miuko.* Where would he take her? What would he do with her once he had her?

While she wavered, the first of the hunters climbed from the ravine. Armed with a pitchfork, he charged her, his features distorted by rage.

Miuko froze.

But he did not see Tujiyazai, concealed by darkness, until it was too late. The demon prince caught the pitchfork, wrenching it from the man's grasp and tossing it aside as if it were no heavier than a matchstick. Sneering, he leaned down and caught the man by the chin.

For a moment, it seemed as if the hunter would lash out at him, but as Miuko watched, the fury drained from the man's face. His fists fell to his sides.

What was Tujiyazai doing to him?

Giving the hunter a little shove, the *doro yagra* released him. He stumbled, landing on his backside among the undergrowth, where he lay, looking about him with a bewildered expression.

"*Doro*-kanai?" he said uncertainly. "My liege, what's happening? What are you doing here?"

Miuko stared at him. Just seconds before, he had been prepared to attack, but now all the hostility seemed to have left him, drawn out like water by a sponge.

Her gaze found Tujiyazai, scarcely visible in the shadows but for his flaming features. He'd said anger was his dominion. Could he control it in others as well as sense it?

He smiled at her. "Well, Ishao? What will it be?"

She glanced over her shoulder. The rest of the hunters were climbing over the lip of the ravine now—arms and legs and smoking torches—looking not like men at all but like many-limbed monsters, fused together by shadow.

She took the demon prince's hand.

Then she was being lifted. She was being settled across his lap. His arms were going around her, and she did not know if he was trying to protect her or trying to possess her, but she knew that as long as Tujiyazai had her, the hunters could not touch her.

She steeled herself for the ride.

But they remained beneath the trees, unmoving.

Tujiyazai looked at the *kyakyozuya* and his men, eyes flickering with sparks only Miuko could see. Then . . .

Heat.

It burst from him like a conflagration, so rabid that Miuko thought for certain it would set the entire mountain ablaze, incinerating every needle on every tree, every spore of moss, every insect chittering in its nest.

It didn't.

Instead, she watched with mounting horror as the man on the ground reached for his pitchfork and stood, launching it back at the approaching hunters.

There was a scream.

A fountain of blood.

The others were turning on one another, too, faces contorted, hands seeking eyes and throats—their original quarry, hiding in the shadows with Tujiyazai, entirely forgotten.

Of them all, the *kyakyozuya* was the only one who seemed unaffected —protected, perhaps, by the spells inked upon his scarf. He shouted at the others, imploring them to stop.

But he did not hesitate to defend himself when they came at him. His sword flashed, slicing a man through the midsection. Blood spattered his white robes.

Miuko gasped.

So this was the true extent of Tujiyazai's power over men. The ability to amplify their hatred and their violence and turn it back upon themselves.

She felt it amplifying her own power, too, except to her it did not feel like heat.

It coursed through her, cold as ice. With the *doro yagra*'s malevolence supplementing her own, she felt formidable, like she could suck the strength from a man's limbs and the light from his eyes. She felt deadly and terrible and bristling with wrath. She was not a girl, now. She was not Otori Miuko of Nihaoi. She was not even Ishao.

For the first time she felt herself capable of being that which Tujiyazai had called her the night they met. A monster. A queen. A dread goddess at whose indigo feet men would place offerings of blood and grain and gold in the hope that she would spare them her fury.

Shao-kanai.

Lady Death.

She hated it . . . and loved it, too, for no man would dare threaten Shao-kanai. No man would catch her or corral her or pinch her into shape like a piece of clay.

If she were a monster, she would at last be free.

Tujiyazai kicked the great black horse, who reared back, throwing Miuko against the demon prince's chest.

She cried out—just Miuko again, poor pathetic Miuko again—and the horse charged away into the darkness, leaving the hunters' torches flaming in the mulch, catching ferns and climbing saplings, while the men tore themselves to pieces on the edge of the ravine.

24

THE TOWER

THEY RODE LONG into the night—over the mountain paths and between the arboreal ridges, the stars spiraling overhead. In other circumstances, Miuko might have found it beautiful. As it was, however, she noticed neither the serenity of the forest nor the splendor of the heavens, for she could not stop thinking of the *kyakyozuya* and his men at the edge of the ravine, hacking and slashing at one another while Tujiyazai watched them with hardly a flicker of his eyelids, as if provoking them to violence was as pedestrian as swatting flies on a summer afternoon.

Sometime near dawn—or so she had to guess, for it was still dark—they reached a castle upon a rocky precipice. It was an impressive sort of place, all massive beams and hand-carved ornaments, that Miuko's mother would have appreciated for its grandeur.

Miuko herself was too tired to appreciate much of anything, and when the *doro*'s servants escorted her to a high tower room, she had only the barest impression of embellished transoms, a porcelain washbasin inlaid with designs of chrysanthemums and butterflies, and a mattress softer than anything she had ever dared to imagine, before she fell into a long, exhausted slumber that did not surrender its hold on her until the following afternoon, when the sun streamed through the shutters, making squares of gold upon the sheets.

Taking quick stock of the room (a viewing nook with a vase of freshly cut branches, a full-length mirror, the washbasin she remembered from

148

the previous night, and a black incense box in the shape of a sleeping cat), she staggered to her feet. There was no time to dwell on the fact that she hadn't brushed her hair or teeth in days. Not being a morning person was a luxury she no longer had. Wobbling across the room on aching legs, she tried the door.

Locked.

He wouldn't make it that easy for you, the demon-voice chided her.

She crossed to the windows next. The shutters, too, were locked; through them, she could see that the castle was on a rocky promontory which overlooked a valley surrounded entirely by mountains. Five stories below her lay a courtyard and a verdant garden, at the center of which Tujiyazai stood, still as a stone.

From this angle, she couldn't see his face, but it seemed to her that there was something forlorn about the slope of his shoulders, the way he hung his head. For the first time, Miuko was struck by how truly and utterly alone he was. He had no friends, no family . . .

Did it trouble him?

Would it trouble her, if she did not make it to the House of December before the curse overtook her?

She searched the room again for means of escape, but the light summer sheets would not be long enough to lower her to the ground, even if she could break open the shutters . . . which, she supposed, was her first task.

What she did find was rather curious, although ultimately unhelpful. As Miuko opened the incense box to check for a secret key—or even incense—a cloud of smoke purled from within, emitting a high-pitched mewing. Startled, she leapt back as the smoke rolled across the bedspread, coalescing into the form of what appeared to be a very small, very adorable kitten. Purring, it butted playfully against her hands, its smoky tail wisping through her fingers.

She laughed, delighted, as it gamboled away from her, pouncing at sunbeams and flecks of dust. "What kind of magic are you, kitten? Where did you come from?"

In response, it began chasing its own tail.

Miuko chuckled. Perhaps Geiki had been right—humans really did have a fondness for cats, didn't they? Seeing no harm in it, she allowed the creature to play and tumble as she examined the stand of the washbasin, trying to determine whether the fine-grained wood was strong enough to leverage against the window locks, and was just about to attempt dismantling it when she noticed the smoke cat pawing at the windows. Outside, another cat—a real one this time, with golden eyes and beautiful calico spots—had appeared on the roof, meowing through the shutters.

Miuko was encouraged. If a cat could make it up so high, perhaps she could make it down too. But she could not think with both animals crying out with increasing urgency for company, and so she opened the incense box again, drawing the magical kitten back into it. "I'm sorry," she said, replacing the lid and stuffing it deep inside her pocket. "I promise you can make friends when we get out of here."

As she spoke, the door opened. Miuko spun, tensed for the sight of Tujiyazai, but it was not the *doro yagra*.

A handful of servants entered, bowing wordlessly. They whirled about the room with the efficiency of the serving class, changing the sheets, carrying pitchers of steaming water for the washbasin, bringing a tray of food and a neat pile of new clothes, including a set of long gloves that reached past her elbows and a pair of narrow trousers to go beneath her robes.

"Good morning," Miuko croaked, feeling only marginally embarrassed by the creak in her voice.

"Good morning," they replied. "Good morning."

But they said nothing more, and if they noticed her blue left hand, clutching the windowsill, they made no sign.

Then, bowing, they whirled out again.

The lock clicked.

Sniffing at the food they'd left, she wrinkled her nose at the fermented soybeans, sticky as mucus, but she was happy to find fresh rice with silky squares of bean curd and tart pickles, the smell of which made her mouth water. None of it appeared poisoned, and besides, she didn't think Tujiyazai would want to poison her, now that he had her. Still, at first she took only a hesitant sip of tea, pausing to see if it would make her choke or perhaps froth at the mouth.

It didn't, and she tucked eagerly into the breakfast, for she'd had nothing to eat since lunch the day before.

Her hunger satisfied, she turned her attention to hygiene. As she disrobed before the mirror, she laid her hand against her stomach. In her reflection, the curse cut across her waist like a shoreline: soft sand, bright water.

Dipping a washcloth into the basin, she noticed that the fingertips of her right hand had turned indigo too. Gently, she prodded each of them, remembering how she'd caught Geiki's hand before he led Roroisho into the forest.

He might have been the last person she'd ever touch, and he was still out there, somewhere. Injured, maybe.

Or dead, said her demon-voice with unseemly cheer.

Miuko ignored the thought. Snatching the washcloth from the water, she began to scour the dirt and dust from her body, the effects of the tea sharpening her wits. That was good. She'd need all her cleverness, and more, to escape from the tower.

25

LAST SON OF THE OGAWA

MIUKO HAD JUST ABOUT decided the only way to escape from her room was through the door, which remained locked, when a servant arrived to escort her to the gardens. For a brief moment, Miuko considered overpowering the girl, for she was diminutive in stature and had the demeanor of a mouse, but she was also accompanied by six well-armed guards in the black-and-silver livery of the Omaizi, so Miuko allowed herself to be chaperoned down the five floors to the garden.

As they walked, she observed that the layout of each floor was the same, with a series of rooms arrayed around a central stair. Given the chance, she could easily make her way out of the keep. From there, she'd just have to find her way to the lower tiers of the castle and then to the mountain roads.

Tujiyazai was waiting for her by the lawn. To Miuko, his horns and flaming features seemed out of place against the backdrop of flowering hydrangeas and petal-blue skies, but she supposed that all anyone else saw was the handsome face of the *doro* and not the demon who had claimed his body.

As she approached, he dismissed her retinue with a wave of his hand. The motion appeared so effortless, it looked as if he'd been doing it all his life.

Perhaps he had. Perhaps the soul of Omaizi Ruhai remained inside his body, tucked into a dark corner somewhere. Were gestures like this evidence that the *doro* could still exercise control over his own limbs? Or plead for help?

"Good afternoon, Ishao," said Tujiyazai. "Did you like my cat?"

Miuko squinted at him, searching his features for a sign that the *doro*'s spirit shared the body with him. "Yes," she said. "What is it?"

"A *tseimi*."[1] He smiled disarmingly, an expression which did not suit him in the slightest. "Cute, isn't it?"

"Unexpected is more like it," she said carefully. "Like the horse."

"The horse?" His brow creased. "You can have it, if you want. But later. Now, I want you to remove your socks and sandals."

She glanced around. Nearby was the castle keep—it loomed over them, five stories tall, with gabled roofs she could probably scramble down, given her demon-strength, but from the lowest roof there was another fifty-foot drop to the courtyard flagstones, and she didn't know how she'd walk away from that. From the castle walls, dozens of windows looked down upon them like black eyes. There could be any number of spectators watching them now.

"Don't be embarrassed." The *doro yagra* clicked his tongue at her. "No one will care. They're my loyal subjects!" His laughter, bright though it was, crackled with anger.

Begrudgingly, Miuko slipped out of her shoes and, at Tujiyazai's insistence, her socks. Feeling exposed and uneasy, she shifted uncomfortably upon the flagstones, warm on her bare, blue soles.

"Now." Tujiyazai took a step onto the lawn, beckoning to her. "Walk with me."

She pictured the luxuriant carpet of grass withering under her footsteps,

---

1 tsei-mi (*tsay-mee*): literally, "smoke eye." The word is a play on the Awaran word for "cat," *tsomi*, meaning "moon eye."

the tender seed heads shriveling, the blades blackening and curling in death.

"No," she said.

The demon prince's features twisted into a mock-pout. "You came to me willingly," he warned. "Don't disappoint me now."

"We both know what will happen if I walk across that lawn."

"Yes." He grinned. "But I want to see it for myself. Come."

Still, Miuko did not budge.

The *doro*'s eyes narrowed dangerously. "*Come.* Or you will force me to do to the inhabitants of this castle what I did to those men in the woods. Do you want their blood on your hands, Ishao?"

Blistered features.

The acrid scent of seared hair.

The smooth arc of the *kyakyozuya*'s blade carving through flesh.

She could not allow that to happen again.

Setting her jaw, Miuko stepped forward, feeling the grass go crisp and brittle, crumbling into dust at the weight of her.

Delighted, Tujiyazai collected her socks and sandals, as if that were the only gentlemanly thing to do, and took her by the arm, ushering her, step by withering step, across the lawn.

"This used to be my family's castle," he explained as they walked. "I used to climb the garden wall there, to the rooftops that led to the women's quarters in servant housing."

Somehow, Miuko could not imagine him without his curved horns and expressionless eye sockets—certainly not as a chubby-cheeked boy peeping on servant girls, who, if they'd known, would have surely been humiliated. Rather than try, she said, "Used to be?"

"Before it was seized by the Omaizi," he said, caressing the dead bloom of an azalea flower, still clinging to its stem, "it was a castle of the Ogawa Clan."

Miuko knew this story well, for it had pervaded her childhood: near the end of the Five Swords Era, the Ogawa and their retainers, sworn enemies of the Omaizi, had ridden on Udaiwa. But before they'd even reached the city, they were slaughtered on the fields that surrounded Nihaoi. A massacre that had given rise to the *naiana*—the fog of ghosts.

"But they were all executed," Miuko blurted out.

"Yes. We were."

They paused in the shade of a maple tree, flush with summer growth. Afternoon sunlight cascaded over the grounds, highlighting the uppermost tier of the keep and throwing into shade several levels of palisades, turrets, and cloisters below.

"You asked my name, the night we met," Tujiyazai said. "My name was Ogawa Saitaivaona, and I was the last of my bloodline to be executed." He spoke softly now, like the seething of an ember. "With my dying breath, I swore that one day, I would have my vengeance on the Omaizi."

"But that was more than three hundred years ago."

"It takes a long time to become a malevolence demon." He eyed her blue toes thoughtfully. "Well . . . for most of us."

He explained to her that for many years, he'd been nothing more than a vengeful ghost, like the girls buried beneath the Koewa manor, but as the years wore on, he'd grown more and more powerful.

"Until you were strong enough to possess the *doro*?" Miuko prompted.

"Indeed." Tujiyazai held out his arms, examining the backs of his hands as a clothier would a bolt of fabric. "It was surprisingly easy, evicting him from his own body. I'd have thought he'd put up more of a fight."

Miuko's hopes deflated like a kite without wind. "What happened to him?"

"Who cares? Now that I'm the Omaizi heir"—again, he laughed, and now she understood that he was laughing at his own cruel joke,

155

possessing the most cherished son of his most ancient enemy—"I am well-positioned to destroy their clan and every last stick of their wretched empire."

"You can't do that!"

He paused, a smile playing across his lips as if her protestations amused him. "Why not?"

"So many people would die."

"Isn't that an acceptable cost? For freedom? From *this?*" Gently, he tugged at the girl's knot in her hair. "Don't tell me you've been happy under the thumb of the Omaizi? Don't tell me you think the systems they've erected are just? You are a *woman* and a *servant,* Ishao. Don't tell me that in Awara, as you now know it, these don't *shackle* you to a man and whatever household you're expected to manage for him. Don't tell me you haven't chafed at these restrictions."

Although she could not agree to sacrificing the people of Awara to the downfall of the Omaizi, neither could she disagree that the rest of what Tujiyazai said was true.

She *was* shackled. She *did* chafe.

The strata of life under the Omaizi was not just.

"Don't tell me you wouldn't tear it all to pieces if you had the chance," the *doro yagra* murmured, his fingers resting lightly at her collarbone. "I could give you that chance. I felt the power surging within you last night . . . and the desire."

A monster.

A queen.

A goddess.

Yes, whispered the voice inside her.

Miuko jerked out of his reach. "The only thing I desire is my freedom."

"Why?" His voice grew petulant. "To run, begging, to Amyunasa's priests? To get rid of the only thing that makes you worth *anything?*"

To another girl, this might have been a harrowing insult. But to Miuko—who had for the vast majority of her life believed that she was neither beautiful nor useful and who had only in the past week discovered that she possessed an assortment of other qualities, like bravery and grit and resilience and loyalty, which were altogether undervalued in women —it was nothing. Perhaps she did not know how she fit into the world anymore, for she was no longer a mere girl of the servant class, but she knew her worth.

She laughed. The sound of it pealed across the gardens, swooping over the lower levels of the castle—the rooftops, the crowns of the trees —before joining the mountain wind, free, even if Miuko herself was not.

At first, Tujiyazai seemed confused. Then he smiled. "Ah. Though we are bound, we two, as the dark and light of the moon are bound for all eternity, you still believe you can escape me."

"Yes," she said, "and I promise you, I won't stop trying."

"Why?" His brow furrowed in puzzlement. "For Geiki? You'll never see the *atskayakina* again."

Miuko's confidence wavered. "You don't know that."

"I know much more than you think, Ishao. He was gone long before we left the forest."

She whirled on him. "What do you mean, *gone?*" Through her mind flashed images of Geiki skewered on one of the hunter's knives, Geiki facedown in the creek, Geiki . . .

No.

Tujiyazai was toying with her. He had to be.

"How would you know?" she snapped.

The demon prince regarded her with burning eyes, his stillness so unsettling that Miuko retreated a step, causing another patch of grass to wither beneath her feet.

"Tujiyazai?" Uncertainty crept into her voice. "Tell me you didn't do something to him."

In response, he merely smiled.

26

THE COST OF VENGEANCE

LOCKED IN HER tower room for the remainder of the day, Miuko decided that the best course of action was to wait by the door, and when the next person entered, hit them over the head and flee to the garden, over the rooftops and to the servants' quarters as Tujiyazai had done when he was human. From there, she could find her way out of the castle. To this end, she positioned the water ewer beside the threshold, so she could seize it when the opportunity arose.

As luck would have it, however, the next person to enter was Tujiyazai.

The ewer came down.

He deflected it neatly, causing it to fall from her hands and shatter into pieces upon the floor. Miuko cursed.

Hefting a paper package under one arm, he shut the door behind him. "That's an odd use for a pitcher."

She backed away, watching him warily.

"Why do you scuttle about so?" The *doro yagra* chuckled. "You are no crab."

She did not smile.

"You're to dine with me tonight."

"No."

As if he hadn't heard her, he laid the paper package upon the mattress. "For you," he said.

"What is it?"

"A gift."

"Another one?"

He simply smiled at her.

Under his expectant gaze, she untied the twine and let the paper fall open. Inside were robes embroidered with golden blossoms and pheasants flying through the sky, tangling suns in their tail feathers. Lifting the heavy collar, she wondered if the threads were of pure gold.

Geiki would know.

If he were here.

If he still lived.

"I don't know what to say," Miuko said truthfully.

"Don't say anything. Put it on."

"I'm already dressed."

"You can undress, can't you?" The demon prince smiled again. "Or do I have to help you?"

Knowing he'd only threaten the people of the castle again if she refused, she turned her back to him, fumbling with the knot of her belt. Slowly, she let the robes fall from her shoulders, aware, with every passing second, of his gaze upon the back of her head, the nape of her neck, the thinness of her underthings.

She was grateful for the narrow trousers and long gloves that covered her legs and arms, but with the collar of her slip dipping past her clavicle and the curves of her breasts visible through the fabric, she felt helplessly exposed.

"Turn around," he said.

She obeyed, grinding her teeth to keep from screaming.

He stepped closer, reaching for the hem of her underclothes, lifting it past the waistband of her trousers until a triangle of indigo flesh was visible, mere inches from his knuckles.

"I could wear your skin like armor," Tujiyazai whispered, his breath grazing her throat. She suppressed a shudder as he splayed his fingers, hovering just above her flesh. "Marvelous."

She tensed. She didn't think he had a knife on him—she hadn't seen a sheath—but he could have hidden a blade anywhere in his finery.

Abruptly, he drew his hand back.

She let out a breath as he retreated a few steps, examining her with a quizzical expression. "I wonder . . ." he murmured, more to himself than to her, as if she weren't listening. As if she weren't even there. He cocked his head at her, eyeless gaze probing.

There was no warning. There was no sign.

But she felt the heat burst from him like a spark alighting upon a pyre.

Miuko's blood ran cold. Whatever she'd felt in the forest—as he'd amplified the malevolence of those around him—was nothing compared to the frigid, blistering rage that flooded her now. It tore through her like a blizzard. She could freeze a man where he stood. She could ice his heart and peel the flesh from his bones. She was cold and fury and terrible to behold.

She felt powerful, and, reveling in that power, she knew he'd made a mistake.

Tujiyazai had made her strong enough to stop him.

Tearing off a glove with her teeth, she leapt for him.

They fought. She: scrabbling, tearing, vicious and feral as a wild thing. He: calmly, curiously, heedless of the way she kicked and scratched, ripping at his embellished robes, digging her cursed fingers into his skin.

Triumphantly, she looked up into his eyeless face, waiting eagerly for his features to shrivel and blacken, to wither and die.

But the *doro yagra* remained smiling, sparks flitting about his teeth as his body began to soften and gray, the flush of health draining from his handsome features.

He laughed—uproariously—as if he'd discovered the secret of immortality or matched an antique teacup to a set his grandmother had long ago given up on as incomplete.

To be frank, it was a little insulting.

"What?" Miuko snarled.

"Do you think you're hurting me, Ishao? You're murdering the body of Omaizi Ruhai." Still chuckling, the demon prince shook his head, and indeed, the monstrous features beneath the mask of the *doro*'s face appeared wholly untouched by her magic. His gaze flicked to her arm, and his smile broadened. "And you're hastening your transformation."

She looked down. The curse was flowing up her elbow toward her shoulder like water filling a pail.

The longer she held on, the sooner she'd be a demon.

Miuko released him.

Gradually, the *doro*'s skin regained its firmness. The color returned to his lips and the shadows beneath his eyes.

Her own skin, however, remained the endless blue of the ocean, the curse now encompassing her entire left arm.

"I'm looking forward to meeting you," Tujiyazai said pleasantly, "the *real* you, one day soon."

Miuko said nothing as she slid her glove back over her fingers and up her arm. Through his shredded clothing, she could see traces of old wounds: some puckered, some glossy, some so faint that if she touched them, she'd scarcely be able to tell they were there.

Seeing her studying him, the *doro yagra* glanced down. "Ah," he said. "My old targets."

"What?"

He let his robes fall to his waist, leaving him bare-chested, with a small bamboo cylinder dangling from a cord at his neck. It was such a simple piece of jewelry, much more plain than the finery he seemed to favor, that

Miuko could not help but wonder what purpose it served. Was it a keepsake from his time as an Ogawa child, perhaps, or —

She frowned. What she'd thought were wounds on the *doro*'s flesh were in fact on Tujiyazai's. Beneath his host's unmarked skin, she could see the demon's arms and torso — the same way she could see his true face — flecked with dozens of scars: names, carved and healed over long ago.

"You recorded the names of your victims?" she asked.

"*I* didn't record them. They were forced upon me."

"What do you mean?"

"I was summoned to dispose of them, like a common executioner." He bared his teeth in distaste. "To call a malevolence demon, one needs only two primary elements: the name of an enemy and enough hate to destroy him. Think about that, Ishao. To some humans, annihilating a foe is worth being scarred forever with his name. When a human is desperate enough for that, they carve that name into their own flesh, and it is carved into the flesh of the nearest malevolence demon — sometimes it was me, sometimes it was another, one day soon it might be you — and we are dispatched to deliver vengeance."

"They make you kill people?" Miuko shivered. If she didn't reach the House of December before the curse claimed her, she would not only be a demon but an instrument of murder, to be used by unhappy men.

"Make us?" Tujiyazai laughed. "Don't you understand yet? Haven't you felt it? We *want* to kill. It is our nature. I suppose I've heard it's possible to refuse an offering of hate. Older demons than I have made thralls of their summoners when they deemed their hatred unworthy of a kill. But killing is what we were made for — we do not decline it when given the opportunity."

"So someone could summon you now?" she pressed. "And you'd be whisked out of here, just like that?"

"Oh, no. I like a good murder as much as the next demon, but I tired of serving humans a long time ago. So I took steps to ensure I could not be summoned." He turned his back. There, visible beneath the *doro*'s smooth skin, she could see words tattooed upon the spine of the demon inside him. Though she could not read it at this distance, it looked like a spell, similar to the one the Doctor had used to freeze the *odoshoya* in human form or the ones painted upon the demon hunter's scarf.

A spell to resist summoning.

"Where did you—"

He faced her again. "As it turns out, priests *are* good for something. Besides eating." He grinned, as if this were some joke they shared between them.

"Do you really eat people?" Miuko asked.

"Why? Do you want to know what they taste like?"

She grimaced.

"Unctuous," he said, licking his lips. Then, abruptly: "I wonder what *you* taste like."

But before she could scream, or recoil, or lift a hand to stop him, he'd crossed the distance between them and grabbed her by the back of the neck, crushing his mouth against hers.

She struggled, but he was stronger, forcing open her mouth with his tongue, wet and unwelcome.

She had only been kissed once before—also by a demon, as *yazai* would have it—and it had caused her to lose everything she'd ever known.

But *this* was worse. The kiss with the *shaoha* had been cold, almost perfunctory, but Tujiyazai was demanding, controlling, entitled, as if she owed him access to her lips and teeth and throat and whatever else he wanted, whenever he wanted.

She staggered under the weight of him, knocking into the porcelain washbasin, which sloshed against her narrow trousers.

It was cold.

And hard.

Hard enough to hurt.

He didn't lock the door when he entered, whispered the little voice inside her. *Hit him on the head and run.*

Seizing the washbasin, which, with the new strength in her demon arms, was lighter than she expected, she brought it crashing down upon Tujiyazai's head.

The porcelain shattered.

He grunted under the impact, releasing her.

Thus freed, she grabbed her discarded robes, ran to the door, and fled.

27

ESCAPE FROM THE KEEP

THE OMAIZI GUARDS were on the stairs. Ducking into one of the side rooms, Miuko cursed the architect who'd designed a five-story keep with only one flight of steps. What if there was a fire? What if a voracious family of insects made a feast of the stairs and devoured them right out from under the feet of the noblemen as they ascended to their rooms? What if a girl held prisoner by a bloodthirsty demon needed to escape before she was used against her will for his nefarious ends?

She pulled on her robes and was just knotting them at her waist when she heard the *doro yagra* shouting from the tower room.

Peering into the hall, she watched the guards leave their posts by the stairs.

She made it down two floors before she was cut off by Tujiyazai's guards flooding up the steps, their black-and-silver regalia winking in the lantern light.

Quickly, she dashed into an empty room, upsetting a painted screen, which crashed to the floor, tangling in her legs. Cursing, she kicked at it as the door slid open.

There was Tujiyazai, still stripped to the waist. Grinning, he gave her a mock bow.

Miuko fled again.

She ended up in a large room, heavily ornamented along the ceiling; perhaps it had been used at one time for war councils or holding court, but it was bare now. Racing to the windows, she wrestled with the shutters, which, to her great fortune, opened easily.

She thrust her head out. It was only a short drop to the roof of the second story, and from what she remembered of the rooftops, a similar distance to the lowest roof. But from there it was still a dizzying fifty-foot fall to the courtyard.

Footsteps sounded behind her.

"There's no escape, Ishao, unless you can fly."

Glancing over her shoulder, she saw the demon prince enter the room. His guards fanned out along the walls, blocking access to any door she might have used as an escape.

Which left her only one option.

She climbed out onto the window ledge, the mountain wind clawing at her hair and clothes, and let herself drop to the roof below.

She slipped, landing hard on the slick tiles, which sent her sliding toward the eaves with nothing but thin mountain air beyond.

Tujiyazai reached the window as she skidded over the edge, catching a glimpse of his face — surprised, she thought — before she fell . . .

Her left hand caught one of the rooftop finials, gripping it with a strength she didn't know she had. Her shoulder jerked. Her body swung, face slamming into the decorative bargeboard beneath the line of the roof. She sucked in a breath, cheek stinging from the impact.

But she was alive.

"Where do you think you're going?" Tujiyazai called down to her. "My guards are already on their way to the courtyard to meet you, provided you don't fall first."

Miuko did not reply.

The shutters below her slammed open. There was the clattering of armor as a guard climbed onto the windowsill.

She dropped, more gingerly this time, alighting on the lowest roof with only a wobble, and sprinted past the soldier to another corner of the castle, where she skidded to a stop, swaying at the sight of the flagstones below.

From this height, she'd probably survive the fall, but not without a few broken bones and perhaps some paralysis, which would drastically lower her chances of escape.

In the courtyard, the Omaizi guards were amassing, armor glinting like stars. Behind her, soldiers were creeping from the window, across the tiles.

Desperately, she searched for another escape.

A roof.

A palisade.

Something.

In the darkness, she spotted a tree, tall and black, growing over the outer wall of the courtyard from the tier below. It had to have been twenty feet from the corner of the roof, much too far for any human to reach.

But she was no longer wholly human, was she?

The tree swayed. In the breeze, its branches waved like eager children at a parade.

And before she could talk herself out of it, she ran for the edge of the roof and jumped.

28

GUARDIAN SPIRIT

AS SOON AS her feet left the rooftop, Miuko knew she wouldn't make it. She was strong, now, but she was not *that* strong. She was going to fall short.

She was going to *fall*.

Then a shadow to her left—

And a body beneath hers, lifting them both over the heads of the Omaizi guards. She clutched at its feathers, struggling to find a hold.

"Ack!" the body said. "You're going to pluck me bald!"

"*Geiki?*"

"Who'd you expect?" he cawed. "Some other *atskayakina* foolish enough to come get you?"

"You're flying!" she cried, laughing. "You're huge!"

"I told you I had more than two forms! Sometimes I'm a *giant* bird!"

She hugged him tightly, first because she did not want to fall off, and second because she wanted the reassurance that he was unharmed, that he was really here—her friend, her bird boy. Her *enormous* talking bird boy, with a wingspan twice as long as his body, casting shadows upon the flagstones below. They soared over the castle grounds, rising high above the courtyard and the shocked Omaizi soldiers, over the tree she'd tried to reach, now rattling with what sounded like laughter in the wind.

Miuko did risk one glance over her shoulder as they flew away, and she saw Tujiyazai at the castle window, his horns wreathed in flame.

Even at this distance, she could feel his anger, hot as an ember in the mountain air.

Geiki beat his wings, taking them higher, the sound of the wind a glorious cacophony that made Miuko shriek with delight.

"What happened?" she asked as they leveled off again. "I thought the demon hunter had you—"

"Not the *kyakyozuya*!" he shouted, the wind carrying his voice back to her. "It was that *vakai* shiny box!"

He'd been toying with the gold cube while he waited for Roroisho to drink her fill at the creek, and he'd discovered, much to his delight but not to his surprise, that he'd been right—it *wasn't* solid. If he pushed *this* part of it and twisted *that* one, the whole thing transformed into a sort of puzzle box.

But it had been a trap. When he opened the cube, there was nothing but a *pop!* and a flash. The sounds of the forest and of the drinking mare disappeared in an instant, replaced by nothing but profound silence and a prison of gold.

"It sucked me inside!" Geiki said.

"Magic?"

He bobbed his head.

That must have been why the demon prince thought the *atskayakina* was gone. *He'd* left the gold box for Geiki on the side of the road. *He'd* set the trap.

"I'm sorry," Miuko said. "I'm the one who let slip that you were an *atskayakina*. Tujiyazai must have known you couldn't resist a golden puzzle box, and . . . No wonder he thought we'd never see each other again."

"He thought *what?*" Geiki cried indignantly. Then he laughed. "Shows how much he knows, huh?"

"How'd you get out?"

"I'm getting to it!"

Smiling, she buried her face in his feathers.

He'd been trying to find a way to unlock the cube from the inside when there was another *pop!* and flash, and he was full-size again, ankle-deep in the creek and face-to-face with none other than the demon hunter, who was holding the puzzle box in his hands.

His robes were bloody. His red scarf was scorched. Fire was behind him on the mountainside, and on the smoky air was the sound of someone screaming.

There in the woods above Koewa, Geiki and the *kyakyozuya* looked at each other.

The demon hunter went for his blade.

But before he could reach it, a loop of rope dropped over his head and shoulders, pinning his arms to his sides. A girl with shorn hair—all hard angles, from her elbows to her cheeks to her chin—emerged from the woods, tightening the rope around him. "Geiki?" she said.

Miuko gasped. "Who was she?"

"I don't know! At first, she looked kind of funny—vacant, you know, like the Doctor's thralls? But Sidrisine wouldn't have known to look for me there, and she *definitely* wouldn't have known what the girl said next."

"What was that?"

"'Go to the Castle of the Ogawa,'" he said, mimicking the girl's flattened tones. "'Miuko needs your help.'"

"*What?* How could she have known something like that?"

"I don't know! Magic?"

Back in the forest, Geiki had made as if to climb onto Roroisho's back, but it was as if the girl was waking from a long sleep, no longer dull and empty but sharp as a fire-striker in temper, and she jerked the reins out of his hands. "That's *my* horse."

"*Her* horse?" Miuko interrupted. "Why would she—"

"*I don't know!*" Geiki answered testily. "How many times do I have to tell you?"

The girl had touched her forehead to Roroisho's neck. "I'm back, girl. Are you okay? Did they hurt you?" Then, glaring at Geiki with stone-gray eyes: "What are you still doing here? Go. Fly."

"But my wing—"

"It's fine!" Her gaze had grown harder, her voice gaining a cutting edge. "Fly, *now*, or you'll never make it in time."

"So you left Roroisho with her?" Miuko interrupted.

"That's the weird thing—"

"*That's* the weird thing?"

"Roroisho seemed glad to see her," he continued. "I don't know if humans can sense these things—"

"And you can?"

"I'm a bird! And I'm telling you, Roroisho *knew* that girl."

Leaving the *kyakyozuya* trussed up in the creek, she had vaulted into the saddle and ridden easily up the slope while Geiki leapt into the air, transforming into a giant bird, his wing healed, just as the girl had told him it would be.

"She was right about leaving then, too," Geiki said as they skimmed the mountaintops. "A few seconds later, and you would've been flat as a flounder."

"Thanks for that image." Miuko paused, watching the constellations high above them. They were flying north, toward the rocky tip of Awara, and the House of December beyond. "It's lucky she reached you in time."

"Yeah. Maybe she's our guardian spirit or something."

Miuko laid her head on his back, weaving her fingers into his feathers

—feeling safe, for all she was hundreds of feet in the air, for the first time in days. "Maybe you're *my* guardian spirit."

"How dare you!"

She chuckled softly and closed her eyes. "Thank you, Geiki," she whispered.

He said nothing—perhaps he hadn't heard her—but the rapid beat of his wings was all the response she needed.

29

GOD'S TEETH

FOR THE REMAINDER of the night, Miuko dozed lightly upon Geiki's back, occasionally opening her eyes to the sight of alpine lakes or the pale ribbon of the Thousand-Step Way winding along a mountainside. By the time dawn crested the horizon, they were flying over a vast expanse of water, dazzling in the sunlight.

Ahead of them, a series of islands rose sharply out of the sea, topped with windblown trees and temple buildings.

"Is that the God's Teeth?" Miuko asked.

"It'd better be!" Geiki cawed. "I'm tired!"

They swooped toward the largest of the islands, where, in a sheltered cove, a handful of boats rocked gently at their moorings. Overlooking the stony inlet, a wide path climbed along the cliff's edge toward a vermillion spirit gate, which opened onto a temple compound of single-story buildings topped with gleaming indigo tiles. From her vantage point in the air, Miuko was treated to a sweeping view of the temple gardens, where priests in straw hats were busy plucking yams from the soil and beans from their stalks.

As Geiki's shadow passed over them, the priests looked up, crying out in surprise. Miuko watched them drop their tools and go scurrying over the stone pathways toward the center of the compound.

"Well," she said wryly, "we've got their attention, I suppose."

From deep inside the temple buildings, a bell began to toll.

Out of courtesy toward the priests, Geiki alighted on the road just outside the spirit gate, sending up a cloud of dust as he landed.

Miuko slid from his back, patting one of his bright blue wings. "You saved my life," she murmured.

"You're welcome." Then, squawking: "Now, if you please . . ."

Politely, she averted her gaze. When she looked back, he was in human form again, without the sling now, his delicate features welcome and familiar.

"Does this mean your debt is repaid?" she asked.

"Oh." He ran a hand through his unruly hair. "It was done when we rode out of Koewa. Snatching you out of the air before you turned yourself into a pancake was just for fun."

She tugged nervously at the tips of her gloves. "So are you . . . this means you're free, right?"

He snorted. "I'm not *abandoning* you to a bunch of priests, Miuko. There's no telling what kind of tortures they'll—"

"Tortures?"

"Kidding! Probably! I don't know. But you won't be alone." He grinned at her. "What kind of friend do you think I am?"

Miuko smiled, but her expression faltered as the priests began hurrying down the hill toward the spirit gate.

"What's the matter?" Geiki asked with a touch of irritation. "Aren't you happy? I thought this was what you wanted."

"It is. I just . . . What if they're like the priests at Nihaoi?"

Afraid. Angry. Bearing spells and torches.

"We'll fly away." He said it so simply, as if the priests, whatever their intentions toward her, were of no more consequence than ants along her path, and she was reminded that she was not the Otori Miuko who'd left Nihaoi seven days before.

She wasn't alone.

"It'll be dangerous," she warned him, "traveling with a *shaoha*."

"Eh. It's already been dangerous."

She could now make out the features of the priests nearest them, the bands of vermillion on their simply cut robes and the cloth handkerchiefs tied about their heads.

Reaching out, she clasped Geiki's hand in her gloved one.

He seemed surprised at first, for perhaps *atskayakinasu* did not hold hands. But then he squeezed her fingers, and, turning, they faced the oncoming priests together.

30

THE HOUSE OF DECEMBER

MIUKO NEEDN'T HAVE WORRIED, for the priests of December were nothing like the priests of Nihaoi. To begin with, they were not the least bit lugubrious. A small welcoming party was soon assembled at the spirit gate, where they greeted Miuko and Geiki with broad smiles and deep bows, and when they heard her tale and saw the blue stain creeping up her arms, they neither recoiled nor attacked. Instead, they rattled their prayer beads, dip-dyed in a variety of indigo hues, and chattered at one another in a flurry of excitement before settling again into their more subdued (although no less convivial) expressions.

A slender young priest with bright eyes and a smattering of freckles stepped forward, gesturing them up the broad path to the temple. "My name is Meli, and I'm a novice here. Our head priest, Hikedo, would very much like to meet you," she said, "but we can show you to your guest rooms if you'd like to freshen up first."

Geiki clapped his hands. "Would we! I could kill for a nap."

Meli laughed, light and musical. The others chuckled. "Luckily, *atska-yakina*-jai, you won't have to."

As they climbed the path, Miuko found herself in a daze. Cool, clean light drifted through the treetops and across her shoulders; a gentle breeze stirred her hair, skimming her neck and cheeks. It was so peaceful, she felt like she should be taking a deep breath, sinking into the stillness the way one might sink into a hot bath.

But after the fear and chaos of the past several days, she found it difficult to believe that they had, in fact, made it.

The temple was going to take them in.

They had *guest rooms*.

They were safe.

So why couldn't she relax her shoulders? Why couldn't she unclench her fists?

If Meli sensed Miuko's inner turmoil, she said nothing, but continued padding alongside her, stopping only to pluck a yellow wildflower from the edge of the path.

Once they reached the temple compound, they left Geiki at his room with another priest, a *hei* with a gap-toothed smile and a sonorous laugh they could hear even as they crossed the gardens to Miuko's room.

Her accommodations were simple but well-kept, with a comfortable-looking mattress, a clean set of priest's robes, and a stack of sun-warmed towels sitting beside a full washbasin and a small earthen vase.

Slipping out of her sandals, Miuko stepped onto the veranda and was about to enter when Meli held up her hands. "Wait! I need to add the finishing touch!"

Quickly removing her shoes, the young priest filled the vase from a pitcher before placing the yellow wildflower in it. Frowning, she turned the stem this way and that until, apparently satisfied, she set it down beside the washbasin again with a flourish. "There!"

Instead of saying thank you, however, Miuko sat down hard upon the veranda, burying her face in her arms.

"I'm sorry!" Meli gasped. "I didn't mean to make you cry."

"I'm not crying," Miuko mumbled into her sleeves.

She felt the girl settle beside her. "Okay . . . then I didn't mean to make you sit down and do whatever it is you're doing?"

"I don't know what I'm doing."

"That's okay. That's why we're here, right? To help you?"

Miuko looked up. In the morning sun, Meli's freckles were a pretty golden color, like glints of light at the bottom of a stream.

The girl smiled encouragingly.

Despite Meli's friendly countenance, however, Miuko still could not bring herself to relax. She hunched her shoulders, digging her hands into her pockets, where her fingers closed around a small, hard object.

Surprised, Miuko withdrew the *tseimi*'s incense holder, gleaming in the morning sun. She'd been so occupied with escaping Tujiyazai, she'd forgotten she had it.

"That's beautiful," Meli said, extending her hand. "What is it?"

Miuko hesitated, but the young priest smiled at her so warmly, she could not refuse. "A *tseimi*." She passed the container to Meli, who lifted the lid, allowing the smoke kitten to flow out onto the polished wood floor, where it began to roll about in a charcoal-colored ball of fluff. "I got it from . . . well, it was a gift, I guess . . ."

Meli ignored her. "A baby!" she cried as the cat purred and rubbed its back along her outstretched fingers. "Hello, baby!"

Her delight was so unassuming that for a second, Miuko was startled. Then she grinned. Together, they watched the *tseimi* prance across the veranda, gallivanting after insects and stray leaves, but it was not long before another cat appeared, drawn to the *tseimi* as the calico at Ogawa Castle had been.

This one was a striped orange tabby who sauntered out of the garden and leapt soundlessly onto the veranda. Surprised, the *tseimi* sprang back, then forward, tumbling ears-over-tail in its excitement. The new cat batted at it playfully, lashing its tail.

"Aw, new best friends!" Meli cooed.

The cats rolled over one another, onto their backs with their paws in the air and back up again like grasshoppers, bounding hither and thither over the floor.

Miuko laughed, at last feeling the tension ease out of her neck and shoulders. She *had* made it. With the priests' help, maybe everything *would* be okay.

Then Meli clapped her hands to her mouth, stifling a cry.

Upon the veranda, the orange tabby was lying on its side, still as a stone.

Miuko bolted upright. "What happened?"

"I don't know!" Gathering the cat into her arms, Meli checked its breathing. Aghast, she glanced up again. "He's dead! One second, they were playing, and the next . . ."

As one, they turned to the *tseimi,* who, having lost interest in the tabby, had traipsed into the garden, where it was now toying innocently with the branches of a nearby gardenia bush.

"Did you know that was going to happen?" Meli asked.

"No! I'd never—" But before Miuko could continue, another cat— this one as black as ebony—appeared in the garden and began trotting happily toward the *tseimi.*

She dove for the incense holder, but even with her demon-reflexes, Meli was faster. Snatching up the lid, the priest called the *tseimi* back inside, the smoke curling up again until it had vanished from the air.

For a moment, both Miuko and Meli held their breath, watching the ebony cat for signs of imminent collapse.

But nothing happened. The cat paused, turned around, and—as if it had not escaped death by a whisker's breadth—promptly trotted off again.

Blinking, Meli cradled the tabby's body to her chest. "What . . . just . . . happened?"

Miuko froze, feeling the girl watching her, like the townspeople of Koewa, like the lugubrious priests of Nihaoi.

Like her father.

Humans, muttered the demon-voice. *How easily they turn. Better to throttle her now before she alerts the others.*

But Meli only spoke sadly, tears welling in her eyes. "Who would give you such a gift?"

Miuko, who had been poised to run — or perhaps to attack, she didn't quite know — hesitated. "A demon," she said cautiously.

"A demon?" The priest bit her lip. Then, shaking her head: "I guess it could have been worse, then."

Miuko's hands fell to her sides. "You don't blame me for this?"

Meli shrugged. "How could I? You said you didn't know." She offered Miuko a small smile. "If this is the kind of thing you've had to deal with, I can see why you need our help."

Miuko swallowed hard. She hadn't known what a relief it would be to be taken seriously by her fellow humans, to be met with compassion instead of fear, to be cared for instead of rejected. To be truthful, she hadn't even dared believe it was possible.

But to think, if everyone had met her with such understanding, what a different journey it might have been!

What a different world.

"Thank you, Meli." Miuko scooped up the incense holder. "Do you have paper and twine to wrap this? We can't have it popping open by accident."

Meli nodded, and while Miuko splashed some water on her face and donned the borrowed robes, the young priest spirited the orange tabby away and returned with supplies to pack up the *tseimi*'s container, which was then relegated to the confines of Miuko's pocket — a reminder that she may have reached the House of December, but Tujiyazai was still intent on claiming her . . . and so was her curse.

Shortly thereafter, Meli ushered Miuko and Geiki to a pergola on the north side of the temple, where they met with the head priest — an elderly *hei* named Hikedo with soft eyes and plump, sun-speckled cheeks. Over refreshments of tea and chestnut cakes, Miuko related their tale (with more than the occasional interjection from Geiki), from the *shaoha*'s kiss upon the Old Road to Geiki's valiant rescue at Ogawa Castle. "And now," Miuko finished, tapping the incense holder in her pocket. "Tujiyazai will be coming after us again. I'm sorry, but I'm afraid we've brought trouble right to your door."

"Trouble or no, we're glad you've come," replied Hikedo. Then, taking a large bite of pastry, which they washed down with an equally large gulp of tea: "Now, we can erect the warding spells that will prevent Tujiyazai from entering the grounds, but we do not know the magic that would prevent his powers from reaching us, even if he is kept out. You say the *kyakyozuya* was immune, somehow?"

"Yes, he wore a vermillion scarf with spells written on it. Do you know where he got it?"

"I do." The head priest reached for another chestnut cake, but, to their disappointment, found the plate empty.

Miuko glared at Geiki, who, having just stuffed the last piece into his mouth, swallowed guiltily.

Sighing, Hikedo collected the crumbs from the empty plate with their forefinger. "Such scarves are made at the House of November," they said, licking their finger thoughtfully, "where demon hunters are trained."

Miuko closed her eyes, remembering the smoke gathering on the horizon as she and Geiki sailed from Udaiwa. "But it's gone," she whispered. "The whole temple was destroyed days ago."

The head priest nodded. "A tragedy. But we are not without options. I will send a messenger bird to Keivoweicha-kaedo—the librarians may have some recourse for us. In the meantime, Miuko, my priests have been preparing some rituals to help you undo this curse. Geiki, might you still be hungry? Meli can show you to the kitch—"

Before they could finish, Geiki was on his feet, grabbing Meli's hand and dashing away as if he knew where the kitchens were to be found, which he of course did not.

Hikedo chuckled. Gesturing to Miuko, they escorted her to a prayer room, where they and eleven others formed a circle around her, chanting and burning incense that seemed to have little effect besides making her sneeze. After a few hours, this was followed by another ritual, which involved the priests painting spells upon her foot soles, palms, and stomach. She was then left alone to meditate upon their power, which she did for about five minutes before her demon-voice intruded upon her contemplations, enumerating in grisly detail the many ways they could murder the priests for forcing her to participate in such a tedious enterprise.

Despite these untoward thoughts — and others Miuko found herself entertaining whenever the priests annoyed her — by the end of the day, she found herself exhausted but satisfied. The curse may not have retreated under the ministrations of Amyunasa's priests, but it had slowed significantly, which gave her reason to hope.

That night, she and Geiki sat on the veranda with Meli, who, much to the *atskayakina*'s delight, had filched a few more airy chestnut cakes for them to share.

"I guess you're not too bad for a priest!" he declared, stuffing one into his mouth.

Seated comfortably between them, Meli gave him a sidelong glance. "And I guess you're not too rude, for an *atskayakina*."

He laughed, spraying crumbs down his robes. "Tell that to Miuko. She thinks I'm very rude."

Miuko smirked at him. "Well, aren't you?"

He grinned. "Yes."

Meli chuckled.

"So how'd you become a priest anyway?" he asked.

"Well . . ." Meli bit her lip, turning to the moon, which was waxing in the east. "I ran away from home."

"Miuko did too!"

"Yes, but not for quite the same reason." Quietly, she explained that her parents had once thought her a boy. "I tried to be one too, for a long time, in order to please them."

"Oh." Geiki looked to Miuko, but she did not quite know what to say. She'd heard that in ages past, some girls were mistakenly thought to be sons, just as some boys were mistakenly thought to be daughters, but she'd wrongly assumed that such people no longer existed.

But people didn't just *disappear*, did they? No, in a culture as rigid as the Omaizi's, there was little tolerance for those who did not conform to their socially sanctioned roles, which meant that transgressors were either forced into hiding, or to places like the House of December, which welcomed all genders, from male to female to *hei*.

"But then you stopped?" Geiki asked. "Trying to please them?"

Meli nodded. "One full moon, when I was thirteen, I was drawn from my bed to the pond behind my father's house. I stood there for hours, staring at my reflection. I stared so long, I was sure I was frozen in place, and the world was frozen too—my parents in their beds, my village, the grass, the trees, the moon itself—all frozen. It hurt, that's what I remember most. It *hurt* to be so static. But then, somehow, I *moved*, causing the water to shatter as if it were glass . . . and when it cleared again, I could see, without a doubt, that I was and had always been a girl." She paused thoughtfully. "Hikedo thinks it was a vision from Amyunasa."

Geiki whistled appreciatively, for such revelations from the Lunar Gods were rare and to be cherished.

Miuko hugged her knees. "Are you glad you left?"

"It's complicated." The girl sighed, shaking herself, and when she continued, she was smiling again, albeit a little sadly. "The only thing I can say for sure is that I'm glad I made it *here,* where I'm accepted for who I am."

Miuko sat back, staring up into the broad face of the moon. When she was younger, she'd hated the moon, for it had always reminded her of her mother: mutable, magical, utterly distant. She had not wanted to think about how her mother had made wishes on the moon, nor how the same moon shone on both of them, no matter how far apart they were.

Now, however, at the House of December, the moon felt different —less changeable, more constant—a presence, perhaps, that was watching over her even now, as it had once watched over Meli, on her journey toward herself.

Miuko hugged her knees a little tighter, as if protecting some very small spark, only recently kindled, within her chest, and as she listened to Geiki and Meli squabbling over the last piece of cake, she sent up a small prayer of thanks to Amyunasa, and the moon, for bringing her here too.

31

A DECISION

OVER THE COURSE of the next two days, the priests tried everything they could to undo Miuko's curse: prayers, incantations, sacred spells. She sat, sweating and cross-legged, through smoke baths, meditations, and the itchy process of having paper enchantments pasted to her spine, like Tujiyazai's tattoo—or, even more nettlesome, to her forehead. She tried to concentrate (really, she did) for she knew the efficacy of the treatments depended upon her mental fortitude as well as the priests' magic, but she could not stop herself from daydreaming of adventures with Geiki—stealing vegetables from the temple gardens or flying upon his back, out over the glassy ocean with the terns and migrating sea birds—and when she did actually succeed in focusing on the task at hand, there was always the demon-voice's constant grousing to contend with too.

It was bored.

It was hungry.

It still wanted to strangle Meli, or Hikedo, or, for that matter, any of the other priests that came within reach.

Under their careful attention, the curse's progress slowed.

But it didn't stop.

And while Miuko tried to ignore the priests' concerned looks or the muttered conversations they had when they thought she could not hear, the looming threat of Tujiyazai was never far from her mind.

He was still out there.

He was still coming for her.

The priests continued to post warding banners along the temple perimeter, but they had received no instructions from the librarians at Keivoweicha, and every day Geiki embarked on more reconnaissance flights to the mainland, searching for signs of the demon prince's pursuit.

Until, on the third day, he returned with news.

Tujiyazai was approaching the tip of the mainland, Geiki said, accompanied by the *kyakyozuya*—who, like everyone else but Miuko, must not have been able to see that the *doro* was possessed. According to the *atskayakina,* the pair were moving quickly, though exactly how quickly, he could not say.

"I'm a bird!" he croaked petulantly. "What do I know about ground travel?"

At this, Hikedo sighed. "I suppose we'll have to rely on the warding banners to keep him out."

"Will that be enough?" Miuko asked.

In response, the head priest only flattened their lips into a grim line.

Later, as the sounds of construction echoed through the compound —more holes being dug, more posts being hammered into the ground —Miuko stood alone in her room, staring at her reflection in the mirror. The blue stain now lapped at her collarbone, forming a crooked seam from shoulder to shoulder, as if she were chained to the sea floor while the tide rose inescapably around her.

Soon it might eclipse her entirely, and she would be a demon: strong, powerful, feared.

But would she still be herself?

Since their arrival, the demon-voice inside her had been soft but never silent, remarking on how easy it would be to kill this priest or that one, the fools, who ordered her to recite these mantras, sit in this prayer room, don't talk to Geiki, help with the washing or the cooking, as if she were a mere servant and not a monster who could drain the life from them with a single touch.

To her surprise, Miuko had often caught herself chuckling at the voice's incessant commentary, or even agreeing with it, which frightened her. She had not always liked herself, of course—more than once, she'd wished she was less clumsy, less loud, less stubborn—but in the past eleven days, these qualities had saved her, sustained her, brought her the kind of friendship she'd never even dreamed of, and she did not wish to lose them.

Then there was Tujiyazai. The banners might succeed in barring him from the temple grounds, but without the spells to protect the priests from his powers, they were likely to meet the same gruesome fate as the hunters above Koewa.

Miuko's face hardened, then, for she knew what she had to do.

Leave.

She'd slip away—in a boat, yes, the following night—to draw Tujiyazai away from the temple . . . and to remove the possibility of her becoming a *shaoha* with so many of her friends nearby.

She would not allow a demon to get them . . . even if that demon was herself.

As she tightened her resolve, someone knocked at her door, startling her out of her thoughts. Miuko slipped her robe back over her shoulders. "Who is it?"

"I'm bored!"

"Geiki!" She slid open the door.

He cocked his head at her. "Want to have some fun?"

She grinned. Together, they sneaked across the grounds, racing to the pergola, where under the stars Geiki transformed into a giant bird. Leaping onto his back, Miuko laughed as they winged over the pointed stones of the God's Teeth, the creaking rope bridges, the windswept trees.

They alighted on the northernmost island, where they discovered an ancient stone gate, twice a man's height and made of white granite they hadn't seen anywhere else on the islands. The gate's features, if it ever had any, had long ago been worn smooth by wind, and now it stood like a silent guardian at the edge of a perfectly round pool.

In magpie form, Geiki hopped from the flat stones that ringed the water and into the shallows, where he fluttered his feathers once or twice before flying to the top of the gate. While Miuko circled the stone columns, tracing their girth with her gloved hands, he transformed into a boy again.

"Hey! Come up here!"

Miuko stepped back. "Get off of that! This is a *sacred place!*"

"Not to me." Plopping down, he kicked his legs over the edge. "Come on. You've got to see this."

Reluctantly, though perhaps appearing more reluctant than she actually felt, she leapt for the top of the gate, her demon legs carrying her high into the air, her demon hands hauling her easily up.

The *atskayakina* patted the rock beside him.

Rolling her eyes, she sat. Below them in the still pool, the heavens were reflected as if in a mirror: every star, every wisp of cloud, every meteor streaking across the sky.

The moon, too, was there, nearly full now—it hung behind them like a pale lantern, making them appear in the reflecting pool only as silhouettes, joined at the shoulder into a single shadow.

"It's beautiful," Miuko murmured. "I wonder what it was for."

"Human sacrifice," Geiki quipped.

"Geiki."

"Kidding!"

"I know."

She felt more than heard him laugh, breathily, though it hadn't been that funny, and they quickly settled into a pattern of familiar chatter, watching the constellations in the water below.

Time slipped by.

A minute.

An hour.

Two.

"It's getting late," Geiki said at last. "The priests will have my ears if you fall asleep during meditation tomorrow."

"Just turn into a bird. Then you don't have to worry."

"Birds have ears!"

"Not the kind you can lose." Sighing, Miuko rested her chin on her knees. She wouldn't be sleeping during meditation tomorrow anyway.

She'd be planning her departure.

A boat. Some provisions. A lonely voyage out to sea.

At least then, Geiki and the priests would be safe.

"This might be one of the last nights I'm human," she said softly.

"Eh." The *atskayakina* shrugged. "Being human doesn't seem that great."

She made a half-hearted attempt at a smile. "It isn't."

"Maybe being a demon will be better?"

"Maybe," she agreed, though she could not bring herself to believe it.

Geiki put an arm around her shoulders, as if drawing her under his wing. "Want to stay out a little longer?" he asked.

Nodding, she leaned into him.

They sat like that for a long time, uncharacteristically silent.

32

THE TWELFTH DAY

MIUKO DIDN'T SEE Geiki at breakfast the next morning, so, after her regularly scheduled prayer session with Meli and the other priests, she trotted off to the *atskayakina's* room to find him.

When she arrived, he was digging through a pile of shiny objects he must have pilfered from the temple: a chain of bells, a gold tassel, a ladle, a brass bowl, a pair of gardening shears. In days past, she would have scolded him, but now the sight of the stolen treasures only made her grin.

Chuckling, she leaned against the doorframe. "What are you doing?"

He spun around, wild-eyed. In his hands, he clutched a traveling sack, which was already stuffed with packets of provisions from the kitchens.

Startled, Miuko looked from Geiki to the provisions and back again. *"What are you doing?"*

"I—" With a nearly audible gulp, he turned away, shoving treasures into the traveling sack by the armful.

"Geiki!" She crossed the room, tapping him on the shoulder.

He jumped. "Ack! Sorry! What? Oh, hi, Miuko."

"Are you leaving?"

The *atskayakina* bit his lip. "We're running out of time."

Her hands went to her throat, where the curse was beginning to creep up her neck. "You don't think I know that?"

"I don't mean *you!* I mean Tujiyazai is still coming, and we have nothing!"

191

"So you're *abandoning* us?"

"Hikedo-jai asked me to go to Keivoweicha," he explained. "Maybe I can get to the library and back before Tujiyazai comes."

Miuko could not help the jolt of anger that surged through her. The head priest? Betraying her? Taking the best friend she'd ever have? She'd thought they were on her side! For a second, she imagined seizing them by the throat, their old body swaying inches above the ground. But that wasn't an appropriate reaction.

Or is it the perfect reaction? whispered the little voice inside her.

Ignoring it, she rounded on Geiki. "Can't you wait?"

One more day. That was all she needed. One more day, and then *she'd* be the one to leave. On her own time. On her own terms. She couldn't be the one left behind this time.

Not again.

Stop him then, said the demon-voice. *You're stronger than him now. Clip his wings.*

Geiki stuffed the last of his things into the traveling sack. "The longer we wait, the closer he gets."

Miuko shook her head. "But I could be gone before you get back!"

"You're too stubborn for that." He tried to smile—failed.

She glared at him. "Is this why you wanted to sneak out last night?"

One last adventure together—she hated that she hadn't realized it, even as she'd felt them saying good-bye.

But it was too soon.

Any time would have been too soon.

"Please, Miuko, they'll all die if I don't go. You know I have to try. It's what you would do, if you were me."

It was true. In planning to leave, to lure Tujiyazai from the temple, she was trying to save the priests too.

But she didn't want to hear it. She wasn't ready. She refused to be ready. Scowling, she stood on tiptoe, bringing them eye-to-eye, and, in the coldest voice she could muster, said, *"Don't leave."*

"I'm sorry." Geiki dipped his head, nuzzling her cheek with his. Then he straightened. "I have to."

Before she could stop him — and because, much as she wanted to deny it, she knew in her heart that it would not be right to stop him — he picked up the traveling sack and threw it over his shoulders.

Knowing what was coming, Miuko lowered her eyes, and when she looked up again, he was on the veranda — a bird of fine size.

He peered over his shoulder, his large black eyes gleaming. "Be here when I get back, okay?" And with a few beats of his massive wings, he was airborne, soaring across the temple courtyard toward the open sky.

33

SHAOHA

THE *ATSKAYAKINA* HAD not gone far when Miuko scowled, digging her fingers into the robe the priests had lent her.

This was wrong.

She'd been wrong.

She couldn't let her last words to him be a demand. She couldn't leave their last moments together steeped in anger.

She'd already endured too many unhappy endings: her mother, riding off into the gloaming; her father, screaming at her while the inn burned. She could not let that happen with Geiki too. Not this time.

The last time.

She raced from the temple as he reached the treetops. "Geiki!"

But he did not hear, or he did not want to hear, because he didn't stop. Flapping his wings, he swept over the canopy.

"Miuko!" Meli dashed from the kitchen, still clutching a paring knife in one hand. "Why are you shouting? What's happening?"

Miuko didn't reply. In the sky, Geiki had reappeared again, but he was gaining distance on her with every passing second.

Hiking up her robes, she sprinted toward the spirit gate. She was swift, now, on her demon legs — carrying her over the gravel, past the gnarled trees — but not nearly swift enough. By the time she reached the cliffs, with the protective banners flapping behind her in the breeze, Geiki was already over the cove, beating his great blue wings. She gripped the woven rope that bordered the path.

He was really leaving.

But before he could make it out of the inlet, his body jerked, as if it had been struck by something. There was a scream.

She watched helplessly as he dropped and spasmed, trying to fly.

On the water, sailing for the island, was a boat, and in the boat were two figures Miuko recognized even at this distance: the demon hunter and the demon prince.

They'd been so much closer than anyone had thought.

The *kyakyozuya* laid down a longbow as Geiki plummeted toward the waves.

Miuko snarled.

He'd *shot* Geiki.

The *atskayakina* was in the water. By some act of divine providence, he appeared to be conscious — and in boy form again — flailing in the waves. Could magpies swim? He seemed barely able to remain afloat.

She took off running, racing along the cliffside and down the slope. In the cove, the boat cruised leisurely up alongside Geiki, and the demon hunter dragged the *atskayakina*'s sopping form onto the deck, where a thin pool of blood formed around him.

Miuko dug her heels into the earth, as if that would speed her approach.

She'd kill them. She'd already stripped off her gloves, her arms a powerful and brilliant blue.

First the demon hunter, the little white gnat. Then Tujiyazai. She didn't care if she killed the *doro* in the process. She was almost a *shaoha* anyway. She'd suck the life from him, and when the malevolence demon slithered from his corpse, she'd pin him by the back of the neck until he shriveled up like the worm he was.

They reached the piers as Miuko hit the shore. On the deck of the boat, Tujiyazai held up his palm. "Stop there, Ishao," he said, his imperious tone carrying easily over the distance between them, "or I will have him killed."

As if she needed further persuasion, the *kyakyozuya* drew his sword, laying the blade against Geiki's throat.

The *atskayakina* gagged, spitting up seawater.

Miuko skidded to a stop so fast, she fell to her hands and knees, skinning them on the splintered dock. Red blood beaded on her blue palms.

She ignored the pain, glaring at the *doro yagra*, then the demon hunter. "What are you doing? You're a *kyakyozuya*! Can't you see that's not really Omaizi Ruhai? He's being possessed!"

"Silence, monster." The demon hunter nicked Geiki's flesh with his sword.

At this distance, she could not see how deep the *atskayakina* had been cut, but she saw him flinch. Heard his small chirp of pain.

She bared her teeth in frustration. She was too far from the boat. If she attacked now, they'd slice Geiki's head from his neck before she'd even made it halfway down the dock.

While her mind raced, she heard footsteps on the gravel road. Panting, Meli appeared beside her, doubled over with the knife still in her hand. "Miuko, what's going on?" Seeing the *doro yagra,* she gasped. "Is that him? Tujiyazai?"

"Go away! Before he uses his powers to—"

Tujiyazai called out to her, then: "Don't fight it any longer, Ishao! You're almost mine now."

Beside her, Meli pointed. "Miuko, your face!"

"What?" Irritably, Miuko snatched the girl's paring knife and lifted it level with her eyes. In the gleaming blade, she caught a glimpse of her reflection.

The curse had covered almost her entire face now—her cheeks, her mouth, her nose—and was closing in around her eyes, moving so quickly that even in the imperfect mirror, she could see it spreading across her skin like blue ink.

"I'll make you a deal," said Tujiyazai in his most reasonable manner. "If you come to me now, before you are Shao-kanai, I will spare the *atskayakina*."

"And the priests?" Miuko glanced again at Meli, who shook her head, tears brightening her eyes.

"If you wish."

She took a breath, feeling the last seconds of her humanity trickling away like water through a sieve.

If this was the end, she had to make it count. She had to go with Tujiyazai to save Geiki, Meli, the priests. Considering that she'd lived an almost entirely ordinary life, that seemed as good an ending as she could hope for.

But she was no longer ordinary, was she? She looked down at her arms — blue and monstrous. She didn't need to be *human* to save her friends.

Gritting her teeth, Miuko laid Meli's knife against her flesh.

Well, that's an idea, said the demon-voice.

In a few moments, she'd be a *shaoha*, and *shaohasu* could be summoned. All it took was hate and a name, and right now, Miuko had both. She just had to carve Tujiyazai's name into her own body, and she would be teleported directly to her target, crossing the distance between them in a flash — quicker than the *kyakyozuya* could kill Geiki, quicker than Tujiyazai could turn Meli into a wrathful monster.

Summoner and summoned.

Girl and demon.

For this one moment, she could be both.

She had to be both.

"Well, Ishao?" Tujiyazai prompted her. "Time is not on your side."

She ignored him, as was his due. Digging the paring knife into her skin, she wrote the name in a few quick strokes.

Tujiyazai.

Her target.

"What are you doing?" His voice was condescending as ever, but now she thought she could detect a quiver of fear in it.

Good.

Let him fear me.

She looked up at him, smiling, though it did not feel so much like a smile now as a snarl, a feral expression, too many teeth and a hiss in the back of her throat. She could almost feel it as the curse closed over her eyes, could feel the sharpening of her senses — she could smell the salt in the air and the iron in Meli's blood, hear the roaring of the ocean and of Geiki's pulse aboard the boat — except there was also, disconcertingly, a clouding of her sight.

Was this what it was like to be teleported to her victim?

Things were going dark.

And cold.

And hazy.

As if the sun had been blotted from the sky.

A shape, wholly indistinct but massive — she could sense that — shifted in the air above her. From somewhere in the darkness came a voice, deep and booming, more felt in the bones than heard: "Hello again."

Miuko spun. "What?"

There was no answer, the silence so resounding that she could not be sure if she'd heard it at all.

Something was wrong. She could no longer see the *doro yagra,* or the demon hunter, or Geiki. She could not even see the priest beside her or the dock under her feet. It was as if they had all disappeared — as if all things had disappeared.

Where was Tujiyazai?

She tensed, gripping the handle of the knife, though she knew she would not need it, for she herself was stronger, quicker, deadlier than any human blade.

But she did not reappear on the deck of the boat. Instead, as her vision cleared, she found herself standing in a patch of weeds, which tugged at the hem of her borrowed robes as she moved to survey her surroundings. All about her was a thick mist, which in days past would have prevented her from seeing farther than a few feet ahead of her, but now she found that with her demon eyes, she could see in the low light almost as clearly as she could in the day—every leaf on every tree was sharp as a blade; even the heavy mist seemed somehow thin, like the water draining from a pot of rice after repeated washing. Through it, a battalion of armored ghosts marched eastward—some on skeletal steeds, halberds angled for combat; others on foot, their worm-eaten banners flapping in nonexistent winds.

And she knew where she was.

There, a burned-out barn. There, the abandoned manor. There and there and there, the fallow fields that formed the unmarked graves of the Ogawa, Tujiyazai's long-dead clan. It was as the villagers had always said: the *naiana* was full of spirits.

Miuko was on the Old Road again.

Somehow, she'd returned to Nihaoi.

PART II

THE FADING, THE HUNGER, AND THE LOST

1

A DEMON, A HUMAN,
A TEAPOT

THE SUMMONING HADN'T WORKED. Tujiyazai wasn't here, among the abandoned fields of Nihaoi, but somewhere far to the north.

With Geiki.

Dropping Meli's paring knife, Miuko pressed her palm to the wounds in her arm, which, although deep, hurt less than she'd expected, but perhaps that was some fortunate side effect of demonhood.

She stilled at the thought. She did not need to check her reflection to know the curse covered her completely now, for she knew it as surely as she knew she was on the Old Road, and that, given the botched summoning, she was already as much of a failure as a demon as she'd been as a servant.

What had gone wrong? She'd carved Tujiyazai's name into her skin. She'd been the closest malevolence demon (except Tujiyazai himself). She should have been transported directly to the demon prince's side, not back to Nihaoi.

She looked up into the darkness. How was it night already?

She did not have time to speculate, however, because a sharp voice interrupted her thoughts: "What are you doing? Get moving, soldier!"

Crying out, Miuko spun around to find a ghost scowling at her from beneath a cloven helmet. He wore leather-coated plates of armor that dangled from his rotting form, and disintegrating gauntlets that revealed finger bones and sinew beneath. He must have been one of the Ogawa bannermen, his corpse decaying somewhere beneath the overgrown fields.

"This is no time for cowardice!" The soldier's teeth chattered as he spoke. "The army waits for no man."

In other circumstances, Miuko might have been afraid of him. But she was a *shaoha* now; there didn't seem much to be afraid of. Idly, she brushed off her pale priest's robes. "It's a good thing I'm not a man, then."

The ghost squinted at her, or at least she thought he was squinting —given that he'd lost both of his brows and most of the skin on his face, it was difficult to tell. "Then what are you?"

Thoughtfully, she examined her hands, blue as water. "I guess I'm a demon."

He laughed, throwing his head back so far, she thought it might roll from his translucent shoulders. "Demon, you are not!"

For some reason, Miuko felt offended. "Have you *seen* me?"

He nodded. "You may have a demon body, but you have the spirit of a human."

"I *what?*"

"Come." He urged her eastward, toward Nihaoi, where she could see the lights of the village temple glittering in the distance. "We dare not tarry."

"Yeah." She rolled her eyes. "Without us, the battle will surely be lost."

"Indeed! Onward!"

She didn't move. "Tell me how I'm human again?"

"Can you not feel it? The two sides of yourself at odds?"

Even as a *shaoha*, Miuko didn't have the nerve to tell him she'd *always* felt at odds with herself, so whatever she felt now was nothing new. She merely shrugged.

"As you are now, you are like a teapot—" he began.

"A *what?*"

For a moment, she felt like Geiki, squawking in disbelief.

For a moment, she wanted to cry.

"A teapot," the soldier continued serenely, "missing its lid. In order to be complete, you must find your lid."

"And how do I do that?"

"You do as demons do, of course. Once you take a life, you will be complete, and there will be no going back to the way you were."

Miuko blinked at him.

Going back? asked a voice inside her.

Miuko startled. The voice was not the raspy, otherworldly demon-voice she'd grown accustomed to, but softer than she'd expected, higher-pitched.

Human?

Perhaps the ghost soldier was correct. Perhaps hope wasn't lost after all.

"You mean I can be human again?" she asked.

He prodded her with the blunt end of his halberd, but it did not, as she expected, slide through her as the ghost girls had done in Koewa. Then again, she reasoned, if mortals could touch other mortals, then spirits could touch other spirits, including ghosts, apparently. Being a demon now (or mostly a demon, anyway), she shrugged the weapon off, causing a cloud of spectral flies to buzz indignantly about the halberd's frayed tassel.

Miuko could not help but smile. That the insects had been so dearly attached to this foot soldier, they'd even clung to him in the afterlife, struck her as rather charming.

"You ask too many questions for a soldier," he told her.

"I'm not a soldier."

"You ask too many questions for a girl."

"I'm not a—"

He sighed. Miuko hadn't thought a spirit without working lungs *could* sigh, but she supposed she brought it out of people, living or not. "I know what you are!" he declared. "You are a teapot, missing—"

"I know," she interrupted. "Missing its lid."

But she did not want her lid. She wanted to be human again.

And until she found out how, all she had to do was refrain from murdering anyone. That seemed simple enough. She'd avoided it for seventeen years already—what was a few days more?

Or weeks? her human-voice added.

Or however long it took to restore her human body?

She turned to the Ogawa bannerman. "How do I become hu—"

But the soldier seemed to have forgotten her, for he had begun marching toward Udaiwa without her, the moth-eaten tassel of his halberd bobbing listlessly from his weapon.

Buzzing, the cloud of ghost flies followed.

She shrugged. She had more important things to do than chase after him.

Like figure out what happened. And get back to the House of December to throttle Tujiyazai until he relinquished her friend.

She glanced around. Overhead, a sliver of moon lay like a fishbone upon a dark slate. The sight of it troubled her, but before she could puzzle out why, hoofbeats sounded behind her, and not ghostly ones.

Someone else was on the road.

The potter? The lugubrious priests?

Father? whispered the voice inside her.

Forgetting for a moment that she did not look like Otori Miuko anymore but like a ravenous, life-draining demon, she whirled in the gravel, eagerly watching the road for the horse and rider to appear around the bend.

What she saw, however, was not her father, nor the lugubrious priests, nor the potter.

It was Tujiyazai. He was galloping swiftly toward her on his great black horse, face alight like a beacon in the mist.

Miuko's thoughts whirled through her mind like dead leaves.

The *doro yagra* was *supposed* to be on a dock at the House of December.

He was *supposed* to be holding Geiki hostage. How could he be here, on the Old Road?

And at night? her human-voice whispered.

Miuko glanced up at the moon again. What had been full only hours before, while she and Geiki explored the God's Teeth, was now nothing more than a slender crescent, no thicker than a fingernail.

The last time she'd seen a moon like that, she'd been on the Old Road. Twelve days ago.

She gasped. The summoning *had* worked. It *had* teleported her to her victim.

Unfortunately, it had also teleported her almost two weeks into the past, to the first night she saw Tujiyazai.

A sudden, deadly whimsy unfurled inside her.

She could kill him now. All she'd have to do was get him off his horse. (She might kill his horse, too, come to think of it.) Then she'd suck the life from the *doro*'s pretty young body, forcing Tujiyazai out of him and into her waiting hands.

He would perish. Her friends would be saved, for they'd never be in danger in the first place.

Miuko's fingers twitched.

The demon prince was almost upon her now. She could feel his power calling to her, building inside her like a cold front. This was her chance.

As the horse charged past her through the fog, she lunged.

2

THE KISS

SHE MISSED.

The horse's tail whipped through her fingers as she took a nosedive into the gravel, tearing her robes and breaking the blue skin of her knees.

Becoming a demon may have given her speed, strength, and the ability to see in the dark, but it had not, apparently, relieved her of her clumsiness.

On the road, Tujiyazai didn't stop. She didn't even think he'd noticed she was there.

But he would. She scrambled to her feet, ready to run after him.

Her human-voice stopped her. *We're not supposed to kill anyone! We don't want to be a teapot, remember?*

Miuko grimaced. She did remember . . . at least, she remembered now that she wasn't pumping with bloodlust.

Abstaining from murder seemed like it might be more difficult than she'd anticipated.

Frustrated, she balled her fists in her robes. Strained to its limit under her demon strength, the coarse fabric tore, leaving the narrow trousers she'd stolen from Tujiyazai exposed to the night air.

Miuko cursed. The priests may have been adept at prayer or what-have-you, but their clothing—

Their clothing.

She paused, staring down at her blue hands. She was a *shaoha*. She was wearing a priest's robes.

A *shaoha* in priest's robes had cursed her on this very road, this very night.

Miuko felt faint.

Was *she* the demon from the Old Road? Had she cursed *herself?*

She peered into the darkness. From here, the road wound northward around the collapsing mayoral pavilion before curving back down toward the Ozotso River. If she cut through the ruins, she could make it to the dilapidated bridge before Tujiyazai ran her past-self over the rail.

But if she did not meet herself at the bridge, she would never be cursed, and if she wasn't cursed, the *doro yagra* would never sense her power as he rode past. After a good dunking in the river—nothing a good nap and a soothing bath wouldn't cure—she'd return to Nihaoi . . . to her father . . . and to the inn, where she'd remain for the rest of her days, never venturing any farther from home than the market at Udaiwa, and only ever in the company of a male relative.

She'd never meet Geiki. She'd never set foot in a gambling parlor (for either humans or *nasu*). She'd never sail in a boat. She'd never ride a horse or save a crane spirit from her violent father. She'd never a stop a man who'd murdered seven girls. She'd never see the God's Teeth or have any adventures at all.

And if she never did that, she'd never discover that all the peculiarities that made her a failure as a girl and a servant could in fact be blessings.

Could she sentence her past-self to a life without that?

Her body knew the answer before her mind did. Swift as the wind, she ran for the bridge—ducking through the collapsed gate of the mayoral mansion, flying through the weed-choked gardens, past a cloven pine that surged toward the sky, crooked as lightning—stronger and faster than she'd ever been in her life.

Reaching the Old Road again, she skidded to a halt. There was her past-self—doe-eyed, fumble-footed—stumbling backward toward the bridge, afraid and desperately clinging to the idea that once she made it home, everything would be normal again.

"Yagra," she heard her past-self whisper.

Demon.

Miuko stepped forward, stubbing her toe in one of the ancient wheel ruts, which made her scream in frustration, and perhaps a little pain.

But one stubbed toe did not stop her from making her move. In the time it took to blink, she crossed the length of the pitted road. She reached out, threading her blue fingers in her old servants' robes, drawing her past-self closer.

She could already feel the desire to kill tingling in her fingers. All she had to do was place her hands upon her own soft cheeks, and then . . .

The withering. The turning of a live body into a corpse, spongy and black with rot. She did not know she could desire something so much, with a hunger she felt in her very bones.

That's me! the little voice inside her cried. *That's us! You can't kill* us!

"Right," she muttered. "Right, right . . . I've already done this. *It must be so."*

And, leaning in, she found her own lips in the darkness, planting the curse that would consume her past-self over the course of the next twelve days, driving her from her village, from her father, into the company of spirits and demons, on adventures she was certain not even her mother had dared to dream of, adventures she would not now trade for anything so trivial as *normalcy.*

3

GOOD INTENTIONS

SHE WAS NOT a good kisser, Miuko realized. Her lips were too cold. Her mouth was too dry.

Embarrassed—and more than a little unnerved—she shoved her past-self away.

For a moment, weakness overtook her, like the dizziness that struck when she stood up too fast or held her breath too long. She fell from the road, tumbling into the weeds as her past-self tottered away, grabbing for the bridge's stone balusters in the mist.

Seconds later, Tujiyazai rode by again.

Crawling from the ditch, Miuko watched her past-self stumble backward into the rail of the dilapidated bridge, watched the *doro yagra* turn in his saddle, mesmerized by the small, cursed human as she tipped head over heels into the river.

There was a splash.

The horse continued over the bridge.

Exhausted, Miuko slumped back into the ditch. Overhead, the stars glistened. In the fields, the ghosts of the Ogawa streamed toward the capital.

It was done, then. Her past-self was cursed. She'd wake upon the riverbank in the morning and make her way back to the guesthouse.

Then the fire.

Miuko sat up among the weeds, frowning.

Did there have to be a fire? If she knew what was to come, then she should be able to stop it. She could warn her father. She could save the inn.

Maybe then, without the chaos of the fire, he would see that she was still his daughter and did not deserve to be banished.

Miuko staggered to her feet, swaying. Something was wrong with her. She felt insubstantial, somehow, like a shadow—strong and dark, but nothing more than a mirror image of something else. Perhaps cursing herself had depleted her energies, and she needed time to recover.

Cautiously, she picked her way over the dilapidated bridge, accompanied by ghosts who marched steadily over the holes and rotten planks as easily as if they were solid ground.

Her progress was halted several times by the sight of villagers on the Old Road: the teahouse proprietor, a couple of farmers, the lugubrious priests, calling her name in the fog. Spying Laido among them, she was sorely tempted to snatch him by the robes and whip him about like a stalk of rice at threshing time, but her human-voice convinced her otherwise.

At last, she reached the faded spells and termite-eaten wood of the Nihaoi gate. Beyond it lay the temple, the teahouse, the smattering of shops, the inn. As she wandered the streets, the slumbering village seemed both so familiar and so small. The old market, the largest structure in what remained of Nihaoi, could have fit in a corner of Tujiyazai's family castle. The overgrown fields, which she'd once thought sprawling and wild, were like patches of moss compared to the mountains she'd seen from Geiki's back.

But when she finally made it to the guesthouse, it was exactly as she remembered: the sandy front garden with its overgrown camellias, the stables to the left, the abalone shells tied to the roof as talismans against fire.

In one of the rooms was a steady light. Perhaps the demon prince was still awake, thinking of the girl on the bridge, obsessing over her plain features and simple robes and the way she'd looked at him—really looked at him—like she could see the monstrousness beneath his pretty, noble face.

Odd that he could not sense her now, as she stood before the inn. Was that because she was not of this time? Or was there another—

Miuko felt a cold spike of giddiness in her chest. If he could not sense her coming, she would have the advantage of surprise—there could be no better time than now to kill him.

You're here to warn our father, her human-voice reminded her sternly. *And you're not to murder anyone.*

Grumbling, she stepped forward, knocking upon the guesthouse door.

There was a shuffling sound within.

And then Otori Rohiro, her father, appeared in the doorway. A lantern cast a warm glow upon his broad shoulders and graying hair, highlighting the pouches beneath his weary eyes.

Miuko brightened to see him. "Fath—"

He slammed the door in her face.

Well, he tried, at any rate. With her new demon-reflexes, Miuko caught the door, shoving it open again with a loud *crack!* The walls rattled.

"Father, wait!" she whispered. "I have to tell you—"

Inside, Otori Rohiro reached behind the shrine of the *tachanagri,* which stood beside the threshold, and withdrew a paper talisman inked with spells. "Out, *shaoha!*" With nearly comedic force, he flapped the tiny scroll at her, brandishing it as if it were a blessed blade, not a yellowed scrap of paper.

"Father, it's me—" Miuko took a step forward, but she was thrust back as if by an invisible hand. She stumbled, retreating over the doorstep and into the night air as her father advanced on her, waving the talisman. "Wait! The inn is in—"

"Begone!" Leaning outside, he hung the strip of paper from a nail over the threshold before slamming the door shut again. "You are not welcome here!"

That's what you said the last time we saw each other.

Miuko scowled up at the talisman, though she dared not touch it. Its words were as indigo as the ocean, as indigo as Myudo,[1] the waters from whence all things came and to which all things returned. It was Amyunasa's color—a holy color—which was why the priests used it, of course.

But it was also Miuko's color—a *shaoha*'s color. To be expelled with it felt to her like a particularly personal sort of betrayal.

Pressing her face to the crack in the door, she hissed, "Listen, the inn is in danger! You have to believe me!"

The light inside went out.

With a growl that sounded frightening and otherworldly even to her own ears, she stormed for the stables. Her father may have been able to prevent her from entering the guesthouse, but he couldn't stop her from saving him and his damned family legacy from his own pigheadedness.

Dragging the troughs from the stables, she filled them with water. Beside them, she set piles of horse blankets she'd retrieved from storage. *There.* She smoothed the topmost blanket with her palms. Now, even if she could not stop the priests from starting the fire, at least someone would be able to—

She paused, fingering the thick wool.

She had seized this very blanket the first time the inn burned. She had dunked it into this very trough before trying to reach her father in the conflagration. She even remembered thinking how odd it was that the trough and blankets should be in the yard.

She had already done this.

And it had not worked.

But Miuko was not ready to give up. Seizing a broom, she used one end to scrawl a message in the well-swept dirt beside the baths, a warning to her father. Then, wrapping herself in another of the horse blankets, for

---

1 **Myu-do** (*mew-doh*): literally, "unknowable place," the before-life and the after-life.

she could not traipse about with her demon face uncovered, she fled the guesthouse.

If she'd been a little less preoccupied, she might have taken a moment to review what she'd written before she left the yard. If she had, she might have reconsidered her phrasing, for what she'd thought was a well-intentioned cautionary note could also be interpreted as a threat: *Tu ifeizikoi.*[2]

You will burn.

She was mostly demon, after all. It was only natural that even her best intentions would come out crooked.

Alas, she did not reread the message. Instead, she fled to the village temple, where she was repeatedly repelled from the grounds by the same sort of warding magic her father had used at the guesthouse. Soon finding herself both exhausted and out of ideas, she curled up in the horse blanket beside the temple gates, where she fell into a deep and dreamless sleep.

---

2 Tu ifei-zi-koi (*too ee-fay-zee-koy*)

4

THE BURNING OF THE INN

MIUKO WAS STARTLED AWAKE by the sound of someone shouting, "Get out! You cannot be here!"

The pebbles of the road swam into focus as she blinked, rubbing her eyes. It was already past dawn; the sun made the grass growing upon the Old Road glisten with dew.

"Evil!" someone cried.

She looked up in time to see a girl rush from the temple gates in a flurry of damp robes and the silty smell of river water. At the gate, she tripped over Miuko's outstretched feet, making Miuko grunt in surprise, before racing off in the direction of the guesthouse.

"Yagra!" someone shouted after her.

Watching the grass wither in the girl's footsteps, Miuko groaned. She remembered this, remembered stumbling over the beggar in the horse blanket.

That girl was us, said her human-voice. *It is us.*

The priests and their torches would not be long in following.

Uncurling from her position on the ground, Miuko flexed her hands, studying them in the morning light. She did not know why, but her fingers seemed strange to her, as if the sun's pale rays penetrated further into her skin now, like light into deep waters.

Shaking her head, she pulled her gloves back on. When the lugubrious priests finally emerged, there would likely be a confrontation, and she did not want to harm them.

Well, not much.

Thanks to the expediency of religious fervor, Miuko did not have to wait long. The lugubrious priests stormed from their temple in their finest ceremonial robes (a little threadbare, but otherwise passable), bearing torches and banners with ink so wet, they were still dripping when the priests left the gates.

"Wait! Stop!" Miuko started up, tightening the blanket over her head like a hood, but her voice, though hoarser, was still the voice of a girl, and so the priests paid her little attention.

Frustrated, Miuko reached for them, intending to tap the last priest on the shoulder—or perhaps grab his sleeve, or his arm, or the back of his neck—but before she could close her fingers around his pale, easily damaged flesh, there was a sound like the wind filling the sail of a boat.

Watch out for the warding spells! the little voice cried.

In an instant, Miuko was thrown back, as she had been by her father's talisman, except this time she did not stumble—she flew through the air, colliding with the temple fence.

The rotting bamboo lattice cracked under her weight, spilling her onto the ground.

Dazed and groaning, Miuko lay there as the oblivious priests marched onward, chanting.

The banners. She should have known that if a tiny scrap of paper could repel her from the guesthouse, warding spells of greater size would also be greater in power.

She blinked. Why wouldn't the sky stop swimming? Why wouldn't the earth hold still? She could not tell whether such unsteadiness was an effect of the priests' spells or part of the general malaise that had plagued her since she was transported to the Old Road, but the time on her back did give her the opportunity to admit that she still had a lot to learn about being a demon. At least she understood this particular lesson loud and clear.

217

Warding spells could stop her.

Good to know.

When the world finally righted itself again, she scrambled to her feet, sniffing the air. Smoke, noxious and brown, lay thick upon the breeze. Drawing the horse blanket about her like a hooded cloak, Miuko raced for the guesthouse.

The lugubrious priests were already standing in formation, chanting mantras, while the villagers amassed behind them, whispering nervously as they watched the flames devour the inn.

From the baths in the back, there was a scream: *"Father!"*

Her past-self.

Miuko felt like she'd been punched in the chest, remembering the heat of the conflagration on her cheeks, the sight of her father standing among the flames.

Above the front door, the paper talisman blackened and shrank in the fire, dispelling the protective enchantment that had thus far prevented her from entering the guesthouse.

Then, just as it had happened eleven days before, came her father's voice: "Miuko, get away from here!" Somewhere inside, Otori Rohiro was hobbling through the rooms, surrounded by flames.

Miuko set her jaw. She had not listened to her father then, and she would not listen now.

Pulling the horse blanket low over her head and shoulders, she pushed past the crowd and into the burning guesthouse.

Inside, all was light and heat and pain. Fire clawed at the walls and spread across the ceiling, roaring. Covering her mouth with her robes, Miuko squinted into the smoke. "Father?"

The kitchen, her human-voice reminded her. That was where she'd find him, scorched across the neck and huddled behind the ruins of the outer wall.

She ran through the inn, through empty rooms where the straw mats were quickly dissolving into sparks, past blazing scrolls and flaming flower arrangements.

There was a crash — the rafters falling.

In the smoke, someone grunted.

Her father?

Leaping the fallen beams, Miuko made her way to the kitchen. The pots were overturned. The water basins were shattered. One wall had collapsed, through which she could see the back garden and the roof of the baths.

And in the corner, cowering from the heat of the flames, was her father, his neck and shoulder blistered and bleeding freely.

Distantly, she heard her past-self shout from the yard: "Father!"

Miuko hunkered down beside him, extending her gloved hand. "Father? Come with me. We have to get out of here."

"Miuko?" He turned toward her. "I thought I told you to —"

At the sight of her, however, his eyes went wide with horror. He backed away, digging at the earth as if he could burrow into the wall to get away from her. "No," he muttered. "No, no. You're not my daughter! Get away from me!"

Miuko drew back, stung. She may have had blue skin and white eyes at this point, but the rest of her features remained the same.

"*Shaoha!*" he shouted.

She glanced toward the back of the inn, where she remembered standing eleven days ago, watching Otori Rohiro's face twist with fear and dread.

"What have you done with her?"

From this angle, her past-self could not see her behind the collapsed wall. Her past-self did not know her father was addressing *her*, the *shaoha*. It had all been a misunderstanding.

A mistake.

Perhaps if she hadn't run away then, her father would have embraced her among the smoking ruins of the guesthouse. Perhaps he would have convinced the priests she was no demon. Perhaps they would have helped her. Perhaps they would have even brought her to the House of December themselves.

Her eyes narrowed.

But it could not be a misunderstanding now. She was kneeling right next to him. She was *right there,* speaking to him. This close, he should have known her, no matter her appearance. She was still his *daughter*.

"Begone from this place!" he roared.

Miuko clenched her fists.

"Go! You are not welcome here!"

She'd wanted to be human again . . . for this? To be reviled by the one person she loved most in the world? To be betrayed? To be cast out? For *this?*

She didn't know when she'd stripped the gloves from her hands, didn't know when she'd crossed the distance between them, didn't know when she'd twined her fingers in his robes, making him cry out in pain.

But she knew when her fingertip brushed his stubbled chin. She knew when she heard him gasp. She knew when she felt the life trickling out of him like water from a spring, flowing into her, giving her new strength, new life. She knew it, and she relished it as she squeezed his jaw between her fingers, hungry for more.

5

HOPE AND DESPAIR

MIUKO WAS GOING to kill her father.

No.

She loved her father. He may have been in the wrong here, but that didn't mean he deserved to die for it.

And we're not a killer, the voice inside her added.

Quickly, she grabbed her father — this time under the arms — and hauled him out from behind the rubble, into the yard, where he wrested himself from her grasp.

"I'm sorry, Father —" she began.

But she'd forgotten that by this time, the priests were in the yard too. They ran at her, waving their banners.

Rohiro jerked away from her. "I'm not your father."

"You are my *only* father," she said softly. "But I don't know if I can forgive you for this."

He blinked, as if seeing her — truly seeing her, both as a demon and as a daughter — for the first time. But it was too late; Miuko could not linger. She scrambled around the lugubrious priests and their damned spells, and, without a backward glance, she fled the village for the second time that day.

Miuko ran as long as she could, but in truth, it was not long, for the ache in her heart was too painful to bear. Gasping, she collapsed on the edge of the Kotskisiu-maru, head in her hands.

Somehow, her father's rejection hurt worse the second time. Before, there'd been pain, yes, but more than that, confusion . . . and the hope that she could one day return.

But what would she be returning to now?

A lifetime of trying and failing to fit in? To be quiet, obedient, feminine? Her father may have indulged her occasional waywardness (while the villagers had barely tolerated it), but none of them had truly embraced it.

Or her.

Maybe that had been enough for her, once, but now that she'd experienced the alternatives—freedom, adventure, acceptance—she knew that even if she got her humanity back, she still might never be able to go home.

For the first time since her misadventures began, she allowed herself to cry. The tears came hot and fast, pouring down her cheeks and falling onto her exposed hands.

As she wept, a voice, small and sibilant, drifted up to her from somewhere on the forest floor: "What tearsss? Why crying?"

Surprised, Miuko straightened, wiping her eyes.

At her side was a spirit no bigger than the length of her arm. The little creature had the face of a woman and the body of a snake, pearly white in the shade, with delicate blue frills by her ears and a pair of useless forepaws, each tipped with a single claw.

Miuko sniffed. "Who are you?"

Shrugging, the spirit plucked at the leaf litter, her forked tongue flicking between her lips. "No one of conssssequenccce. What troublesss, *shaoha*-jai?"

Although all her mother's stories told her that any spirit who claimed they were "no one" was not to be trusted, Miuko was too surprised by the little spirit's boldness to be cautious. Besides, she was a *shaoha*.

"Aren't you afraid of me?" she asked.

"What reassson to be ssscared?"

Miuko lifted an eyebrow. "How about that I could kill you?"

"Uhula isss not ssstrong. Many can kill me." The spirit's head swung back and forth meditatively. "Yet none have sssucccceeded."

That seemed fair.

"Why crying?" Uhula repeated.

Perhaps sorrow and exhaustion had worn away Miuko's defenses, because at that moment she wanted nothing more than to let all of her inadequacies and disappointments spill from her: unsightly, irregular, damaged, deficient, each one proof of just how much of a failure she really was.

She bared them all to the spirit: how she couldn't save Geiki at the dock; how she couldn't stop Tujiyazai when she'd had him within reach; how she couldn't save her father's guesthouse; and for all her power and foresight, how she couldn't seem to change anything at all about the events of the past.

Uhula listened with both patience and sympathy, nodding as rhythmically as a monk falling asleep at prayer. "Hopelesss," she murmured.

Yes. Perhaps it *was* hopeless. Perhaps the next eleven days were doomed to repeat themselves exactly as they'd done the first time: the inn would always burn. Geiki would always be captured. Miuko would always end up a *shaoha*.

"Why keep trying?" Miuko moaned, laying her head on her arms. It would be so much easier to stop here, to let things pass as they were destined to.

"No ussse," the little snake agreed, tugging at something deep within Miuko's pocket. The *tseimi*'s incense holder—she'd forgotten she had it. "All isss ssset."

No, the voice inside her whispered. She could not leave Geiki in Tujiyazai's hands. He was her friend. He needed her to come rescue him the same way he'd swept out of the sky at the castle, strong and swift as the North Wind.

Trembling with the effort, Miuko lifted her head, feebly slapping Uhula away from her robes.

The shadows had shifted positions upon the forest floor. How long had she been sitting here? How much time had she lost?

"I can't," she said weakly. "I have to stop Tujiyazai—"

"No ussse." The spirit had crept even closer, Miuko realized now, hovering at her shoulder. "Ssstay."

Miuko wanted to obey. It would be so easy to remain here, sinking slowly into the mulch as the night closed in about her, allowing the falling leaves to cover her like a winter blanket . . . She could not kill the *doro yagra* without risking her human spirit, and if she couldn't kill him, then she couldn't stop him, so why . . .

Unless there's another way.

She blinked, struggling to clear her thoughts. There had to be another way. She knew it somehow, had found the answer already, in some dusty corner of her memory. . . .

Something is wrong, her human-voice said. *Get up.*

As if in response, the little snake hissed. "Ssstay. Elssse disssappointment. Elssse catasssstrophe."

GET UP.

Snarling, Miuko wrenched herself away from Uhula, who recoiled, baring her tiny fangs. Suddenly, Miuko saw that the snake was not a lonely little spirit at all but a spirit of despair, her many heads floating around Miuko, picking at her hair and clothing with their tiny claws, crooning in their soft, reasonable voices to give up, to remain where she was, to stay with them. She was a failure as a daughter and a monster and a friend, so why keep trying to prove she wasn't? Wouldn't it be nice never to let anyone down again? All she had to do was sit here, just here, just like this forever . . .

"Get away from me!" She lunged wildly for the nearest head, fingers reaching for one of Uhula's many throats.

The spirit hissed — all her blue frills rippling in alarm — and fled, slipping out of Miuko's grasp and skimming away over the ground, leaving a flurry of dead leaves and a foul, bog-like odor in her wake.

Miuko slumped back down, exhausted. All around her, the light was dimming, turning the twisted trunks and tangled thickets of the Kotskisiumaru into snarled shadows, bristling with darkness. She groaned. She'd lost almost an entire day to the despair spirit.

But now that Uhula was gone, Miuko's head was clearing already, running brisk as a mountain stream.

She would not give up. She would not abandon Geiki. Perhaps she could not kill Tujiyazai, but if she'd learned anything in her limited time as a spirit, it was that there was more than one way to stop a demon.

Talismans. Banners. Spells scrawled in holy ink.

And she knew exactly where to find the ones she needed, for she'd learned about them in the dusty alcoves of Keivoweicha eleven days ago, upon an illustrated scroll — *the only one with pictures!* Geiki had said.

The House of November, where demon hunters were trained.

If she could reach their forested mountain temple, the priests of Nakatalao would surely know how to stop Tujiyazai without harming the body of the *doro*. But she had to be quick, she thought, remembering the sight of smoke in the west. The temple would not be standing much longer; in two days, while Geiki and her past-self were sailing across the bay, the House of November would be destroyed by some unknown calamity.

Could she make it in time? She didn't know, as she struggled to her feet again, brushing dead leaves from her robes, but she knew she had to try.

6

FERAL SPIRITS

MIUKO HAD LESS than forty-eight hours to reach the House of November before both it and the mountain upon which it stood became an *oyu* — a blight bereft of all life, both mortal and spirit.

She remembered watching the smoke rise from the mountaintops as she and Geiki crossed the bay, remembered that creeping sense of dread, illogical as it seemed at the time, that she was somehow connected to the destruction. Now, here she was, bound for the temple, and she could not help feeling like she'd been right.

She was walking into a trap.

But who set it? the little voice inside her wondered. *And for what purpose?*

Strong as she was, racing over the countryside on her demon legs, she did not have the power to obliterate an entire mountain; nor, as her experience with the spells of the lugubrious priests had taught her, could she enter a warded temple to slaughter its inhabitants, whether she wanted to or not.

No, there were other elements at play, both formidable and unseen.

From a farmer's hut, she stole a water gourd and food to sustain her, although the fresh cucumbers and handfuls of summer berries did little to replenish her energy, and as the hours wore on, her pace slowed. She felt diluted, somehow, thin and diffuse as ink in water.

By dawn, she could walk no more. Stumbling from the Ochiirokai, she curled up in the hollow trunk of a tree, where she plummeted into sleep and did not wake again until the bright rays of the midday sun struck her face.

Stirring, she rubbed her eyes . . . and screamed.

The sound echoed through the forest, disturbing several sparrows from their nests and causing a squirrel to fall from its branch, landing with a squeak in the mulch.

In the tree trunk, Miuko stared at her gloved hands. She could almost see through them to the shadows of the forest floor, as if her body were nothing more than a silk veil or a rice paper screen. Frantically, she rubbed her palms on her thighs, as if that would make them opaque again.

It didn't.

Moreover, it made her realize she wasn't merely becoming see-through. Her own hands seemed to sink partway into her legs, as if her body was losing not only its visibility but its very substance.

Was this how the curse worked? Twelve days of transformation, followed by a couple days as a demon, and then . . . nothing?

"You're in trouble, *shaoha*," a voice creaked from overhead.

In the treetops, there appeared the head of an old man, sitting atop a bulbous body and six spindly legs, all clothed in what appeared to be a tattered garment of leaves.

Out of habit, Miuko screamed again.

Grimacing, the old man plugged his ears with two twiggy fingers. "Stop that. You already woke me up, eh? You can't do it again."

Guiltily, she bowed. "I'm sorry. I just . . . Who are you?"

He grinned at her through his beard of lichen, revealing broken stumps for teeth. "Whose forest do you think you're in, *shaoha*?"

Miuko stared at him, open-mouthed. *Daiganasu,*[1] forest spirits, were

---

1 daiga-na (*dye-gah-nah*)

supposed to be noble, stately, more like the cloud spirit, Beikai, and less like . . . whatever this creature was.

Feral, the little voice inside her said. Like he might gobble her up if given half the chance.

Her mother had always said spirits survived on belief. If one were left alone too long, without prayers or offerings, they could become wild, growing horns and fangs. Perhaps that was happening to the spirit of Nogadishao Forest,[2] which bordered this segment of the Thousand-Step Way.

Still, Miuko bowed again, for even a wild spirit deserved her respect. "Apologies for waking you, *daigana*-jai. What do you mean, I'm in trouble?"

The spirit scuttled closer, climbing from one branch to another like an insect. As he neared, Miuko realized he was much bigger than he looked from afar, his tremendous weight making the trees dip and sway. "Just look at yourself," he said.

She glanced down at her fading body. "Do you know what's happening to me?"

"You're dying. Odd, eh?"

"*Dying?* I didn't think spirits could—"

"Oh yes, we die. Not often, but we die . . . alone, alone, always alone. Our trees burn. Our shrine crumbles. We're neglected and forgotten, growing weaker and weaker until at last our domains perish, and we fade from the world like shadows . . . alone . . ." Nogadishao shrugged, causing great clods of dirt to fall from his joints. "But you're not alone, are you? I'm here, eh?"

"So why is this happening?"

The *daigana* stroked his beard, studying her with eyes of little white

---

2 No-ga-dishao (*noh-gah-dee-shaoh*): literally, "where-face-sword," or, to be poetic about it, "The Place One Goes to Face Death by the Sword." In the language of Awara, the forest's full name is Nogadishao-daiga, "daiga" meaning "forest."

mushrooms. "You don't happen to be a redundancy, do you? A copy? Another you? An . . . *other* you?"

Miuko gaped at him. "How did you—"

"Pah. You're not that special. It's happened before, eh? Sometimes there are two of the same spirit where only one should exist. You are an intruder here, *shaoha*! A shadow."

"So what happens to the shadow, if it doesn't belong?" she asked.

"It's . . . er . . . *expunged.*"

"*What?*"

"Expunged!" He waved his arms as if dispersing a cloud of smoke. "Ha ha!"

Miuko examined her fading fingers. Her body was losing substance much more quickly than the curse had claimed her. Judging by the opacity of her limbs, she estimated she was already a quarter transparent. If she retrieved the spells from the House of November the following morning, she'd be able to catch Tujiyazai in Vevaona that night, perhaps after her past-self saved the crane girl. Much longer after that, however, and she would likely be too transparent and too weak to stop him.

But she couldn't allow herself to think about that.

"Of course," Nogadishao continued, "if you'd only eat something, it'd probably stall the process. You look famished, eh?"

As if in response, Miuko's stomach growled. "I had some vegetables—" she began.

"Pah. Vegetables. I mean, have you *eaten?*"

The way he said it made her fingers curl. For a moment, she imagined laying her palm to someone's cheek, dreaming of the sweet, cool sensation of their life draining from their flesh . . .

"You mean have I killed anyone?" she gasped.

"That's what you do, eh? That's what sustains you."

No! her human-voice protested. But she could not say it. . . . Not truthfully, at any rate. Somehow, she knew that taking a life would rejuvenate her, giving her more time to stop the *doro yagra,* just as she knew that without it, she would be too slow to make it to the House of November.

Again, she felt that hunger rising inside her. The forest spirit was within reach now, peering curiously at her from beneath his overgrown brows. All she had to do was kill him, and she'd have the strength she needed to reach Nakatalao's priests before the massacre.

But even as she imagined lunging for him, she could see another path unfolding before her, twisted as a climbing vine. As a lone *shaoha,* she'd have little hope of convincing the priests of her good intentions (such as they were in her demon-addled brain), but if she persuaded the forest spirit to *carry* her to the temple gates, she would not only make it to the House of November in time, she would also have the legitimacy of the *daigana's* company to encourage them to help her.

If a feral spirit like him could be considered legitimate, that is.

It's better than eating him and losing our humanity for good, said her human-voice, and, much as she didn't want to admit it, Miuko had to agree.

How to convince him, then? She had nothing to offer but an empty water gourd and a magical cat that killed other cats, neither of which would be useful to a forest spirit.

But he was desperate and wild and lonely, and she could capitalize on that. Without a shrine, without devotees to pray to him or leave him offerings, he was not so far from becoming a shadow himself.

Abruptly, she flung herself to the ground, prostrating herself before the *daigana,* who recoiled. "Nogadishao-kanai," she said, pressing her forehead to the earth. "I am glad I found you."

"No, no, no, no. I found *you,* eh? Discovered you in my woods shrieking like a *baigana.*"

"On the contrary," she lied, "I have been sent to find you, for you are the only one who can help me."

"Help a *shaoha*?" He cackled. "I'd rather eat my beard!"

"I am only part *shaoha,* and it was for this reason I was chosen. You already observed, O Wise One, that I am not of this time, and it is true! I am an emissary sent from the future, tasked with preventing a terrible calamity, and for this I require your assistance."

There was a pause, and Miuko squeezed her eyes shut, praying he would not see through her falsehoods.

From somewhere overhead, the *daigana* grumbled testily. "Get up. This is worse than you screaming, eh? I can't hear a thing you say when you're mumbling into the dirt like that."

Straightening her torn clothes, Miuko sat back on her heels.

The forest spirit stuck his chin on one of his gnarled fists, his white eyes waggling in what she assumed was curiosity. "So, you're an *emissary,* eh?"

She had his attention, then. That was a start.

She cleared her throat. "Indeed. You see that I wear the clothes of a priest? That is because I have been ordained by the disciples of Amyunasa to carry out a mission of utmost importance." She gestured to her robes, keenly aware of every rip and smudge and scorch mark. Anyone else would have been immediately suspicious of her ragged appearance, but the *daigana* seemed just eccentric enough to overlook it. "No human could have survived out of her own time long enough to succeed, which is why I was the only option."

"And what terrible calamity are you supposed to prevent, eh?"

She inhaled deeply, schooling her features. "Tomorrow at dawn, the House of November will suffer a grave tragedy. The priests will die, the temple will burn, and the mountain upon which it stands will become an *oyu.* Only I can prevent this from happening, and only you can help me, for, without you, O Paragon of Swiftness, I cannot make it to the temple in time."

Nogadishao sidled closer, smelling of sap and boar-scent and rot. "You need my help?" he asked softly.

"Yes."

"You . . ." He turned the words over between his rotten teeth, as if he hadn't tasted them in centuries. ". . . need *my* help."

"Yes," she repeated, "and if you help me, your name will never be forgotten. Shrines will be built in your honor. Worshippers will flock to your forest. Never again will your woods be neglected, for you will be Nogadishao-kanai, Savior of the House of November."

Her declarations rang through the trees with the kind of grandiosity reserved for grifters and false prophets, and for a moment, Miuko felt guilty for lying to him.

Then again, she reasoned, she could not say for certain whether or not her words were false. There was still the possibility that they might stop the ruination. There was still the possibility that the priests might be saved. Who knew? The *daigana* might get the adulation he so desired, and Miuko might not be a liar after all.

For his part, Nogadishao seemed momentarily dumbfounded. Then his broken grin widened. His mushroom-cap eyes swelled. His entire body seemed to come alive — the ferns along his legs uncoiling, moths fluttering from between his ears. Dropping to the forest floor, he beckoned wildly to her, beaming like an eager child at the door of a sweet shop. "What are you waiting for then, eh? Climb on!"

7

DEMON AT THE GATES

CLINGING TO THE FOREST SPIRIT as he scrambled through the treetops, Miuko explained their next moves. First, they had to convince Nakatalao's priests to help her stop Tujiyazai without resorting to murder. Then they'd need to persuade the priests to evacuate the House of November. That done, Miuko would continue alone to Vevaona, where Tujiyazai would soon track her past-self to the inn.

Eventually she slept, and sometime before dawn, she woke to find that she and the *daigana* had arrived at the back entrance of the temple grounds. A vermillion gate stood before them, its protective spells so deep and powerful that even at a distance of twenty yards, Miuko could feel the warding magic pulsing between her eyes.

"Stop here," she said, sliding down one of Nogadishao's legs.

Beyond the gate lay the temple compound, which for the most part was obscured by a thick screen of trees. Here and there, slanting tile rooftops appeared to sprout directly out of the canopy, as if the forest had sprung up around the buildings, making them as much a part of the woods as any ancient cypress or towering pine. In fact, the only structure that did not merge seamlessly into the mountainside was a five-tiered pagoda standing on a nearby rise.

She glanced at the sky, pale in the pre-dawn light. "We need to get their attention."

"Say no more, *shaoha*!" Puffing out his chest, the forest spirit drew himself up to his full height, rising to three times her size, and bellowed so loudly the nearest treetops rattled with the force of it. "COME OUT, PRIESTS! WE ARE ON AN URGENT MISSION FROM THE FUTURE!"

Grimacing, Miuko clapped her hands over her ears. "Agh! Warn me next time, will you?"

Nogadishao cackled. "You're delicate for a demon, eh?"

Having been alerted thus, the priests quickly gathered on the other side of the gate, where they equipped themselves with magnificent painted banners nearly sparking with magic.

"What kind of spirit is *that*?" someone asked.

"It's a *daigana*," another replied.

"Not that one! The other one."

Grinning widely, Nogadishao lifted his arms. "The *shaoha* and I have come to request the aid of the priests of Nakatalao!"

There was a pause. Then: "You're with a *shaoha*?"

Someone pointed. "*That's* a *shaoha*?"

"I thought she was a legend!"

Grumbling, Miuko ground a twig to bits beneath her heel. "Hurry it up, will you?"

The forest spirit lifted his mossy brows. "They're priests, *shaoha*. They need a little pomp, eh?" Then, to the assembly: "Where is your head priest?"

One of the men, broad as a boulder and as solidly built, stepped through the gates. Unlike the others, he wore a sash, flaming in color and reminiscent of the demon hunter's enchanted scarf. With the steady confidence of an old warrior, he twitched it into place as he and his bannermen approached.

The throbbing between Miuko's temples increased.

"I am the head priest of Nakatalao," the man said, stopping ten paces from her. "What request would a demon and a *daigana* make of the House of November?"

Up close, he did not appear as old as Miuko had expected a head priest to be. With the wrinkles only just appearing at the corners of his eyes, he couldn't have been much older than her father.

She opened her mouth to reply, but Nogadishao threw open his arms again, nearly swiping her across the face. "A request of utmost importance!" he declared. Grinning, he explained in extravagant terms how Miuko was no mere demon but a great hero dispatched from the future to stop the demon Tujiyazai and prevent a terrible tragedy from befalling the House of November.

Miuko cringed. With his unruly beard and molting bark skin and the forest creatures scurrying around his joints, he looked foolish, babbling about time travel and grave purposes. How could the priests possibly believe a story like that?

How could she possibly have thought this plan would work?

"What is the nature of this tragedy?" the head priest asked.

"I don't know." Miuko shivered in a sudden wave of cold. "But all of you die, and it happens soon—shortly after dawn—so you have to evacuate before it comes."

All around her, the other priests began muttering.

The head priest silenced them with a wave of his hand. Turning to Nogadishao, he bowed. "It is a rare honor, *daigana*-jai. When I took my vows, not one of our order had spoken with a spirit in decades, so I must assume the circumstances of your visit are quite serious. Tell me, should we do as the *shaoha* asks? Is she worthy of our trust?"

Beside her, Nogadishao scratched his belly, dislodging an irate weasel from one of his armpits. It hit the ground, chittering angrily, and scrabbled back up his leg, where it secreted itself within a patch of ferns. "She may be a demon, but she's not a *bad* demon, eh? She believes in me, and no one has believed in me for many years." One of his mushroom eyes turned toward her thoughtfully. "Yes, you would do well to listen to her and clear out of here as soon as you can."

"Sooner than that." Rubbing her arms, for goosebumps had appeared on her blue flesh, Miuko glanced at the clouds, which were turning rosy with light. "We're almost out of time."

The head priest sighed. "We will craft you two spells, *shaoha*, for exorcising this demon and binding him in an object so he cannot harm anyone else. Pray that *yazai* does not find us for aiding a demon." Turning, he gestured to the other priests, issuing orders to evacuate the temple while he prepared the spells.

As soon as he was gone, Nogadishao raised his arms and stamped his two front feet, causing the weeds on his shins to tremble. "Victory!" he crowed. "Am I not convincing, *shaoha*? Am I not impressive? Ha ha! No calamity shall occur here today!"

Miuko wanted to celebrate with him, but she could not seem to escape the uneasy chill in her bones. It seeped through her, making her tense and impatient.

She was relieved, therefore, when the head priest finally reemerged from the temple grounds. Flanked again by his bannermen, he presented Miuko with two bamboo cylinders strung upon a simple cord.

"These spells have been written for you alone to use," he said, lifting one of the cylinders. It was small, no longer than her thumb, with a stoppered top and a slip of paper inside. "One to exorcise a spirit and one to bind it."

She took them, frowning. The cylinders looked so familiar, she was certain she'd seen their like before.

"What's the matter?" Nogadishao muttered.

The head priest scowled. "You're displeased?"

"No, I just . . ." Her voice trailed off.

She *had* seen a cylinder like this before. The memory of it flashed through her mind: a castle tower, a forced kiss, a fight . . .

She'd seen it on the neck of the demon prince.

What had he said when he found her in Vevaona, the night after the slaughter at the House of November?

I had an errand to run nearby.

Her mind reeled as a red glow touched the mountainside, spreading over the forest canopy and the tiled roofs until it reached Miuko and the *daigana* at the back gate.

The bells rang, signaling sunrise.

And it all fell into place: the chill in her heart, the rawness of her nerves, the hunger burning in her hands. She should have recognized it sooner, from the forests above Koewa, only . . . she had not expected to encounter it here.

But she should have known. The answer had been right in front of her.

Who had the power to incite the kind of massacre that had occurred here—that would occur, *now*, if Miuko didn't stop it?

Only Tujiyazai.

8

THAT DREADED DAWN

MIUKO SEARCHED THE TREE LINE for the demon prince's flaming visage, his twisted horns. After their first meeting in the Kotskisiu-maru, Tujiyazai must have realized his disguise was imperfect. *You see me?* he'd asked, surprised. *As I am?* If Miuko knew he was not the *doro,* cherished son of the ruling Omaizi Clan, but a demon . . . that meant, with the right magic, she could unseat him. As a preventative measure, he must have ridden to the priests of Nakatalao, the only ones with the power to bind him in the *doro's* body.

And the only ones with the power to exorcise him from it.

Had he already gotten his binding spell? How much time did she have before he forced the priests to slaughter one another, as he'd done to the hunters above Koewa?

As she scanned the woods for signs of Tujiyazai, a surge of cold coursed through her. Someone inside the temple complex screamed.

The priest's bannermen recoiled as the sounds of violence erupted from the House of November. Through the trees, Miuko caught glimpses of the priests attacking one another in front of the pagoda, seizing whatever weapons they could lay their hands on: ceremonial urns, ropes, salvers of burning oil, which flew through the air, catching on trees and wooden cloisters.

"It's Tujiyazai!" she shouted at the head priest. "He's here already! You all have to run!"

Beside her, Nogadishao flexed his gnarled hands and gnashed his broken teeth. "Is this it, *shaoha*? Is this the calamity we have been preordained to stop?"

"No!" Miuko tried to shove him toward the woods, away from the temple, but his great bulk did not budge. If Tujiyazai could twist priests into murderers, what could he do to a *daigana*?

She could not bear to find out.

"You have to get out of here!" She shoved him again, hard enough this time to cause him to stumble back in alarm. "Please, Nogadishao, you're in danger—"

"HA! I *AM* DANGER!" he roared.

Miuko wanted to argue with him, but her attention was drawn by the head priest and his attendants charging toward the spirit gate. "No!" she cried. "Stop!"

But no one listened to her. No one ever listened to her.

Baring her teeth, Miuko yanked off one of her gloves and ran at Nogadishao, striking him with the flat of her palm. For a second, his life force flowed into her, bright as sap and just as sweet, before she reared back again. "RUN!" she screamed.

Yelping, the forest spirit scrambled out of her reach like a kicked dog. "But *shaoha*, this is why you brought me here, eh? We're supposed to—"

But she didn't let him finish. Surging with renewed energy, she launched herself at him again, her fingers curved into cold, murderous hooks. *"I TOLD YOU TO RUN!"*

With one last confused glance at her, he galloped away from the temple, disappearing into the woods with an anguished howl.

Miuko had no time to make sure he'd escaped. Donning the priests' spells like a necklace, she pulled her glove back on and raced to the temple. The vermillion gate had caught fire, its protective spells vanishing as the indigo ink bubbled and evaporated in the conflagration. Without hesitating, she vaulted through the flames and dashed up the path while priests fought around her, grappling and clawing with their bare hands as more fires licked at the trees and wooden cloisters.

She found the head priest fighting off his own disciples in front of a towering idol of Nakatalao. Banners had become garrotes. Poles had become pikes. Of them all, only the head priest seemed unaffected, as immune to Tujiyazai's powers as the *kyakyozuya* had been.

Miuko dashed through the melee, dragging him away from his attendants, who turned on one another as soon as the head priest was out of sight. "It's too late!" she cried as he wrenched out of her grasp. "You have to get away from here. If even one of you escapes, you can still rebuil—"

But a roar from the forest made the words turn to ash on her tongue.

Nogadishao? Her heart sank. Had she failed to save him after all?

But it was not the *daigana*.

From above the treetops, the immense form of a spirit rose—a giant with stone skin—so large he threw the entire temple into shadow. Flames burned in the pits of his eyes and along his sloping shoulders, igniting the forest as he crashed toward the House of November.

The earth trembled, shaking the trees and causing the temple buildings to sway on their foundations.

The head priest inhaled sharply. "That's the spirit of our mountain," he said. "Only now it is a *yasa*."[1]

Horrified, Miuko watched as the creature demolished a painted portico with a single swipe of its massive forepaws.

So this was what Tujiyazai's powers did to spirits.

It turned them into demons.

"He must have sensed a disturbance here and come to stop it." The priest turned his bloodshot eyes on Miuko. "What evil have you brought upon us?"

---

1   ya-sa (*yah-sah*): literally, "evil form."

She smacked him across the face with her gloved hand, startling at the violence of it. Had she meant to strike him?

She didn't have time to wonder. "You have better things to do now than reprimand me, priest," she growled. "The entire mountain is going to become an *oyu* if you don't snap out of it. Now, listen to me. *Can you bind the mountain* yasa?"

He should have been afraid of her—and perhaps he was—but the slap seemed to have awoken the warrior's spirit she'd seen in him earlier, because he nodded. "I can. What will you do, *shaoha*?"

Miuko gripped the spells which hung around her neck. "I'm going to find Tujiyazai and put a stop to this."

With that, she dashed up the mountain toward the pagoda. She could not sense the demon prince beyond the unearthly cold that transfused the grounds, but from the peak of the ridge, she would be able to spot him, wherever he was among the devastation.

As she reached the pagoda steps, another earthquake shook the temple. Turning, she watched the mountain *yasa* demolish the idol of Nakatalao, swinging his flaming arms as the priests jabbed at his stone feet like dozens of stinging ants.

Then, out of the corner of her eye: a flash of vermillion. The head priest in his bright sash was running toward the fallen statue as his disciples fought and died around him. Racing to the foot of the *yasa*, he slapped a slip of paper to the giant's ankle.

A spell.

From her vantage point at the pagoda, Miuko watched the head priest lift something in his palms—a rice bowl, she thought, a simple rice bowl —and with a roar, the mountain *yasa* began to vanish, sucked downward as if into a drain, his great form shrinking until he was no taller than a tree, a rooftop, a fencepost, a water pitcher, a grapefruit . . .

The earth stilled.

Out of the corner of her eye, Miuko caught sight of a familiar figure, tall and elegant, strolling serenely through the courtyard at the heart of the temple.

Tujiyazai?

But before she could look closer, there was more movement near Nakatalao's broken statue. As the head priest clasped the rice bowl to his chest, one of his disciples, bearing a black eye and clad in bloodied robes, limped from the wreckage. Screaming, he rushed for the head priest, running him through with a kitchen knife.

In and out and in and out—the blade flashed in the morning light.

Upon the hillside, Miuko screamed.

In the courtyard, Tujiyazai paused, glancing about as if searching for her.

Once, at Ogawa Castle, Miuko had thought him lonely; but now, seeing him encircled by such unrepentant destruction, she understood that he could never be lonely, because he did not desire company.

No, what he desired was subjugation, and that meant he would always be alone, above all others.

Unless she stopped him.

By the fallen statue, the head priest dropped to the ground, the rice bowl containing the mountain spirit tumbling from his lifeless hands. With a pained cry, his killer dropped his knife and hobbled from the scene.

The cold ebbed from Miuko's bones as she raced down the pagoda steps—Tujiyazai must have been withdrawing his power. In the gardens and among the trees, sprawled across thresholds and hanging out of windows, the priests of Nakatalao lay dead and dying.

She could have stopped for them. A part of her wanted to.

But it was already too late.

It was not too late, however, for her to save the priests at the House of December.

Reaching Nakatalao's fallen idol, she tore the vermillion sash from the head priest's body. If she could get the spells to Amyunasa's priests before the week was out, they would know how to protect themselves from Tujiyazai when he arrived at the God's Teeth.

Pulling the wrap around herself, she circled back toward the courtyard, where she'd last seen the demon prince. All was quiet now, except for the flames, which greedily devoured the temple buildings, tearing down walls, roofs, even the pagoda on its hill.

She crept through the ruins, her senses sharpened with the thrill of the hunt, until she spied him through a burning prayer hall. He was meandering along one of the paths, watching the fire crackle around him as if it were an opera—stirring, magnificent—and he, its only patron.

Unspooling the exorcism spell from its cylinder, Miuko stalked him through the smoke.

Then: movement along the walkway.

The disciple who'd murdered the head priest had survived. Dazed, he hobbled toward the demon prince. "*Doro*-kanai, what are you doing? Do you know what happened here? I had the most terrible visions . . . I think . . ." A sob bubbled up in his throat. "I think I may have done terrible things—" Unable to walk any further, he pitched forward, landing face-first at Tujiyazai's feet.

Kneeling, the *doro yagra* smiled, almost benevolently, and in one fluid motion, drew a knife across the priest's throat. With a sort of bland curiosity, he watched the blood pour from the wound, onto the gravel.

He's distracted, whispered the little voice inside her.

Now was her chance.

Miuko leapt from the shadows, heedless now of being heard. The undergrowth crashed around her as she dashed for Tujiyazai's crouched figure. She was almost there. She just had to reach him before he—

A sudden pain caused her to stumble. Words were appearing on the flesh of her arm, carved there as if by some invisible hand.

No, her human-voice muttered. *Not words.*

A name.

Miuko was being summoned.

No! Not now. Not when we're this close! She charged forward, determined to catch him. All she had to do was hold out long enough —

Tujiyazai was standing now. Perhaps he'd heard her behind him. He was beginning to turn.

But she was too fast for him, still pumping with the energy she'd sapped from Nogadishao.

Another second more, and she'd have him.

She lifted the exorcism spell, the thin paper uncoiling around her fingers, her palm, her wrist . . .

And then she was gone, leaving the *doro yagra* standing alone on the footpath while the House of November blazed around him.

9

A TWIST OF FATE

MIUKO ARRIVED SHRIEKING and did not stop.

Gone was the smell of burning buildings. Gone was the crackling of the trees. They had been replaced by cramped chambers and the stifling odors of medicine and incense—herbs swaying from the rafters, pots of liniments crammed onto the shelves.

A doctor's house.

"You terrible woman!" someone cried. "How dare you intrude—"

Snarling, Miuko whirled on a paunch-bellied man sitting at breakfast. Though it was not long past dawn, he reeked of wine, as if it seeped through his pores in place of sweat.

She did not know how she knew this was the man whose name had been etched into her arm, but she knew it as surely as she knew the hunger in her fingertips and the power in her limbs. At the sight of him, some deep-rooted instinct reared up inside her like a blast of cold, starving for a kill.

It didn't matter who he was.

It didn't matter what he'd done.

She was a malevolence demon, and she'd been summoned to strike him down.

Don't! cried the little voice inside her. *We're not supposed to—*

Miuko lunged.

Screeching, the doctor sprang to his feet—in his haste, striking his head on the underside of one of his own shelves—and, before Miuko could reach him, he slumped to the floor in a heap.

Fortunately, knocking himself unconscious likely saved his life, for the surprise was enough to halt Miuko in her tracks.

Her human-voice was right. She did not want to kill this man.

She *wanted* Tujiyazai.

She must have been the nearest malevolence demon when she'd been summoned, which meant she could not be far from the House of November. There still might be time to catch the demon prince before he reached her past-self in Vevaona.

Coiling the exorcism spell back into its bamboo cylinder, she raced out of the doctor's house, expecting to find herself somewhere upon the Thousand-Step Way, perhaps in Nogadishao's woods.

But the sight of her surroundings stopped her short.

She was not on the Ochiirokai. She was not even in a forest.

She was on a wide path between melon fields, which sloped from the doctor's house all the way down to a white sand beach and the glittering spear of an unfamiliar inlet striking eastward from the sea.

No.

Spinning, she searched the horizon for the temple fire.

There it was — so far to the north that the billowing smoke appeared, at this distance, as little more than a faint haze, like that of a cooking fire or a stick of incense.

Miuko let out another shriek. She'd been so close — a few seconds longer, and Tujiyazai would have been hers — and the loss of all those priests, the mountain *yasa,* and Nogadishao, too, whatever had happened to him, would have been worth it.

Would it? her human-voice asked.

She ignored it, lashing out at the doctor's shuttered windows, which snapped like kindling under her fists.

Much more than a day's journey lay between her and Vevaona now.

Even with the energy she'd drained from Nogadishao, she'd never be able to catch Tujiyazai before she became too weak to stop him.

She screamed again—wrathful, impotent, grief-stricken—tearing at her own clothes. She'd failed. She was going to fade from the world like a bad dream, leaving Geiki and the priests at the mercy of the demon prince.

"Did you do it?" someone called.

A skinny girl, as sharp in the cheekbones as she was in the knees, rode up on a gray horse. Dismounting before Miuko, she tossed her close-cropped hair out of her face. "Did you kill him?"

Miuko stared at her—the girl's arm, like Miuko's, was bleeding from a series of deep cuts.

The summoner.

"*You!*" Miuko leapt at her. *This* was the person who'd wrenched her away from the temple? *This* was the person who'd kept her from the demon prince? "*You* did this?"

Yelping, the girl tried to flee, but Miuko caught her by the back of her robes and flung her to the ground.

"How could you?" Miuko leapt on top of her, clawing at her clothes. "How dare you?"

"He killed my father!" Underneath her, the girl bucked and struggled with a wiry, rabid strength that belied her slender frame. "He was too drunk to see he'd mixed up my father's medication, and he *murdered* him! You were *supposed* to kill him!" She thrashed, almost knocking Miuko off of her.

Miuko shoved her back down. Pulling off a glove with her teeth, she reached for the girl's pointed chin.

STOP! her human-voice cried.

Again, Miuko ignored it. She wanted this. She needed this.

To punish someone. To kill something. To bring it to its swift and fatal conclusion.

But the voice would not be silenced. *You can't! A skinny girl with short hair? A girl on a gray horse? Look up, Miuko! Don't you see? It's*—

Blinking, Miuko glanced up at the girl's dapple gray mare, where several loops of rope hung from the saddle.

"Roroisho?" she whispered.

The horse nodded, although she was not a sentient horse, so she was likely nodding for other reasons, perhaps pertaining to the fly buzzing at her left ear or a persistent crick in her neck.

But it *was* Roroisho—Miuko would have known her anywhere by now. The same horse she and Geiki had ridden inexpertly out of Vevaona; the same horse that, according to Miuko's hurried calculations, would be left there tomorrow morning, when the *atskayakina* would come knocking upon her past-self's door, declaring jubilantly that the innkeeper had given them a horse—

With a cry, the girl kicked Miuko off of her. "If I knew you were going to try and kill *me*, I would've thrown myself into Izajila and saved us both the trouble of summoning you!"

This is Izajila? the little voice murmured as Miuko glanced toward the inlet. *That means*—

Miuko was near the shrine of Beikai, Child of the North Wind, who owed her a favor.

A slow smile spread across Miuko's lips. Perhaps the summoning had not interfered with her plans after all. Perhaps, in fact, it had been instrumental to her success.

If the girl rode to Vevaona now (she could make it on horseback, if she rode hard enough), she could leave Roroisho in the temporary care of Miuko's past-self. Then she could travel on foot to the forests above Koewa to rescue Geiki from the demon hunter, tell him to fly to Ogawa Castle, and collect her horse again. Meanwhile, Miuko could redeem the favor Beikai owed her. The cloud spirit had said they could not carry humans, but Miuko was no longer strictly human, so Beikai should be able to transport her directly to Tujiyazai, wherever he was on the Thousand-Step Way, and there, with the spells she'd collected from Nakatalao's priests, Miuko could stop him once and for all.

It was so perfect, it almost seemed like destiny.

The only problem was, the girl was already leaving. She was already on her feet, dusting off her robes as she staggered toward her horse.

"Wait!" Miuko scrambled after her. "Please, I need your help!"

The girl didn't even look back. "You were the one who was supposed to help me! Go away!"

"Please, I just need you to take your horse to Vevaona and give her to a girl named Otori Miuko—"

The girl let out a curt laugh as she grabbed hold of Roroisho's saddle horn. "Are you kidding? No way."

Panic took hold of Miuko then.

The girl wasn't going to help her.

Without Roroisho, Geiki and Miuko's past-self would be caught by the ghosts on the Ochiirokai or mobbed in Koewa. Geiki would end up captured by the demon hunter, and Miuko would end up dead upon the flagstones of Ogawa Castle.

They wouldn't have a shred of a chance.

She grabbed the girl's shoulder. "Please, wait! If you'd just let me explain—"

With a grunt, the girl jerked out of her grasp.

For a second, Miuko could feel her future disintegrating around her, quick as sand running through her fingers.

All this power? All this opportunity?

It could not be for nothing.

She would not let it be for *nothing*.

From the depths of her memory, Tujiyazai's words arose like smoke: *Older demons than I have made thralls of their summoners when they deemed their hatred unworthy of a kill.*

Miuko had not killed the doctor (though that had been by accident more than by design), and that meant she didn't have to *ask* for the girl's help.

She could take it.

Don't, her human-voice whispered.

Miuko scowled. The girl wasn't giving her a choice, was she? She *had* to do this. She had to save Geiki. And the priests.

And herself.

The same instinct that had told her she had to kill the doctor now told her how to take a thrall. Almost unconsciously, she lifted her exposed hand to the girl's breastbone, over her heart.

The girl's breath caught in her throat. Her pupils expanded.

Between Miuko's fingers, there was a sizzling sound, like ice dancing upon a stove. The girl cried out, stumbling backward and clutching her chest.

And it was done.

The girl straightened, her gray eyes as dull as any of Sidrisine's thralls. For all that her sharp and slender features had not changed, she did not even look like the same girl anymore, Miuko thought, but like a doll, to be clothed and posed as her owner saw fit.

What have we done? whispered the little voice inside her.

Miuko swallowed, trying to ignore the guilt pooling in her belly. Quietly, she explained what the girl was to do next: ride to Vevaona, leave the horse at the guesthouse for Otori Miuko, rescue a boy in the forests above Koewa, and tell him to fly immediately to Ogawa Castle. After that, she would be released from her thrall and could do as she pleased.

Duly, the girl climbed onto Roroisho's back.

"It'll only be a few days," Miuko said, more to reassure herself than the girl, who had shown no reaction to her orders at all, "and then you'll be free again."

Again? her human-voice whispered.

What she'd done hit her then, as it had not before, making her insides slick with nausea. She'd taken the girl's *freedom*. She'd stripped her of her choices, the way Miuko, too, had been stripped of her choices every day of her life.

To speak as she wanted. To go where she wanted. To *be* what she wanted.

Gone.

Miuko had been a girl of Awara for seventeen years, and it had only taken three days as a demon for her to bend another person to her will. It hadn't even been that hard—the power had been there, and she'd used it.

All she'd had to do was not question herself.

Silently, the girl turned Roroisho northward, toward Vevaona.

"Wait!" Miuko cried.

At her command, the girl stopped.

Reaching up, Miuko tried to take it back. She pressed her fingers to the girl's chest, trying to send her free will pouring back into her body like water coursing from a spring. She pushed harder, ordering herself to make it happen.

It didn't.

Miuko had taken something from her, something vital and precious, and even though it would be returned again in a matter of days, Miuko never should have taken it in the first place. She'd made a mistake, and some mistakes could not be unmade.

Some choices, one could never come back from.

Defeated, Miuko let her hand fall to her side. "What's your name?" she asked softly.

The girl's response was toneless, bereft of the spark that had infused it mere moments before: "Kanayi."

"I'm so sorry, Kanayi."

But Kanayi did not reply, and after a moment, they parted ways in silence.

10

THE FAVOR

ONCE THE ENERGY Miuko had drained from Nogadishao had dissipated, she was left feeling fainter than ever. On the way north to Beikai's shrine, the weakness in her fading limbs forced her to stop several times beside the road, where she felt herself seeping slowly into the moss like spilled blood.

At this pace, it wasn't until sunset that she arrived at the shrine, stumbling up the steps to Beikai's stone idol, where she collapsed, accidentally knocking several offerings from the altar. Lacking the strength (or the will) to replace them, she touched her forehead to the cool floor of the shrine.

"Beikai-jai, it is I, Otori Miuko," she prayed. "You owe me a favor. I have come to collect."

The idol did not answer.

The sun disappeared into the water.

There, among the gifts of wine and coins and paper, Miuko fell into an exhausted slumber from which she did not awaken until much later, when a blast of icy wind blew her robes up to her thighs.

She bolted upright with a cry, jerking her tattered garments back into place.

The night sky was overcast, and beneath the clouds, Beikai, Child of the North Wind, stood before the shrine, radiant in their gauzy white robes.

"You look different," they said, cocking their head at her. "Is that a new sash?"

Miuko glanced down, remembering the vermillion wrap she'd stolen from Nakatalao's head priest. She'd almost forgotten—she had to get it to the priests at the House of December before Tujiyazai came for them.

The spirit pursed their lips. "No, that's not it. You've been transported from your true place in time, haven't you?"

How does everyone keep guessing that? her human-voice wondered.

Beikai snapped their fingers, drawing Miuko's attention. "Well, what do you want? I'm a busy spirit, you know. I don't have time to dilly-dally with *shaohasu*."

Not wanting to irritate the cloud spirit any more than she already had, Miuko explained her request in a hurry: "I need transportation to the House of December, so I can tell the priests to make sashes like these, and then to Tujiyazai—"

"Tujiyazai?" the cloud spirit interrupted. "I thought he was a legend."

"He's very real, and very dangerous, and I need to stop him."

"Can you, though?" Beikai squinted at her. "Stop him?"

Miuko clutched both bamboo cylinders in her fist. "I have to. The priests made these spells especially for me. I'm the only one who can use them."

"Tch." The cloud spirit flicked their fingers at Miuko's body, nearly transparent in the dim light. "You'll be half gone by morning, *shaoha*. With the kind of shape you're in, you haven't got the stuff to defeat a demon as powerful as Tujiyazai."

"That's why we have to go *now*. The longer I wait, the weaker I'll get."

"So don't wait. Leap forward to where you belong. You'll be strong enough in your own time to destroy whomever you please."

We don't want to destroy—the little voice began, but before it could continue, Miuko rushed eagerly at Beikai, barely stopping short of clasping the cloud spirit's softly glowing hands. "Can you do that? Take me forward through time?"

"Not at all."

"Then how?"

"You need Afaina, the God of Stars. He's the only one that can help you now."

"Can you take me to *him*, then?"

Beikai crossed their arms. "I could, but I only owe you one favor, *shaoha*. I can take your sash and warn your priests, or I can take you to Afaina, but I won't do both."

Miuko bared her teeth at the spirit. "But that's not fair!"

"Fair?" They straightened, and for a second, they seemed much taller than their old wrinkled form would suggest. "I am a *cloud spirit*. You are a *demon*. I decide what's fair, and *you* deal with it."

For an instant, Miuko was overcome with the sudden urge to wrap her hands around Beikai's shriveled neck, but the faintness in her spectral limbs told her such an assault would be ill-advised. If she was too weak to fight Tujiyazai, she would certainly fare poorly against a demigod. In lieu of an attack, she settled for a good, old-fashioned glower, but this was neither an effective threat or a persuasive argument, so nothing happened.

Miuko bit her lip.

The decision seemed obvious. She had a handful of hours, at most, before she became little more than a phantom, at half her strength and fading by the second. A few days after that, and she'd be almost entirely translucent, stranded in the wrong time and too weak to reach the God's Teeth before she dissolved into nothingness.

She *had* to ask the cloud spirit to take her to Afaina, who would transport her to the dock eight days hence. Then she would use the spells to exorcise Tujiyazai from the *doro*'s body and bind him inside one of the salt-eaten pilings . . . or a fishing float . . . or a worm. The demon would be defeated, Geiki and the priests would be saved, and they would have no need for the vermillion sashes at all.

Except . . . her human-voice began. *Even if Beikai takes us to Afaina, there's no guarantee he'll help us.* She could spend her final days marooned in some distant corner of Ana without any way of returning to help her friends, now or in the future.

Geiki.

Meli.

Hikedo.

No, she had to protect them now, while she still could.

With a certainty she did not quite feel, Miuko removed the red wrap and extended it to Beikai. "Please warn the priests at the House of December that they will need more of these in eight days, when Tujiyazai will arrive on their shores."

"Huh," the spirit said. "You surprise me, *shaoha*. At my age, that isn't easy to do." Taking the sash, Beikai swept their arms wide. Mist rose from the inlet, purling over the cliffside and across the floor of the shrine, where it swirled up their human form, obscuring them completely.

Miuko bowed. "Thank you."

The fog buffeted about her, as if in annoyance, before ascending into the sky, taking Beikai with it. A dusting of raindrops spattered Miuko's upturned face as she watched the spirit sail northward.

Surprised, she touched her cheeks, dampening her gloved fingertips. The last time she'd been on the Thousand-Step Way, the skies had been perfectly clear, without even the slightest chance of rain.

Now, with Beikai heading north, there were showers in the forecast.

Miuko allowed herself a small grin. She didn't know how she was going to locate Afaina before her time ran out. She didn't know if she'd ever make it back to the future. But at this moment, she could not help wondering if the despair spirit had been wrong after all. Maybe she *could* change things.

All it took was a favor from a demigod.

11

BAIGANASU

SIGHING, MIUKO EXAMINED her gloved hands, transparent enough now that she could almost read the inscriptions on Beikai's altar through her palms. The cloud spirit had been right—she was in no position to defeat Tujiyazai. Given the state of her phantom body, she didn't even think she was strong enough for the trek back to the Ochiirokai, which left her only one option: she had to find Afaina.

The only problem was, she hadn't the faintest idea how to do that. With a moan, she slumped against the back of Beikai's idol, sliding to the floor with her head in her hands, as if that would make her think more clearly.

Unfortunately, she was prevented from forming a single coherent thought by a burst of commotion at the front of the shrine. Peering around the statue, she watched, openmouthed, as a troupe of monkeys cavorted out of the trees. Dressed in short red robes, they ambled up the steps of the shrine, where they immediately seized upon the gifts left at the cloud spirit's altar.

"Look, look!" one cried, donning a paper chain as if it were a crown. Then, stuffing a stale rice ball into her mouth: "Old Grouch leaves us a feast this time!"

Miuko gasped. These were *baiganasu*, monkey spirits, like the ones she'd seen in Sidrisine's gambling parlor. They'd said there was another troupe near Izajila, hadn't they? Perhaps this was that troupe. Hooting, they rummaged through Beikai's offerings, testing coins with their teeth and slurping at half-rotten peaches, spitting the pits onto the ground.

Her mother had warned her about *baiganasu*. Although monkey spirits were often said to lead lost travelers to safety, they, like *atskayakinasu*, were also tricksters, and Miuko could recall several tales where men, stranded in the wilderness, had followed *baigavasu*—or "monkey lights"—off of cliffs or into the dens of hibernating bears. To prevent such mishaps from occurring too frequently, humans often left gifts for *baiganasu* at the borders of the wilds or roadside altars, where the monkey spirits could collect them by careening past on their magical sled, skimming hither and yon over the landscape in a rush of wind.

While she was lost in thought, a small *baigana*, nose-to-stubby-tail no longer than her forearm, peered over the statue. His little eyes widened as he shrieked, "Ah, ah!"

Immediately, the *baigana* in the paper crown was at his side. Gathering him to her chest, she pointed at Miuko. "You're not Old Grouch!"

"Old Grouch?" Miuko scrambled to her feet. "Do you mean Beikai? No, I'm—"

A moldy orange struck her, followed by a flurry of incense ashes, which drifted about her like snow.

"Hey!"

"You're a *shaoha*!" Screaming, the monkey spirit flung a bottle of wine in Miuko's direction. "Demon Lady! Demon Lady!"

She caught it with her demon-reflexes, smashing it over the altar in a spray of liquor and glass. "My *name* is Miuko!"

The *baigana* bared her teeth in what was either a threat of violence or a mocking smile. "My *name* is Miuko!" she screeched. Then, taking up another bottle, she smashed it upon the steps.

Whooping, a second *baigana* drew a short sword from a scabbard he wore on his belt. "My *name* is Miuko!" he cried.

"Stop copying me!" Miuko snapped, which naturally prompted a loud chorus of "Stop copying me! Stop copying me!" as the *baiganasu* danced around her, wagging their bottoms.

She ground her teeth, fighting the urge to grab them by their stringy little necks and squeeze them until their eyes popped from their skulls.

But she couldn't do that.

Not after Nogadishao. Not after Kanayi.

Seeing that she refused to fight back and was therefore of little entertainment value, the monkey spirits slowed. A few of them jabbered in what Miuko suspected was disappointment. "Why you don't fight us?" asked the one in the paper crown.

"Do you *want* me to fight you?"

"No, no. Not really."

"Great."

The *baigana* seemed to consider this, tugging thoughtfully at her chin fur. "What you're here for then?"

"I'm stuck." Miuko shrugged, feeling the faintness of her ghostly form. "A few days ago, I ended up in the past, but I need to get back to my own time to stop a demon and save my friends, except I need Afaina for that, and Beikai wouldn't take me to him."

"Old Grouch!" The *baigana* with the sword sheathed it with a *clack*.

Miuko managed a smile. "Yeah, I guess they are a grouch, aren't they?"

"Old Grouch!" The other monkey spirits booed. "Old Grouch!"

The one in the paper crown nodded. "Yeah, yeah. When our sled gets stuck under the tree, we say, 'Can you help us, Old Grouch?' But they say, 'No, no, I can't be *bothered* with common *baiganasu*.' Now we scavenge in Old Grouch's leftovers, or else we get no offerings, and so we die." Squinting, she eyed Miuko appraisingly. "But maybe you help us, Demon Lady? And then we help you?"

Miuko sighed. "I'd love to help, but I don't see how—"

"You need go somewhere, yes? Neinei"—here the monkey spirit gestured to herself—"and her *baiganasu* have sled. You free sled, and we take you where you want to go."

A flutter of hope appeared in Miuko's chest. "You can take me to Afaina?"

"Afaina?" Neinei chortled. "No, no. Who knows where the God of Stars lives? Not *baiganasu*. Instead, we take you to Kuludrava Palace,[1] yes?"

Miuko frowned. Kuludrava Palace was an ice court, home to Naisholao,[2] the January God. By all accounts, it was located somewhere deep in the northern heart of Ana, where the mountains rose black and jagged as a series of spear points. "Why would you take me there?"

"What? You don't know?"

"No?"

"Big trouble comes to the House of November, yes? It makes an *oyu*, yes? It's very sad. Nakatalao runs away, and no one can find him at all."

Miuko sucked in a breath. The November God had vanished? It was unheard of. She hadn't even known it was possible.

Then again, she hadn't known it was possible to befriend a magpie spirit or summon herself to the past or any number of heretofore unimaginable happenings that had most certainly happened, so perhaps the concepts of "possible" and "impossible" were hazier than she'd assumed.

"You don't know?" Neinei repeated.

---

1 **Kulu-drava** (*koo-loo-drah-vah*): literally, "dancing crystal."

2 **Na-isho-lao** (*nah-ee-shoh-laoh*): literally, "spirit-snow-attendant." After the creation of Rayudana, the Summer King, it is said that Amyunasa formed from the primordial waters the Five Divine Mysteries, deities of the cold months; and first among these were Naisholao and Nakatalao, twins of January and November, who were brought into existence at the very same time—one by Amyunasa's left hand and one by their right. Thought to be closest among all the Lunar Gods, they are said to share a special connection, which explains why Nakatalao's disappearance may have been particularly troubling to his sister Naisholao.

"No," Miuko murmured. "I didn't."

"Everyone knows. Naisholao calls an emergency council. Many gods go to the palace to see what can be done."

"Including Afaina?"

"No, no, Afaina is far away, okay? He likes nobody. He sees nobody. *Other* gods go to Kuludrava Palace, and you ask *them* to take you to Afaina, yes?"

Miuko blinked. "Oh, yes! Please! Only . . ." She flexed her spectral hands. "You said your sled was stuck under a tree? I don't know if I'm strong enough to—"

"Yes, yes," Neinei interrupted. "You're very weak. We know."

"Yeah, thanks, and the only way I'll get stronger is if I return to my own time, and that won't happen without Afaina."

"No, no, not the *only* way." Solemnly—so solemnly, in fact, that Miuko, who had already grown accustomed to the *baiganasu*'s animated mannerisms, was more than a little unnerved—Neinei extended her forepaw, fingers looking almost human in the low light. "You need to eat, yes?"

12

SLEIGH RIDE

"WHAT?" MIUKO BACKED into the statue of Beikai, knocking her head against the hard stone. "I can't eat you!"

"No, no, not all of me." Neinei flicked her fingers distastefully. "Just some of me. You eat some, you get stronger, yes? You free the sled, and we are all happy."

"You eat Yoibaba too!" declared the one with the short sword.

"Yes, yes!" The littlest *baigana* did a flip. "Me too!"

Neinei smacked him away. "No, no, not you."

Eagerly, the other monkey spirits began prancing around Miuko, offering up their furred hands as if they were children begging for sweets.

She licked her lips, feeling herself salivating at the thought of their ripe little lives draining into her, just a sip from each of them, like a sampling of different teas.

Gently, Neinei took one of Miuko's gloved hands. "We want this, yes? We know the risk. We still choose it."

"I don't want to hurt you," Miuko whispered.

"It's not hurt if it's gift. We help you, you help us. That's how it works, yes? Everyone needs everyone, and no one gets what they want alone."

Miuko felt the other *baiganasu* frolicking around her, brushing against her with their small furry bodies and filling her senses with their pungent furry smells, and she could not help but smile at their antics. "Okay," she said.

Cheering, they gamboled out of the shrine, leaving Miuko to trail after them.

"Keep up, Demon Lady!" Neinei scolded her.

"I'm trying!" Ducking into the undergrowth, Miuko followed them into the woods. After Beikai's recent showers, the air smelled earthy and the ground was spongy underfoot. In the darkness, a few of the monkey spirits conjured *baigavasu* to light their way, the glowing orbs bobbing eerily through the trees.

Gradually, they made their way deeper into the forest, where the trees towered over them, some thicker in circumference than the entire troupe lined up nose-to-tail. At the sight of them, Miuko's stomach twisted. "I don't know if I can do this," she said to Neinei, who was padding alongside her with the littlest *baigana* dozing on her back.

"So?" replied the spirit. "Who has to know? Not you. You only have to do."

Miuko did not know how to argue with that logic, and so she remained silent.

Her misgivings resurfaced, however, at the sight of the trapped sled. Constructed of warm, faintly glowing wood, it was pinned beside a large boulder; which had, by accident or by design, prevented it from being smashed to bits when a tree had come down on top of it. Unfortunately, the tree, while not the largest in the forest, still had enough girth to make Miuko imagine several graceless ways in which she might be crushed to death beneath it.

"Okay, okay," Neinei said, pointing. "Time to work, Demon Lady."

Swallowing her nervousness, Miuko slid off one of her gloves. One by one, all but the baby *baigana* filed by her, touching their fingers to her bare palm. Their energy flowed into her, so brilliant and tart it brought tears to her eyes. She bit her lip, fighting the urge to grab hold of the spirits, to suck the life from them as she would a bushel of kumquats.

Finally, the last of the *baiganasu* lurched away from her, gray in the face. Miuko glanced down—her hands were more opaque now, more solid. She flexed them, feeling energy coursing through her veins again.

Neinei, who looked a little peaked, shooed Miuko toward the boulder. "Hurry, hurry!"

Obediently, Miuko tugged on her glove again and vaulted onto the stone while Neinei organized the weary-looking troupe into various positions around the sled, where they would be ready to pull it loose once the tree was lifted.

Miuko crouched beside the trunk, digging her hands into its rough bark. "Ready?" she called.

The monkey spirits tightened their grip on the sleigh.

"Heave!" Neinei cried.

Grunting, Miuko hauled on the tree, legs straining, back tightening, arms pulling. The branches trembled. Bits of dried moss crumbled under her fingers.

"Heave! Heave! Heave! Heave!" the *baiganasu* chanted.

A crack of light appeared beneath the trunk.

"Now!" Miuko shouted.

Screeching, the monkey spirits yanked the sled out from under the tree a split second before Miuko's arms failed her. The enormous trunk slid out of her hands, striking the boulder with a crash that shook the entire forest.

The *baiganasu* cheered as she collapsed against the fallen tree, her limbs aching with the effort. "Demon Lady! Demon Lady!"

Scrambling into the sleigh, Neinei removed the seat back, which had been jammed in place by the weight of the tree, and withdrew from behind it a smooth, bone-white whistle, which she quickly checked for damage. "Yes, yes." She chuckled. "Fine, fine."

Squeaking, the littlest *baigana* plugged his ears.

The others quickly followed suit.

Belatedly, Miuko was about to do the same when Neinei lifted the whistle to her lips and blew.

The sound that emerged from it was enormous. No, it was *gargantuan*. It reverberated through the woods in an ugly, guttural roar, causing dry pine needles to drop from the canopy in a sudden, mildly painful shower.

Miuko cried out, clapping her hands to the sides of her head, but she was too late. The bellowing of the whistle was already fading.

For a moment, all was still.

"What was that?" She dismounted from the boulder, landing beside the sled. "A little warning would have been—"

"Demon Lady," the baby *baigana* interrupted her. "Watch out for the boars."

"The boars?"

"The boars!" Clapping gleefully, he pointed to the woods behind her, where a pair of giant, glowing boars in jingling tack were charging pell-mell out of the forest.

Miuko yelped, leaping aside just in time to avoid being trampled.

The colossal swine, nearly as tall as Miuko herself, skidded to a stop in front of Neinei, who patted their mustachioed snouts fondly.

"What do you have boars for?" Miuko asked.

The *baigana* clicked her tongue, as if the answer should be obvious. "Who you think pulls the sled?"

"I thought it was a magical sled!"

"Yes, yes, pulled by magical boars." She gestured to the rest of her troupe, who quickly yoked the animals to the sleigh. "To Kuludrava Palace now, yes?"

Still a bit mystified, Miuko laughed. "Yes!" She climbed into the back of the sled, where the monkey spirits crowded around her, hugging her legs and clinging to her arms.

With a screech, Neinei flicked the reins.

The boars lurched forward, jerking the sled so hard Miuko was thrown backward, colliding with the monkey spirits, who squealed with delight and shoved her back into her seat.

And they were off—helter-skelter through the trees, with Neinei and Yoibaba yanking at the reins while the rest of the *baiganasu* careened from one end of the sled to the other at every twist and turn.

Miuko laughed. When she'd flown with Geiki, they'd crested mountains. They'd touched clouds and breathed starlight. But they'd ultimately been removed from Ada and its riotous, unruly nature. Now, however, she felt wholly a part of the world—equally riotous, equally unruly—as the sled crashed over the hills, scraping against rocks and ridges, splashing through streams, picking up speed with every mile. They zigzagged wildly across the landscape, howling as they passed mountains, cities, shores, a surprised cormorant fisherman, a herd of water buffalo, a hundred dyed bolts of cloth drying in the breeze.

Before she knew it, dawn came, and then night, and when the sun rose again, the world had changed. They sped through forests that moved like armies, past mountains with spirits drumming upon their peaks, over seas as clear as crystal, with palaces sparkling below the waves.

Abruptly, they hurtled downward, diving into a deep cavern starred with luminescence, where Miuko temporarily locked gazes with a tall demon queen, her dark hair cut short across her forehead, before the sled whisked Miuko upward again.

Clinging to the rail, she joined the *baiganasu's* screeches of delight. Ana was nothing like she had ever seen! More than that, it was like nothing she'd even dared to dream. She could not help but think of her mother and how much she would have loved it, how she would have devoured every sight, every sound, every phantasmagoric scent wafting up from the volcanic fissures and meadows of drunken, chittering flowers.

Gradually, the boars slowed to a trot, towing the sled across a vast field of ice, which filled a valley that by Miuko's reckoning had to measure at least fifty miles across. Atop the ridges, black spurs of stone jutted toward a sky ribboned with light, rippling and swaying in curtains of every color imaginable: petal and coral and sea anemone, fern and powder and dawn.

Neinei pointed. After their sleigh ride through Ada and Ana, the *baigana* seemed to have regained some of her vigor, her cheeks a healthy red. "Kuludrava!" she shouted.

Built on top of the glacier, the January God's court was a castle of scalloped ice so clear and blue, it appeared like crystal. Aquamarine walls soared upward like chipped glass, with icy waterfalls cascading from ledge to ledge, forming curtained alcoves among the towers and rooftops.

As the boars slid to a stop in front of the palace, the sled skidded across the ice, slamming sideways into the wall. Cheering, the *baiganasu* tumbled onto the glacier floor, where they bowed, like magicians after a particularly impressive trick.

Miuko clapped, which caused them to bow again, this time with additional flourishes. "Thank you!" she said, climbing from the sled. Since they'd left Beikai's shrine, her body had become more than half transparent, making her appear like a ghost at the edge of the snowfield.

Another few days, and she'd disappear entirely.

She inhaled deeply, staring up at the slick walls.

Don't worry, Geiki, her human-voice whispered. *We're coming for you.*

13

THE KULUDRAVA PALACE

BEYOND THE GATES lay an enormous courtyard garden, dotted with boulders and trees made of ice, among which a number of spirits had already convened: fox spirits, flower spirits (wilting pitifully in the cold), bog spirits, little spirits of the hearth with bodies of glowing coal. As far as she could tell, she was the only demon present.

And the only mortal, her human-voice chimed in.

Quickly she surveyed the castle, which towered above her in seven tiers of powder blue ice carved with exquisite facades—balconies, columns, dragon-faced downspouts—with silvery lights glimmering from the eaves like hundreds of captured stars. The sheer height of it made Miuko's head spin.

"What you wait for, Demon Lady?" Neinei asked, tugging at her robes. "You find transportation to Afaina now, yes?"

"Yes, yes!" The other *baiganasu* swarmed around her, hopping up and down. "Demon Lady! Demon Lady!"

"Shh!" Miuko hissed, with a nervous glance at the other spirits. She didn't know how they would react to a demon in their midst, but she was certain she did not want to find out. "Do you have to call me that?"

They chortled. Scrambling up to her shoulder, the littlest monkey spirit pawed at her hair. "Demon Lady," he whispered.

She stroked the top of his head fondly. "It doesn't look like any of these spirits are powerful enough to know where Afaina lives," she observed. "Where are the higher spirits?"

"Up, up, up, up," jabbered Yoibaba, pointing toward a flight of stairs flanked by a pair of crab spirits clad in red, spiny armor.

Miuko glared at Neinei. "You didn't tell me there'd be guards!"

The *baigana* shrugged. "What you think? They just let anyone go see the gods?"

"How am I supposed to get past them? I'm not exactly inconspicuous here."

Yoibaba cackled. "Neither are we!" With that, he and a couple of the others darted into the crowd. Moments later, across the courtyard, there was a shriek, causing several of the spirits to flurry about in dismay.

The guards at the steps moved to investigate.

"Okay, okay, we go!" Neinei declared.

Miuko did not have to be told twice. Lowering her chin and arranging her hair about her face, she entered the crowd, trying not to step on any toes or roots as she moved quickly toward the steps. All about her, she could hear the other spirits whispering about the *oyu* at the House of November and the disappearance of Nakatalao. Naisholao and the other gods were gathered in the topmost tier now, they said, conferring about how to locate their missing brother.

But Miuko had never been very good at blending in, and as she wove through the garden, the *nasu* began to take notice. Some of them merely looked at her curiously, as if they had not seen her like before, but others must have recognized her, for they were clearly frightened. A mouse spirit squeaked and fled to a corner. The fox spirits chittered and snapped. A *tachanagri* with deep green skin creaked and transformed into a tree, petrified except for the trembling of its leaves.

"*Yagra,*" someone muttered.

"What is *she* doing here?"

Face burning, Miuko bowed her head. In that moment, she could not help but miss Geiki. The *atskayakina* would have been yammering about the red nose of that grief spirit or the stink of that swamp spirit, anything to ease her mind.

But she'd left him behind, and her only way back to him was forward. And upward.

With the crab guards still busy at the other end of the garden, she climbed the slippery flight of steps while several of the *baiganasu* cavorted around her, screeching (as quietly as they could) with unparalleled delight.

The second floor was filled with more powerful spirits: fire spirits, meadow spirits, spirits of icebergs with crystals continually forming and melting on their white cheeks. They reacted with distaste as the monkey spirits skipped among them, upsetting tables and overturning chairs.

"Ah," Miuko said, "so each floor has more and more powerful spirits, with the gods at the very top, is that it?"

Neinei nodded. "Now you get it."

Picking up her robes, Miuko hurried through the throng, ignoring the hissed complaints and warding signs made by the spirits as she passed. Gripping her hair, the littlest *baigana* made faces at them, baring his teeth and wagging his tongue.

She had made it to the center of the floor when she was halted by a low, burbling voice: "Er . . . *shaoha*-jai, pardon me, but you are not allowed here."

Irritably, she turned to find a slick green frog spirit standing at her elbow. He was dressed in servants' robes, with the knot of a head servant at his waist. Behind him, the other spirits clustered nearby, watching like marketgoers eager for a public scandal.

"I'm afraid your *baiganasu* companions must return to the first floor," he continued apologetically, "and you, unfortunately, must leave the premises altogether, for demons are not permitted in the court of Naisholao."

Ignoring him, Miuko eyed the steps and considered making a run for it. But with the crowd closing in around her, she doubted she'd make it far.

"Just get rid of her already!" one of the fire spirits snapped.

"So . . . er . . ." The frog spirit's throat bulged uneasily. "Yes . . . I regret to inform you, *shaoha*-jai, that you must depart immediately."

Miuko considered him for a moment. He was a stuffy little creature, half her size. Even in her weakened state, she might have been able to fight him off, particularly if she siphoned some of his life force first.

Fortunately, she didn't have to, for Yoibaba appeared at her side again. With a sharp cry, he drew back his sheathed sword and struck the frog spirit in his narrow green shins. "YAH! Go, Demon Lady! Go!"

Seizing the opportunity, she swept past the frog spirit with the *baiganasu* at her heels.

"Guards!" the frog spirit croaked from behind her. "Guards!"

As Miuko and the other spirits made for the stairs, more crab soldiers in spiny armor came running toward her, bearing lances like forked claws. Yelping, the monkey spirits clambered over them, pinching their long mustaches and pulling at their antennae.

Panting, Miuko dashed past the spirits to the third floor, followed by an intrepid snow spirit and the *tachanagri* she had frightened in the garden. Together, they erupted from the stairwell into a mass of airy wind spirits and whiskered dragons and lake spirits with robes of rippling water, and were running for the next flight of steps when a voice like the creaking of an ancient forest echoed through the palace: *"SHAOHA!"*

Miuko skidded to a halt on the icy floor. She knew that voice.

She looked around, eagerly searching for the forest spirit she'd thought she'd lost at the House of November, and found him galloping through the throng like a spider, his beard flying comically about his face.

She ran toward him, laughing with relief. "Nogadishao! I'm so glad to see—"

But he did not smile, and he did not slow down. Before she realized what was happening, he was towering over her, roaring, and lashing out at her with three of his hard, bark-skinned hands.

14

WRATH OF THE FOREST

THE LITTLEST *BAIGANA* squeaked as Miuko twisted sideways, sheltering him from Nogadishao's claws. The forest spirit's thorny fingers tore across her arm—or at least they would have, if they hadn't passed through her as if she were little more than a shadow. For the first time since she began fading from the world, Miuko counted herself lucky for it.

"What are you doing?" she cried, lifting the baby monkey spirit from her shoulder and depositing him in Neinei's arms. "It's me!"

"*You* killed them!" Nogadishao wailed. With a start, Miuko realized he was crying, large dribbles of sap flowing down his craggy features and congealing in his beard. "You murderer! You scum! You foul, stone-hearted *vakaizu*—"

Miuko dove aside as he scuttled toward her, swinging his arms. "What are you talking about? I tried to stop it! I tried to stop *him*, remember? Tujiya—"

"LIAR!" Catching her across the chest, the *daigana* flung her into the crowd of *nasu*, who dropped her unceremoniously.

As she struck the icy floor, the armored guards closed in with their forked lances, poking and prodding at her like crabs fighting over a dead fish. Rolling out of their reach, Miuko scrambled to her feet again in search of an escape.

But a contingent of crab guardians had already blocked the stairs, and more were marching toward her through the crowd.

There was no way out.

Nogadishao charged her again, ignoring the *baiganasu*, who tore at his beard and eyebrows. From atop his head, Yoibaba gestured with his short sword. "Out the window, Demon Lady!"

Miuko reacted without thinking. She ran—the spirits scattering around her like minnows fleeing before a heron—and, reaching the window, shimmied onto the rooftops.

Outside, the wind whipped by her, lashing at her hair and clothing as she clung to the window ledge. Though the walls were steep and made of ice, they were also pitted with windows and viewing galleries, verandas and arches and slanting roofs.

She could make it.

If her spectral body did not fail her.

She did not have time to waver, however, because a moment later Nogadishao—with a few of the monkey spirits still clinging to him—came crashing through the wall beside her, shattering the ice into chunks that fell to the glacier floor in large misshapen heaps.

"You told me you were an emissary from the future!" the *daigana* cried, swiping at her. "You said you needed my help!"

"I did!" Miuko leapt out of his way, grabbing a fourth floor balcony and hauling herself up. "I just didn't think you'd help me if I told you the truth!"

"What's the truth? You saw a feral old *daigana* and thought you'd take advantage of him? You promised him importance? You promised him greatness? You knew he'd do anything for that, eh?"

Miuko wanted to stop, then, for she knew he was right. She'd lied to him. She'd manipulated him. She'd exploited his weaknesses the way Tujiyazai had once exploited hers. It had seemed harmless at the time—nothing more than a little trick, like Geiki might have pulled—but hearing him now, she understood that it had not been harmless at all.

Abandoning their ineffectual assault on Nogadishao, the *baiganasu* clambered around her, pointing at handholds, ledges, fissures in the ice. "Go, go!" they cried. "Go!"

"I'm sorry, Nogadishao!" she shouted. "I'm so sorry!" With the forest spirit scrabbling at her heels, she began to scale the palace walls—past the fourth floor and swinging through a window into the fifth, where she slipped past mountain spirits, sea spirits, even a star spirit, come down from their place in the heavens, and back out through a covered balcony, where she scrambled along a decorative cornice and began climbing again.

But she was weakening. The higher she climbed, the faster she felt her strength draining from her ghostly limbs, making her fumble.

Behind her, chaos reigned. Cries of alarm went up among the higher spirits as Nogadishao lunged after her, screaming, "I listened to you, *shaoha*! I believed in you! I *vouched* for you! And you betrayed me!"

Miuko flinched as each word cut her, true as any blade. She fumbled, her strength slipping, as she pulled herself around a corner, clinging desperately to the wall as the wind tore at her fading body.

Yoibaba, the only *baigana* still keeping pace with her, jabbed his short sword upward. "Don't stop, Demon Lady! Almost there!"

She smiled at him weakly and continued to climb.

Through the windows, she spied the other monkey spirits wreaking havoc as they bounced from railing to ceiling, off the heads of more powerful *nasu* and back outside again, following in the *daigana*'s wake. More than that, other spirits were ascending through the palace now too—the tree goblin Miuko had startled on the first floor, the snow spirit that had raced up the steps from the second, a fire spirit with sparks for hair, and even a dragon, iridescent beneath the aurorean skies.

She was nearly at the seventh floor when Nogadishao ripped out a chunk of wall and hurled it at her, narrowly missing the side of her head. "Liar! Traitor!" he shouted. "Scum!"

Miuko gasped as a shard of ice cut her cheek. Her weakened fingers slipped.

"Use this, Demon Lady!" Perched upon a ledge, Yoibaba jammed his sword into the ice.

She grabbed the hilt, grunting, as Nogadishao leapt for her from below. With a shriek, Yoibaba dove into the safety of a sixth-story window, narrowly avoiding being knocked from the wall by the *daigana*'s bulk.

In one last burst of energy, Miuko hauled herself upward with trembling arms, tumbling headfirst onto the top floor veranda, where she was thrust across the ice by the forest spirit, who emerged, roaring, from the night air.

She scarcely had the chance to survey her surroundings—a vaulted hall, several figures arrayed on thrones of obsidian—before twin bolts of light, each glimmering like the winter skies outside, shot across the chamber: one for her and one for Nogadishao.

No! her human-voice cried.

Was she strong enough to take it? Was she solid enough?

She did not know, but she knew she could not let Nogadishao be hurt again, not on her account. She launched herself in front of him, catching the attack squarely in the chest. It seared through her, bitterly cold, and she dropped to the floor again, tears frosting on her fading cheeks.

As she lay there, stunned, someone swept by her in thick white robes that could have been the richest fur or the deepest snow. The figure took one look out the balcony and whirled back to Miuko and Nogadishao, glaring at them with eyes as small and red as winter berries. "What have you done to my palace?"

Miuko groaned, hoping she had faded enough now to disappear into the floor; for standing over her was Naisholao, the God of January and Queen of Kuludrava Palace.

15

OH, GODS

IF MIUKO HAD NOT already been shocked senseless by the sight of the January God, she almost certainly would have fainted when she got a good look at the rest of the chamber. There was Naisholao, of course, but also Tskadakrikana,[1] the February God, a tall female spirit with crimson feathers for eyelashes; Cheiyuchura,[2] the April God, whose exposed skin was covered with flowers in perpetual cycles of blooming and dying—morning glories, chrysanthemums, lotuses, azaleas, honeysuckle, and more that Miuko could not name; and lastly, Satskevaidakanai,[3] the September God, his old man form nothing but water and thundercloud, with lightning flickering in his twisting hair and beard. There were more obsidian thrones in evidence—perhaps the other gods had yet to arrive at Naisholao's council—but the presence of four Lunar Gods was more than enough for Miuko's poor befuddled mind to contend with.

Meanwhile, her human-voice was, rightfully, panicking. *What are we doing? That's a god! Those are gods! Oh, gods. We should be bowing! Groveling? No, bowing. Don't just lie there, Miuko! We have to do something!*

"Shut up," she muttered.

---

1 **Tskada-krika-na** (*tskah-dah-kree-kah-nah*): literally, "awakening-thaw-spirit."

2 **Chei-yu-chu-ra** (*chay-yoo-choo-rah*): literally, "tea-life-young-love."

3 **Satske-vai-da-kanai** (*sah-tskeh-vye-dah-kah-nye*): literally, "destructive-sky-physical-lord," or simply, "Lord Typhoon."

Above her, Naisholao's plump cheeks flushed a furious pink. "Excuse me?"

"Sorry!" Miuko groaned, rolling over until she was prostrate upon the floor. Through her ghostly limbs, she could see, within the ice, swirling bands of soot and sediment from some ancient age, frozen there for eons like a merle of blackbirds in mid-flight. "I didn't mean you, Naisholao-kanai! I was just—"

Talking to yourself, the little voice finished for her.

"Shh!"

"Crazy demon," Satskevaidakanai grumbled in a voice like the rolling of thunder.

"I'm not crazy, my lord," Miuko protested. "My name is Otori Miuko, and I've come to—"

Before she could ask for their help, however, Nogadishao lunged past her, grabbing at Naisholao's fluffy robes with his gnarled fingers. "Don't trust her, my lieges! She lies!"

Miuko made a face she was glad no one could see. *Crazy. Untrustworthy.* What were they going to call her next? *Too emotional?* It seemed that being a demon in the spirit world was akin to being a woman in Awara.

The gods recoiled from the forest spirit as he leapt at them, flakes of bark molting from his chest and taloned hands.

"She said we'd save them!" he cried. "She said we'd stop it! She *promised!* You must punish—"

But he was not permitted to finish his sentence. Satskevaidakanai snapped his fingers, sending a clap of thunder through the vaulted chamber, and the *daigana* shrank to the size of a coin. Chirruping in surprise, he plummeted to the floor, where he hopped once or twice, no longer a towering six-legged spirit but a tiny, bearded cricket.

Tskadakrikana let out a laugh like the cracking of an ice floe.

Naisholao rubbed her temples. "I can't be bothered with this now."

Lifting an arm, she summoned from the back of the chamber an armored giant, made entirely of the same faintly glowing ice as the rest of the palace. It emerged from the wall, its joints crackling and snapping, and with great lumbering steps crossed the floor, scooping up Miuko with one hand and catching the *daigana* — still in cricket form — with the other.

"Dispose of them," Naisholao said, puckering her small, red lips in a moue of distaste. "We have more pressing matters to attend to."

"What? Wait, no!" Feebly, Miuko struggled as the giant shambled toward the balcony from which she and Nogadishao had initially entered, but the icy fingers merely tightened around her waist, causing her to gasp.

From inside the giant's other fist, she could hear the forest spirit squeaking: "But she was there, my lieges! She was there when the House of November burned! You want to know who's responsible for Nakatalao's disappearance? It's *her!*"

Miuko froze.

The *daigana* was convinced she was to blame for the massacre, but he hadn't been there, not really. She'd forced him to flee before the mountain spirit arrived, before it became a *yasa,* before the head priest bound it to prevent it from destroying more of the temple.

"He's right!" she cried, straining against the giant's cold grasp. "I was there! I'm the only one who knows what really happened when the temple burned! You can't throw me out of here, or you'll never figure out how to get Nakatalao back!"

The January God raised a hand, halting the ice giant before it hurled both Miuko and Nogadishao into the night air. "Explain yourself, demon."

Emboldened, Miuko bowed as best she could while still caught in the giant's enormous fingers — which was to say, not very well. "I have information I think will be valuable to you, Naisholao-kanai," she said breathlessly, "and in return for it, all I request is your help."

Lightning flashed through Satskevaidakanai's form. "You dare demand a favor of us?"

Miuko swallowed. "I don't demand, my lord, but I have to ask, for my friend's life depends on it."

"Friend?" Naisholao's beady eyes blinked in a mixture of amusement and confusion. "Since when do *shaohasu* have friends?"

"I'm not just a *shaoha*," Miuko replied, "and I can explain why, but I don't have much time. You can see that I'm out of place—I'm from a future six days from now, but I'm fading too fast to make it back there. If I tell you what I know, will you grant me an audience with Afaina, who can return me to where and when I belong?"

"No!" the *daigana* creaked from within the giant's other fist. "Liar! Murderer!"

Ignoring him, Naisholao glanced at her fellow gods, some of whom nodded. Satskevaidakanai grumbled, low and dangerous, like thunder.

At last, the January God returned her attention to Miuko. "Tell us what you know." With a flick of her wrist, she gestured to the ice giant, who released Miuko and Nogadishao from its hold. "And we shall decide whether your knowledge merits this reward."

Swaying slightly on her feet, Miuko nodded, for this seemed as good an outcome as she could have hoped for. The cricket-*daigana* must have had other ideas, however, for he came tumbling out of the giant's palm, chirping angrily. At a glance from Satskevaidakanai, however, he settled for seething upon the floor.

Miuko winced as she checked her ribs for damage, though she was relieved to find that although she was more transparent than ever, she seemed to have sustained nothing worse than a severe bruising. Inhaling deeply and with only mild agony, she told the gods about the kiss upon the Old Road, Tujiyazai in the *doro*'s body, the journey north with Geiki, the standoff at the dock, the bungled summoning, the decision to curse herself, the spells she'd acquired at the House of November, the sudden appearance of Tujiyazai, the head priest binding the enraged mountain spirit in a rice bowl at the ruined statue of the November God.

"If you free the spirit," she finished, "you can return him to his original form. The mountain will have life again. The *oyu* will vanish. The temple can be rebuilt, and there can be new priests. Maybe then Nakatalao will return."

For a moment, the gods were silent. Tskadakrikana's feather-lined eyes widened, making her appear more startled than ever. All the flowers upon Cheiyuchura's skin blossomed at once, obscuring their features in a riot of multi-colored blooms. Satskevaidakanai brooded like a distant storm.

Then Naisholao rushed Miuko, who yelped and prepared to run, but despite her heavy robes, the January God was swift on her feet. She slammed into Miuko, nearly bowling her over.

Nogadishao cheered.

But, deep within the folds of Naisholao's clothes, Miuko wasn't entirely sure she was actually being attacked. She thrashed and sputtered, more confused than anything, and in that moment she could not help but think of Geiki, sitting across from a campfire in the Kotskisiu-maru, waving his good arm at her.

Miuko let out a hiccup of laughter. "Are you happy or mad?" she cried. "Happy–mad?"

At her words, Naisholao drew back, smiling. "Thank you, demon."

Though she was so weak she could barely stand, hope flared in Miuko's chest. She clasped at the January God's hands, which were surprisingly warm, like life sleeping snugly beneath a snowbank. "Does this mean you'll help me?" she asked.

But before Naisholao could respond, a sudden pain lanced through Miuko's arm. She doubled over, clutching her wrist.

Blood ran through her gloved fingers, staining the fabric red.

Surprised, Naisholao pulled back Miuko's sleeve to examine the cuts as they formed into syllables.

Another name.

"You're being summoned," she said.

Miuko nodded, already feeling herself disappearing the same way she'd disappeared at the House of November. "Please," she begged, "we have to hurry. Will you take me to Afaina, Naisholao-kanai?"

Nogadishao chittered angrily from the floor. "No! You have to pay! You have to be punished!"

Miuko winced. Another incision. Another syllable. There could not be many more before the summoner's carving was complete.

Into her hands, the January God pressed a bell of brightest silver. "Ring for my emissary, Otori Miuko. He will take you wherever you wish to go."

The cricket-*daigana* was shrieking now, launching himself at Miuko, mandibles snapping.

As the pain seared through her arm one last time, Miuko bowed to the gods, wondering where she would end up next: Udaiwa, the Ochiirokai, some far-flung corner of Awara she'd never even heard of? Gratefully, she clasped the bell to her chest. It didn't matter. Wherever she found herself, she would be one step closer to returning to the dock . . . and to Geiki.

With that thought, she vanished, leaving only a few drops of red blood behind.

16

THE DESPERATE LOVER

WHEREVER MIUKO REAPPEARED, it was unbearably hot, and several people were screaming at once. The loudest was a pretty girl of sixteen or seventeen, half clothed and shrieking unintelligibly as she cowered behind a sturdy (if uninspired-looking) boy, also half clothed. He was screaming at a second girl, whose unruly black hair kept floating about her face as she brandished a knife at him, while he shouted repeatedly at her to "CALM DOWN, SENARA!" and "STOP OVERREACTING!"

Senara, however, seemed to have no intentions of doing anything of the sort, for she kept jabbing the blade in his direction, blood dripping from the cuts in her arm onto her abundant, petal-pink robes. "*Overreacting?* You said you loved me! You said you'd marry me! You promised me sons, remember? Fat, healthy ones! I gave myself to you—I *ruined* myself for you—and now you're marrying *her?* You're giving *her* the sons you promised me?" Gesticulating wildly, she pointed the knife at the other girl, who took the opportunity to screech even louder than before. "NO, HAWI! What else am I supposed to do?"

Miuko's spectral knees buckled, throwing her to the floor. Through the faint outlines of her thighs, she could see flecks of straw in the dirt. Was she in a barn? Looking up, she saw clothes abandoned among the sacks of grain. Perhaps Hawi and the loud girl had been engaged in some sort of midnight tryst when Senara had interrupted them.

"You're not supposed to try to *murder* me!" Hawi bellowed. Then, seeing Miuko: "AH! What's *that?*"

Groggily, Miuko glared at him from her position on the ground. She may have been exhausted by her ascent of the Kuludrava Palace and discombobulated by the summoning, but it seemed clear to Miuko that if Senara had lain with this boy before marriage—regardless of any promises he may have made her—she was, according to the customs of Awaran society, damaged goods; and, being damaged goods, she now had limited opportunities for the marriage and fat sons she so longed for. If the rest of her community found out she'd slept with Hawi, the best she could hope for was a future as a burden to her family, until she died or there were no more male relatives willing to keep her. Given that her choices now were to live in disgrace while he married some other girl or to summon a malevolence demon to kill him, Miuko was not surprised that Senara had opted for the malevolence demon.

Whirling, Senara spied Miuko on the floor. "Go on!" she shouted. "That's him! That's him right there! Kill him!"

A part of Miuko wanted nothing more, for the same demon-instinct which had propelled her at Kanayi's drunken doctor drove her now. She could hear Hawi's blood pulsing at his jugular. She could taste his sweat upon the air. He smelled *succulent*, like the plump bud of an apricot, sweet with lust.

But she was too weak now to attack him; and, more than that, she had sworn never to use her powers like that again.

When Miuko did not move, Senara flung herself at Miuko's feet in a rush of pink cloth and floral perfume. "Please!" she begged.

Taking the loud girl by the arm, Hawi collected their discarded clothing. "Come on," he said, "let's get out of here."

The girl sniffled, pointing at Senara. "What about her?"

He shrugged. "What about her?"

At his words, Senara seemed to wilt, curling in on herself like a sunscorched blossom. Even her wild hair appeared to deflate a little.

285

Reaching the door, Hawi pulled the loud girl out into the night, where they quickly vanished down a wide dirt lane, leaving Miuko and Senara alone in the barn.

"I'm sorry," Miuko whispered, shaking her head. "I just couldn't do it."

"It's okay." Senara let the knife fall from her fingers. "I don't even know if I really wanted you to. I just . . . I didn't want him to get away with it, you know?"

Miuko nodded. Hefting Naisholao's bell, which seemed heavier now than it had been minutes before, she staggered to her feet.

"Where are you going?" Senara asked.

"To stop a demon and save a friend."

"I didn't know malevolence demons had friends." Perking up again, Senara hitched up her robes and followed Miuko into a fenced yard that overlooked a valley, gray-blue with shadow. In the village below, lights were gathering along the road, and distressed voices could be heard upon the still air.

"Was that screaming?"

"I think it came from the barn!"

With great effort, Miuko shook Naisholao's bell, the sound of it pealing through the valley, cool as starlight on a frozen sea.

With a look of wonderment, Senara turned this way and that, as if she could trace the echoes ringing off the mountains. "What was *that*?"

"Transportation . . . hopefully."

Overhead, a half moon shone down upon them, marking the sixth night since Miuko had kissed herself upon the Old Road. Somewhere out there, the *kyakyozuya* was hunting her past-self in the forests above Koewa. Somewhere out there, Tujiyazai was riding toward her on his great black steed. Somewhere out there, Geiki had trapped himself inside the puzzle box.

Was Kanayi searching for him now, inching closer to regaining her freedom?

Miuko hoped so.

As she searched the sky, another chime echoed through the heavens. From out of the high, wispy clouds, a giant white weasel, tall as a horse and three times as long, sprang toward the earth. With otherworldly grace, he bounded down into the yard, skittering to a stop before Miuko and Senara with hardly a sound.

Gasping, Senara threw herself upon her hands and knees, her robes rippling gently about her.

Ignoring her, Miuko bowed to the weasel. "Did Naisholao send you?"

On the ground, Senara sat up again, pawing her hair out of her face. "What do you mean, *Naisholao?* What kind of demon are you, anyway?"

Miuko, however, did not respond, and neither did the weasel, for he was not a talking weasel. Instead, he took the bell from Miuko with his forepaws and attached it to a silk ribbon around his neck. Crouching, he chirped encouragingly at her, as if urging her to climb onto his back.

She hesitated. She didn't know what she'd been expecting—something instantaneous, probably, like teleportation—but with her phantom body more than half transparent now, she didn't know if she'd be strong enough to make it to Afaina riding on the back of a giant weasel . . . even a magical one.

Turning to Senara, she studied the girl's simple, flowing robes and the knotted belt of the peasant class at her waist. A farmer's daughter. Like Miuko, Senara's options had always been limited—to marry, to manage a household, to bear and raise children—but her illicit romance with Hawi had narrowed her opportunities even further.

The lights on the road grew closer; the voices, louder. The villagers would reach the barn soon.

"Senara," Miuko said softly. "Do you want to come with me?"

Surprised, the girl jumped to her feet. "Leave the village? I can't do that! My family is here, all my friends . . ."

"You summoned a demon to kill your lover. What do you think will happen when they find out?"

Senara moaned, hiding her face in her hair.

"Please . . . I could use your help."

"What does a demon need *my* help for?"

In answer, Miuko lifted her gloved hands, barely visible in the dim light. "I'm growing weaker," she said. "I don't know how long this journey will take, but if it's longer than a day, I don't know if I'll be able to hold on."

"Where are you going?"

"Does it matter?"

Senara bit her lip, glancing back at the village.

A figure crested the rise. In the light of his lantern, he could be seen squinting at the yard. "Senara? Is that you?"

"That's a demon!" someone else cried, joining him.

"And a *giant weasel!*" said another.

As if to say he was much more than a giant weasel, thank you very much, Naisholao's emissary squeaked indignantly.

Grunting, Miuko pulled herself onto his back, where she turned to Senara, extending her hand. "Come on. There is so much more out there than this."

The girl's eyes glittered—with tears, or perhaps excitement. "For a girl?"

"For anyone brave enough to look."

The villagers were leaping the fence now, shouting and swinging their lanterns, but Miuko did not waver.

A smile flooded Senara's face. Taking Miuko's hand, she scrambled up behind her as the villagers raced across the grass.

"I'm scared," she whispered.

Miuko grinned back at her. "It's scary out there . . . but it's wonderful too."

With a great leap, the white weasel launched himself into the sky, and Miuko and Senara were off, leaving behind the villagers, the yard, the valley, bounding from one cloud to another, toward new lives, new adventures, new dreams—and, yes, danger and death too, perhaps.

But that was a risk anywhere.

17

A DISTANT STAR

AS THE NIGHT wore on, Miuko found herself growing fainter, thin as a trail of smoke rising from a dead candle. She faded in and out of consciousness, glimpsing a furrow of mountains here, a ribbon of shoreline there, but though the view shifted and changed, the sensation of Senara's arms about her waist never wavered.

Dawn came, then dusk. Dimly, Miuko was aware of a sunset—arcing across the sky and turning the weasel's fur to a brilliant, heavenly gold —and Senara's breathless gasp.

Then nothing.

Sleep, maybe. Or a glimpse of the oblivion that awaited her if she failed.

But it was only a glimpse. When she woke again, it was night—the sixth night since the kiss upon the Old Road—and below, the ocean was black and seamless as a mirror, reflecting every star in the heavens, with the white weasel dancing like a snowflake through the darkness.

"You're awake!" Senara cried.

Miuko made a sour face. "For now!"

"How much farther?"

"How should I know?" Then, because the words reminded her of a certain, foolish *atskayakina*: "I'm a *shaoha*!"

Senara laid her chin on Miuko's shoulder, her wild hair whipping about them both. "That means nothing to me!"

Despite her grouchiness, Miuko laughed.

But her laughter failed upon her lips. She felt drained, all of a sudden, like she could breathe nothing, could hold on to nothing, because she was vanishing into nothing.

Gasping, she clutched at the weasel's fur as Senara's hands tightened around her, but Miuko slid through the girl's embrace as if she were little more than mist. With a faint cry, she pitched sideways, sliding from the weasel's back.

"Miuko!" Senara screamed.

But she was already plummeting toward the waves below. The air whistled through her hair and along her sleeves, making them billow about her like wings, except they were not wings, and they could not carry her.

Something flew from her pocket, shrieking, "Eee! Look what trouble you've gotten me into now, *shaoha!*"

With her quick demon-reflexes, Miuko snatched the thing out of the air, cradling it carefully between her gloved fingers.

A little bearded cricket.

"Nogadishao?" she cried. "What are you doing in my pocket?"

His antennae waggled angrily. "Waiting for my chance to strike you down, but it seems like gravity is going to do that for me!"

Miuko glanced down. The ocean was rushing toward her like a black slate, like a flagstone courtyard.

Could she survive the breaking of every bone in her body?

Could her organs?

Or would she simply slip through the surface like the spectral creature she had become, dissipating into the currents like spilled ink?

Fortunately, she did not have to find out, for out of the heavens came Naisholao's emissary, squeaking frantically as he raced toward her.

Miuko jammed the cricket-*daigana* unceremoniously into her pocket, beside the *tseimi*'s incense holder (which through all her otherworldly adventures she had somehow managed to hold on to) as Senara reached out from the weasel's back, snagging Miuko's hand in hers.

For an instant, Miuko was certain she'd slide right through Senara's fingers.

For an instant, she tasted sea spray.

They both cried out as Naisholao's emissary twisted upward again, away from the undulating waves, as Miuko struggled onto his back. "Why did you do that?" she breathed.

Senara tossed her hair out of her face, her cheeks flushed with excitement. "You mean, save your life?"

"Yes. I'm a demon, remember?"

"A lying, murdering demon!" Nogadishao piped up from her pocket.

The girl let out a startled laugh. "Who's *that?*"

"A stowaway," Miuko grumbled.

The little forest spirit chewed ferociously at the lining of her pocket. "I am a *daigana!*"

Senara poked him lightly. "Of what? A tuft of grass?"

Miuko snickered.

"You should have let her fall!" Nogadishao scolded the girl. "Everyone would've been better off, you included, eh?"

Senara shook her head. "Oh, I don't think so. I'm having a grand time, actually! Besides, you would have died too!"

"It would have been worth it!" Then, hissing, he retreated into Miuko's pocket to pout.

Senara squeezed Miuko gently. "What happened back there? Why did you fall so suddenly? Why is there a *daigana* with you? And why is he a cricket?"

Miuko closed her eyes. Tonight was the night Tujiyazai had cornered her past-self in his castle and used his powers to inflame her own. It was the first time she'd intentionally used her touch to drain another living being.

Were she and her past-self connected?

Was that why, on the day of the massacre, her past-self had discovered the curse surging up her legs? Because her demon-self had used her powers against Nogadishao and Kanayi?

"It's a long story," she said at last.

Senara chuckled, settling her chin in the crook of Miuko's shoulder again. "We have nothing but time."

To this, Miuko had no rejoinder, so she told the girl her story, and as she did, she found herself remembering who she was and who she'd been —a girl, just a girl, who wanted to be human again.

She'd almost forgotten. She'd been so absorbed in stopping Tujiyazai, and then in returning to the dock, that she'd grown quite accustomed to being a demon—or *mostly demon,* as her human-voice reminded her—and regaining her humanity had become something of a dream, uncatchable as a distant star or a fleeting shape in the *naiana.*

But she *lived* dreams, now, didn't she?

She'd traveled to Ana. She'd bargained with gods.

Nothing was out of her reach.

Crawling to the lip of her pocket, Nogadishao was silent, his forelegs plucking thoughtfully at her robes, as she recounted the bungled summoning spell on the docks, the mysterious voice she'd heard greeting her — *Hello again*—before she arrived at the abandoned fields, her failed attempts to change the past, the tragedy at the House of November.

Did he believe her now?

She hoped so.

Her story caught up to the present as the sun rose over the waters, and they found themselves circling a small, rounded island, where Naisholao's emissary let out a low, throaty whistle. Lower and lower they drifted, until the weasel's paws touched the ground.

Kneeling, he allowed Senara and Miuko to dismount. The cricket-*daigana* hopped from Miuko's pocket up to her elbow, and then to her shoulder, where he perched, looking about him curiously.

Rocky and barren, the island was about the size of the guesthouse at Nihaoi, with nothing but a few dips and hummocks marring its otherwise gentle slope.

"Is Afaina coming?" Miuko asked, turning to Naisholao's emissary.

But he merely whistled again, and before she could catch his snowy fur, he had bounded off in a blaze of white light, leaving the three of them in the middle of the endless ocean.

Miuko gaped after him.

Did Naisholao trick us? the little voice inside her whispered.

No.

No.

Afaina was not here. He had never been here. The January God had lied to her. She and her *vakai* weasel had abandoned Miuko upon this island, where she could not stir up further trouble before she faded from the world.

And that would not be long now, for she was very nearly transparent, little more than a shimmer in the sunlight.

She howled, searching for something to throw, although of course she found nothing. She then tried to kick at the stone, but even that exhausted her, and she sank to her knees, watching the pebbles through her disappearing body.

Nogadishao leapt from her shoulder, chittering in alarm. "Where is he, eh? Where's this god we're supposed to meet?"

Miuko reached for the ground, but her fingers slid through it as if they were nothing. "I thought I was so close," she murmured. "Just one more favor, and I would've been home. I would've been able to . . . And now I'm stuck here, and you're stuck with me. I'm so sorry."

Hugging her arms, Senara looked about her, clearly trying not to cry. "It's okay. . . ."

"No, it's not," Miuko and Nogadishao replied at once.

There was a long, uncomfortable silence.

Then the waves shuddered. All around them, enormous bubbles rose to the surface, churning the sea. The island trembled, throwing Senara to her knees in a puddle of pink robes.

"What's happening?" she cried.

"How should we know?" the cricket-*daigana* shouted.

But the answer was soon to be evident, for something—something huge, bigger than Nogadishao in his true form, bigger than the mountain spirit Miuko had seen at the House of November—was rising from the water.

18

GOD WITH A THOUSAND EYES

PETRIFIED, MIUKO AND SENARA clung to each other, trying not to topple from the island's sloping shores as Afaina appeared above them, gargantuan in size. He had the form of a young man, long-haired and naked to the chest (as well as below, although that part of him remained submerged), and upon his head he wore a crown of stars which revolved slowly in dazzling, ever-shifting ellipses.

He rubbed his startlingly blue eyes, as if he'd only just awoken. "Hello again," he said in a deep, booming voice.

Senara jerked out of Miuko's grasp, as if she'd experienced a static shock.

"What's wrong?" Miuko hissed.

"Nothing. I just . . ." The girl bit her lip. "I could've sworn I've heard those words somewhere recently. . . ."

Above them, the God of Stars cleared his throat. In the center of his forehead, another eye opened, this one the clear turquoise of a lagoon. "I mean, hello," he said. "I thought I felt a tickling upon my knee."

"Oh, gods." Horrified, Senara glanced at the shore, which was the same rough texture as Afaina's bare skin. "We're standing on him."

Chirping in dismay, Nogadishao hopped up her billowing robes and onto her shoulder.

Miuko bowed, hoping they hadn't caused any offense. "Greetings, Afaina-kanai. My name is Otori Miuko, and as you can see, I do not belong in this time. Before I vanish from this world, I have come to ask for your

296

help in returning me to my proper place upon the docks at the House of December, four days from now."

"Or you could not, eh?" the cricket-*daigana* piped up. "Let her be expunged, I say!"

Afaina blinked. In fact, several of his eyes blinked, opening and closing along his throat and chest.

"Aren't you there already?" he asked.

"What? I'm right here in front of you."

More eyes, in hues ranging from the crystal blue of Kuludrava Palace to the near-black of the ocean floor, appeared along his arms. "On the contrary, you never left. You're standing there still, with the priest's blade in your hand."

She glanced down, half-expecting to see Meli's paring knife in her palm, but her gloved fingers remained empty and translucent. "I don't understand."

"Maybe he's saying you're dreaming, eh?" Nogadishao said. "Maybe all this has been nothing but a dream!"

Senara nudged him with her fingertip. "Stop that. We're not dreams."

He tugged at her hair. "Speak for yourself. If I'm a dream, then I'm not really a cricket, eh? And you're still in your village, nice and cozy with what's-his-name. Wouldn't that be nice?"

The girl's eyes glistened, and for a second Miuko thought she might start crying, but she merely dashed the tears from her lashes and lifted her chin. "It would be a lie."

After a pause, in which Afaina appeared to be staring off into the distance, or at some nearly indiscernible specks floating upon the air, he cocked his head curiously. "This is no dream." Then, to Miuko: "You were also never at the dock. You remain captive to the one you call *doro yagra*."

"But how can that be?"

Around his head, the crown of stars turned, constellations flashing in the sunlight. "Time is a river with many tributaries, Otori Miuko. Along one, you are already a demon, having feasted upon your own father as his guesthouse burned to the ground. Along another, you remain human, for, sensing misfortune ahead of you, you turned back upon the Old Road eight days ago, and Tujiyazai, never having seen you, rode on to Udaiwa, where he proceeded to raze Awara to the ground. In that timeline, not even Nihaoi was spared." The god inhaled deeply, causing another set of eyes to open along his ribs. "I can smell the smoke from here."

Miuko stomped her foot—which, even if she'd been stronger, would have had little effect upon the hard surface of his kneecap. "But those things didn't happen in *this* time. In *this* time, my friend is waiting for me, and he'll die if I can't get back to him."

Upon Afaina's body, there now appeared hundreds of eyes, all of them opening and closing as they looked upon temporal variations only the God of Stars could see. "Many will die if you return. Many will die if you don't. When you see existence as I do, then death has no meaning. I am alive —or you, in your frustration, have killed me. Your friend escapes—or his throat is cut. There is no difference."

"There is to me! Come on, there must be something you want, something I can give you?"

He yawned, as if his attention was already drifting away. "You can't bargain with me, Otori Miuko, for you have nothing I need."

Desperately, Miuko looked to Senara (who was biting her lip again, apparently as lost in her thoughts as Afaina himself), and then, with less hope, to Nogadishao, who shrugged.

The God of Stars yawned again. "Everything exists somewhere else, in some other time." Languidly, he began to sink back into the waters, each of his eyes closing as they turned to other timelines, other possibilities.

He was not really here at all, Miuko realized with disappointment.

He never had been. At this very moment, he was in a dozen other worlds—perhaps one where the Omaizi Clan had not defeated the Ogawa outside Nihaoi; perhaps another where Miuko's mother had not ridden into the verge hour that night but stayed with her family another day, another week, another year.

Perhaps, in Afaina's eyes, she'd never left.

To the God of Stars, all things were possible, and because all things were possible, none of them mattered. He floated through time like a raft in an infinite ocean, utterly unmoored from his surroundings.

But Miuko was not unmoored, and to her, everything mattered.

Every moment she had.

Every choice she made.

Every person she loved.

Unlike Afaina, she was not disconnected from the world, because she was not alone.

"Wait!" she cried, flinging up her transparent hands to catch his attention. "I have something for you, Afaina-kanai, something I do not think you have in any of your many tributaries."

He paused, his eyes focusing and unfocusing as the waves lapped at his colossal chin. After a while, he lifted an eyebrow. "Oh?"

Digging into her pocket, Miuko withdrew the incense holder. With trembling fingers, she untied the twine and unwrapped the paper, lifting the lid. "A friend," she said.

In an instant, the smoke cat sprang forth, tumbling out onto Afaina's knee in a wispy ball of smoke.

"The *tseimi*!" Senara threw herself to her knees, cooing happily. Then, looking up at Miuko accusatorily, "You didn't tell me it was *this* cute!"

"It's not just cute," Miuko explained as the smoke cat rolled onto its back, pawing at the air. "It's also immortal. I'm afraid it was too dangerous to let loose in Awara, but here it's no danger at all."

Every one of Afaina's eyes was open now, thousands of them, even the ones upon his kneecap, where Miuko and Senara had to hop out of the way to avoid stepping on his eyeballs, and every one of them was trained upon the *tseimi*. From the ocean, he lifted an enormous hand, dripping seawater, and laid his fingers gently against the edge of the island.

"Huh," he said.

The smoke cat trotted over to him, leaping up the damp ridges of his fingertips, where it immediately began batting at a loose strand of kelp, chasing it across Afaina's knuckles.

"A cat." The god chuckled, sending ripples across the water. "In no other timeline do I have this."

Purring, the *tseimi* hopped back onto the island and curled up between three of Afaina's eyes, which stared at the fluffy creature adoringly.

Miuko bowed again, extending the incense holder in her palms. "I offer him to you," she said, "if you'll return me to where and when I belong."

With a tenderness she did not think possible for a being of such great size, he lifted his hand, careful not to disturb the dozing kitten, and plucked the incense holder from her, enfolding it somewhere within his flowing beard.

"Otori Miuko," he said, amusement still rumbling in his voice. "I accep—"

"Wait." Senara laid a hand on Miuko's arm.

Miuko, feeling like she'd already waited long enough, scowled at her but remained silent.

A devious, knowing smile crept across the girl's lips. "There's something else you have to do, Afaina-kanai, for I believe you've already done it."

Several of the god's eyes turned on her, though others remained fixated on the slumbering *tseimi*. "Oh?"

"*You're* the one who took her from the dock in the first place!" Senara declared. "'Hello again!' Why would you say that unless you'd met her before? I mean, it was the first time for Miuko, but it wasn't the first time for you, because you've met her now!"

"Uh, what? Wait. You—" Miuko stumbled over her own thoughts, remembering the moment she'd been transported from the God's Teeth.

There *had* been a figure nearby—something immense, obscuring the entire sky—and a voice, deep as the deepest chasms of the sea: *Hello again.*

Her summoning hadn't gone wrong at all.

It had merely been interrupted.

"That was *you?*" Miuko cried.

For a time, the God of Stars seemed to ponder this, his many eyes blinking and winking in mesmerizing patterns. At length, all of his eyes but the main two closed, and he looked down upon Miuko and Senara thoughtfully. "I suppose it was," he said with some amusement. "You are correct, little human."

Blushing, the girl bowed.

Miuko, however, was furious. "Why would you do that? I could have stopped him on the dock! I could have—"

"I did it because you gave me a cat," Afaina interrupted, "and because the little human asked me to, and because in four seconds, you will agree that it was for the best."

Snarling, Miuko readied a retort, but instead her hand fell to the necklace of spells the head priest had given her.

If Afaina hadn't taken her to the past in the first place, she would have been forced to kill the *doro,* Omaizi Ruhai, in order to evict Tujiyazai from his body. In taking that one life, she would have lost her humanity forever.

Because of this moment, right here, she still had a chance to defeat him without destroying herself.

"Oh," she said.

"Ha ha!" Nogadishao chirped. "Four seconds exactly!"

Afaina extended his palm. "Are you prepared, Otori Miuko?"

Yes! the little voice inside her cheered.

But she did not reply. Looking to Senara, who still appeared rather pleased with herself, and the cricket-*daigana*, creaking on the girl's shoulder, Miuko shook her head. "What about my friends?"

The god hummed deep inside his chest, and for a second, all his eyes fluttered—open and closed and open and closed—like thousands of wings. "There is much turmoil ahead," he said at length. "I will place them where they will be needed most."

Miuko turned to Senara, who flung herself into Miuko's arms in a riot of soft robes and wavy black hair, nearly dislodging Nogadishao from his perch.

"Thank you," Miuko whispered to her. "I hope one day we'll meet again."

The girl squeezed her tightly. "I know we will."

"What about me, eh?" Nogadishao chirruped irritably.

Releasing Senara, Miuko bowed to him. "I thank you too, *daigana-kanai*." Then, climbing into Afaina's hand: "And you, not least of all, God of Stars. I won't forget this."

"No one else will, either," he rumbled, closing his fist about her, gentle as an embrace, "if the world survives."

Then she was soaring upward into the sky, waving to Senara and the cricket-*daigana* below.

"Good-bye! Good-bye!" they shouted, shrinking in size until they were no more than a splotch of pink upon the hard stone of Afaina's kneecap. "So long, *shaoha!*"

"Good-bye!" she cried as the air clouded, swirling around her like mist, until their faces were lost from view.

Clutching Afaina's thumb, she squinted into the shadows. Yes! There was the god's other hand, reaching for a figure in the darkness. Briefly, she caught a glimpse of a priest's robes fluttering through the air.

That's us, her human-voice whispered.

The God of Stars chuckled. "Hello again."

All of a sudden, she felt wooden planks beneath her feet. Above her, Afaina's hand was withdrawing, and in the center of his palm, she saw another eye, as blue as her own flesh.

It winked.

And then it was gone, replaced by the slap of the waves, the scent of blood, and an unmistakable blast of heat as Tujiyazai's voice reached her: "Well, Ishao? Time is not on your side."

Miuko grinned, pulling the exorcism spell from around her neck.

That's what you think.

19

A VISION OF SHAO-KANAI

ALL WAS AS Miuko had left it: the blazing sun, the glinting waves, the gulls circling noisily overhead. On the deck of the boat, Geiki lay motionless at the point of the *kyakyozuya*'s sword, while Tujiyazai stood upon the dock, his triumphant voice softening into uncertainty as Miuko's past-self vanished from sight.

The only difference was that Miuko did not reappear in her old position beside Meli, facing the *doro yagra* at a distance of twenty paces.

Instead, she materialized directly behind him, so close she could feel the heat cascading from his shoulders like a cloak.

Around his neck, he still wore the simple necklace strung with the binding spell he'd taken from the House of November.

"*Doro*-kanai!" the demon hunter shouted.

Tujiyazai turned, and in a single scorching gaze took in Miuko's transparent figure, quickly regaining substance now that she'd returned to her proper place in time.

"How did you do that?" Geiki started up, accidentally nicked himself on the *kyakyozuya*'s blade, and shrank back again. "Why are you *see-through?*"

In the distance, there were shouts from the temple.

The demon prince eyed her thoughtfully. "Where have you been, Ishao?"

"That's not my name." Before he could react, she yanked the cord from around his neck and slapped the exorcism spell to his chest with such force that he staggered backward, stumbling on the uneven planks.

For a moment, the slip of paper flared brightly, the indigo ink flickering like shadows crawling upon a piece of coal.

Miuko reached for the second spell—the one that would bind him.

But Tujiyazai did not emerge from the *doro*'s body. Regaining his footing, he straightened, cocking his head at her as if puzzled. On his chest, the spell fizzled out, smoking like a snuffed candle.

He began to laugh.

Miuko backed away. The exorcism spell should have driven him from the *doro*'s body. It should have had him oozing onto the dock like pus from a sore.

Instead, the demon prince peeled the spell from his chest, shredding it into dozens of tiny pieces with his graceful fingers. "After your tantrum in the castle, I thought you might react with some form of foolishness. I don't yet know precisely how you pulled it off, but it appears I was right." Parting his robes, he bared his chest to her.

There, over the *doro*'s heart, was a tattoo, freshly carved.

Miuko looked down at the bamboo cylinder she'd taken from him. Empty.

Tujiyazai had *imprinted* himself with the binding spell.

Of course, the little voice inside her moaned.

She should have been expecting it. He'd already used a tattoo to prevent himself from being summoned. Why not use one to bind him in the body of Omaizi Ruhai forever?

Now Tujiyazai could not be exorcised, and if he could not be exorcised, he could not be stopped.

Behind her, she heard the *kyakyozuya* shift stances. "The *doro* would not need a spell to bind him in his own body. Who are you, monster? How long have you possessed him?"

Tujiyazai chuckled. "Long enough."

With a roar, the demon hunter leapt at the *doro yagra*, his blessed blade flashing in the sun.

Seeing her chance, Miuko ducked beneath him, yanking Geiki from the boat.

"Ow!" he cried, clutching his injured side.

"Hurry up!" As Tujiyazai and the *kyakyozuya* clashed, she half-dragged, half-carried the *atskayakina* toward shore.

Meli sprinted out to meet them, her tall form draped with a vermillion sash Miuko was certain she hadn't been wearing when she'd raced to the docks the first time.

"When did you get that sash?" Miuko cried.

The priest pulled Geiki's arm over her shoulder. "A cloud spirit delivered one over a week ago, telling us to replicate as many as we could."

Beikai.

Miuko smiled. Her favor had been redeemed.

Together, she and Meli helped Geiki to shore while the sounds of battle rang behind them. Leaving the *atskayakina* in the priest's arms, Miuko dashed back to help the demon hunter.

He was moving quickly—slashing, stabbing, his sword flickering in and out, down and sideways—but none of his strikes were landing. Tujiyazai was too fast, too strong; he didn't even need a blade to deflect the *kyakyozuya*'s attacks, evading them with unnatural swiftness.

The *doro yagra* sighed, as if he found the entire exercise wearisome, and the next time the demon hunter came at him, he caught the man's wrist, snapping it neatly, and slammed him face-first into one of the pilings.

Blood coursed from the *kyakyozuya*'s nose and mouth. His body went limp, collapsing onto the dock, where Tujiyazai stomped upon his chest several times, apparently out of nothing more than spite.

"Stop!" Miuko cried.

Dusting off his hands, the demon prince faced her with flames dancing in his eye sockets. "Resistance is a waste of both my time and yours. You will come with me eventually, Ishao." He leveled a finger at Geiki, the only person on the dock without the spells to protect him from Tujiyazai's power. "Perhaps you will do it to spare your friend the penalty of my wrath?"

Miuko glared at him, but he was not finished.

"Or perhaps you will do it because you finally accept the truth: you are a *demon*. You were meant to destroy. You will come with me because devastation is your *nature*, Shao-kanai. One way or another, it is inevitable."

Shao-kanai. Murderer. Un-maker.

Lady Death.

At last, Miuko understood what Tujiyazai wanted.

Everything. With the demon prince fueling her powers, she would be capable of obliterating both Ada and Ana in a matter of days, from the tallest peaks to the lowliest beetles to the Lunar Gods themselves, rendering it all to dust. She would be a tool of vengeance, unleashed upon the world.

And if she ever lost her humanity, she would do it gladly, for then she would crave such desolation as much as Tujiyazai did.

At that moment, the sound of chanting reached her. Amyunasa's priests were storming the shoreline, each of them clad in a vermillion sash like Meli's.

"Where did they get those?" Tujiyazai growled.

Miuko bared her teeth at him in a feral smile. "Wouldn't you like to know?"

He retreated as the priests advanced with their warding banners, opening up a space for Miuko, who could feel the magic buzzing between her teeth, before closing ranks again. The *doro yagra* glared past their rippling spells, fire blazing along his horns.

"Is this it, then?" he demanded. "You choose them over me?"

Straightening, Miuko met his gaze. "I will *never* choose you."

Behind her, Geiki cheered.

Meli shushed him.

"So be it." Tujiyazai leapt into the boat and pushed off from the dock, his entire body aflame now, bright as a beacon on the morning sea. "But if I can't have *you*, then no one can have *anything!* You're going to regret this choice, Ishao! I'll make certain of it!"

20

THE CRONE

GEIKI'S FIRST REACTION, after he'd heard the entirety of Miuko's strange and otherworldly tale, was to jab a finger in her direction and declare with a triumphant cackle, "You're old!"

Perched on the edge of his mattress, she scowled. "No, I'm not."

"You're seven and a half days older than you were this morning. You're an old lady! You're a crone!" Lowering his head, he pressed his palms together in a gesture of mock respect. "I bow to you, O Ancient One."

She swatted at him. "I can't believe I missed you."

"Of course you missed me!" He preened. "I'm a delight."

Despite herself, she grinned. If the *atskayakina* was feeling well enough to sit up in the temple infirmary and tease her, it was a good sign.

She could not say the same of the *kyakyozuya,* however, for he remained unconscious in the bed by the window, where the afternoon sunlight streamed through the trees outside, dappling his bruised and bandaged body with shadow.

Geiki shook his head. "You know the worst part of it?" he asked.

"What's that?"

"You used our only favor with Beikai on *fashion accessories.*"

Miuko scoffed. "Those 'fashion accessories' saved everyone from being turned into violent killers!"

"Yes, but think of *me* for a second, will you? I could have had riches beyond compare!"

"You don't want riches beyond compare." She poked him in his uninjured side, partly to annoy him, partly to reassure herself that she was well and truly solid again. "You want the opportunity to *steal* riches beyond compare."

"Isn't that what I said?"

She laughed.

As the hours passed, the angles of light shifted, creeping along the straw floors. In the temple courtyards, the priests prepared to leave for the mainland, assembling banners and inking vermillion sashes. No one knew quite what Tujiyazai had planned for Awara, but everyone understood that the demon prince did not make empty threats.

At Geiki's bedside, Miuko toyed with the binding spell—the only spell she had left—wrapping its cord around the tip of her gloved pinky.

"What?" the *atskayakina* demanded. "What's the matter with you?"

"What are we going to do, Geiki?"

"Sleep, most likely. You should have done it already. You've earned it."

"I haven't earned anything. Tujiyazai is still out there."

The *atskayakina* shrugged. "Well, *I* earned it, then."

"How?"

"By getting shot!"

"*Geiki.*"

"Kidding!" He grinned. "Mostly."

"He's going to do something terrible," she said, letting the necklace fall against her chest. "I know it."

"The priests are going to the mainland tomorrow morning. We'll have enough spells to protect people by then."

"*Some* people, maybe, but not everyone. The only way to protect everyone is to stop him."

The *atskayakina* fidgeted with his sheets. "Yeah, but how? We can't get him if he's still inside the *doro*'s body."

From his bed by the window, the demon hunter stirred and groaned. "Force him out," he croaked.

"*Kyakyozuya!*" Geiki cried, flapping his hands at the wounded man as if to shoo him from the infirmary. "Don't go thinking about chopping anybody now. Miuko may be a demon, but she's not like other demons. She's a *good* demon."

The demon hunter moaned. "I can see that."

The *atskayakina* opened his mouth to reply, but Miuko laid a hand on his shoulder. "Go get Meli."

He gawked at her. "But I've been shot!"

"You can still walk, can't you?"

"Only painfully!" Whimpering, he hobbled dramatically from the infirmary, though neither of his legs had been injured.

Miuko stood, approaching the demon hunter's bed the way one might approach a wounded steer—he may have been incapacitated, but he was still dangerous.

She needn't have been so cautious. The *kyakyozuya*'s face was swollen and purple, his nose broken, his lip split. Both his wrist and his ribs were bandaged, and he seemed to be having trouble breathing.

He squinted at her through one of his bloodshot eyes. "You're not entirely a demon, are you?"

Nope, her human-voice said cheerfully.

Miuko shook her head. "I still have my human soul. I'll have it until I take my first life . . . or until I figure out how to get rid of this curse for good."

"That's a new one for me."

"Yeah." She rolled her eyes. "Me too."

One corner of his bloodied mouth twitched, as if he were fighting a smile. "So . . . what kind of a demon is possessing the *doro*?"

"A malevolence demon called Tujiyazai."

"Tujiyazai? He's a legend."

"Yeah," said Geiki, reappearing in the doorway with Meli. "A legendary *vakaizu*."

To Miuko's surprise, the *kyakyozuya* laughed. Startled, she leapt back, readying for a fight, but he merely laid a hand over his bound chest, for laughter seemed to pain him.

Meli clicked her tongue, gently nudging Geiki out of her way as she crossed to the demon hunter's side. "If you're well enough to disturb our other patient, perhaps you're well enough to be moved out of the infirmary."

"Oh no!" the *atskayakina* said, flinging himself back onto his mattress, where he pulled the sheets up to his chin. "My recuperation may have been set back by days or even months, just because Miuko didn't want to fetch you herself. I must stay here!"

The priest chuckled. "That arrow hardly scratched you. You're far too quick to have been seriously injured by something like that."

Peeping over the edge of the covers, he grinned.

Sighing deeply, Miuko turned back to the *kyakyozuya*. "Anyway, we can't force Tujiyazai out of the *doro*. I tried the only exorcism spell I had, and you saw how that worked."

"Heh." The demon hunter cringed as Meli inspected his wounds. "You think a *kyakyozuya* only knows one way to exorcise a demon?"

Forgetting that he'd once hunted her, and had only mere hours before threatened to kill Geiki, Miuko grabbed his arms eagerly. *"What?"*

He groaned, for she'd also forgotten that he was gravely injured.

"Miuko!" Taking her firmly by the shoulders, Meli forced her back.

"Sorry!" Awkwardly, Miuko patted his arm, and even retreated another step to give him peace of mind. "You were saying?"

He grimaced as the priest resumed checking his wounds. "All men have two forms, one of Ada and one of Ana."

"Body and spirit," Meli said. Then, tightening one of his bandages with only slightly more force than necessary: "All people have them, actually, whether they're men or not."

The demon hunter winced. "Yes, of course—and in all people, the body and spirit belong together. It is the law of nature."

Miuko crossed her arms. "So . . . ?"

"So you need the host's original soul. No matter how powerful the possessing spirit, the host's original soul will always oust him."

"Omaizi Ruhai?" In her excitement she reached for the *kyakyozuya* again, but this time refrained from touching him. "We need the soul of Omaizi Ruhai?"

The demon hunter nodded. "The problem is finding him. He may not be in his body anymore, but he's technically alive, so he won't be in Myudo, which means he could be anywhere in Ada *or* Ana."

Remembering the sprawling, nautiliform cities and far-ranging arbors she'd seen on her ride with the *baiganasu,* Miuko groaned. The lands of Ana were simply too vast to search, and the time they had was simply too short.

"Hmm." Meli tucked the last of the demon hunter's dressings into place. "I think I know a way," she said thoughtfully. "It's an old ritual of the priesthood, rarely used, but if it works the way I think it does, then we should be able to locate the *doro*'s soul tonight."

21

THE MOON DOOR

THE RITUAL, as it turned out, involved the reflecting pool Miuko and Geiki had discovered the night prior (or eight nights prior, depending on one's perspective). "It's called the moon door," Meli explained, and in generations past, the December priests had used it to locate lost human souls, severed from their bodies and adrift in the wilds of Ana.

On the night of a full moon, the priests could send the soul of a volunteer through the pool and into the spirit world, where, if their intentions were true, they could discern the location of the lost soul. Upon gaining the information they sought, the volunteer's spirit would then return to their body, and the physical journey to retrieve the lost could begin.

There was one problem, however.

"The magic is strongest when the volunteer knows the lost soul," Meli said, "and I don't know about you, but *I've* never met the *doro*."

"Maybe Hikedo-jai?" Miuko suggested hopefully.

Unfortunately, as they discovered when they proposed their plan to the head priest, not one of Amyunasa's disciples had ever met the true Omaizi Ruhai; for men of the nobility did not, as a rule, comingle with reclusive priests.

"Or *atskayakinasu*," added Geiki.

Having traveled with Tujiyazai from the mainland, the *kyakyozuya* had at least spent the most time with the *doro*'s body, which he insisted made him the best candidate for the ritual, but Meli protested that his wounds were too grave.

314

"I'm not going to let you drown while you're under my supervision!" she declared with such finality that the demon hunter sank meekly back into his mattress.

"It's got to be me, then," Miuko said. "I'll do it."

The *kyakyozuya* shook his head. "You're a demon."

"I've got a human soul. That's all I need, right?"

Meli frowned, her usually serene expression troubled. "You'll have to be careful. I don't know exactly what it's going to be like on the other side of the moon door, but I've heard of volunteers getting lost in the spirit world, never to find their way back to their bodies again. It'll be dangerous."

"Danger? Ha!" Geiki puffed out his chest. "I know him well."

"*You're* not volunteering," Miuko pointed out.

"Yes, but I'll be in close proximity to the volunteer, won't I?"

"Oh, so you're coming with us?" She feigned surprise. "I thought you didn't want to set your recuperation back."

The *atskayakina* scowled. "I already missed one adventure. If you think I'm going to sit this one out just because of a few minor, valiantly earned flesh wounds, you don't know me at all."

Leaving the *kyakyozuya* to recover at the temple, Miuko, Geiki and the priests set off near midnight, with the waves slapping softly against their boats. To the south, a macabre crimson glow cloaked the horizon where the Awaran mainland lay. The priests murmured uneasily as they took up their oars.

"That's Tujiyazai's doing," Miuko said, also attempting to row — though, strictly speaking, she did not know how. "It has to be."

"Good thing we're going to stop him, then." Geiki patted his satchel, which had been loaded with provisions and a change of clothes for each of them, for he and Miuko planned to begin their search for the *doro*'s soul as soon as they knew where to start looking.

Crossing the narrow strait, the priests moored at the rocky island, where by the light of their lanterns they scaled the narrow path to the moon door. There, they arrayed themselves around the pool, sitting cross-legged upon the flat stones that lined the rim.

Under Meli's direction, Miuko waded into the water. In Omaizi society, girls of the servant class were discouraged from swimming, but thankfully Miuko had at least learned how to float practicing in the guesthouse's cedar tubs while her mother cradled her beneath the surface.

She had not done it in years, not since she'd outgrown the baths and her mother had vanished from her life, but the memory of it filled her now as she lay on her back with the water lapping at her cheeks and her hair floating around her like a cloud. Inhaling deeply, she closed her eyes, feeling Meli's hands—as gentle as her mother's had been—guiding her toward the center of the pool.

"Once I leave the water, we're going to start chanting," the young priest whispered to her, "and the ritual will begin."

"And all I have to do is stay focused on the soul of a boy I've never met," Miuko said. "Easy."

Meli squeezed her shoulder, giving her a warm smile. "Don't worry. You've done stranger things than this." With that, the young priest kicked away from her, swimming with long, smooth strokes toward the granite arch at the edge of the water, where Hikedo helped her onto one of the flat stones. Behind them, Geiki was hopping nervously from foot to foot, a dancing silhouette against the face of the moon.

Slowly, the priests began to chant in low, resonant tones, their voices rising and falling in hypnotic rhythms that thrummed in the rocks and the water and Miuko's very bones, until the air itself seemed to vibrate.

The wind died.

The sound of the breakers, gnashing at the cliffs below, dropped to a dull whisper.

A ripple disturbed the surface of the reflecting pool, although there was no breeze to make it. Miuko felt it splash over her cheek, wetting her lips.

"What was that?" Geiki cried.

"Shh!" she said. "I'm trying to concentrate!"

The priests continued chanting, their voices vibrating through every grain of sand on the shore, every drop of water in the pool, every fiber of Miuko's demon body, thrumming with magic—

And then, between one breath and the next, she was gone.

22

LOST SOULS

PASSING THROUGH the moon door felt like being sucked through a drain, with a gasp and a gurgle, sent floating along a stream like a fallen leaf or a discarded tail feather. She flew through the air, faster than Geiki —faster, even, than the *baiganasu*'s sled—slipping through the dewy clouds and skimming the round chin of the moon, while the earth flowed beneath her, rippling and shifting, as if the positions of its cities and villages, its hills and valleys were as formless as water.

A part of her understood that her body was still in the reflecting pool —in fact, she could still see her body, and the pool, and the priests, looking down upon them as if from a great and dizzying height—but Miuko herself was no longer there.

She was in Ana, searching for the soul of Omaizi Ruhai.

At the thought of him, the world spun beneath her, settling upon some penumbral country, through which the tall, broad-shouldered figure of the *doro* walked, his handsome face taut with fear.

Miuko gasped.

Or rather, her body gasped.

Back on the God's Teeth, her body floundered in the reflecting pool, dropping below the surface and struggling upward again, sputtering.

Was she drowning?

She clawed at the water, sending it splashing into her eyes and mouth. Through her blurred vision, she caught glimpses of figures upon the shore: a boy with windblown hair; a ring of priests, plump as hens in their nests.

"Miuko! Are you okay?" The boy reached for one of the priests—young, tender—shaking her shoulder. "What's wrong with her, Meli? Hey, Miuko!"

Instead of words, a snarl emerged from Miuko's throat, causing the boy to leap back, crying, "Ah! You're not Miuko!"

And it wasn't.

Without her human soul, the demon part of her had been given free reign over her body, and now bloodlust flooded through her veins, colder and wilder than anything she'd yet experienced. She thrashed toward the edge of the pool, starving for touch, for life.

But Miuko couldn't return to her body yet. The entire world was counting on her.

She wrenched her attention away from the moon door, back to Omaizi Ruhai's soul. He hadn't been lost for very long, she realized, having been ambushed by Tujiyazai one night in the southern prefectures less than two weeks before the *doro yagra* ran her off the dilapidated bridge.

Since being ousted from his body, Omaizi Ruhai had been on his own adventure. Stumbling through the spirit world, he'd fought off demons and bargained with trickster spirits, escaped from ogres and befriended a lonely *tskemyorona*[1] with a shadowy centipedal body and two glowing fireflies for eyes. To Miuko's surprise, he'd done it all with a good-natured flexibility she never would have expected from a member of the nobility, much less the son of the *yotokai*. At times, the *doro* even seemed to relish gallivanting through Ana with a pack of goblins or other low spirits, whom he appeared to enjoy helping as much as he enjoyed their help.

As the weeks passed, his surroundings shifted: cities dissolving into plains; plains swelling into mountains; mountains melting into pastures

---

1   tske-myoro-na (*tskeh-meeoh-roh-nah*): literally, "not-alone spirit." In Awara, *tskemyoro* is the hair-raising feeling that one gets in the presence of certain uncanny phenomena, or, in English, the "heebie-jeebies." A *tskemyorona*, therefore, is a heebie-jeebie spirit.

dotted with sheep. Rivers rushed past, roaring like dragons. From somewhere in the distance came the sound of the ocean.

But always Omaizi Ruhai remained fixed on his destination. Throughout his trials and the occasional caper, he moved with a steadfast resolve, his dark eyes set upon the shapes of hills in the distance, glimmering with lanterns.

Udaiwa.

In that moment, though Omaizi Ruhai was a man of the Great Houses and she was a servant-girl-turned-demon, Miuko felt a strange kinship to the *doro,* for it had not been that long ago when she, too, had wanted nothing more than to make it home.

To her village.

To the inn.

To her father.

A sharp cry yanked her awareness back to the reflecting pool, where her body had reached the shallows. Choking and spitting, she splashed through the water, weighed down by her sodden robes.

The priests had not stopped chanting. They remained immobile on the shore, placid as cattle. Her body was nearly upon them now, so close she could almost feel their energy emptying into her ravenous fingertips.

Suddenly, something hit the water beside her. A lantern. It fizzled out, smoking, as another struck her in the shoulder. She hissed.

"Sorry!" the boy shouted. He darted past the priests, picking up a third lantern. "Don't be mad!"

She ducked as he hurled it at her, but she continued to advance. The boy might be too quick for her to catch, initially, but the tall priest and the older one beside her—ample as an overripe peach—would be easy pickings.

With a growl, she tore the gloves from her hands.

Miuko's spirit panicked, flying down at her body like they would become one again as soon as they touched, but she passed through herself as if she were a ghost. Whirling upward again, she tried to moan, but she didn't have the lips or throat to do so.

Meli had already told her how to return to her body, and it wasn't by blundering into it like a moth batting at a flame. She had to gain the information she sought in the spirit world.

She had to find the *doro*.

So she fixed her attention again on Omaizi Ruhai, and from her perspective in the air, she saw him stagger through a series of fallow fields, passing a kiln, an abandoned farmhouse, a burned-out barn.

Nihaoi.

He was somewhere near Nihaoi.

But Nihaoi was dangerous for a son of the Omaizi, and as Miuko watched, the ghosts of the Ogawa—his family's ancient enemy—surfaced around him, crawling from the earth with calls for vengeance on their rotten tongues. Overwhelming him quickly, they marched him at swordpoint through a collapsed gate and into a ruined garden, where a cloven black pine forked into the sky like reverse lightning.

Far to the north, her body had reached the edge of the reflecting pool. She had grabbed the head priest by the collar and was dragging them toward her, reaching for their throat with her curved blue fingers.

But Miuko knew that pine. She knew that gate. She knew that garden.

The ever-shifting landscape of the spirit world winked out.

She was back in her body, shoving Hikedo away from her and falling back into the shallows. "I'm sorry!" she gasped. "Did I hurt you?"

Dazed, they shook their head as the other priests helped them to their feet. "That was close, wasn't it?"

"Miuko?" Meli asked, fear rippling in her musical voice. "Is that you? Are you back?"

Geiki did not wait for an answer. He charged into the pool, tackling

Miuko so hard she was knocked back into the water, landing hard on her bottom.

"Ow!"

"Sorry!" He nuzzled her shoulder, like the bird he was, and continued, quieter this time, "I thought for a second you were gone for good."

Sighing, Miuko leaned into him. "No, just gone long enough to attack the most important person on the island."

The *atskayakina* laughed. "What do you mean? You didn't attack *me*."

"Wish I could say the same of you." She gestured to her scorched robes, where the lantern had struck her.

His eyes widened guiltily. "Meli did that."

Miuko flicked water at him. "Liar."

"You don't know that!" he protested, helping her from the pool. "You were off in Ana, trying to find the soul of some fancy boy—"

"Which I did."

"So you can't know who threw what lanterns at whom."

"It worked, then! You found the *doro*'s soul?" Meli piled towels and fresh clothes into their arms. "Do you know where you're going next?"

"Yes." Miuko stood, wringing water from her hair. She'd spent seventeen years gazing out at those abandoned fields, but she'd only entered that crumbling gate nine nights ago, racing past the cloven pine, to the dilapidated bridge, where she'd set herself upon the path she trod now.

The soul of Omaizi Ruhai was being held in Nihaoi's old mayoral mansion.

"We're going home," she said.

23

THE RAZING OF AWARA

AS MIUKO AND GEIKI prepared to depart, Meli looped a vermillion scarf around each of their necks. "There are four extra in your pack for any mortals or spirits who might need them," she said, tugging the cloth into place about Miuko's shoulders. "Good luck."

Already in his giant bird form, the *atskayakina* squawked. "We'll need it."

Miuko bowed to her. "Thank you for all you've done for us."

The young priest embraced her swiftly, her cheek warm against Miuko's hair. "Thank you for what you're about to do."

Slinging their provisions over her shoulder, Miuko climbed onto Geiki's back. With a flourish of his great blue wings, he bowed to the priests, who bowed solemnly in return, and leapt into the sky.

Over the ocean they flew, skimming the black waves, as the wind kissed Miuko's cheeks, tangling its fingers in her hair. Releasing her hold on Geiki, she let her arms fall to her sides as she inhaled the sharp, salty air.

It tasted like freedom.

Like danger and possibility.

She closed her eyes, and in that roaring darkness, she thought again of her mother, astride her stolen horse, galloping through the fallow fields toward an unknown future.

"What are you doing?" Geiki cawed, startling her out of her imaginings. "If you fall off, I'm not going to catch you!"

Grinning, Miuko embraced him again.

A surge of heat struck them as they sailed over the mainland, and Geiki quickly banked westward to avoid being tossed about by the scorching wind. Below them, great swaths of devastation marred the landscape: fields and forests burning, smoke upon the mountains, cities like cinders, crawling with fire.

Tujiyazai had warned her, hadn't he?

If I can't have you, then no one can have anything.

He meant to destroy the world, and the destruction had been swift. As the first rays of the sun reached them from the east, they saw refugees streaming along the roads, and corpses, aflutter with vultures, lying in blood-soaked meadows. In some places, however, the land seemed untouched — almost deserted — nothing but abandoned carts and baskets overturned, their contents spilling into the ditches for the monkeys to scavenge.

"He's following the Great Highways," Miuko said, pointing at a strip of road unwinding below them.

"Why?" Geiki asked. "Do you think he figures that's how he can do the most damage?"

"Maybe." She glanced to their right, where, not far off, a nearby city seemed to have gone entirely unscathed. "Or maybe he has another destination in mind."

"Well, it looks like he's heading south. That narrows the possibilities to . . . pretty much anywhere in Awara."

"Udaiwa. It's got to be Udaiwa."

"Why?"

"It's the heart of Omaizi civilization. If he wants vengeance for his family, that's as good a place as any to start." She paused, remembering what Afaina had told her about the alternate worlds he'd seen. "In another timeline, he struck there first."

The *atskayakina* flapped his wings, speeding them onward. "He won't be far from Nihaoi, then. We'd better hurry."

They soon outstripped the destruction, pausing briefly so Miuko could check Geiki's wounds, but they dared not linger long. Every time they stopped to rest, the violence threatened to overtake them again—smoke on the horizon, the scorching heat of Tujiyazai's powers on the back of Miuko's neck.

Again and again they fled, chased off by the sounds of devastation in the distance.

"How is he moving so fast?" Miuko wondered, glancing behind them as flames roared across an orchard. "He shouldn't be able to travel that quickly in the *doro*'s body, even on horseback."

They got their answer on their second night in the air, when Geiki, flying on little sleep and ignoring the strain from his injuries, was struggling to remain alert. Wings faltering, he swooped low over a forest canopy, where every so often they'd plunge another few feet, making Miuko's stomach drop.

"Let's stop for a while," she said, patting his shoulder. "You need a rest."

"Can't," he grumbled.

"You have to."

"If Tujiyazai's heading for Udaiwa, he's going to pass the Kotskisiumaru. That's my home. I have to warn my flock."

"We'll never reach them if you don't keep up your strength."

As if in protest, Geiki lifted them higher for another few seconds, but then he sighed and, with a weary flap of his wings, began to drift toward the treetops in search of a place to land.

Miuko ran her gloved fingers through his feathers. "Don't worry. We'll reach them in time."

As they descended, however, there was an explosion behind them. Crying out, Miuko glanced back as the whiskered head of a river spirit erupted through the canopy. Roaring, it coiled upward, its scales glinting silvery blue in the moonlight as a small figure clung to its neck.

Even at this distance, Miuko could not mistake the way his face burned in the darkness.

"Tujiyazai's riding that river spirit!" she shouted.

"That's not a spirit," Geiki replied grimly. "That's a *yasa*."

She shook her head. So that was how the demon prince was moving with such speed. He was turning spirits into monsters, riding them south toward the capital.

Bellowing in what might have been pain, the river *yasa* fell back into the trees, the rest of its body coiling and surging through the forest in twisted spirals.

Geiki sped onward, beating his wings, but they had not gone far when there were shouts from below.

"There, in the sky!"

"The monster!"

"Shoot it down!"

Geiki pitched sideways as a volley of arrows burst through the treetops, but he was too slow. An arrow caught Miuko in the shoulder. Screaming, she toppled from the *atskayakina*'s back, the air whistling by her as she hit the canopy, smashing into tree limbs, eating facefuls of leaves.

"Miuko!"

There was a *whoosh* of air as Geiki dove after her.

Then his wings were around her, so soft that for a moment, they muffled all the sound in the world.

And together, they struck the ground.

24

MANY REUNIONS,
NOT ALL OF THEM MERRY

MIUKO GROANED, stirring beneath Geiki's wings. Around them, the woods were thick with shadows, which loomed dark and deep beneath the gnarled trees. Moonlight filtered through the canopy, illuminating the *atskayakina*'s fallen form: curled feet, rumpled feathers, closed eyes.

"Geiki?" she said.

He didn't move.

Nearby, something crashed through the undergrowth—twigs snapping, branches breaking. On the air, there was the sour smell of sweat and fear.

"Geiki." Miuko sat up, shaking him, but still he did not wake. *"Geiki."*

Standing, she took hold of his not-inconsiderable bulk and began hauling him, bit by bit, behind the shelter of a half-rotten log; but before she could hide him completely, a group of people burst through the trees.

Men. Seven of them, in ages ranging from younger than Miuko to decades older. They were peasants, judging by their clothing, and each of them carried a hunting bow and arrows, which they trained on her now, shouting.

"Don't move!"

"We heard evil was coming from the north, and here you are!"

Placing herself between them and Geiki, Miuko snarled. "It isn't me! And I'm not evil!"

"But you came from the north!"

One of them, a man with green robes and close-set eyes, loosed his arrow. Miuko dodged, hearing it strike a tree behind her.

Her lip curled. For a moment, she wished she could blame their fear and anger on Tujiyazai's powers, but the demon prince was too far away to affect them, and besides, those ensorcelled by him did not speak.

No, these were just men.

Angry, terrified, ignorant men.

They converged on her, firing arrows, drawing short sickles normally used for harvesting.

She tried to do battle with them, but even with her demon-enhanced abilities, she was no fighter. An arrow skimmed her arm. Another found her thigh. Roaring, she caught one of the boys by the collar and threw him into a tree, where he landed in a groaning heap.

Someone sliced her across the back. Another arrow embedded itself in her side.

She screamed, seizing the nearest man and flinging him to the ground so hard, he lay there among the dead leaves, dazed and wheezing.

But she was still outnumbered, and now she was bleeding freely — her shoulder, her arm, her thigh, her ribs. Blood dripped down her back, hot and wet.

The men closed in again.

But before they could reach her, a loop of rope flew from the shadows, ensnaring one of their bows. The others cried out fearfully as thunder echoed through the woods.

No, not thunder.

Hooves.

From the trees, another rope fell over the oldest man's shoulders, yanking him to his knees. A gray blur galloped from the darkness, pulling to a stop beside Miuko.

"Roroisho!" she cried.

The dapple mare snorted in greeting. Upon her back, Kanayi, the girl Miuko had once taken as her thrall, stared down at her with a grim expression in her gray eyes.

"Oh. It's you."

Miuko plucked the arrows from her ribs and thigh. The wounds were painful, but in truth they should have pained her more than they actually did. It seemed her demon body recovered swiftly; though, at the rate she was accruing injuries, not swiftly enough. "Kanayi," she said, "what are you doing here? Where—"

"Ah!" one of the men cried, pointing with his harvesting blade. "What's that girl doing on that horse?"

"Leaving!" Kanayi snapped, urging Roroisho onward. "You're on your own, demon!"

But the horse refused to budge. Growling, Kanayi kicked her heels, but the mare did little more than lay her ears back.

"What's wrong?" Miuko cried, glancing over her shoulder. "Get going!"

"I'm trying!"

They were too distracted, too inexperienced in battle, and while they squabbled, the men attacked.

An arrow grazed Miuko's scalp. Another flew at Kanayi—a sharp metal point gleaming in the low light.

But before it could strike, Miuko leapt up, catching it by the shaft and snapping it in her strong demon fingers.

Kanayi gasped, her stony expression melting into surprise. Then it hardened again. "This doesn't make us even!"

"Fine!" Miuko tossed the halves onto the ground. "Then get out of here, so I don't have to protect you too!"

But the girl did not leave. Twirling her last length of rope, she caught the green-robed man by the arm, forcing him to drop his sickle. One of the boys charged her, but Miuko intercepted him, his blade nicking her cheek, and hurled him away.

The green-robed man scrambled to his feet, glancing wildly about him. His men were scattered, stunned, bleeding—no match, apparently, for this demon and a girl on a horse.

So he called for a retreat. Shouting to one another, the hunters gathered their wounded and fled into the forest.

Grimacing, Miuko limped back to Geiki, who could evidently sleep through anything, including the threat of impending demise.

Wordlessly, Kanayi dismounted, collecting her ropes into neat coils, which she hung from Roroisho's saddle.

"Can you help us?" Miuko asked from where she crouched, bleeding on the ground. "I wouldn't ask if it was on my own behalf, but my friend is injured . . ."

Sighing, the girl glanced at Roroisho as if asking for permission.

The horse snorted.

"Fine." Glaring down at Geiki's unconscious form, Kanayi chewed the inside of her cheek, a muscle twitching along the hard line of her jaw. "Is this the same *atskayakina* you made me rescue?"

Miuko nodded.

"Looks like I saved him for nothing, I guess."

"He's not dead! He's just—"

The girl regarded her coldly.

"I'm sorry," Miuko said quietly. Not knowing what else to do, she bowed. "For what I did to you."

Kanayi scoffed.

"I know it doesn't help," Miuko continued, "but I promise you, I'll never do anything like that—"

"Stop." The girl cut her off. "I said I'd help you. I didn't say I'd listen to your apologies."

Closing her mouth, Miuko nodded.

In silence, they checked Geiki's unconscious form, but aside from the lump at the back of his head, he appeared to be miraculously unharmed by the fall. While Kanayi wet a cloth for a cold compress, Miuko stroked the *atskayakina*'s feathers, ignoring her own injuries. "Geiki, Geiki. Get up, you silly bird," she whispered, but when that yielded no results, she flicked him in the beak.

That's not going to help, the little voice admonished her.

"Yes, but it makes me feel better," she grumbled.

Kanayi scowled at her. "Who are you talking to?"

"My human soul."

"You have a—" The girl shook her head, tossing Miuko the compress. "Forget it."

Miuko laid the wet cloth against the back of Geiki's head. "It was lucky, you coming by when you did."

"Coincidence. Cutting through this forest is the quickest way home."

A clamor in the woods stopped Miuko from replying. Was it the men, returning with reinforcements? Or Tujiyazai, riding the river *yasa*? Wincing at the pain in her wounds, she pushed herself to her feet again, though in her current state she did not know how she would manage if she had to fight again.

But whatever was coming, it did not smell like the river, or like humanity for that matter, but like the wild, dark earth—new shoots and sap and decay—and it was approaching fast.

She tensed, crouching in front of Geiki like a wolf in front of her den.

What emerged from the shadows, however, was neither man nor demon. It rambled toward her on six legs, bulbous body swaying like that of a spider, with a girl—looking both disheveled and exhilarated in her tattered pink robes—riding upon its back.

Cursing, Kanayi reached for her rope, but Miuko stayed her hand.

"Nogadishao! Senara!"

No longer in cricket form, the *daigana* skidded to a halt in front of her. "Fancy finding you here, eh?" His mushroom eyes waggled. "Are you the one wreaking havoc in my forest?"

"This is *your* forest?"

"That's how he transformed back!" Senara scrambled down one of his branch-like legs as if she'd been doing it her entire life. "As soon as we reached the trees, *pop!* He wasn't a cricket anymore!"

"Is that an *atskayakina?*" Nogadishao nudged Geiki with one of his gnarled toes. "Noisy creatures. I'd eat their beaks for breakfast if I could."

Miuko slapped him away. "That's *Geiki.* I told you about him."

"Geiki, eh?"

"Yes."

"Maybe just his tail, then."

Senara clicked her tongue at the forest spirit, who had the good grace to look ashamed, then proceeded to wash and dress Miuko's wounds while plying her for all that had happened since they'd parted. The girl was nearly as brisk and efficient as Meli, pausing only when Miuko introduced Kanayi, who, seeming a bit bewildered by the warm welcome Nogadishao and Senara had given Miuko, was shifting uncomfortably beside Roroisho.

"Oh! You're *Kanayi!*" Ignoring the girl's obvious discomfort, Senara threw her arms around her as if they were not strangers but dear old friends.

Kanayi stiffened. "And you are . . . ?"

"Why, I'm Senara, of course!" She laughed, as if this were all the explanation required. Then, turning to the gray mare: "And you must be Roroisho!"

The horse nodded, nosing gently at the girl's outstretched palm while Kanayi, discreetly inching out of reach, mumbled, "That's not her name."

"The God of Stars must have known we'd all meet up here," Senara said, tying off Miuko's last bandage. "Nogadishao and I have been trying to get back here ever since Afaina dropped us off. We only just arrived this evening."

"It's good you did," Miuko said, testing her limbs, which, thanks to Senara's ministrations and her own demon-healing, already felt better. "Geiki and I still need to get to Nihaoi. His flock is in danger, and I need to find the *doro*'s soul to oust Tujiyazai from his body. Nogadishao is the only one big enough to carry us both there."

The *daigana* grumbled. "What am I, a pack horse?"

"You're a generous spirit," Senara reminded him.

"But am I really?"

Laughing, she patted the end of his bedraggled beard.

He huffed, letting out a gust of air that smelled of moist earth, and reached for Geiki.

"Carefully!" Miuko cried as Nogadishao lifted the *atskayakina*'s limp form onto the widest part of his back.

"I am being careful, you wretched *shaoha*!" the forest spirit scolded her, tying Geiki in place with a few loose vines. "Get up here and watch him yourself, if you don't trust me."

But she didn't climb up yet. Reaching into her carrying sack, she withdrew the spare scarves Meli had given her and doled them out to the others.

"For protection against Tujiyazai's powers," she said.

Kanayi did not reply, but she took the scarf all the same.

"They're beautiful!" Senara declared, looping one about her neck before winding the other about Nogadishao's.

"We have only one left," Miuko said, climbing onto the *daigana*'s back.

"For the *doro,* when we find him. He'll have to get close to Tujiyazai to reenter his body, and we can't have him turning into a *yasa.*"

"Will that work on a disembodied spirit?" Senara asked. "It might just pass through him."

Miuko fingered the scarf, her travel-roughened hands catching on the fine cloth. "Meli said they'd work on spirits."

"Then I guess we'll have to try!" Senara scrambled up in front of her, causing Miuko to sputter and swat at her cloud of hair, and turned to Kanayi, standing still as a stone at Roroisho's side. "So? Are you coming with us?"

For a moment, Kanayi made no answer. Then, with enviable ease, she swung up into the saddle. Her gray eyes flashed.

"No," she said. Clicking her tongue, she turned Roroisho south, toward Izajila, and together they disappeared into the shadows.

25

STRANGE COMPANY

DISAPPOINTED BUT UNSURPRISED by Kanayi's departure, Miuko and the others continued south, hoping to outpace Tujiyazai. The demon prince had once claimed he could sense her, like a fragrance from a farther room, and Miuko could now sense him too, raging southward, the edges of his power dancing upon her back like flames.

Shortly before sunrise, Geiki awoke, complaining of a headache and a crick in his neck, though, miraculously, he appeared none the worse for his fall. "The gods must be on my side!" he crowed. "Praise the many gods who are on my side!"

"What'd I tell you, eh?" Nogadishao, scuttling along the forest floor, muttered to Senara. "Noisy creatures."

The girl shushed him.

"You're in poor company if you want quiet, *daigana*-jai." The *atska-yakina* nodded at Miuko, who was removing the bandages from several of her injuries—which had, thanks to her demon-abilities, already healed from the night before. "Have you heard the voice on this one?"

"I have. Like the yowling of a hundred cats, eh?"

"Like the screeching of a hundred hawks," Geiki agreed.

"Like the—"

In truth, they could have carried on like that for ages, but, as Miuko reminded them tartly, they did not have the time. They had a *doro*'s soul to find, a malevolence demon to stop, and Geiki still had to evacuate his flock in the Kotskisiu-maru. Sufficiently chastised, he departed soon thereafter and did not return until afternoon, when he came plummeting out of the smoky auburn sky in magpie form, alighting on Miuko's shoulder with only minimal snarling in her hair.

She stroked his head with a gloved finger. "Did you get them out in time?"

He nodded, cawing weakly, and hopped into her lap, where he curled up in the nest of her arms and promptly fell asleep.

As the smoke thickened, Nogadishao left the shelter of his woods, scrambling down the river valley that would eventually lead them to Nihaoi. What a sight they would have made, Miuko thought. Not only did their strange company include girls—scandalously unescorted—but were they riding a half-feral forest spirit? And was one of them in fact a blue-skinned demon?

But there was no one around to spit at them or demand they return to their kitchens. The few farmhouses they passed were either deserted —doors ajar, open trunks overturned in the yards—or locked up tight, with spells painted across their shutters and pinned above the thresholds.

To the east, Udaiwa still stood, and that was a relief, at least, for it meant Tujiyazai had not reached the capital yet.

As the verge hour descended upon them, the *atskayakina* stirred, hopping out of Miuko's arms and onto Nogadishao's back, where he shapeshifted into his boy form.

Startled, Senara turned around. "Oh!" Seeing Geiki in his blue robes, she blushed. "*You're* Geiki!"

"Uh-huh. We met this morning, remember?" He ran his hands through his windswept hair, tousling it further. Then, noticing her staring: "Ack! What's the matter with you? Why does your face look like that?"

Flushing an even deeper shade of pink, she hid her face in her hair. "I'm sorry! I just didn't expect you to be so . . ."

"Handsome?"

She laughed. "Yes!"

"Miuko should have warned you. I'm a very handsome bird."

Miuko rolled her eyes.

"Chatter, chatter, chatter," grumbled Nogadishao. "I liked it better when you were unconscious, eh?"

Even Geiki fell silent, however, as they entered the abandoned outskirts of Nihaoi. A haze lay upon the fallow fields, dense with foreboding. Behind them, a red glimmer danced wickedly upon the northern horizon.

Tujiyazai could not be far now.

As they neared the village border, Miuko's head began to ache. The spells upon the spirit gate must have been renewed since she'd left, for now they hummed with power, throbbing painfully behind her eyes.

"Stop," she said faintly. "We have to go around."

"What about your father?" Senara asked.

Peering past the gate, Miuko looked longingly toward the ramshackle houses and broken-down shops of Nihaoi. Was Otori Rohiro there, huddled in the guesthouse or sheltering in the temple with the lugubrious priests?

Did it matter? The last time she'd seen her father, he'd cast her out of his life as if she meant no more to him than a torn umbrella or a broken vase, wholly beyond repair. He'd already done it twice. Even if she could have entered the village, she didn't think she could endure it a third time.

"Tujiyazai will strike Udaiwa before he ever bothers with Nihaoi," she said, removing the last of her bandages and flexing her newly healed limbs. "My father will be safe behind the spirit gate as long as we can get the *doro*'s soul before Tujiyazai's powers reach the village. Let's keep moving."

Twilight fell as they crossed the dilapidated bridge, but the waning moon was bright enough for them to see flotsam in the Ozotso River: barrels, baskets, charred scraps of wood . . .

Bodies.

Floating face-down in the water.

Whimpering, Senara buried her head in Nogadishao's mossy shoulder.

Miuko felt for the binding spell she wore around her neck, but as her fingers closed around the bamboo cylinder, a blast of heat washed over her.

In the distance, a scream flickered and died.

Senara startled, clutching Miuko's arm. "Oh no," she whispered. "Is that—"

"Tujiyazai!" someone shouted. Over the hillside, a slender figure was galloping toward them on a misty-gray horse, almost glowing in the dim light.

"Kanayi?" Miuko called.

"Miuko!"

"Roroisho!" Geiki cried as the mare drew up next to them, sides heaving. "You beautiful animal, I never thought I'd see you again!"

Miuko stared at Kanayi, doubled over and breathing hard in the saddle. "What are you doing here?"

"Tujiyazai's coming!" the girl gasped. "He—"

She was interrupted by more screams, followed by a crash—something huge and wooden falling—and heat, hotter than Miuko had ever felt, like a wildfire.

"I was heading for Izajila when I saw him. Tujiyazai. He didn't even make it to Udaiwa before he turned off the Great Highway and started walking straight toward Nihaoi."

"So you came to warn us?" Miuko asked, surprised.

"I knew you were here, trying to stop him," Kanayi snapped. "Don't make a big deal of it."

"How close is he?" Senara asked.

"Close. His powers are already starting to affect the outskirts of the village."

Miuko leapt to the ground.

Her father was back there.

He may not have wanted to see her—at least not as she was—but she could not let him fall victim to Tujiyazai's powers.

"Miuko, wait." Geiki slid down after her, touching her elbow gently.

She looked up at him with panicked eyes. "I have to. My father—"

"We'll do it."

She shook her head. This was *her* village, *her* responsibility. She had to save them, or at least she had to try. "But—"

Nogadishao turned his craggy face toward her, eyes waggling. "It's a mission of utmost importance, eh?"

"Just do whatever you have to, to stop this," Kanayi agreed, her jaw set in a hard line. "We'll get the villagers to safety."

Swallowing, Miuko looked from one of their motley assembly to another: the forest spirit, two murderous girls, a dapple gray mare, and Geiki, who winked at her.

"Go on," he whispered.

"Thank you," she said, and, without waiting for a response, she turned and fled toward the old mayoral mansion . . . and the soul of Omaizi Ruhai.

26

SACRIFICES

THE GHOSTS of the Ogawa were out. As Miuko sped across the fields, they climbed from the earth—armor creaking, scabbards rattling against their thighs—to relive the same fateful march they had made every night since their charge on Udaiwa more than three hundred years ago.

Only tonight, with Tujiyazai's help, they might actually see the stronghold of their enemies fall.

Not if we find Omaizi Ruhai first, the little voice inside her said grimly.

The moon door had shown her he was being held somewhere inside the old mayoral mansion, so she ducked through the crumbling gate and into the overgrown garden. Darting past the cloven pine, she raced through bedchambers, kitchens, and sitting rooms, where visiting dignitaries had once gathered to discuss politics, philosophy, and the dowries of their daughters.

She found all of them empty—dusty and deserted—until at last she spied movement in a small storeroom on the outskirts of the complex.

Creeping closer, she peered around the doorframe. Inside, the wooden floors had rotted away, revealing gaps of gravel and weeds among the decomposing planks. One of the outer walls had collapsed, allowing moonlight into the dim interior, where it shone, pure and silver, upon the disembodied soul of Omaizi Ruhai, slumped in a corner.

His young, handsome face looked so familiar—the same face she'd seen Tujiyazai wearing for weeks—but there was a kindness in his spectral features, a humor in the shape of his mouth, that Tujiyazai never could have mustered even if he possessed the *doro*'s body for a thousand years. The *doro*'s spirit watched warily as a ghost soldier prowled back and forth in front of him. "Something's happened," the soldier muttered, his disintegrating features looking rather cross, as far as Miuko could tell. "I should have been relieved of my post by now. What is taking so long? I am no warden. I am a soldier! I should be marching upon my enemies, not childminding this pathetic excuse for an Omaizi!"

He thumped the butt of his halberd against the rotten floor, causing a swarm of ghost-flies to go buzzing about his head in dismay.

Miuko almost laughed. The *doro*'s guard was the same phantom she'd met the night Afaina had deposited her on the Old Road.

He'd mistaken her for a soldier then. If she could convince him to do the same now, she might easily escape with Omaizi Ruhai's lost soul.

She just hoped she'd be better at impersonating a man now than she'd been at the library, when she'd had Geiki's illusions to help her.

Standing, she straightened her shoulders and swaggered into the storeroom. "What are you doing, soldier? Get moving!"

The guard rattled his halberd at her. "About time! It took you long en—" He glared at her suspiciously—or as suspiciously as he could with neither eyelids nor eyes to speak of. "You're not the one who's supposed to be relieving me."

"Of course I . . ." Miuko's voice trailed off. Through the collapsed wall, she could see the phantom army of the Ogawa streaming eastward across the barren farmland. She watched, horrified, as one of the ghosts nearest Nihaoi suddenly grew taller, talons sprouting from his fingers. Beside him, another of the soldiers roared, revealing a gullet ringed with spines.

Yasasu.

Tujiyazai must be drawing closer.

"Of course I am!" She forced her attention back to the guard. Digging inside her pack, she felt for the only vermillion scarf she had left. "Can you

341

not see? I am a soldier, here to guard the Omaizi prisoner. Onward with you, now! The army waits for no man!"

The guard crossed his arms. "You are not a man."

Against the wall, the *doro*'s disembodied spirit straightened. He did not seem shocked at her appearance, or even particularly fearful, as another human might have been, but curious . . . and expectant, as if he did not quite know what to make of her. "Are you a demon?" he said.

"No, this is no demon." The Ogawa soldier beamed, as if struck by his own deductive brilliance. "She is a teapot! Missing its—"

Miuko sighed. The ruse had been a long shot anyway. "My *name* is Otori Miuko."

He bowed to her. "And I am Pareka, bannerman of the Ogawa."

"Okay, you're right, Pareka. I *am* a teapot. But I'm still here for the prisoner." She tried to shoulder past him, but he blocked her with surprising swiftness, his halberd falling between her and the *doro*'s soul.

The flies buzzed angrily.

If she'd been mortal, she could have swept right through him, but she was one of the *nasu* now too (or mostly, anyway), and the weapon's shaft felt dangerously solid against the flat of her hand.

Tensing, Omaizi Ruhai drew himself into a crouch, looking from Miuko to Pareka as if he could not be certain whom to trust: the ghost soldier who'd imprisoned him, or a blue-skinned demon who'd appeared out of nowhere to claim him.

"This is the son of my great enemy," Pareka said. "I am tasked with guarding him, and I will not relinquish him to a *teapot*."

From Nihaoi, Miuko felt Tujiyazai's powers blazing outward in widening spirals, expanding across the fields and warping more of the Ogawa soldiers into twisted, monstrous versions of themselves.

Hurry, her human-voice whispered.

342

"Get out of my way," she growled.

But Pareka leveled his weapon at her, taking up a fighting stance in front of the *doro*. "Are you a teapot?" he demanded. "Or are you my enemy?"

With a snarl, she knocked the halberd aside. Dashing to the *doro*, she flung the last vermillion scarf over his head, sending up a prayer to Amyunasa that it would not pass through his spectral form.

"Hey!" The soul of Omaizi Ruhai blinked, confused, as the cloth settled neatly over his shoulders. "What is this?"

It worked! the little voice inside her cried.

"Protection." She grabbed his hand, pulling him to his feet. "Come on. We have to—"

But a blow to her side knocked her to the ground.

Above her, Pareka was transforming. Horns grew from his helmet. Fangs sprouted from his cloven jaw.

Tujiyazai's powers had reached the manor.

Pareka staggered back, startled. "Teapot?" His voice quivered. "What is happening to me?"

Miuko's gaze raked across the storeroom, searching for a way out. "You're a solider," she said, trying to calm him.

But Pareka was growing larger and more terrible by the second—new arms, eyes, heads—barring their escape. They had only seconds before he lost his mind entirely and became a *yasa*, bent on destruction.

"Remember?" she asked. "You're a bannerman of the Oga—"

As if sensing his old enemy nearby, Pareka rounded on the *doro*'s soul, snapping and slavering.

Miuko stepped back, in her clumsiness tripping over a small round stone, which rolled beneath her heel, almost throwing her to the ground again.

A stone.

Something harmless, into which a spirit could be bound.

No! her human-voice protested. *We have only one binding spell, and if we use it now, we won't have it for Tujiyazai. We'll have to—*

"You're a soldier," Miuko whispered to Pareka as she scooped up the stone. "Don't you remember?"

Please remember.

Pareka paused, looming over her.

"Please." She reached for the spell, unspooling it from its bamboo cylinder. "I don't want to do this to you."

I don't want to do this to me.

But he was not a soldier anymore. He was a *yasa*, mindless, monstrous, void of everything but the desire for destruction. Bellowing, he lifted his halberd to strike.

But Miuko, gripping the binding spell, did not flinch.

She'd meant to use it on Tujiyazai, but she'd never get the chance if she didn't return the *doro*'s soul to his body.

And she could not do that if Pareka cut her down first.

As the blade sliced through the air, she slapped the binding spell against the *yasa*'s exposed ribs. He turned, the tip of his weapon just missing the *doro*'s scalp, as Miuko lifted the rounded stone, drawing his spirit into it as smoke is drawn into the lungs. Desperately, he clawed at the walls, his talons raking across the timbers, causing splinters to shower the storeroom like rain.

But it was no use. His spirit thinned and shrank, sinking inexorably into the stone.

"I'm sorry," Miuko cried, and she did not know if she was sorry for Pareka, or for herself, or both. "I'm sorry!"

Tears wet her cheeks as the soldier's twisted spirit vanished, until not even the spectral flies remained.

It was done.

He'd been bound.

Wiping her eyes, she pocketed the stone as the soul of Omaizi Ruhai got to his feet.

The spell was gone. Even if she succeeded in exorcising Tujiyazai from the *doro*'s body, she now had only one way to stop him.

She'd have to kill him.

"What just happened?" the *doro* asked. "Hey, why are you crying? What kind of spirit are you anyway?"

Miuko shook her head, unable to speak.

She'd just surrendered the possibility of ever being human again. She'd known it, and she'd done it, because she'd had to. And now, in the end—if she succeeded, anyway—she would finally become the *shaoha* Tujiyazai had always wanted her to be: powerful, perilous, and utterly, devastatingly alone.

27

IF THE WORLD SURVIVES

AT THAT PRECISE MOMENT, Miuko wanted nothing more than to curl up in a corner of the storeroom and mourn for what she had to do next. After all, it wasn't every day that she resigned herself to losing her humanity in order to save the world from a ravening demon, and she could have used a little time to adjust. If there was one thing she'd learned from growing up in Nihaoi, however, it was that things ended, whether you wanted them to or not, and rarely in the way you hoped. In such circumstances, the best you could do was tighten your belt and carry on.

And carry on she did. Pulling the *doro*'s soul behind the shelter of the collapsed wall, she explained their predicament—which, to his credit, he accepted without either argument or protest.

"Okay," he said, fanning out his hands as if trying to arrange his thoughts, "so you're telling me this demon, Tujiyazai, who took my body, is actually one of the Ogawa, and now he wants to destroy everything my family's ever built."

"Yes."

"And you're not really a demon but a girl from this little village."

"Yes."

"And you want me to retake my body because you *are* actually kind of a demon, and you're the only one who can stop Tujiyazai before he brings the entire world crashing down around our ears, but *first* we have to get through *that*." He pointed to the fields beyond the storeroom, now teeming with *yasasu*, the twisted forms of the Ogawa soldiers clashing and

346

bellowing as if the malice that had sustained them all these centuries had erupted as suddenly and violently as water from a geyser.

Miuko nodded. "That's about the size of it."

Abruptly, the soul of Omazi Ruhai put his head between his knees. "Hooo . . ."

She reached for his shoulder. "My liege?"

He batted her away. "Don't 'my liege' me. I think we're a little past that at this point, don't you?"

She managed a faint smile. "Only a little?"

"Ha!" He looked up again, his dark eyes twinkling. "You're funny, demon."

She stood, extending a gloved hand to him. "Call me Miuko."

In similar circumstances, a lesser man might have refused the overtures of a woman and a demon. Indeed, if she'd made such an offer only a few weeks before, Omaizi Ruhai might have rejected both her proposal and her assistance. But perhaps he'd always been a little more open-minded than the other boys of the Great Houses, and perhaps a month wandering through Ana as a disembodied spirit had cracked him open even further, for now he grinned and clasped her hand in his. "Okay, Miuko. Call me Ruhai."

She smiled as she helped him to his feet. "Are you ready, Ruhai?"

"Hardly." He smirked.

Sighing, she hitched up her robes. "That sounds about right."

Together, they dashed from the mayoral mansion into the masses of Ogawa *yasasu*. The monster soldiers scratched and snarled, lunged and tore at them. One caught the edge of Miuko's robes, which shredded in his claws. She tripped, pitching forward as the others converged on her.

But before she hit the ground, Omaizi Ruhai caught her, pulling her to her feet again. "You're clumsy for a demon!"

"And you're rude for a *doro*!"

He chuckled, but his amusement was cut short when one of the *yasa* slashed him across the arm. He grunted, but he didn't stop running.

Panting, they made it across the dilapidated bridge, racing up the hill to the village border.

The temple was on fire. Its tiled roof had collapsed, and the ruined garden was ablaze, illuminating the smashed spirit gate lying in splinters upon the ground. Miuko couldn't see anyone in the smoke—there was no sign of her friends or of the villagers—but in the distance, someone shrieked.

A wave of heat passed over Miuko's skin, fluttering her torn robes.

"Tujiyazai is close," she said. "You'd better hide now."

The *doro*'s spirit nodded. "Keep him distracted, Miuko. I'll get as close as I can before I jump back into my body."

"Don't let him know you're coming."

"I won't." With an encouraging half-smile, Omaizi Ruhai slipped away, vanishing quickly into the shadows.

Sliding her gloves from her hands, Miuko stepped over the broken gate and into Nihaoi.

It was deserted. Doors were ajar. Blood stained the gravel. Nothing moved in the darkness but the smoke from the temple flames.

She passed a body, dead-eyed on the side of the road.

The teahouse proprietor.

She tried not to look closely, tried not to wonder what had happened. Where were the rest of the villagers? Had they been gored upon their verandas? Drowned in their wells? Around every corner, she feared she'd see Nogadishao and Senara hacked to pieces, Kanayi dead beneath Roroisho's corpse, Geiki—

She bit her lip, forcing her thoughts away.

At last, she came to the guesthouse—still standing, though its door had been kicked in and there were signs of a struggle among the camellia bushes.

Father.

Her breath caught in her throat.

But she did not have time to search for him, for as she approached, Tujiyazai emerged from the inn, his face blazing bright as a torch, his horns wreathed in flames.

"I've been looking for you, Ishao."

28

BY MEANS OF A TRICK

MIUKO LIFTED HER CHIN as she neared the demon prince. "Here I am."

Though Tujiyazai was dressed in the same finery he'd worn at the dock, he no longer looked the part of the *doro*. The hems of his robes were muddied, the rich fabric streaked with soot. Through a tear in his sleeve, she could see a bloody scratch running the length of his forearm.

Someone had gotten close enough to strike him.

This thought gave her hope.

But he lifted a hand as she reached the camellias, halting her in her tracks.

Inwardly Miuko cursed, counting the paces between them. At this distance, there was no guarantee she'd be able to distract him long enough for Ruhai to sneak up behind him, and she certainly wouldn't be near enough to catch him when he was finally expelled from the *doro*'s body.

No, she had to get closer than this.

Tujiyazai tilted his head at her curiously. "When I sensed you nearby, I thought surely you must have been racing home to protect your precious little village from my wrath. Imagine my surprise when I found it entirely undefended."

Miuko's courage wavered. Undefended? Did that mean her friends had failed? Her gaze flickered to the inn—its darkened windows, its damaged doorframe.

Was her father inside?

Was he alive?

She could not allow herself to think about that now.

Schooling her features, she forced her attention back to Tujiyazai, who was still watching her intently. "This village doesn't care about me," she replied. "Why should I care about it?"

His eyes narrowed before the flesh of his face turned to ash again. "Why, then, are you here?"

"I'm here for you." Sucking in a breath, she took another step forward, and, when he didn't stop her, another.

"To kill me?" He glanced at her bare hands. In the silence, she thought she heard him shift uneasily in the gravel.

"To join you."

She was only eight paces away now.

But where was Ruhai?

Tujiyazai laughed, stopping her again. "I seem to recall you saying you'd never join me."

"That was when I had hope." Reaching for the simple cord at her neck, she took the bamboo cylinders that had once held the spells from the House of November and crushed them in her fists.

"Empty?" For a moment, he stared at the fragments, brow furrowed in surprise. Then he stepped toward her, radiating heat. "Do not play games with me, Ishao."

She swallowed. In the shadows, she saw Ruhai hovering at the corner of the guesthouse.

As if sensing the direction of her gaze, Tujiyazai began to turn.

"I'm not!" Quickly, Miuko flung herself to her knees. To her surprise, tears beaded on her lashes. "Please. I don't want to be alone."

The demon prince's footsteps crunched in the gravel.

Five paces.

Two.

He was close enough now for her to reach, but still Ruhai did not approach.

What was he waiting for?

Tujiyazai's voice drifted over her, dry as smoke. "If you truly wished to surrender to me," he murmured, touching the edge of her scarf with his long fingers, "you would not come to me wearing the protection of the priests."

Meekly, she bowed her head.

But her human-voice panicked. *We can't let him take it from us! It's the only thing shielding us from his powers! Without it, we'll—*

But Miuko had to hold his attention—*she had to*—for Ruhai, for Geiki, for her father, for her friends and the villagers—and so she did not flinch when Tujiyazai lifted the vermillion scarf from her head.

At once, heat flared around her—scorching, deadly—but inside she felt it only as a searing cold, racing down her throat and carving into her chest, hollowing her out from the inside.

No!

Another wave of heat buffeted her, lifting her to her feet.

Tujiyazai's fingers closed around her upper arm. "Someone should have told you, Ishao. You cannot bluff when your opponent holds all the cards." He leaned in, whispering softly into her hair. "I don't know what you thought you were going to accomplish here, but it doesn't matter. I'm smarter and stronger than you'll ever be."

"Maybe." Miuko turned to him, her teeth feeling sharp on her lips. "But you have only yourself, and I have so much more than that."

As she spoke, Ruhai rushed from the shadows. A breeze stirred her robes.

Sparks flew from Tujiyazai's eye sockets. "What did you do?" He spun, one hand extended as if to stop whatever attack was to come.

But the soul of Omaizi Ruhai was too quick. He slipped beneath Tujiyazai's arm and dove into his chest, straight and sure as an arrow.

The demon prince staggered backward, gasping. His fine-boned hands roved across his torso, as if searching for a wound, but they found none. "What did you do?" he snarled again, rounding on Miuko, his flaming horns tracing bright arcs through the smoky air. *"MIUKO?"*

At the sound of her own name, she smiled. "Come out, Tujiyazai. Come out to play."

29

A WOMAN OF AWARA

"NO!" TUJIYAZAI ROARED, stumbling toward her on limbs that no longer seemed quite under his control. His teeth gnashed — two separate sets of them. His demon features slid and shuddered beneath his human ones.

He was coming apart. From the *doro*'s collarbone, a shoulder surfaced.

"Is it working?" Ruhai shouted from within him.

Tujiyazai's arm emerged from the *doro*'s body, his skin as vibrantly red as Miuko's was blue. She stared at it: the clawing hand, the flesh scarred with names. He'd been young — he must have been close to Miuko's age when he'd seen his family slaughtered by the Omaizi.

When he'd died the first time.

Now she was going to kill him again.

Even if it cost her very soul.

She seized his wrist with her bare hand. In an instant, she felt his life force flowing into her, scalding her veins.

Tujiyazai's head arose from the side of the *doro*'s neck, his face swathed in flames. "If you kill me," he snarled, "there will be no going back."

"I know."

"You'll be a demon. You'll be like me."

Still, she did not release him. "I know."

His crimson flesh paled. "Will you destroy yourself to destroy me?" he demanded. "Don't be foolish, Miuko! This isn't what you want."

"I know." But she dug her fingers into him all the same, willing herself to drain him, willing his body to wither like a worm in the sun. "But you must be stopped."

Tujiyazai writhed in her clutches. Freeing his other arm from the *doro*'s body, he grabbed her free hand, as if he meant to pull her off him.

But he didn't, or he couldn't.

He had been stronger than her, once, but no longer. He was too divided, too alone—battling Ruhai's soul for control of the *doro*'s body, and battling Miuko, who was siphoning off more and more of his strength with every passing second, for his very spirit.

"I'm sorry," she whispered.

"So am I." To her surprise, he smiled—his fanged expression dripping with self-assurance. "You could have been magnificent."

"What?" She jerked in his grasp, but his grip only tightened.

Something was changing. She felt her strength waver, like a cold breeze against a fire. In the fields, the ghost *yasasu* were shrinking, their tusks and talons retracting as they returned to their spectral forms, marching eastward again as if they'd never been interrupted.

In an instant, Miuko was reminded of the forests above Koewa: the first hunter, advancing with his pitchfork, Tujiyazai catching him by the chin, all the rancor draining from his body, leaving him bewildered at the edge of the ravine.

Tujiyazai was withdrawing his powers.

But why?

"Miuko!" someone shouted.

She turned to see Geiki, in boy form, running toward her, his wild hair scorched, blood coursing from a cut at his brow. Beside him, leaning heavily on a cane, limped an older man: broad-shouldered, blistered at the neck, face bruised almost beyond recognition.

But to Miuko, it didn't matter how beaten he was, or how long it had been since she'd seen him. She would have known him anywhere.

Her father.

He wasn't wearing one of the priest's vermillion scarves, but he, like the ghosts, seemed to have shed the spell of Tujiyazai's malevolence.

"Daughter!" he cried.

A sob rose in her throat.

He saw her.

He *knew* her.

But she would not be his daughter anymore, after this.

"Stay back!" she shouted.

Geiki skidded to a halt, stopping Otori Rohiro beside him. "Miuko, your skin!"

She glanced down. Through the slits in her robes, she saw the color shifting along her legs. A tide receding. Blue shadows retreating up her ankles and calves, leaving her paler than she'd been in weeks.

Tujiyazai's grip on her hand tightened.

He was stripping her of her malevolence—just as he'd done to the hunter in the forest—and because she was a *shaoha,* a malevolence demon, he was also stripping her of her powers.

She looked up, meeting Tujiyazai's solemn gaze. His skull-like features dimmed and blurred as her demon-sight left her. Though she could not see it, she could almost feel the curse ebbing from the sides of her face, seeping down her ears and throat like ink.

She was becoming human again.

"I never wanted this," he murmured. "But I can't let you kill me."

For a moment, she was afraid. The curse was slipping away so fast, and her demon-strength with it. Could she drain him before he drained her?

If she failed, he would be weakened, but eventually he would regain

356

strength, growing more and more powerful on his own bitterness until one day, maybe generations from now, he would return to complete the destruction of Awara.

Then she was furious. She yanked him toward her. "You mean you could have gotten rid of my curse *at any time?*"

Power blazed inside her. She didn't need a curse to feed her malevolence, for she was a woman of Awara. She was something to be restricted, excluded, suppressed, subjugated, owned. She had anger enough to fuel her for a hundred lifetimes, to kiss a thousand more girls and make a thousand more *shaohasu*.

Tujiyazai thought she could have been magnificent? A magnificent weapon, perhaps. An instrument. An object.

But she was already magnificent, just as she was, and with a shriek, she wrenched him from the *doro*'s body. He slithered onto the ground, flopping and gasping.

He was going gray, his limbs withering, his fire dimming. He fought and pulled, trying to break her hold on him.

But he had not relinquished his hold on her either. The curse was flowing down her arms now, faster and faster, flooding out of her where he clutched her hand in his.

"Don't," he whispered.

Commanded.

Even now, as he lay dying at her feet.

Pitiful, her human-voice muttered.

The curse slid down her wrist. Her demon-malevolence had almost left her, but she knew she still had enough strength in her for this.

"Good-bye, Ogawa Saitaivaona," she whispered. "May you find peace at last."

He said nothing. His horns curled in on themselves as the flames that surrounded his face flickered and died.

The spirit of Tujiyazai, last son of the Ogawa, collapsed beside the Old Road leading to Udaiwa, where his clan and their bannermen had been slaughtered by their enemies so many centuries before.

His hand dropped from hers, fading into nothing before it even struck the ground.

30

MORTAL AND DIVINE

MIUKO STARED AT the spot where Tujiyazai had vanished. There, a spiked tuft of weeds. There, a pebble, black as an inkstone. There, a cracked seed hull carried and dropped by some passing sparrow.

But no demon. There was not even a trace of heat left where he'd fallen. Was he gone?

Had she killed him?

Miuko stared at her hands. One was now creamy in hue, almost disappointing in its ordinariness, but the other—the one Tujiyazai had held as he drained her of her curse—remained a startling oceanic blue.

Beside her, Omaizi Ruhai staggered to his feet, touching his torso and thighs as if to reassure himself that he was in his own body at last. "Is he gone?" he asked. "Did it work?"

Cold pulsed through Miuko's fingertips, ravenous and wicked. Miuko backed away. "It isn't safe, Ruhai. You have to leave—"

"Miuko!" Across the Old Road, Geiki barreled toward her, followed closely by her father.

"Daughter!"

She recoiled. "STOP!"

The *atskayakina* halted, yanking Otori Rohiro so sharply, his cane clattered to the ground.

But Miuko's father was just as stubborn as she was—*si paisha si chirei*—and he slipped from Geiki's grasp, hobbling to her on his broken foot.

As he reached for her, a quiver went through her demon fingers, chill as a glacial wind.

"NO!" She retreated again, hugging her arms to her chest, as if that would keep her humanity inside her. Doubling over, she waited for her hunger—the *shaoha*'s hunger—to overtake her, as violent and inescapable as an avalanche.

But nothing happened.

Somewhere inside her, a little voice, rougher and deeper than her own, grumbled, *I'm the one who got us here. I'm the one who kept us alive. I'm the one who killed Tujiyazai. And this is all I get? One hand? One measly hand?*

"What?" Miuko stared at her blue fingers, which made a rude gesture at her.

"What?" Geiki peeped through his arms, where he'd hidden his face. "What's happening? Are you evil now?"

She shook her head, mystified. "I think . . . I'm okay?"

"Good-okay or evil-okay?"

Neither! her demon-voice snapped.

"Both," she murmured.

"What does that mean?" Dumbfounded, the *doro* glanced at the *atska-yakina,* who shrugged.

"How should I know? I'm a bird!"

"You're a *what?*"

Ignoring them, Miuko flexed her fingers in wonderment. Somehow, thanks to Tujiyazai's efforts to disarm her, she had become both human *and* demon, girl *and shaoha,* mortal *and* spirit.

Otori Rohiro dashed to her, falling to his knees at her feet. "I thought you were a demon. I thought you were gone. I didn't know . . . I couldn't see . . . I'm sorry, Miuko. Please, forgive me."

Her blue hand reached for the back of his neck, her fingers curved into claws.

Aghast, she slapped it aside, tucking it into the folds of her robes.

Her demon-voice grunted with displeasure.

Kneeling, she kissed the crown of Rohiro's head. "You're my only father," she said softly.

With a cry, he pulled her into his embrace, weeping freely into her shoulder. Not one to be left out, Geiki threw his arms around them too.

Ruhai shifted awkwardly, utterly at a loss for what to do in the face of such impropriety.

Unfortunately for him, there were stranger improprieties ahead.

"Oh, *shaoha!*" someone called in a creaking, sing-song voice.

Miuko looked up, beaming. There, upon the Old Road, were the rest of her friends: Kanayi, with half her face bandaged, and Roroisho (completely unharmed and utterly splendid); Senara, limping beside them but smiling effusively; and Nogadishao, who carried upon his back several villagers in varying states of consciousness and shock.

The *doro* raised his eyebrows. "You've got some peculiar friends, Miuko."

In the past, she might have been embarrassed by such a statement, but now she only grinned. "Thank you."

The corners of his mouth twitched. "I hope you consider me one of them."

"Friends, huh?" Geiki slapped the *doro* on the shoulder. "Tell me, *doro-jai*, just how grateful *are* you for your new friends? Grateful enough to offer some kind of reward to your valiant rescuers, maybe?"

"*Geiki.*" Miuko rolled her eyes.

"What? I'm not saying we deserve riches beyond compare, but I'm also not *not* saying that either, if you know what I mean."

Gently, Otori Rohiro drew him away from the *doro*. "Everyone knows what you mean, *atskayakina*-jai."

Miuko grinned as her blue hand unclenched. She may not have been all human. She may not have been all demon. But whatever she was, after all that had transpired, she knew one thing for certain: for the first time in her life, she was finally, wholly, unabashedly herself.

31

THE UNCONVENTIONAL WORLD OF NIHAOI

FOLLOWING TUJIYAZAI'S DEFEAT, Omaizi Ruhai departed immediately for the capital, where he would be needed to help his father's government contend with the devastation in the north. Over the next several months, however, he returned to Nihaoi as often as his duties could spare him. Soon, he became a regular visitor to the failing village — helping the lugubrious priests to reconstruct the burned temple, tending to the teahouse gardens, overseeing the workers he'd brought in (at Miuko's request) to repair the Old Road — and on days when the work went long, which it usually did, he would rent a room at the guesthouse, where he could be found sharing meals with Miuko and Rohiro, Geiki, Senara, and Kanayi, with Nogadishao peeping in from the veranda.

Perhaps, in other times or to other eyes, such a sundry gathering might have been unseemly, but the *doro*, much to everyone's delight, had always had a transgressive streak in him — and, after his strange journey through the spirit world, he found he had less and less patience for the rigid conventions of Omaizi society. In the evenings, when the faint sounds of clattering dishes and after-dinner chatter could be heard drifting from the village houses, he often joined Kanayi in the stables — for in fact horses were one of his passions, as evidenced by the beauty of his great black steed, which had been found grazing in the alpine valleys near Ogawa Castle and was quickly returned to him.

At Ruhai's request, the horse was stabled in Nihaoi, under the care of Kanayi, who was, though she did not say so, both pleased and honored by the responsibility.

Roroisho, who had become rather accustomed to the copious amounts of adoration lavished on her by the villagers (and by Geiki in particular), was at first a little peeved to share any attention at all with the *doro*'s fine horse, but she was an adaptable creature; and besides, both Kanayi and Geiki adored her more than enough to make her the best-loved horse for many miles around.

Things were changing in Nihaoi. In addition to Omaizi Ruhai, Nogadishao had also become a common sight in the village, scuttling up and down the roads, shedding seeds that sprang into saplings overnight. At the back of the inn, where he slept beside the baths, the villagers often left him offerings of melons and coins, and after a month of their attentions, he began to look significantly less wild. His beard transformed. His eyes became actual eyes. Fewer woodland creatures skittered along his limbs, though there were always two or three nesting somewhere on him.

For his part, Geiki flitted between his flock, which had returned to the Kotskisiu-maru, and the inn, where he helped raise new beams and thatch the rooftops, though he could most often be seen searching the abandoned ruins with Miuko, digging up the skeletons of the Ogawa soldiers so the lugubrious priests could finally give them proper burials and lay their souls to rest.

The *atskayakina* found numerous treasures this way, although he almost always dropped each of them as soon as he unearthed the next.

More telling than the presence of spirits or nobles, however, was the change in the villagers themselves. They did not balk when Kanayi rode by on Roroisho. They did not try to prevent Miuko from walking about unescorted. Once he'd recovered from his injuries, Laido even apologized to Miuko for chasing her from the temple the morning after she was cursed, to which her gloved demon-hand promptly responded by slapping him across the face.

The thing simply had a mind of its own. Within a few days of Tujiyazai's attack, she'd discovered that it could easily find ways to divest itself of ordinary gloves, mittens, swaddles, and slings, so she'd had to commission a buckled glove that could not be removed except with the help of her other hand.

Thanks to this glove, the lugubrious priest suffered no more than a bit of a shock and a sudden reddening of the cheek.

"Apologies, Laido-jai!" she said, stuffing her demon-hand into her pocket.

He should apologize for his breath, muttered the little voice inside her.

Though Miuko knew it to be ill-mannered—and inaudible to anyone but her—she could not help but laugh, and she didn't even bother to smother it.

The priest smiled weakly, rubbing his cheek.

Change was not confined to Nihaoi, either. The seasons shifted, with summer sliding leisurely into autumn. The days retracted. The leaves turned. From the north, there was news that life had returned to the House of November. Squirrels had been spotted scurrying among the burned trees, and birdsong could be heard upon the air. One traveler even brought word that a young *kyakyozuya* had arrived to restore the order of Nakatalao's priests.

That change would come slowly, but others would be swift. Shortly after the fall equinox, Omaizi Ruhai arrived in Nihaoi with an invitation for Kanayi to apprentice with the *yotokai*'s stablemaster, who had long been searching for anyone—male, female, or *hei*—competent enough to meet his exacting standards. It was an unconventional hiring, to be certain, but, as was quickly becoming apparent, the *doro* was interested in collaborating on an unconventional new world.

On Kanayi's last day in the village, Miuko saw her off at the spirit gate. "Will you be okay in Udaiwa?" she asked, stroking Roroisho's soft nose.

Kanayi shrugged. "Okay as anywhere, I guess."

"Well, if you ever need anything—"

"I know better than to call you." But she smiled to take the sting out of her words.

Miuko laughed. "I'm serious!"

"Oh yeah? How do you think this job will go, if the first person who harasses me loses an arm to a *shaoha*?"

"Smoothly!"

Grinning, Kanayi looked east, where the warm autumn sun was rising over the hills of Udaiwa. "Well ... I guess I'll keep that in mind." Then, as was her way, she turned and, without any further farewells, she and Roroisho rode off toward their new lives in the capital.

Not long after that, Nogadishao returned to his forest, accompanied by Miuko, who, with the help of her somewhat diminished demon-strength, built him a shrine on the edge of the Thousand-Step Way. With little more than an altar and an urn for incense, it was not nearly as large or as well-constructed as Beikai's, but that didn't seem to matter to the pilgrims on the Ochiirokai. Even before the shrine was completed, offerings began to appear: rice cakes, bits of lichen, mushroom caps. These were soon joined by several crude wooden statues, each of an old man with a long beard, hands pressed together in a posture of utmost serenity.

The forest spirit picked one up, waggling it like a doll. "What's this?" he demanded. "Is this supposed to be me?"

Miuko took it from him, gently settling it with the others. "It could be a good likeness, if they gave it more arms."

"Pah."

"What's the matter? I thought you wanted followers."

He scuffled in the dirt, refusing to meet her gaze. "Followers aren't the same as friends, eh?"

Touched, she laid a hand on his mossy shoulder. "You consider me a friend?"

"I consider you a nuisance!" he declared, shaking her off. Then, his voice softening: "But I suppose I've gotten used to you."

She bowed to him. "If I promise to visit, will that make you happy?"

"Yes!"

"Then I promise."

He clapped his hands, causing a mouse to emerge from the crook of his elbow and scurry up into his beard. "Excellent!"

The offerings at Nogadishao's new shrine were not the only evidence that tales of Miuko's adventures were spreading throughout Awara. As the repair of the Old Road progressed, travelers began to trickle into Nihaoi, where they stalked Miuko through the village, begging her to tell them of her strange journey through Ada and Ana.

Disliking the attention, Miuko often made herself scarce, roaming the abandoned fields or stopping by the Kotskisiu-maru to visit with Geiki and his flock. Though she was most often alone and unescorted, for she no longer feared either men or spirits, she didn't think anyone even noticed, for unattended girls were becoming a common sight in Nihaoi.

They came alone—some old, some younger than Miuko, some dressed as boys, some upon horseback—or occasionally in pairs, friends or sisters, cast out from their homes or seeking to escape them. In their first days, they stayed at the inn, where Otori Rohiro welcomed them as heartily as he would his own daughter, but they quickly found more permanent homes above shops or on restored farms, where they began to till the soil.

They were not the only arrivals, either. *Heisu* came to Nihaoi too, and girls like Meli, for word was quickly spreading that the House of December was no longer their only option.

Curiously, the shifting demographics of the village coincided with the sudden appearance of a new shrine. It simply showed up one day, beside the dilapidated bridge—which was, thanks to the construction efforts of Ruhai's workers, dilapidated no more. The shrine was plain in appearance—even plainer than Nogadishao's—and as far as Miuko knew, no one had been seen praying there, but inside it there could occasionally be found an offering of a withered flower or a gnarled purple root shaped like a human hand.

Senara was instrumental in resettling the newcomers in Nihaoi. She had remained at the guesthouse to help Miuko and Rohiro, and they soon discovered that she had more talent as a servant than Miuko possessed in her little toe. She cleaned spotlessly. She cooked excellently. A quick study in accounting, she was soon managing their ledgers and making business connections as easily as she made friends, and she used both to find their guests places to live and work and gather in peace.

Given her affability, she soon found herself the center of considerable romantic attention and even entertained the affections of one or two suitors, although as she confessed to Miuko over a steaming pot of jasmine tea, she hadn't really given the affairs much thought.

"I suppose I'm having too much fun on my own!" she declared happily.

"What?" Miuko asked, setting down her teacup, miraculously un-chipped. "Does this mean you're no longer interested in all those fat sons you wanted?"

"Oh, maybe one day!" Senara winked at her. "But perhaps not yet."

A few months ago, Miuko would have envied how easily Senara fit into the serving class, but, truth be told, Miuko no longer cared about fitting in. As repairs were completed and the villagers, old and new, began to settle into their new ways of life, she spent less and less time in Nihaoi and more on her own, or with Geiki, taking flights over the fields and forests of the Ozotso River valley.

Otori Rohiro noticed, of course; but, knowing his daughter, he did not object. Instead, he quietly packed her meals—with extra for the *atskayakina*—and left the lanterns burning when she was out late.

One cool November evening, Miuko and Geiki stood at the spirit gate, watching the sun fall in the west. So much had changed since she'd been cursed. The Old Road had been restored. The ditches had been cleared of weeds. The lights in the nearest farmhouses glowed with warmth.

Wisps of the *naiana* still drifted over the fields, and, though she no longer possessed her demon-sight, she knew the remaining ghost soldiers—the ones who had not yet been unearthed—were making their nightly march on Udaiwa.

Reaching into her pocket, she felt for the stone that contained Pareka's soul.

"Are we ever going to get him out of there?" Geiki asked. "The *kyakyozuya* said he could do it."

"I know." Miuko sighed. She'd been meaning to make the trip to the House of November for over a month, but with the reconstruction of the village and the settlement of the newcomers, there had always been a reason to stay.

Even now, there was Senara, her father, the inn.

But there were reasons to go, too: a fluttering in her heart, a restlessness that had always been inside her—and inside her mother too, as she was now unashamed to admit—a longing for new horizons, strange encounters, and daring adventures, the likes of which most people would only ever hear of in stories.

"What's the matter with you?" Geiki demanded suddenly. "Why are you so quiet? It's creepy."

"*Creepy?*"

"Coming from you? Yes!"

She laughed. "Are you ready for another adventure, Geiki?"

"Oh yes." He slung an arm about her shoulders, drawing her so close she could smell the scent of the wind on him. "I've got a good feeling about you, you know."

A week later, on the first night of December, they bid farewell to Senara and Rohiro in front of the guesthouse. He embraced Miuko, kissing her on the crown of the head. "Your mother could never call this place home either," he said. "You're more like her than I ever imagined possible."

She smiled. "Not in a bad way, I hope?"

"Never." He smiled back. "You'll have a place here whenever you wish to visit."

"And make sure you visit often!" Senara added from behind him.

Miuko bowed to them both. "I will."

Geiki, standing in the yard in giant bird form, flapped his wings impatiently. "Yes, okay. You'll miss her. She'll miss you. Blah, blah, blah." He squawked. "*Atskayakinasu* could tell a whole tale in the time it takes you to say good-bye."

"So?" Senara chided him. "We're human."

"Mostly." Grinning, Miuko climbed onto Geiki's back, and they took off into the cool twilight air. Over the wild blue countryside they flew, like a pair of heroes from some ancient tale or a constellation limned in stars, and not once did she look back, for she did not need to—she had the support of her loved ones behind her, and the big, beautiful world ahead.

ACKNOWLEDGMENTS

Five novels in and I still get wonderstruck by the fact that I am an author, doing this thing that I love so much, and I am so grateful for the amazing and exceptional people who have given me the opportunity to do it.

To my agent, Barbara Poelle — what a thrill and a pleasure and an honor it's been to work with you. I'm grateful for your good humor, your steady hand, your sharpness. Thank you for always reminding me that I can do this and telling me when (not!) to panic. Many additional thanks to the incredible team at IGLA — I am so fortunate to be one of your authors.

Thank you to Catherine Onder for saying yes. Thank you for believing that even my most experimental, out-of-the-box ideas will somehow all come together . . . and thank you for letting me know when they won't! Working with you has been a joy and a dream — I'm so proud of the work we have done together.

To Emilia Rhodes, thank you for taking the reins and guiding this book into the world. From our very first conversation, I was blown away by your enthusiasm and your thoughtfulness, and I'm excited to be in such good hands as we move forward.

Behind every book is a team of wonderful, dedicated people, and I am grateful to be working with one of the best. My deep, deep thanks to the editorial team at Clarion Books and HarperCollins: Gabby Abbate, Mary Magrisso, Anna Leuchtenberger, Stephanie Umeda, Emma Grant, and Emily Snyder. Enormous gratitude to the publicity, marketing, school and library, and sales teams for getting my books in front of so many readers, with particular thanks to John Sellers, Tara Shanahan, Lisa DiSarro, Audrey Diestelkamp, Taylor McBroom, Amanda Acevedo, Patty Rosati, Colleen Murphy, and Rachel Sanders. I can't believe how lucky I am to have you on my team — thank you, thank you.

I am enamored with the cover and interior of this book. Thank you to Celeste Knudsen, Kotaro Chiba, and Natalie C. Sousa for putting this story into such a perfect package.

Thank you to Tommy Harron, the HarperCollins audio team, and all the narrators for your work on *A Thousand Steps into Night* and *We Are Not Free*. You have gone above and beyond for these books. So much gratitude to you for bringing these stories to life.

Thanks and admiration to Sean Berard, Shivani Doraiswami, and the rest of the team at Grandview LA. Sean, thank you so much for both your hustle and your patience — I'm endlessly grateful for you running with each of my projects, walking me through every step of the process, and always sitting me down to remind me that I belong in the room.

A heartfelt thank-you to Ariel Macken for helping me create the language of Awara. The words we made together have shaped this world from the very beginning, and I am so grateful.

I owe a huge debt of gratitude to my readers. Profound thanks to Ben "Books" Schwartz and Rachel Wirth, whose feedback challenged me to question, deepen, and crystallize the ideas about hierarchy, transgression, and power that have become the backbone of this project — thank you, my friends, for all your guidance and support. To Parker Peevyhouse, whose friendship, encouragement, and keen sense of surprise have bolstered me from the very first line to the twistiest of twists — thank you for being my ideal reader. Christian McKay Heidicker, your advice on writing "cozy horror" helped me to find the voice of this project and brought the spirit world of Awara to life — thanks so much for always encouraging me to dig into the specific, the weird, and the wonderful. To Kaitlyn Sage Patterson,

Misa Sugiura, Karolina Fedyk, Mikaela Moody, Emily Skrutskie, Gabe Cole Novoa, Tara Sim, and Isabelle Felix—thank you for your time, advice, and generosity. Your insight and expertise have been a gift, and I am immensely grateful for your feedback.

Special shout-outs to the Highlights Foundation, where I wrote the very first words of the very first draft of this book; to Tiffany Jackson, for helping me figure out the puzzle of the "coin demon"; to Alex Villasante, for the book recommendation; and to Matt Kitagawa, for the playlist. Thank you all.

As always, my love and gratitude to my family for their encouragement and support. To Mom, Dad, and Auntie Kats, for giving me so many opportunities to imagine, create, and grow. To Cole, for loving me. To Mom, Chris, Jordy, Cole, Uncle Gordy, Matt, and Terry—thank you for sharing our very first trip to Japan, the trip that inspired this book. I don't know how a family vacation comprising eight people, three weeks, and five cities could go so impossibly well, but *it did*. Thank you for making so many memories with me—I'll treasure them forever.

Finally, I'd like to extend a huge hug to my high school friends. I can't believe how lucky I am to have found you, or, more accurately, to have been found by you. It wasn't always easy being different and awkward and a nerd, but you showed me how to embrace it. Your acceptance and support shaped so much of who I was and who I've become, and I'll be eternally grateful to have spent those four years with so many kind, smart, quirky, creative, generous, brave, extraordinary girls (and David!). You inspired me then; you inspire me now. I love you, and I'm so thankful for all of you.